Laws of the Hunt PLAYERS GUIDE™

WRITTEN BY CORANTH GRYPHON, JESS HEINIG AND CYNTHIA SUMMERS

CREDITS

Written by: Coranth Gryphon, Jess Heinig and Cynthia Summers

Development by: Cynthia Summers and Jess Heinig

Editing by: Lindsay Woodcock

Previously published material has appeared in: Laws of the Night, Laws of the Wild, Laws of the Hunt, Oblivion, Halls of the Arcanum, The Inquisition, World of Darkness: Sorcerer, The Shining Host, The Autumn People, World of Darkness: Mummy

Art direction by: Richard Thomas

Layout and typesetting by: Aaron Voss

Art by: Laura Robles

Playtesters: Nathan Brown, Michael Dent, Earle "Glas" Durboraw, Kenndra Durboraw, Randy Edmonds, Bernadette Groves, Tim Harris, Christopher Hooker, James Lai, Anthony Macedo, Jennifer "Joie" Martin, Jeremiah McCoy, Kevin Scheidt, Billy Trozzo, Chris White

SPECIAL THANKS TO:

Richard "Big Bird" Dansky, for many productive late-night discussions, frequently involving food.

Jess "Streltsy" Heinig, for offering to teach the Brujah Thaumaturgy.

Ian "Siouxie" Dunteman, for finally correcting me on "Eat That Bug."

735 PARK NORTH BLVD.
SUITE 128
CLARKSTON, GA 30021
USA

Laws of the Hunt
PLAYERS GUIDE ™

TABLE OF CONTENTS

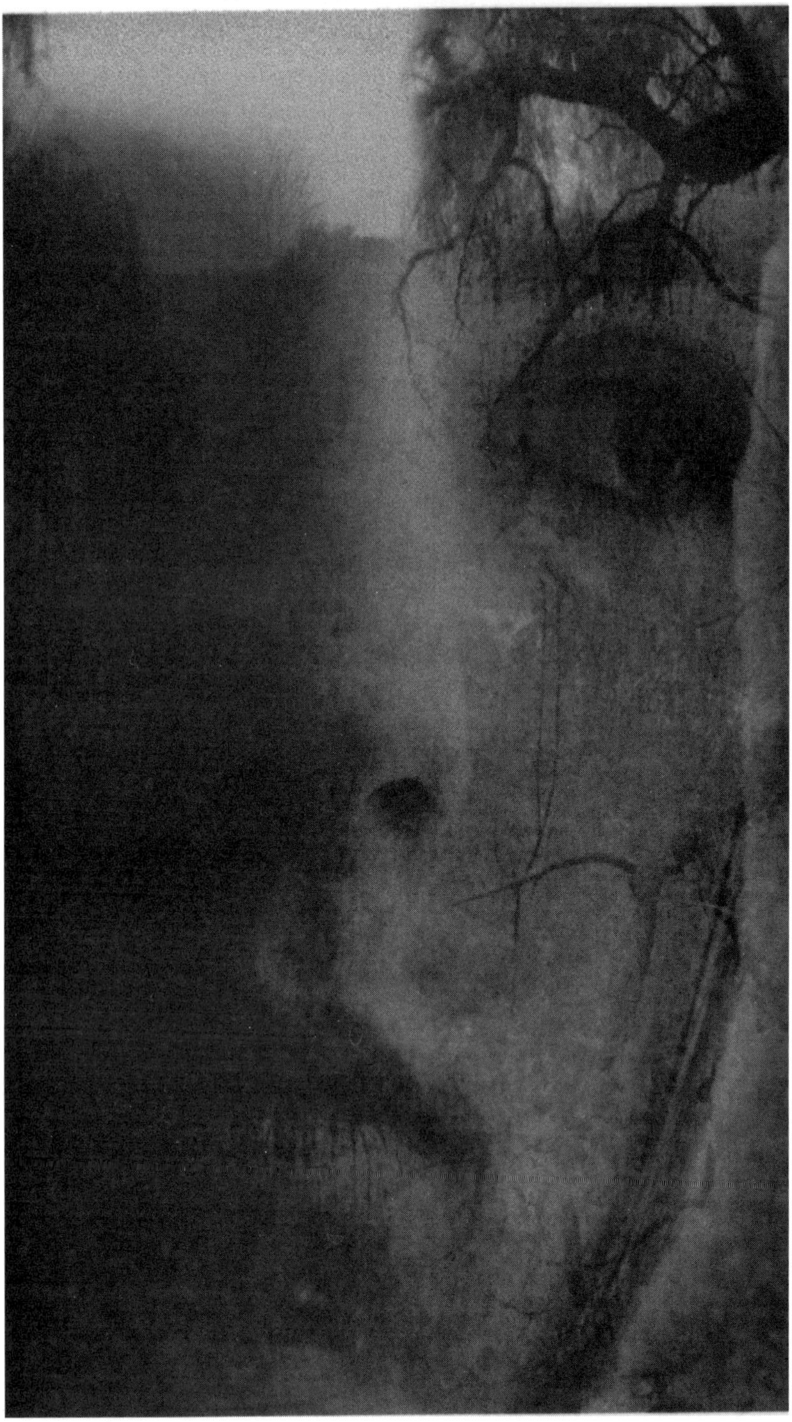

Introduction

But when the darkness sets in, their true beauty
Is revealed only if there is a light from within.
— Elizabeth Kübler-Ross

Think back to when you were a child. Games were full of make-believe. Cowboys and Indians, hide and seek, even playing with trucks and dolls all involved dreaming up worlds of adventure each day. As you got older, complex rules often replaced free-floating imagination as the basis for your amusement.

With **Mind's Eye Theatre**, you can have both. Instead of sitting around a table describing what your character is doing, you become your character, acting out the scenes in which you are involved. If you have never done any sort of roleplaying, you can think of it as a long-running improvised play, with the world as your stage.

ORIGINS

Laws of the Hunt Players Guide is part of the **Mind's Eye Theatre** series. It contains all the information necessary to create and run mortal characters but occasionally refers back to other **MET** supplements. To make best use of this supplement, you should have **Laws of the Hunt** and one other

MET book, such as **Laws of the Night, Laws of the Wild, Oblivion** or **The Shining Host**.

Laws of the Hunt Players Guide is derived from the tabletop books in **World of Darkness: Sorcerer, The Inquisition, Halls of the Arcanum** and a few other sources. You do not need to own or be familiar with any of these books to use this supplement; however, the background material contained in these books can be a useful source of additional information.

HOW TO USE THIS BOOK

This book was intended as a companion to **Laws of the Hunt**, and when we started out, we decided to only put in the new material and direct folks to the other books for things like Attributes, Abilities and Influences. However, we found that many folks liked having certain material at hand, to avoid carrying extra books and to make sure that everything needed was in one place, especially during character creation. So, in deference to your wishes, here's just about everything you'll need to create your character and the rules you'll need for playing in the games.

Chapter by chapter, here's how it breaks down:

Chapter One: Magical Society — These describe the various societies that many sorcerers have found comfort and refuge in. From preferred paths, to outlooks, to magical style, the sorcerous array themselves.

Chapter Two: Character Creation — Here is all the necessary infomation to create any sorcerous character, from Attributes to Backgrounds to Merits and Flaws. This material can also be used for creating Dauntain and mummies.

Chapter Three: Hedge Paths and Theurgy — The nitty-gritty of being a sorcerer, here are the hedge paths (several of them having their first outings ever) for the sorcerously inclined, and Theurgy for those with other purposes.

Chapter Four: Rules, Systems and Drama — In addition to the rules about bidding and challenges, there is information about the Umbra as it relates to sorcerers, spirits and suggestions for making the magic a little more magical.

Chapter Five: The Dauntain — These folks should have been in **Laws of the Hunt**, but owing to a couple of mishaps and space problems, they got bumped and landed here. You can create Dauntain characters either using the material provided here or in **Laws of the Hunt** if you see something you want there. All the necessary material for playing a Dauntain is included here.

Chapter Six: Mummies — The Reborn — Here is a complete work-up for creating and playing mummies, revised according to **World of Darkness: Mummy, Second Edition**. You can create mummy characters using the steps provided in the back, with the material given in the front of this book.

Appendix: FAQ — All the little (and not so little) questions come to roost here.

THE WORLD OF DARKNESS

The World of Darkness is the backdrop for our game. It is a dim and tarnished reflection of the normal world in which we live. The landmarks are the same; the cities are where the map says they should be. Yet a dark undercurrent runs through this world. Monsters howl on their nightly hunts, sinister forces prey upon the unsuspecting, and magic still lives. It is an eerie world, and your character must adapt in order to survive. Danger lurks in every shadow, and there are a lot of shadows here. Welcome to the World of Darkness — pray that you make it through the night.

LIGHT AT THE END OF THE TUNNEL

Even though much of the game focuses on isolation and conflict, there must always be a sense of hope to keep things in balance. Everyone needs something to believe in, a goal to strive for, a way to make a difference. Even in the World of Darkness, you can take time to smell the roses, have a picnic or celebrate a friend's birthday. Characters are not just combatants in an endless struggle: They are also people seeking to understand the world around them. Enjoy both the dramatic moments and the quiet times, for they all provide a means of self-discovery that is an important part of roleplaying.

STORYTELLING WITH MORTALS

The World of Darkness is not simply a playing field for supernatural creatures such as vampires, werewolves and mages. It is comprised of people on whom the vampires must feed, activists who are attempting to preserve or destroy the face of Gaia and the unknowing masses who move in the sunlight of the world.

Among those faceless automatons are a rare few people who have discovered within themselves some spark of power or awareness. Some use these abilities for the good of all; others hoard the benefits for themselves. These small lights shining in the mundane sea make up the focus of this book.

Many people ask why someone would want to play a mortal character when **Mind's Eye Theatre** offers such a wide range of supernatural roles. It can be a good way to learn the basics of the system, allowing new players a chance to get their feet wet without trying to swallow an entire cosmology at the same time. More experienced players might enjoy the challenge of trying to match mortal powers against the supernatural, acting either as allies or enemies.

There are two ways a Storyteller can use mortal characters. First, human servants or hunters may be included in a standard **Vampire**, **Werewolf**, **Wraith** or **Changeling** game. Alternately, the Storyteller may decide to run an all-mortals chronicle, focusing on the interaction between the worlds of the mundane and the supernatural. This can be especially exciting if there are two chronicles running side by side, one mortal and the other supernatural, with each reacting to the other's advances.

MIXED CHRONICLES

Sorcerers are human. This may seem to go without saying, but the wide range of nonhuman roles available in **Mind's Eye Theatre** makes that small fact a unique asset. Many supernaturals arrogantly assume that mortals are just not a threat and dismiss them out of hand. Very often, dearly bought experience teaches them otherwise — those supernaturals who lived through the Inquisition are not likely to disregard mortals again.

There are several roleplaying challenges available to players whose characters are much closer to "home." It is easy to let your imagination go completely when playing a vampire or werewolf. Taking on the role of a mortal, especially one who is unaware of the shadow world around her, is more of a challenge. In addition, it provides a greater opportunity to explore your own humanity. This is especially true when the mortal is set against a background of supernatural characters. Humanity is an aspect mostly lost to vampires and wraiths and largely alien to the Garou and changelings. For mortal sorcerers, maintaining human ties in a world which constantly seeks to turn them into monsters (both literally and metaphorically) can be difficult indeed.

Finally, there is a difference in intensity that comes from a mortal perspective. Mortals don't have the forever of vampiric or wraithly existence. They don't have the escape of changelings or the mighty forms of the Garou. The issue of immediacy becomes much more relevant to these characters, giving them an element of frantic activity. For mortals, the clock is ticking and "do or die" becomes a very apt motto.

MORTAL TROUPES

Time is not the only danger mortals face. Storylines that are trivial for supernatural beings can be dangerous to someone with only his wits and a few spells at hand.

The prospect of Storytelling a game with a troupe of mortal characters becomes even more exciting when one considers the relationships they often have with other inhabitants of the World of Darkness. Kindred see most mortals as servants, food or, more rarely, as potential childer. Many Garou hold mortals in contempt, though a few tribes have taken a less forgiving stance, viewing humans as a threat to Gaia. Wraiths and Spectres covet the life these mortals take for granted and may rage as they watch opportunities wasted. Little wonder, then, that most supernatural beings shun mortals or try to eliminate them entirely. The protagonists of every other **MET** game have suddenly become your antagonists! This provides a wonderful change of pace.

And then let's consider what happens when there are no clear "good guys." So the mortal has decided that vampires are foul creatures, and he wants revenge on the one who killed his wife and Embraced his daughter. What's going to happen when he encounters his vampire daughter, who is struggling to retain her Humanity in the face of her new state? Is she something evil to be destroyed? What if she's in love with another vampire, and she'll face down her father before she lets him destroy her lover? Who's the "bad guy" here? The daughter, because she's a vampire? The father, who's hunting? Let's throw a twist on that and say the father is hunting under the aegis of the Inquisition. Does he disobey his superiors to save his daughter, or does he follow orders and consign her to a horrific death, hoping that her soul will be saved like the Inquisition claims? Now who's the bad guy? Mortals (and roleplaying) thrive in such morally muddy situations.

Humans have a remarkable capacity for both great good and great evil, as well as creativity and ingenuity, by dint of the spark of Humanity that runs in all of them. This can surprise supernaturals who thought they'd seen it all. Jaded vampire elders, regal sidhe lords, grizzled Garou warriors and ancient wraiths can all recall when mortals have given them some new marvel. Hitler, Mother Theresa, Da Vinci, Thomas Edison, Idi Amin, Amelia Earhart, Hammurabi — who knows what each mortal is truly capable of?

RULES

Once all is said and done, **Laws of the Hunt Players Guide** is about telling a story. However, to keep things running smoothly and to provide a sense of balance, the game needs rules. Rules enable a character to perform feats that the player cannot or should not, such as shoot a gun, cast a fireball or swing from a chandelier. The rules should be taken in context, with interpretations based upon what is best for the current story and the game as a whole.

The rule system is designed to fit seamlessly into the flow of play, providing a fast and simple resolution to complex situations without disrupting the scene. This allows you to preserve the illusion of reality while still making things work. Remember, characters don't know anything about game mechanics, so players should keep such out-of-game discussions to an absolute minimum. Every time you break character to discuss the rules, the tapestry of the story is torn apart.

WINNING AND LOSING

Most games we learned as children had definite winners, usually determined after the game was over. This is not the case in **Mind's Eye Theatre**. Here, the game reflects life. There are no ultimate winners and losers. There are only temporary victories and setbacks as characters strive for their goals.

As in life, there are consequences for your actions. Each story is a strand in a vast web connecting each to the others, a rich and complex tapestry into which your character is woven. Your part may be large or small, but it is vital to the story as a whole. Chronicles can be as short as a few hours or as long as months. Either way, the tale never truly ends.

THE ONLY RULES THAT MATTER

Most rules are at the Storyteller's discretion, but some limits are written in stone. **Mind's Eye Theatre**, unlike other types of games, can bring out strong feelings and emotions. You are interacting in person with other players instead of just describing what your character is doing. These rules are simple and easy to follow, but they are necessary for the safety of everyone involved. The objective of live-action is to broaden and enhance the game, not to increase the possibility of harm.

#1 – IT'S ONLY A GAME.

This is the most important rule of all. If your character dies, if your plot falls apart, if your allies betray you — it's only a game. Too many times, a hothead will forget this and ruin the game for everyone. Remember to leave your character at the door. Do not bring problems from real life into your stories, and don't bring game problems into the outside world. If your significant other's character stabs your character in the back, that does not mean it's time to get your own apartment. Rather, it's probably time to take a deep breath and regain your perspective.

#2 – NO TOUCHING. NO STUNTS.

This means none whatsoever, even if consent is given. Things have a way of getting out of hand and it's better not to chance any unpleasantness. No horseplay should happen at all. This means no swinging from objects, running or jumping. Just because your character is tough and can take a 20-foot fall does not mean you can. If you have any doubts about whether something is safe, do not try it.

#3 – NO WEAPONS.

Props have an amazing way of enhancing the game, but real weapons should stay at home. It doesn't matter if that sword goes well with your character's concept or how responsible you are with your dagger. That does not prevent some moron from running around the corner and impaling himself on it. Even toy guns are forbidden. Remember when Laser-Tag was big and the cops shot some kid who thought it would be a good idea to point his weapon at them? Enough said.

#4 – NO DRUGS OR DRINKING.

Well, duh. Drugs and alcohol do not create peak performance. It's one thing to play a character who's stoned or drunk, another thing entirely to actually be inebriated while roleplaying. At best, bringing such behavior into a game is in poor taste. At worst, it's illegal. Don't do it.

#5 – NOT EVERYONE IS PLAYING THE GAME.

While "freaking the mundanes" can be amusing, remember that a game can confuse or startle people passing by. Be considerate of non-players in your vicinity, and make sure that if you are in a public area, your game actions are not going to alarm anyone watching. Attempting to explain to suspicious Bible-thumpers or the police that you weren't really performing a Satanic ritual, you were just creating a Ward against a hostile spirit is an exercise in futility.

#6 – THE RULES ARE FLEXIBLE.

This is what we at White Wolf refer to as the Golden Rule. Put simply, what the Storyteller says goes. After playing a while, some groups find that they don't like the way things work, so they come up with different ways to perform existing effects. The Storyteller may also decide to change some things for game balance or to better suit the style of his chronicle. This does not mean that players can take it upon themselves to decide they are not going to follow the rules. Feel free to come up with suggestions, but get your Storyteller's approval before putting them into play. It's likely he will go along with any reasonable ideas, provided that they are fair and internally consistent.

#7 – HAVE FUN.

Not "win." Not "go out and cause chaos." Just "have fun." That is the overall objective of a game, after all. As stated before, there are no winners or losers, only players. Enjoy the ride and don't worry about how it ends.

LEXICON

Apprentice — A sorcerer who is just beginning her studies. Commonly used to refer to those sorcerers capable of only Basic applications within a single path.

Arcane — A mystical veil used by certain sorcerers to guard their identities.

Astral Plane — The layer of the Periphery connecting the Higher Umbra to the physical world.

Counterspell — A means of using sorcery to negate hostile spells.

Deep Umbra — The part of the spirit world that lies very far away from this reality, the equivalent of deep space.

Familiar — A spirit who has contracted with a sorcerer for mutual service.

Gaia — Mother Earth. The collective consciousness of the Tellurian.

Gauntlet, the — A mystical barrier separating the physical and spiritual worlds.

Hedge Wizardry — The most common mode of sorcery. Also called *Hedge Magic*.

Madwand — A Solitaire who had no teacher and learned everything on her own. Often considered a derogatory term.

Mana — A generic term for the mystical energy used by sorcerers to power their spells. Each magical heritage looks at this energy in its own context and calls it by a different name.

Mentor — A sorcerer's teacher or sponsor. Though sometimes played in-game, these characters are most often handled behind the scenes.

Mundane — Mortals who are incapable and unaware of magic. Used as a derogatory term.

Numinae — The various powers learned by mortals. The singular form is Numina. There are two main categories of Numinae: sorcery and Psychic Phenomena. Some also consider True Faith a type of Numina, though it is usually combined with Theurgy.

Otherworld — Another name for the Deep Umbra, specifically the realms which many consider alternate realities.

Path — A linear progression of related magical effects. Spells are the required elements of a path, whereas rituals are learned separately. Each mode of sorcery has its own collection of paths which practitioners of that style may employ.

Penumbra — The layer of the Periphery connecting the Middle Umbra to the physical world.

Periphery — The part of the spirit world, lying just on the other side of the Gauntlet, that mirrors the physical world.

Praxes — The technical term for the paths of Hedge Wizardry. Singular: Praxis.

Priest — A general term for any sorcerer who has True Faith and studies Theurgy. Different religions have their own specific titles.

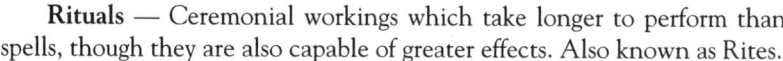
Rituals — Ceremonial workings which take longer to perform than spells, though they are also capable of greater effects. Also known as Rites.

Shadowlands — The layer of the Periphery which forms a bridge to the Lower Umbra.

Solitaire — A sorcerer who belongs to no magical society or traditional heritage.

Sorcerer — A general term for any mortal who uses magic. This does not include true mages or psychics.

Sorcery — The array of spells and rituals known to mortals. This includes both Hedge Wizardry and Theurgy.

Spell — A common magical effect, usually cast relatively quickly.

Tellurian — All reality, including the physical and spiritual worlds. Some say that our Tellurian is but one universe among many alternate realities.

Theurgy — An alternate form of sorcery practiced by those mortals possessing True Faith.

True Faith — The measure of a character's belief in a higher power and the rare ability to call upon that power in times of need.

Umbra — The spirit world; everything that is not part of the physical world. The Umbra is broken up into the Higher, Middle and Lower realms. In common usage, this term refers primarily to the Middle Umbra.

Umbrood — A technical term for any being native to the Umbra.

Underworld, the — A common term for the realms of the Lower Umbra.

Via — Latin for road, this is the name given to the paths of Theurgy. Plural: Viae.

Repeat after me:

"I am not a wizard. I am not a vampire. I do not drink blood, worship Satan, or kill animals or people. I am playing a fantasy game. None of this is real."

Is that clear, clear as in "crystal"? As in "I know that!" As in "Do Not Pass Go, Do Not Collect $200, Do not go on the talk show circuit and brag about drinking blood"? Cool. Let's get busy playing.

If it's *not* clear, throw this book and any others like it in your possession into the nearest trash can and go seek mental help. Please don't make your illness other people's problem.

Thank you.

MIND'S EYE THEATRE

These terms are common to all **Mind's Eye Theatre** systems. They describe rules and mechanics rather than in-game terms.

Abilities — The extent of a character's expertise in various fields, measured in Traits. These cover talents and skills as well as general and specific knowledge.

Archetypes — Basic personality types used to specify Nature and Demeanor.

Attributes — These descriptive Traits measure a character's innate Physical, Social and Mental capabilities.

Backgrounds — Advantages that a character has acquired during her history, also measured in Traits.

Bidding — A process of risking Traits in an attempt to win a challenge.

Challenge — The system by which conflicts between characters are resolved through the bidding of Traits and the use of Rock-Paper-Scissors.

Chronicle — A series of stories all centered upon one major plot or theme.

Corpus Levels — The wraithly equivalent of Health Levels.

Experience — Awarded to characters as they progress through the story, these Traits are used to purchase advantages or overcome existing limitations.

Health Levels — A measure of how injured your character is at any given time.

Humanity — Similar to Attributes, these descriptive Traits portray your character's virtues and ties to her community.

Narrator — Someone who has the authority to adjudicate rules and resolve disputes. This person assists the Storyteller in running the chronicle.

Negative Traits — Similar to Flaws, these represent defects in the character's Physical, Social or Mental make-up.

Scene — A short period of time in which a specific activity takes place. This may be a single discussion or an entire battle. Scenes typically last about 10-15 minutes.

Simple Test — A feat in which the character's efforts are not being actively resisted or countered. Also used for purely random events, such as environmental or situational effects. No Traits are bid or lost in Simple Tests.

Static Test — A more applied effort in which the skills and attributes of a character come directly into play in the result. Though not directly resisted by other individuals, the character must still risk a Trait when attempting these actions.

Story — One or more game sessions that take place within a short amount of time, such as over a single weekend.

Storyteller — The person running the game. The Storyteller has final authority over all game activities.

Test — The system for resolving conflict. **Mind's Eye Theatre** uses Rock-Paper-Scissors to provide for a random outcome without using external props, such as dice or cards.

Turn — The amount of time it normally takes to perform a single action. One combat turn is about 10 seconds.

Chapter One: Magic Society

Snowflakes are one of nature's most fragile things;
But just look what they can do when they stick together.
— M. Kelly

Magic is real. Not the stage illusions provided for an evening's entertainment, but the ability to change reality. It has survived from the first moments of creation through the ages of Myth and Reason. And contrary to what most mundanes believe, it is still around today.

So too are the rare individuals who study the mystic arts. These practitioners move through the world like the wind, some moments a quiet breeze, other times a storm. They go by many names: witch, wizard, shaman, high priestess, cunning man, wise woman. Here, these names are bound up into the simpler "sorcerer."

MAGICAL SOCIETIES

Humans form communities. It is a common behavior, especially when we feel different from the people around us. Sorcerers are no exception.

There are countless mystical organizations throughout the world. Some are very old, passing down their traditional ways from mentor to apprentice, generation to generation. Others are more recent in origin, perhaps with a newly rediscovered heritage or a freshly created one.

The common thread that binds these people into groups is shared philosophy and beliefs. It matters little whether a sorcerer was raised with a particular group's mindset or adopted it after she came into her power. Either way, the heritage she claims has a direct impact on the way she practices magic.

HEDGE WIZARDRY

Knowledge is power. When a person truly understands the world around him, he ceases to be a mere observer. By learning the world's secrets, he becomes an active participant in his own life. This is the goal of hedge wizardry. The most common form of sorcery, these arts are practiced by countless traditions throughout the world.

One person discovers a Truth. She shares it with someone else, and the two begin to create the framework for an ideology. When enough people have come to accept this ideology, it becomes doctrine. Over time, the beliefs weave themselves into the tapestry of the world, providing a heritage of known techniques to those students who seek enlightenment.

The practice of magic is no different. If one person does something over and over, it's called habit or personal preference. If a hundred people do the same thing, it becomes tradition or dogma. The practice is then passed from teacher to student, each setting the path more firmly in place. Though there are countless such roads carved into the landscape of reality, any given individual usually follows only one of them.

TOOLS OF THE TRADE

Each sorcerer must choose a magical style. This describes the paradigm and techniques used in her practice of magic. Most often, this style is the result of the sorcerer's own heritage, though some individuals have adapted existing models to suit their own unique flair.

Many practitioners rely upon symbolic expression, such as chanting, runes or words of power. Others may use dance, musical instruments, blood rites or herbs as a means of expressing their intent. The list of tools is almost endless, though some of the more common systems are listed later in this chapter along with the groups that practice them.

While the debate over which form of magical practice is the most potent is long and heated, the proof, in the end, is in the pudding. All of the styles listed here have been in use throughout history, all to effect. It is up to you to select a style and set of tools which best fit your character concept.

THE ANCIENT ORDER OF THE AEON RITES

The Aeon Society is a group of Western Hermetics, formed in 1872 by Master Johannes Agrippa. In his work, *The Aeon Rites*, the Master claimed to have been shown the true origins of magic by a group called the Secret Watchers. This collection of ascended beings then proceeded to guide Agrippa in the creation of this order. Gathering his closest friends and colleagues, Master Agrippa formed what he called the Aeon Tabernacle. Though the members of this ruling body have changed over the years, the Tabernacle still controls all aspects of the AOAR from its main chantry house in Amsterdam.

Though similar in style and heritage to groups like the Order of the Golden Dawn, this society holds a different temperament. Acts of charity and goodwill are the mainstay of the order, with advancement in the hierarchy being determined not only by magical competence but also benevolence. Some outsiders believe that this kindness and good humor is too pervasive, and wonder if there is something going on behind the scenes.

The Tabernacle's recruitment policy doesn't help the situation. The AOAR is very active in seeking out new members, even soliciting practitioners from other mystical societies. Consequently, the AOAR has a reputation as a "poacher" within the global occult community. This is offset somewhat by the members' good deeds and general demeanor. Magicians from this order are usually calm and collected when others lose their heads, equally well-versed in etiquette and magical theory and generous to their fellow magicians and the mundanes around them. They are also most likely to encourage magicians put off by the increasingly dark tone of other occult groups and personality cults to throw away the black robes and pursue the sacred mysteries.

When a high-ranking devotee joined the Sons of Tertullian in 1948, a war ignited between the AOAR and the Sons, nearly decimating the AOAR. The order dropped out of sight in 1960 and has kept a fairly low profile since then, working quietly in small covens and shelters. The recent expansion of spiritual awareness caused a resurgence of interest in the order. At last count, the Aeon Society had numerous members and chantries in several major European and North American cities.

Preferred Paths: *Daimonis, Enchantment, Spirit Calling, Summoning*

Magical Style: *The Aeon Rites* resembles a blend of the Kabbalah with ancient Greco-Egyptian texts, including the *Corpus Hermeticum*, filtered through Agrippa's own unique perspective. The book puts great emphasis on symbolism, leading to the extensive use of classical tools: cups, wands, swords and pentacles. Other geometric forms are also common, including the sacred Pythagorean solids: triangles, squares, circles and hexagrams. In addition to Latin, Greek and Egyptian, many members of the AOAR also know Enochian,

the legendary angelic tongue. Astrology plays an important magical role, as does sacred mathematics. "High ritual" doesn't even begin to describe the elaborate procedures of the AOAR.

Quote: *There is a better way. Discard the tarnished traditions you were taught by others and step into the light of truth. Come, let us show you how.*

THE FENIAN

Less of a magical society than an extended family, these Irish shapeshifters boast of an unbroken lineage to the Tuatha de Daanan. Though just about everyone would like to claim such a heritage, the Fenian can back up their claims with magical powers, unearthly talents and inhuman family.

Many Fenian are kinain, carrying the blood of one of the Celtic kith: boggans, clurichauns, ghille dhu, selkies or sidhe. Others are Kinfolk, usually of the Fianna tribe. However, this magical heritage also comes with a price. All members of this clan suffer a strong geas, an inherited oath binding them to the honor of their family. In addition to allegiance to their society and kin, the Fenian are dedicated to the protection of nature and humanity against the Wyrm. With such allegiance and heritage come additional threats that most sorcerers do not usually encounter, such as fomori or Dauntain, and with each death, the old folk grow rarer still.

Though a common element in many Celtic legends, these half-fae magicians today number less than a few dozen. New members are not recruited; rather, the Fenian treat discovery of a long-lost descendant like a family reunion. This sense of reverence and joy is one of the few things preserving the clan's spirit through the shadow times. By honoring their history and singing the old songs, the Fenian will preserve their legacy for another generation. That is all that matters.

Preferred Paths: *Shapeshifting* (required), *Fascination*, *Weathercraft*; access to Fae Arts/Realms or Fianna Tribal Gifts (if the Fenian is properly related through Merits such as *Kinain* or *Kinfolk*)

Magical Style: Because the Fenian are innately magical beings, they treat all of their powers as part of a blood inheritance. Fenian magicians must decide whether to concentrate on sorcery or the powers of their supernatural relations. You may purchase one of these domains at normal cost, and the other counts as a Fringe Power (see Chapter Three). In either case, you always pay normal cost for the path of *Shapeshifting*. However, to reflect the Fenian reliance upon this legacy, you may not raise any other Praxis, Gift or Art to a higher level than your current rating in *Shapeshifting*.

Each Fenian bears a geas (see the Flaw on p. 100, no additional Traits conferred), which she must uphold, else she risk losing her gifts. If a Fenian breaks her geas, she is down four Traits in any challenge involving her magic. Her magic will not return to her until she has sought out a Storyteller and detailed how her character is atoning for the trespass. While the Fenian is actively atoning for the mistake, she is two Traits down in her attempts to work magic. When the powers that be (and the Storyteller) deem the transgression paid for, the Fenian may use her full Trait pool in challenges.

Quote: *What's the matter, lass? Why the sad face? Life is a time of joy. Drink, dance and be merry, for tomorrow — well, we'll deal with that later.*

MOGEN HA CHAV

Known as the Shield of the 36, this fraternity of Jewish scholars is based in Brooklyn, New York. They believe in the existence of 36 upright humans who protect the world through their essential goodness. The Shield is dedicated to the task of keeping track of and protecting these individuals, for if they were to die, the world would fall into darkness. Begun as a student cabal at the Kabbalistic academy in Genoa, this group spends its days trying to learn the identities and locations of the 36 and protecting them once they're found. Since the world hasn't fallen to darkness yet, apparently the Shield is doing well.

All members of the Mogen Ha Chav are Jewish males, most above 40 years old. Jewish tradition dictates that only older, preferably married, men are allowed to study the Kabbalah. Such wisdom requires experience; only

HISTORY OF THE KABBALAH

Originally, there was not one Kabbalah but many. Each covered a different topic: such as philosophy, medicine, theology, science or magic. The latter text is what most people today think of when they hear the term. Though still deeply rooted in Hebrew mysticism, the lore and systems contained within this work have found their way into several magical traditions over the last few centuries.

There are various ways to spell the word, the most common being Qabalah and Kabbalah. The former usually refers to non-Jewish, Hermetic or Western versions of the lore, and the latter is universally accepted as the traditional form.

Though the first written texts of this name date back to the first century B.C., the origins of this wisdom are much older. Some claim that they derive from the ancient *Key of Solomon* itself. This legendary treatise held the answers to all worldly questions — names of power, ceremonies of enchantment and consecration, circles of protection, healing, even the calling and binding of spirits.

those scholars who are properly "grounded" in life are considered ready to study Kabbalah without danger. The oldest scholar of the group, the Baal Shem Tov (or Master of the Good Name), is almost 100. The rest range in age from 97 to as young as 45. All wear the traditional tzitzis, beard and yarmulke demanded by Orthodox Jewish tradition.

Currently, the Shield maintains its main house in Brooklyn, NY. While their most active mission is the protection of the 36, these men also practice gematria and cast traditional horoscopes, which can yield some surprising information. Their resources are considerable — a network of informants, an astonishing occult library and wealth to provide for the Shield's daily needs.

Preferred Paths: *Divination, Healing, Summoning, Warding, Weathercraft*

Magical Style: The Mogen Ha Chav follows the Kabbalah, studying the Sephiroth of the Tree of Life. These sorcerers perform most spells and rituals in their original Hebrew. Divination uses traditional astrology or horoscopes, and other secrets are revealed through the study of gematria and numerology. The maintenance of a devout Jewish life — keeping Torah — is essential to the Shield.

Quote: *Earth is too great a treasure to leave without protection. Though our task is a hard one, we must endure. There is no other way.*

THAL'HUN

Not everyone believes in magic. Interestingly enough, this is true even among the ones who practice it. The Thal'hun tentatively fall into the category of technowizards, those people who use their own unique form of science to duplicate the arts of sorcery. In the case of this society, the story goes much deeper.

The Thal'hun claim to be the heirs to an ancient extra-terrestrial science. Millions of years ago, the Hui:xa fled their dying planet, Bars'hm. Three hundred members of their race, known as the Jeva, set out to find a new home for their people. The rest passed into a place outside time and space, sealed away in a city-sized ship until another planet could be found.

One of the Jeva, a being by the name of Khuvon, made his way to Earth. He walked among the earliest civilizations, many thousands of years ago, teaching them lore of his people. Unfortunately, there was no translation for many of the concepts used in his advanced science. Lacking any other way of framing his words, people understood his techniques to be magic. This misperception continues even today.

Khuvon last walked among his followers in the early 1960s. He gathered about him seven disciples to whom he revealed the secrets of resonance and vibration. These visionaries formed the Star Council of Zoraster in order to teach others this forgotten lore, preparing for the time when the Hui:xa will return from their self-imposed exile. Of the original seven, three have died.

The four original councilors and the three successors lead the Thal'hun from their headquarters in San Francisco, California.

The Thal'hun do not consider themselves an occult society. They do not welcome seekers of mystic lore or students of other magical systems. Instead, the Thal'hun find new members from the ranks of UFOlogists and visionary inventors. New initiates (a:xa) are taught the ancient language of Luz'at. This sacred tongue holds the secrets of thal — the power of harmonics.

Preferred Paths: *Coiling, Conjuration, Hellfire, Mentalis, Summoning, Weathercraft*

Magical Style: Thal'hun practice the remnants of Hui:xa technology, a strange blend of crystallography, meditation and vocal toning. While they use crystal rods, spheres and cones to focus these resonances, the key to thal lies in the mastery of Luz'at. Members of the fellowship spend years learning this difficult language as well as the mental discipline necessary to manifest its concepts in reality.

Quote: *There is no magic, only the secrets of sound and thought. We have moved beyond superstition, instead rediscovering a science older than the human race.*

PRIESTS

Unlike their scholarly counterparts, those sorcerers who follow the paths of *Theurgy* rely more upon divine guidance than accumulated lore. Though the effects are similar to the effects of sorcery, the mindset and manifestations of the two powers are often very different. Priests do not see themselves as causing these effects but rather as the recipients of a divine gift. At most, the priest is a conduit through which the light of her patron flows.

Regardless of what religion they follow, priests all have one thing in common: a deep-seated belief in some supernatural agency. This may be the kami of Shinto, the one God of Christianity and Judaism, even the formless void known to the followers of Buddhism. This supreme force has many faces and even more names, but above all else it has power.

In addition to manifesting this divine support as True Faith, priests are able to learn the powers of *Theurgy*. However, because of their dedication to a religious framework, Theurgists may learn only the paths of sorcery that conform to their chosen ecclesiastical model.

Both the spells and the rituals of *Theurgy* take the same amount of time as other forms of sorcery. This may be spent in prayer and meditation or in performing the benedictions and mudras of one's faith. Usually, the only material focus for these feats is a holy symbol or token appropriate to the chosen religion (e.g., a cross for Christianity, a pentacle for a Wiccan, a yin-yang symbol for a Buddhist). Some sects do rely upon vestments of office and

other paraphernalia to help the priest form the proper mindset for the working. Many would argue that these liturgies and ceremonies are just another magical style, one of a different heritage but no less steeped in symbolism than the sorcerous praxes.

Though Christian terminology is used often throughout this section, it is only because of its greater familiarity in the West. Many other religions trace their roots back as far or even farther, and their Faith is no less intense.

BALAMOB

Descendants of the ancient Mayan shamans, the Balamob are found throughout Mesoamerica. Known to the native people as Children of the Jaguar, these mystics have preserved the old ways for thousands of years. Both h'men (sorcerers) and itzamna (priests) are common within the sect, each group honoring the spirits in its own way. Each "soul-carrier" is dedicated to a particular wayob (spirit-guide). The shaman's power over the spirit world comes from his study and service to this totem.

There is no formal organization among the Balamob. The sect keeps to its traditional homelands: the Yucatan peninsula, Belize, Guatemala, El Salvador and Honduras. Even Western recruits eventually settle in Central America. Most do not associate with outsiders, though visitors who honor the spirits are treated cordially. Kinfolk who study the old ways are also welcome, especially those related to the Balam, or werejaguars (see **Bastet** for more information).

Initiates to the Balamob usually come from the local tribes and native peoples. However, in recent times, a few anthropologists and other foreign

A WORD ON TOTEMS

The original meaning of totems and spirit-guides has been lost in pop culture. The calling of a shaman by her totem is the same as the calling between God and a Christian priest. It is not simply a matter of behaving in a certain way or adhering to arbitrary rules. The life of a shaman is filled with the essence of her spirit guide. Every thought, every action, every belief is filtered through this perspective. A shaman of the jaguar does not simply talk about defending her homeland — that service is her entire reason for existence. She can no more ignore the bans and strictures of her totem than you can ignore breathing or sleeping. Don't make the mistake of assuming that just because a sorcerer can talk to the spirits, she is a shaman. The path is a way of life all its own.

scholars have been allowed to join. This is not common, and the elders of each sect go to great lengths to make sure their dedication to the spirits is sincere.

Neophytes are taught about Xibalba, the spirit world or Umbra. Once she understands the basic cosmology and requirements of the Balamob, the initiate is taken to one of the ancient Mayan temples. From this sacred site, she undertakes a vision quest, journeying into the spirit world in search of her life-guide. If the spirits find the candidate worthy, she will be greeted by her totem, who will ask if she wishes to serve. Not all initiates have the strength or dedication to make this commitment — some wander the spirit world aimlessly until the ritual ends. If a sorcerer is rejected by the spirits, she is still allowed to study with the sect, though only the most basic rites will be available to her.

Preferred Paths: *Alchemy, Conveyance, Spirit Calling, Shadows, Shapeshifting, Totem Link*

Magical Style: Balamob believe their power comes from the Wakah-Chan, the World Tree that binds the physical and spiritual planes together. Its sap (ch'ulel) flows through the veins of all living beings. By shedding blood and other bodily fluids, chanting and drinking hallucinogenic brews, the sorcerer may call upon the power of the spirits who inhabit the Tree. Ritual dance also allows communication with these spirits, as native cultures have known for thousands of years. Because they are usually rural magicians, Balamob often lack "book learning" but still master *Lores* through oral tradition. Western initiates tend to be more academically inclined.

Most Balamob also learn the Mestizo language, a derivative of ancient Mayan. Though not considered sacred or magical, this is the language spoken by the elders of the sect. Younger initiates keep trying to convince the elders to teach in English or Spanish, but the wise ones feel that too much is lost in translation.

Quote: *Do not be fooled by what you see on the surface. The true strength of the spirit comes from within. And our strength grows. The faiths of our invaders have become brittle, like an old wineskin. Soon it will be time to reclaim the tribal lands, returning them to the old ways.*

SOCIETY OF LEOPOLD

Though the Society is generally thought of as one that hunts sorcerers and supernatural beings, such lines are never clearly drawn in reality. Within its ranks are several sects that practice *Theurgy* in one form or another, from the healers of Saint Claire to the necromancers within the Sons of Tertullian. However, even though tending to the injured (*Via Medicamenti*) and receiving divine guidance (*Via Oraculi*) are generally tolerated, other forms of practice are not so well favored.

The two groups below, officially part of the Society, often stray outside the guidelines set forth by the Office of the Censor. As such, they work hard to keep their mystical practices quiet lest they themselves attract the attention of the Inquisition. Any Theurgist who wishes to practice within the Society must register with the Office of the Censor. Failing to register is not a crime, *per se*, but it is a serious breach of protocol, an act of insubordination and an invitation to further investigation by the Censors.

Those Society members who practice *Theurgy* see it more as divine providence than any form of magical working, but they also recognize that scholarship and knowledge can take someone far beyond where faith alone could lead. Prayer and formal liturgy form the heart of their practice, and a Theurgist's works are intrinsically bound up in the vestments, symbols and rituals of her religion. Without them, her magic will not work, and she might even be taken for one of the enemy.

BRETHREN OF ALBERTUS

These Inquisitors take their direction from the teachings of Albertus Magnus. Magnus believed that magic was evil, but one must learn it in order to combat it most effectively. The Brethren, commonly called Albertines, are known within the Inquisition for their command of *Theurgy*, and they have wielded this command with great success against the supernatural.

The Albertines are not always trusted, however, as most Inquisitors firmly believe that "white" magic is merely the first step toward practicing "black" magic. Because no Inquisitor-General has ever outlawed *Theurgy*, the Albertines continue to practice without interference from their superiors. Some Inquisitors whisper that they have some sort of mystical hold over the Inquisitor-General, and any appointment of a trained Albertine Theurgist to the Inquisitor-General's personal council only provides grist for the mill. The Brethren are also frequently targeted for investigation by the Order of St. Peter, which investigates magicians, witches and warlocks.

Though the Brethren live and work alongside their fellow Inquisitors, rumors crop up now and again about a private Cenaculum where they study their mystic arts. Any Brother asked about such a thing usually scoffs at the suggestion. The Albertines are justifiably proud of their sect's heritage; they were among the first to freely admit women into their ranks, and women continue to occupy a prominent place in the sect.

Preferred Paths: *Alchemy, Conjuration, Enchantment, Illusion, Mentulis, Summoning, Theurgy, Warding*

Magical Style: The Brethren practice their "magic" with an eye toward allaying the fears of their colleagues in the Inquisition. Not a few refuse to cast anything when there is a member of the St. Peter Order present. Many use highly hermetic trappings, particularly with regard to angels, while others create their own unique rituals that don't look much different from Catholic ritual (especially to those unfamiliar with such).

Quote: *Anything which comes of the Divine cannot be evil. The simple fact that we can perform these wonders proves that claim. Someday people will learn that it is the heart, not the outward acts, which determines good and evil.*

THE ORDER OF SAINT MICHAEL

A retired Roman soldier named Antonius is credited with founding the Order of Saint Michael in A.D. 413. Originally formed to venerate the archangel Michael, the Michaelites attracted a great many ex-soldiers looking for a way to redirect their martial talents. Like many Christians of the day, they believed that the Second Coming was near and that the Church was not ready for the fierce battle predicted in the Revelation of John. Because they were trained as exorcists as well as soldiers, the Michaelites were frequently summoned to communities where demonic possession or infestation was feared.

The order saw a significant downturn in membership over the next thousand years. By the time the Society of Leopold relocated to the Monastery of San Michele, built by Antonius himself, in 1488, the Michaelites had been reduced to a dozen at best. However, after the Society subsumed the order, the small sect reorganized and seemed to find new life under the Society's direction.

The Michaelites are not concerned with hunting the infernal in things (e.g., vampires, werewolves, sorcerers, etc.) but with discovering its direct presence and sending it back to Hell, preferably as painfully as possible. A highly militant order, its initiation process is much akin to basic training. All members are skilled in the use of weapons, for these warriors of God believe that Faith sometimes needs a helping hand. This belief is also apparent in their Theurgic practices.

Preferred Paths: *Cursing, Daimonis, Divination, Enchantment, Fascination, Hellfire, Warding*

Magical Style: Rather than focusing on the abstract applications of theology like the Albertines, the Michaelites learn how to call upon divine authority in its most direct forms. *Cursing* (*Via Tormentum*) and *Hellfire* (*Via Ignis*) allow them to evoke the wrath of God, whereas *Daimonis* (*Via Geniorum*) and *Warding* (*Via Defensorum*) deal directly with the dark forces they encounter. The Michaelites usually avoid elaborate rituals, as they rarely have time for more than the briefest prayers before plunging into battle.

Quote: *Darkness takes many forms. Our brethren seek that which is hidden in mortal frames, but our quest is simpler. If the tangible manifestations of evil are driven from this world, the lesser darkness will fade on its own.*

NEPHITE PRIESTHOOD

According to the Book of Mormon, the first Westerners to find the Americas came not with Columbus but almost a thousand years earlier. Fleeing the Holy Land, the family of Lehi crossed the great ocean to the New World in the sixth century A.D. With them came a prophet named Nephi, a man touched with the vision of God.

When Joseph Smith wrote down the story of these travelers in the early 1800s, few people believed him. When Brigham Young, Smith's successor, led the first members of the Church of Latter Day Saints to the Salt Lake Basin, the full tale of the prophets was still not known. It was not until 1849, when Nephi appeared in the dreams of Uriah Spence, that those lost visions were restored.

Spence was a man of simple piety and great intellect. He accepted the wisdom of Nephi and, with it, the charge of the Nephite Priesthood. Over the next decade, he selected other men of equal heart and faith to stand beside him, teaching them the secrets that had been revealed to him. Thus was the new Priesthood born. Its divine mission: to protect the people of New Zion until the Second Coming of Christ, when all those who are apostate will bow before the Messiah and repent their evil ways.

As the end of the millennium draws near, the Nephites have let fall their shroud of secrecy. New recruits are drawn from the Mormon community. The newly initiated, called deacons, are then taught the ways of Nephi and the deeper history of their people. After a year or two of study, they become full priests, leaving their temples to wander across New Zion (the western United States). Some Nephites travel to Mexico and Central America, searching for archeological proof of Lehi's arrival in the New World. When such "evidence" is found, the Nephites declare these sites sacred ground, defending them from all "trespassers" — even ones whose families have lived in the area for centuries.

Preferred Paths: *Daimonis, Divination, Enchantment, Healing, Hellfire, Necromancy, Weathercraft*

Magical Style: The Dust Prophets, as they are often called, are all devout Mormons. Prayer and religious ceremony are the only acceptable means of performing "magic" — though again, no member of the Priesthood would ever acknowledge that he is actually performing magic. Many prayers are spoken in Reformed Egyptian, a language descended from the tongue Lehi and Nephi spoke. "Spells" invoke the names of celestial beings as manifestations of the Holy Spirit. Dust Prophets will never call upon God or Jesus directly — though the great powers may be petitioned, no Nephite would be blasphemous enough to demand such aid.

Quote: *As it was in the days of our forefathers, so it is today. The word and ways of the Prophet must be preserved against those who do not believe. The end* *times are coming, and those who do not know the Truth must be made to understand.*

UZOMA

The original practitioners of Ifa came from the Yoruba tribe in what is now Nigeria. Though most of the elders are still located there, younger members of the sect have taken their faith into the broader world. Most Uzoma are either amused or offended by other religions descended from their beliefs, though a few prefer to honor the similarities rather than the differences.

Most Uzoma operate as babalawo (priests). To them, interaction with the Orisha is a matter of service and dedication. The degenerate custom of dealing with more than one Orisha — even called by another name — is foreign to them. As such, each Uzoma priest is limited to *Alchemy* and the paths taught by the Orisha she serves.

Orisha	Title	Preferred Paths
Elegba	Opener of the Ways	*Conjuration, Conveyance*
Obatalá	Father of the Universe	*Conjuration, Mentalis*
Ogún	God of Iron and War	*Coiling, Hellfire*
Orunmila	Keeper of Wisdom and Truth	*Divination, Mentalis*
Oshosi	Patron of Hunters and Scouts	*Divination, Summoning*
Oshún	Queen of the Sweet Waters	*Fascination, Illusion*
Oyá	Mistress of Winds and the Dead	*Necromancy, Weathercraft*
Shangó	Master of Fire and Thunder	*Hellfire, Weathercraft*
Yemayá	Mother of the Waters	*Healing, Watercraft*

Though priests are the most common practitioners within the Uzoma, other sorcerers — known as bokor — exist as well. These warlocks are not well-respected, however, by others of their sect. Using the power of the Orisha without their blessing is considered selfish, and the motivations of such individuals are highly questionable. On the other hand, the bokor are still looked upon with more favor than the Nhanga — Uzoma infernalists.

Most new initiates (asogwe) are Yoruba. However, all asogwe must journey to the homeland of the Orisha. Non-Africans are not forbidden to join the priesthood, though few make it through the initiation period. A European might be able to understand the Orisha intellectually, but the one who can feel them in his heart is quite rare.

Preferred Paths: *Alchemy, Conjuration, Divination, Healing, Weathercraft*; those who serve as shamans in tribes may tailor their magics to that which serves the tribe best. Bokor often practice *Conjuration, Divination, Hellfire, Mentalis, Necromancy* and *Summoning*.

Magical Style: These folk often practice African-style magics, and hold strong belief in animism and shamanism. They invoke the spirits through supplication and offerings, such as dance or a carving. Such offerings and invocations are varied according to the spirit involved — Ogún may find battle-cries or a well-made weapon to be more appealing to him than the flute music and bowls offered to Oshún. Also, proper spirit etiquette is extremely important; once a favor is granted, the petitioner should thank the spirit for her help, lest the spirit find the shaman ungrateful. Bokor often work without such niceties, but at peril to themselves.

Quote: *Come, my friend, let us talk of the spirits. You may see them as beings from another world, but that is not so. They are the world — its very breath. Only when you see the Orisha as I do can you be in harmony with what is around you.*

OTHERS

Literally thousands of societies and covens exist throughout the world, each with its own history, rules and requirements. The few groups described in this chapter are a tiny fraction of the whole. Vows of secrecy and loyalty are common: Many societies have developed a sort of siege mentality and perhaps not unjustifiably. The World of Darkness is a strange and dangerous place, and there is undeniable safety in numbers.

SOLITAIRES

Not all sorcerers are members of a mystical society. Many prefer to walk their own road as wizards or priests, free from the ties of others. Some do this by choice; others are simply not fortunate enough to have found a mentor.

Though they're isolated and self-taught, Solitaires are often very good at what they do.

Solitaires range in age from curious children to elderly spinsters. They can be from literally any walk of life, any age, any background. A teenager starts dabbling in witchcraft, looking for revenge against her teasing classmates, or an older antiquarian begins his quest after finding an obscure magical text. Some are wealthy eccentrics who practice for amusement; others practice in their parents' basements, searching for something to believe in. Some have never realized that sorcerous communities exist at all, and others have seen too much of such societies and have abandoned them. The only thing these sorcerers have in common is a command of strange forces.

Solitaires must still select a personal magical style, though each sorcerer's particular method may draw from many diverse systems. It is not uncommon for a Solitaire to borrow bits and pieces of a dozen different cultures. No wonder, then, that Solitaires are both pitied and envied by the followers of more rigid traditions.

Preferred Paths: None.

Magical Style: Solitaires quite literally borrow from every resource that looks good to them, but they stick with whatever they choose. Their rituals are often elaborate and chockablock with all manner of snippets of different magical styles, from personal bloodletting to sand painting to inscribing runes.

Quote: *I've been at this for a while, I've got my own way of doing things, and I'm pretty happy with it. So if you don't mind, I'll just stick with it. Now please excuse me, I can't let the cauldron boil over....*

Chapter Two: Character Creation

All my life I've wanted to be somebody.
But I see now I should have been more specific.
— Jane Wagner

CHARACTER CREATION SUMMARY

- **Step One: Inspiration — Who are you?**
  - Create a character concept
  - Choose Nature and Demeanor
- **Step Two: Attributes — What are you like?**
  - Prioritize Categories (Physical, Social, Mental)
  - Select Attribute Traits: 6/4/3
- **Step Three: Advantages — What do you know?**
  - Choose three Abilities
  - Choose Background and Influence Traits: 5
  - Choose your character's sorcery style
  - Select paths: Five Basic spells
- **Step Four: Assets — How dedicated are you?**
  - Record starting Humanity (4) and Willpower Traits (1)
  - Choose Negative Traits, if any
  - Purchase Merits and Flaws, if any
  - Spend freebie Traits (5)
- **Step Five: Spark of Life**

STEP ONE — INSPIRATION

The first step in creating any character is a concept. To play the role, you first need to define the role. Before translating anything into game mechanics or trying to write up statistics or Attributes, you need to get a feel for what it is like to be that person. A good rule of thumb is this: If you were forced to play your character with no Traits, no powers, nothing — just as a personality and a name, could you do it for a week? More important, would you enjoy doing it? If not, then you have not finished coming up with a character concept yet.

PERSONALITY ARCHETYPES

Humans instinctively wear masks. We spend every moment of our lives playing roles of one type or another. Our minds are made up of many layers and personalities, some which we pretend to be, others that we present naturally.

Personality archetypes are a way of defining our various selves. The psychologist Carl Jung developed the concept of archetypes to describe the fundamental concepts residing in the universal unconscious of humanity. They help us make sense of things, enabling players to better understand their characters and to relate them to their own lives.

Archetypes are the molds for an infinite number of different personalities. They represent broad templates and patterns, not absolute standards. Characters do not really fit into such neat and tidy categories. Each individual varies from the pattern in many ways. However, archetypes are handy starting points when describing your character's origin and concept.

NATURE AND DEMEANOR

The key to the use of archetypes is the interaction between the character's inner and outer selves. Your Nature is your true (inner) personality, the calling of your heart. Most people do not wish others to know them intimately, and therefore create a facade behind which they can hide their true self. This false front is your Demeanor. It may be as consistent as your eye color or may change as frequently as your mood. An extraordinarily open, honest or simple-minded individual may even have the same Demeanor and Nature.

Archetypes have a practical impact on the game, for your character's Nature defines the limits of what she will and will not do. On the positive side, if your character is forced to perform some action that violates her Nature and Demeanor, she may call for a free retest against such mind control. However, an opponent may also use your Nature against you, calling it as a Negative Trait in an appropriate challenge.

Players may draw their Natures and Demeanors from the following list, but these are just the beginning. Storytellers and players are encouraged to develop new archetypes, creating a truly unique personality for your character.

ARCHITECT

Your sense of purpose goes beyond your own needs. You strive to create something of lasting value for those who will come after you: to found a town, create a company or in some way leave a permanent legacy. You gain satisfaction by creation.

BULLY

You are a ruffian, a tough guy who delights in tormenting the weak. Power and might are all you respect, and you see it as the only way to survive this dog-eat-dog world. The emotions of kindness and pity are not foreign to you, but you tend to hide from them and from your own sense of weakness.

CAREGIVER

You want to make a difference for those around you, helping them when they need support. People depend on your stability and strength to keep them steady and centered. This does not mean you automatically neglect your own needs and wants, but you do have a tendency to put the common good before your own happiness.

CONNIVER

What's the sense of working hard when you can get something for nothing? You always try to find the easy way out. Some might call what you do swindling or outright theft, but you know that you only do unto others before they can do unto you. Trickery is a game and you get great pleasure out of outwitting someone.

CRACKERJACK

You're the best. Everyone knows it. Or at least, that's the plan. You've got a reputation to uphold. You always like to show off, to prove to people that you've got what it takes. While this can get you into trouble, it just makes it all the more impressive when you walk away unharmed

CRITIC

Nothing is ever perfect. You accept nothing without careful scrutiny and examination, pointing out the blemishes in order for the good to be recognized. Your standards are high for everything, and you insist that they be met. You are never satisfied with anything that is less than ideal, unless it is yourself. After all, you are not a perfectionist.

CURMUDGEON

Cynicism is your middle name. You tend to take everything seriously and find little humor in life, though you may have a wickedly barbed wit. You have a clear understanding of how things really work, especially when they involve the circus of human endeavor. While this has not completely taken the joy out of your life, you have little tolerance for the stupidity of others.

DAREDEVIL

You love gambles and seize any opportunity to take a chance. The outcome is secondary compared to the thrill that the risk affords. You thrive on the high of not knowing how things are going to turn out, taking chances rather than going with the known.

DEVIANT

There are always people who do not fit in, and you are such a miscreant. You are not so much an aimless rebel as an independent thinker who does not belong in the society that raised you. You don't give a damn about other people's morality, but you do adhere to your own strange code of conduct. Deviants are typically irreverent, and some have truly bizarre tastes and desires.

DIRECTOR

You despise chaos and disorder, leading you to take control and organize things in order to suppress anarchy. You like to be in charge, live to organize, and habitually strive to make things work smoothly. You trust your judgment implicitly and tend to think of things in black-and-white terms. Either the people around you support your efforts, or you will be forced to find some way of dealing with those who oppose you.

EXPLORER

Your primary reason for existence is to experience the excitement of finding new people, places and things. You are not looking for any particular thing, just anything that has not been discovered yet. Once you have uncovered your newest find, it's off to the next adventure. Explorers tend to have (often short) lives that others consider unstable or even reckless.

FANATIC

You are consumed by a particular cause. It is the primary force in your life, for good or ill. Every ounce of blood and passion you possess is directed toward your cause; in fact, you may feel guilty about spending time on anything else. You and those around you may suffer, but your cause is everything. The end justifies the means. You must describe your cause in your character history and define how it affects your behavior.

GALLANT

You are as flamboyant as you are amoral. Some see you as a rogue or a scoundrel. A consummate actor, you are at home in the spotlight, soaking up the attention (if nothing else) from those around you. Gallants vary widely in their moods and ambitions, sharing only the love of the spotlight.

HUNTER

You live for the thrill of the chase. Nothing satisfies you quite like running your prey to ground. Some hunters find more pleasure in watching and stalking their prey from the shadows, knowing they can strike at any time. It is the hunt that gives you pleasure, not the kill. In the end, though, the weak must fall so that the strong survive.

JESTER

You constantly seek the humor in any situation, often to battle the tides of depression inside yourself. You hate sorrow and pain, and constantly try to take others' minds off the dark side of life. Occasionally, you're so determined to be cheerful that you make light of truly serious subjects at inappropriate times. Some Jesters manage to escape their pain and find happiness, but many are never so lucky.

JUDGE

As a facilitator, moderator, arbitrator, conciliator and peacemaker, you always seek to make things better. You pride yourself on your rationality, your judgment and your ability to deduce a reasonable explanation when given the facts. You struggle to promote truth, but you understand how difficult it is to ascertain. You respect justice, for that is the way through which truth can reign.

LONER

You are always alone, even in the midst of a crowd. You are the wanderer, the hunter, the lone wolf. Though others might think of you as lonely, in truth you simply prefer privacy to the company of others. There are many different reasons why this might be so: you do not understand people, people dislike you, or you are simply lost in your thoughts. Regardless of the reason, you keep your own counsel.

MARTYR

Many people possess the instinct for self-sacrifice, but few act upon it. You, however, do not shy away from the course. Your desire to give of yourself may stem from a profound sense of love or duty, or from low self-esteem. Whatever the reason, you are able to endure significant suffering because of your beliefs and ideals.

PALADIN

You are dedicated to some higher purpose that sustains you, but you recognize that there is a proper time and place to pursue this goal. Sometimes it is more beneficial in the long run to work with such obstacles, rather than confront them directly. Your goal might be a specific objective with a concrete resolution or a code of behavior that you have sworn to uphold.

PEACOCK

You have lived a pampered life. Only proper, since you are the best and the prettiest, and you have no trouble letting anyone know that. Unfortunately, that nasty world out there does not always see things your way. You wish someone would come along and make things better so you can go back to playing the trophy.

PENITENT

You have sinned, but somehow you will find a way to make things right. In some cases, your crimes are obvious. Nobody can forgive you for them, so you try to find a way to balance the scales. Maybe your unworthiness stems from a more personal cause. Here the quest is to prove your self-worth, to earn the right to the life you have been given.

REBEL

You are independent and free-willed, so much so that you are unwilling to join with others. You desire only the freedom to walk your own path. A maverick, you've occasionally pulled stunts to spite those who tried to fence you in. Those who try to control others are in for a rough time with you.

SAGE

You are the wise one, the advisor, the scholar. You have seen many things, uncovered many secrets. It has not always been easy, for wisdom has come at a high price, but you would gladly do it all again to know what you do. Mundane concerns are secondary to your quest for knowledge. Now if only those around you would pay heed to your advice.

SENSUALIST

Life is shallow, often pointless, so have a good time while it lasts. You are a hedonist, sybarite and party animal. The words austerity, self-denial and discipline have no place in your life. You prefer instant gratification. While you don't mind a little hard work, there had better be a good time waiting for you at the end.

SUPPLICANT

You live to serve others. This could be a divine calling or dedication to some individual. Either way, you find it easier to comply and follow your

master's wishes than to make decisions for yourself. This support and service allows you to maintain a sense of order and reason in your life.

SURVIVOR

No matter what, you always manage to survive. You can endure, pull through, recover from, outlast and outlive nearly any circumstance. When the going gets tough, you get going. It may mean sacrificing things (or people) to keep going, in the end, you'll still be standing.

TRADITIONALIST

You believe in the time-honored traditions. What was good enough for your ancestors is good enough for you now. You resist change of any sort, always striving to preserve the status quo. Some respect your orthodox and conservative beliefs, while others simply see you as an old fogey. Even when things are breaking down, you cling to the old ways rather than gamble on change (which is, in your opinion, usually worse).

VISIONARY

Very few are brave or imaginative enough to look beyond the suffocating embrace of society and mundane thought in search of something more. Though you might have your head in the clouds, that gives you the best perspective. You may be a spiritualist, a shaman, a New Age mystic, a philosopher or an inventor. Whatever your path, you have the ability to see beyond the bounds of conventional imagination and create new possibilities.

STEP TWO – ATTRIBUTES

Attributes are Traits that describe your character's basic potential. **Mind's Eye Theatre** uses an open-ended scale to gauge the relative strength of the character's body, personality and intellect. Rather than the numeric ranking found in most tabletop games, **Mind's Eye Theatre** uses adjectives to express your character in descriptive terms. While any such labels could be applied, in practice it makes more sense to have common terms that are familiar to the players. It does not contribute to the flow of a scene if a player has to stop a challenge to ask what the Trait "Obsequious" or "Perspicacious" means.

SELECTING TRAITS

The first step in assigning Traits is determining which Attribute category is most important. Again, this is based upon your character concept. For sorcerers, Mental Traits are usually the most crucial, but for some, personality (Social) or physique (Physical) may be more relevant.

Once you have put the categories in order, you need to select specific Traits that describe your character in each of those areas. For now, we will only talk about the positive qualities of the character. Assign six Attribute Traits to the primary category and four for the secondary area. The least important facet gets only three.

When building your character, select Attributes that are appropriate to your initial concept. While some people chose Traits based upon based upon number-crunching optimization, this robs you of the joy of playing an intricate and balanced individual. Here is a list of common Traits. A more detailed description can be found later in this chapter.

NEGATIVE TRAITS

In addition to the positive Attribute Traits that a character possesses, she may also have some not-so-desirable qualities. These are referred to as Negative Traits and are chosen from the same categories as the other Attributes. Each Negative Trait taken allows the character to select one additional positive Attribute Trait. It does not matter which category (or categories) these Negative Traits come from, though a maximum of three in each category is recommended. Of course, you are under no obligation to take any at all if you do not wish. Keep in mind that while Negative Traits are useful for describing your character in more detail (as well as providing freebie Traits), an opponent may use them against you during a challenge.

Negative Physical Traits: *Clumsy, Cowardly, Decrepit, Delicate, Docile, Flabby, Lame, Lethargic, Puny, Sickly*

Negative Social Traits: *Bestial, Callous, Condescending, Dull, Inarticulate, Naive, Obnoxious, Repugnant, Shy, Tactless, Untrustworthy*

Negative Mental Traits: *Forgetful, Gullible, Ignorant, Impatient, Oblivious, Predictable, Shortsighted, Violent, Witless*

BIDDING TRAITS

Attribute Traits are used in a descriptive manner when initiating a challenge. While players can think of ways to use nearly any Trait in a given situation, not all Traits from the category in question are appropriate to the specific circumstances of a challenge. If your character is trying to kick someone, *Resilient* is not an appropriate Trait to bid as part of the attack. Likewise, if your character is trying to read an opponent's thoughts, *Creative* might not be an appropriate Trait to bid.

When an opponent bids a Trait that you feel is completely unrelated to the declared task, politely tell her that you are not going to allow its use. If she is insistent, reevaluate your grievance. If you still cannot agree, ask any witnesses for their opinions. Then, if there is still deadlock and no one is willing to compromise, seek out a Narrator to make a ruling. This form of appeal should not occur often. Instead, learn to handle confrontations on your own, quickly and calmly.

SIMPLIFIED BIDDING

For simplicity sake, a Storyteller may wish to permit players to ignore the subtleties of Traits within each category. This would allow, for example, any Physical Trait to be used in any Physical Challenge. This approach is particularly useful when you have a number of novice players trying to learn the rules. Eventually you will want to grow beyond this convention and only use Traits that are appropriate to the situation at hand.

PHYSICAL TRAITS

Athletic: You have conditioned your body so that it responds well in most situations, especially competitive events.

Uses: Competitions, duels, running, acrobatics, grappling.

Brawny: Your physique is characterized by bulky muscular strength, suitable to any type of directed efforts.

Uses: Punching, kicking or grappling in combat when your goal is to inflict damage. Power lifting. Any feat of strength.

Brutal: You are harshly aggressive and capable of taking nearly any action to succeed.

Uses: Fighting an obviously superior enemy.

Dexterous: This Trait represents a general aptitude involving the use of your hands. It is equally valuable to a pickpocket and to a sharpshooter.

Uses: Weapon-oriented combat (*Melee*), picking pockets

Enduring: You have a persistent sturdiness and hold out well against physical opposition. Bullets may not bounce off you, but you can roll with a punch.

Uses: When survival is at stake, this is a good Trait to risk as a second, or successive, bid.

Energetic: You possess a strong internal drive that propels you. In physical situations, you can draw on a deep reservoir of enthusiasm and zeal.

Uses: Combat, running.

Ferocious: You exhibit savage intensity and extreme physical determination. When confronted by obstacles, you waste no time in eliminating them.

Uses: Any time you intend to do serious harm, or when angry.

Graceful: This Trait represents control and balance in motion and the use of your entire body. It is commonly found in athletes and dancers.

Uses: Defense in combat. Whenever you might lose your balance. Dancing, athletics, gymnastics, acrobatics.

Lithe: Your body is characterized by flexibility and suppleness.

Uses: Acrobatics, gymnastics, dodging, dancing, swimming.

Nimble: Light on your feet, and skillful in moving; general agility.

Uses: Dodging, jumping, rolling, acrobatics and hand-to-hand combat.

Quick: This represents your speed and reactions.

Uses: Defending against a surprise attack, running, dodging, attacking.

Resilient: This Trait describes your knack for resisting damage or surviving in adverse environments, as well as your ability to recover quickly once injured.

Uses: Resisting adverse environments. Defending against damage in an attack.

Robust: You are resistant to physical harm and damage, both in resisting the effects and recovering quickly.

Uses: Defending against damage in an attack. Endurance-related actions that could take place over a long period of time.

Rugged: Hardy, rough and healthy. You are able to shrug off wounds, pain and injury to continue.

Uses: When resisting damage, or any challenge that you enter while injured.

Stalwart: Physically strong and steady, you are a rock in a stormy sea. You tend to be uncompromising against opposition.

Uses: Resisting damage, or when standing your ground against overwhelming odds.

Steady: More than simply physically dependable and balanced, you are unfaltering and have a firm control over your efforts.

Uses: Weapon attacks. Fighting in exotic locations. Piloting ships over difficult waters.

Tenacious: You possess great physical determination, mainly through force of will. You often prolong physical confrontations, even when it might not be wise to do so.

Uses: Second or subsequent Physical Challenge.

Tireless: You have a runner's stamina and are less taxed by physical efforts than most people. Like the pink rabbit, you just keep going, and going, and going....

Uses: Any endurance-related challenge. Second or subsequent Physical Challenge with the same foe or foes.

Tough: You possess a harsh, aggressive attitude and refuse to submit.

Uses: Whenever you're wounded or winded.

Vigorous: This is a combination of energy, intensity and resistance to harm. A punch means nothing, and a gunshot wound just pauses you for a minute.

Uses: Combat and athletic challenges when you're on the offensive.

Wiry: This Trait represents tight, streamlined, muscular strength. This is found in a number of people, most often dancers and martial artists, and most likely to be possessed by smaller, non-bulky folks.

Uses: Punching, kicking or grappling in combat. Acrobatic movements. Endurance lifting.

NEGATIVE PHYSICAL TRAITS

Clumsy: You lack physical coordination, balance and grace. You are prone to stumbling and dropping objects.

Cowardly: In threatening situations, saving your neck is all that is important. You might even flee when you have the upper hand, just out of habit.

Decrepit: You move and act as if you are old and infirm. You recover from physical damage slowly and tire easily.

Delicate: You do not withstand stress well and are more susceptible to injury than most.

Docile: You lack physical persistence and often back down rather than stand up for yourself. It is not a matter of being afraid; you simply do not like conflict.

Flabby: Your muscles are underdeveloped. You cannot apply your strength well against resistance.

Lame: One or more of your limbs are disabled. The handicap can be as obvious as an artificial arm or as subtle as a weak knee.

Lethargic: Your actions are deliberate and drowsy. You suffer from a serious lack of energy or motivation.

Puny: You are weak and inferior in strength. This could be caused by a diminutive stature, or simply atrophied muscles.

Sickly: You are feeble and respond to physical stress as if you were suffering from a debilitating illness.

SOCIAL TRAITS

Alluring: You have an attractive and appealing presence that inspires desire in others.

Uses: *Fascination*. Seduction. Convincing others.

Beguiling: This Trait represents the skill of deception and illusion. You can twist the perceptions of others and lead them to believe what suits you.

Uses: Tricking others. Lying under duress.

Charismatic: You have a talent for inspiration and motivation, the sign of a strong leader. You could be a Gandhi... or a Hitler.

Uses: In a situation involving leadership of any sort.

Charming: Your speech and actions make you fascinating to be around. You have a knack for getting what you want.

Uses: Convincing or persuading.

Commanding: You have an impressive way of speaking and people tend to follow your suggestions.

Uses: Summoning. Ephemera. When you are seen as a leader. Giving orders

Compassionate: Your feelings of care or pity for others run deep, and your kindness shines through.

Uses: Defending the weak or downtrodden. Defeating major obstacles while pursuing an altruistic end.

Dignified: Your posture and bearing come across as honorable and aesthetically pleasing. You carry yourself well.

Uses: Defending against Social Challenges, or an attempt to make you look foolish.

Diplomatic: You are tactful, careful and thoughtful in speech and deed. Few are displeased with what you have to say.

Uses: Very important in intrigue and leadership situations.

Elegant: You have a way about you that suggests refined tastefulness. Even though you do not need money to be Elegant, you exude an air of richness and high society.

Uses: High society functions. Defending against Social Challenges.

Eloquent: This Trait highlights your talent for speaking in an interesting and convincing manner. You can give moving speeches and sermons, and your incantations are a work of art.

Uses: Convincing others. Swaying emotions. Public speaking.

Empathetic: You can identify and understand the emotions and moods of those you encounter.

Uses: Guaging the emotions of others. Not useful to defend against Social Challenges (might make it easier for you to be affected!).

Expressive: You have the ability to articulate thoughts in interesting and meaningful ways, whether spoken or written.

Uses: Acting. Public speaking. Any social situation in which you want someone to understand your meaning.

Friendly: Even after a short conversation, most find it difficult to dislike you. You fit in well with everyone you meet.

Uses: Convincing others. *Fascination*.

Genial: You are cordial, warm and pleasant to be around. If someone doesn't have a smile, you're happy to offer one of yours.

Uses: Mingling at gatherings. *Fascination*. Generally used in a second or later Social Challenge with someone.

Gorgeous: You are beautiful or handsome, born with a face and body most people desire.

Uses: Attracting attention. *Fascination*.

Ingratiating: You know what to do to gain the favor of people who know you. This is commonly used when dealing with the more powerful entities called through the paths of *Daimonis* or *Ephemera*.

Uses: Dealing with superiors. Defending against social and emotional powers.

Intimidating: You have a frightening or awesome presence that causes others to feel timid. Some find this useful in dealing with the weaker entities summoned through *Ephemera*, or when attempting to spar with something summoned through *Daimonis*.

Uses: Attempting to cow opponents. Inspiring fear. Ordering others around.

Magnetic: People feel drawn to you. Those around you are fascinated by your speech and actions.

Uses: Seduction. *Summoning*. *Fascination*.

Persuasive: You can propose believable, convincing arguments and requests. Useful for debate, persuading someone who's on the fence, or borrowing someone's prized ritual chalice.

Uses: Persuading or convincing others.

Seductive: You know how to entice and tempt others. You can use your good looks and body to get what you want. This is applicable to either gender.

Uses: Seduction. Subterfuge. *Fascination*.

Witty: You are cleverly humorous; jokes come easily to you, and you can be a very funny person when you wish to be.

Uses: At parties. Entertaining others. Goading or insulting someone.

NEGATIVE SOCIAL TRAITS

Bestial: You have a dark, animal element in your nature that manifests in your actions or appearance. This may be clawlike fingernails, heavy body hair or unnatural appetites.

Callous: You are unfeeling, uncaring and insensitive to the suffering of others. Your heart is a frozen stone. While this may make you more resistant

to certain emotional effects, it also makes it much harder for you to evoke such feelings in others.

Condescending: You just can't help it; your contempt for others is impossible to hide. Even when you try to smile, it often comes across as a sneer.

Dull: Those with whom you speak usually find you boring and uninteresting. Conversing with you is a chore. You do not present yourself well to others.

Naive: You lack the sophistication, worldliness or maturity that most adults possess. Perhaps you came from a simple background, maybe you had a sheltered upbringing, or you may be just plain ignorant about the ways of the world.

Obnoxious: You are annoying or unappealing in speech or behavior. People don't like being around you and have no qualms about telling you why.

Repugnant: Your presence disgusts and frightens everyone around you. This is more than just physical appearance, for it also covers body odor or similar unpleasant personal qualities. Needless to say, you make a terrible first impression.

Shy: You are timid, bashful and socially hesitant. It's not that you do not want to interact with others, you just seem to be unable to try.

Tactless: You have a habit of doing or saying things that others find inappropriate to the social situation. It's not what you say; it's how you phrase it.

Untrustworthy: You are perceived to be untrustworthy and unreliable. This may because of your behavior or rumors that people have heard. This Trait could come into play when you are trying to persuade someone to believe or assist you.

MENTAL TRAITS

Alert: You are mentally prepared for danger and can react quickly when it occurs.

Uses: Preventing or anticipating surprise attacks. Defending against mental attacks.

Attentive: You pay attention to everyday occurrences around you. When something extraordinary happens, you are usually ready for it.

Uses: Preventing surprise attacks. Noticing hidden things or foes.

Calm: You can withstand an extraordinary level of stress without becoming agitated or upset. You are a wellspring of self-control.

Uses: Resisting commands that provoke violence. Whenever a mental attack might upset you. Primarily for defense.

Clever: You are quick-witted and think well on your feet. This resource-fulness is equally applicable to planned artistic endeavors as it is to finding solutions on the spur of the moment.

Uses: Tricking someone. Using sorcery.

Creative: Your ideas are original and imaginative. You have the ability to devise unusual solutions or come up with an inspiring design. A requirement for any true artist.

Uses: Creating anything. Solving puzzles. *Enchantment*.

Cunning: Crafty and sly, you possess a great deal of ingenuity.

Uses: Tricking others. Using sorcery.

Dedicated: You give yourself over totally to your beliefs. When something is important, you stop at nothing to succeed.

Uses: Useful in any Mental Challenge where your beliefs are at stake. Defense against memory-altering powers.

Determined: Once your mind is made up, you are fully committed. Nothing can divert you from your chosen course.

Uses: Staredowns. Useful in a normal Mental Challenge. Casting or resisting forms of mind magic.

Discerning: You can look at a situation and pick out details, subtleties and idiosyncrasies. Flash and dazzle do not distract you.

Uses: Noticing the unusual. Numina. *Divination*.

Disciplined: Your mind is structured and well-ordered, giving you an edge in battles of will.

Uses: Staredowns. Sorcery. Defending against external control. Good as a follow-up bid when attempting to maintain concentration.

Insightful: You have a talent for looking at a situation and gaining an understanding of it.

Uses: Investigation. Numina.

Intuitive: Understanding comes easily to you, usually without conscious thought. This is the "gut instinct" Trait.

Uses: Numina. Understanding people. *Divination*.

Knowledgeable: You possess detailed information about a wide variety of topics. This represents book-learning and formal education.

Uses: Remembering information your character might know. Using a *Lore* Ability. Useful during rituals.

Observant: Your depth and clarity of vision allows you to pick out the important aspects.

Uses: Picking up on subtleties that others might overlook. Investigation.

Patient: Tolerant, perservering and steadfast. People take you very seriously if you threaten to wait all night.

Uses: Staredowns. As a second or successive bid during mental battles.

Rational: You believe in logic, reason, sanity and sobriety. Your ability to reduce concepts to a mathematical level helps you analyze the world.

Uses: Defending against emotion-oriented mental attacks. Not used as an initial bid.

Reflective: You are capable of self-recollection and deep thought. You consider all aspects of a situation before choosing the correct course. The mark of a serious thinker.

Uses: Meditation. Remembering information. Defending against most mental attacks.

Shrewd: You are sharp and astute. You keep your wits about you and accomplish mental feats with efficiency and finesse.

Uses: Defending against mental powers. Solving puzzles.

Vigilant: You are constantly watchful, never letting your guard down for a moment.

Uses: Defending against investigation, or vampiric Disciplines such as *Forgetful Mind* and *Command*. Defending against surprise attacks. More appropriate for defense than attack.

Wily: You are sly and full of guile. You can easily trick and deceive others.

Uses: Tricking others. Lying under duress. Sorting through confusion. *Illusion*.

Wise: You have an overall understanding of the workings of the world.

Uses: Giving advice. Dispensing snippets of Zen. Defending against mind control.

NEGATIVE MENTAL TRAITS

Forgetful: You have trouble remembering even important things. This includes personal information as well as skills and practical knowledge.

Gullible: You are easily deceived, duped or fooled. Perhaps you take things at face value, or are just a little too trusting of others.

Ignorant: You are uneducated or misinformed, and never seem to know anything. Maybe you never made it past grade school, or your superior prefers to keep you in the dark.

Oblivious: You are generally unaware of what is going on around you, often because you are lost in your own thoughts or distracted by a task.

Predictable: Because you lack originality, even strangers can easily figure out what you intend to do next. People could set their watches by you.

Shortsighted: You rarely look beyond the superficial. Details of perception and long-term consequences are usually lost on you.

Submissive: Spineless and timid, you have difficulty standing up for yourself. This may be the product of abuse, upbringing or supernatural influence.

Violent: You fly into rages at the slightest provocation. This is a Mental Trait because it represents mental instability and lack of control.

Witless: You lack the ability to process information quickly. You are often foolish and slow to act when threatened. This is the "deer in headlights" Trait.

STEP THREE – ABILITIES

While many actions in **Mind's Eye Theatre** can be carried out through standard challenges or roleplaying, this is not always the case. Abilities are the skills and talents used to simulate some of the more dramatic or difficult tasks your character is capable of performing.

Sorcerers may select three Ability Traits to represent their accumulated knowledge. Additional Abilities may be purchased through Experience or with freebie Traits, as described later in this chapter. A character may select a given Ability Trait more than once. This would denote a high degree of expertise in one particular skill, or represent a broad range of specialties within that field.

USING ABILITIES

There are many ways to use Ability Traits. Perhaps the most common is when attempting to use a particular skill in game. For example, if your character needed to hack into a database, *Computer* is the obvious choice. A Narrator will specify the amount of time required to use the Ability, either having you act out the attempt or asking you to drop out of play for the duration of the task. Use of an Ability may even require you to pass a Simple or Static Test, with the difficulty determined by the nature of the attempt. For example, you may be required to bid one of your Ability Traits in *Computer*, comparing your total Traits in that Ability against the security rating of the system. Like any challenge, if the attempt fails, you lose the Trait.

RETESTS

In many cases a challenge is resolved in a single test. However, some circumstances permit a character to renew her efforts for that challenge. While certain Merits, spells or other magical powers can grant a second chance, the most common method for calling a retest is through the use of Ability Traits.

By sacrificing a Trait in an appropriate Ability, you may call for a retest on any feat. While any Traits originally bid remain lost, it is still possible to win the overall challenge. Regardless of the outcome of the retest, the Ability Trait is gone for the remainder of the game session.

ABILITY TRAITS

Some of the more common Abilities are described below; however, this list is by no means exhaustive. Imaginative players are free to come up with other Abilities that reflect their characters' skills, or find them in other **Mind's Eye Theatre** books. Bear in mind that some Abilities have been represented by Traits (such as *Seduction*). Of course, the Storyteller has final say over what Abilities are allowed in game.

ANIMAL KEN

This Ability represents your understanding of animal behavior. Given time, you could train an animal to peform simple tasks (i.e., fetch, stay, attack, etc.). When you command the animal, the animal must make a Mental Challenge to understand and follow the order. Difficulty is based on the animal's level of domestication and the complexity of the task. You may also attempt to calm an injured, frightened or attacking animal by defeating it in a Social Challenge. You can also use this to guage what an animal will do in a given situation.

AWARENESS

This Ability allows you to notice things that are not of the physical world, including the presence of magic. This talent covers the spectrum of sensory perception that is outside the range of most mortals. This Ability may be used to call for a retest on any form of magical detection or evaluation. Direct or focused effects are beyond the scope of this talent, including the deep probes of *Mentalis* and the rituals of *Divination*.

BRAWL

You are adept at using your body as a weapon, including unarmed combat ranging from dirty infighting to highly stylized martial arts. *Brawl* is used for punching or kicking, grappling and holding, thus enabling even a character who is stripped bare to present herself as a formidable foe.

COMPUTER

With this Ability, you can use various desktop programs, email and navigate the Internet. You can also engage in less savory activities, such as infiltrating systems, avoiding security measures and accessing privileged information. A Narrator may require a Mental Challenge to accomplish these or similar acts, based on system security accessibility, time and equipment. Failure means your activities have tripped a security measure, which may lead to investigation by mortal or supernatural agencies.

COSMOLOGY

The Umbra holds many unseen secrets. You know some of them. This Ability covers not only the "geography" of the spirit world, but also information about the inhabitants and conditions found in the various Realms. You may ask a Narrator for a Static Mental Test to see how much you know about a particular situation or location. At Storyteller discretion, you may also use this Ability if attempting to identify an Umbrood (speaking to it, however, is the purview of other Abilities, such as *Linguistics*).

CRAFTS

You have knowledge of master artisan techniques, such as calligraphy, gem cutting, weaving, sewing or glassblowing. This Ability may require either a Static Mental or Physical Test to determine the quality of any creation. You should select a particular craft when this Ability is purchased, and must purchase separate Traits for each craft you practice. This Ability also allows you to judge the work of others in your field or make repairs.

DODGE

This talent represents your knack for getting out of the way of injury. You've learned to duck, weave or evade blows that would strike slower or less alert opponents. *Dodge* may only be used to call for a retest against any attempt to strike, grab or injure you.

DRIVE

The majority of adults have at least some familiarity with modern vehicles. You have put special effort into learning how to operate cars or motorcycles, making you better at avoiding collisions and using your vehicle as a weapon. This Ability also enables you to follow other vehicles and avoid tails yourself, though these actions would require a Physical or Mental Challenge with the other driver. You can even perform stunts with your vehicle, taking it places most others would never dare. A Narrator may call for a challenge in such circumstances, with a difficulty based upon the vehicle type, road conditions and the sort of stunt you wish to perform.

ELECTRONICS

You have practical knowledge concerning the function and repair of electrical and electronic devices. This expertise may have come from formal schooling or it may represent an intuitive knack for dealing with such technology. You may use this Ability to determine what a particular device is use for, as well as how to operate it. This skill also enables you to repair a broken or damaged piece of equipment or even jury-rig something on the fly. Most applications of this Ability require a Static Physical or Mental Test based upon the tools and materials at hand, as well as the amount of time you can spend working on the apparatus.

ENIGMAS

You have a knack for — if not a fascination with — riddles of both the physical and intellectual varieties. When posed with a conundrum of some sort, you may request a Static Mental Test to gain insight into the solution. A Narrator will assign a difficulty depending on your relative familiarity with the problem and what information you already have.

FIREARMS

You are familiar most types of guns and other projectile weapons. The most common use of this Ability is in combat. However, by passing a Static Physical or Mental Test, you may be able to make minor repairs or alterations to your weapons. A character without this Ability may still use a gun, but does not benefit from the Trait bonuses the weapon provides.

INVESTIGATION

You possess the learned skills of a diligent researcher. This sort of attention to detail is often found in private detectives, government agents and scholars. Those who hunt the supernatural also make great use of this Ability. When dealing with certain situations, you may request a Static Mental Test with a Storyteller to see if you have overlooked any clues or to uncover information through formal inquiry.

LINGUISTICS

Due to innate curiosity or quest for knowledge, you have taken the time to learn multiple languages. These languages can be anything from ancient hieroglyphics to foreign tongues and complex dialects. For each Trait in this Ability, you may select one language in which you are fluent. This skill allows you to speak privately with someone who also knows the language, or to read and write texts written in that tongue. It also gives you a chance to determine what language a person is speaking, even if you do not know it yourself. This latter use requires a Static Mental Test, with a difficulty based upon how close the target language is to one with which you are familiar.

LORE

Contrary to popular opinion, even sorcerers do carry field guides about the various types of supernatural beings. It is a rare mortal indeed who knows anything about vampires or werewolves beyond what she has seen in the movies. You, however, do have specific and accurate information on these creatures. This may be the result of diligent study on your part, or perhaps a past association with some other type of supernatural creature. Either way, you are able to separate fact from myth, rumor from misunderstanding. Each

Lore Trait must be purchased separately in the specific topic you have knowledge of: vampires, Gypsies, mummies, changelings, mages, werewolves and other Changing Breeds, wraiths or spirits. The Storyteller has final say on what *Lores* may be purchased.

MEDICINE

You are adept at treating the injuries, diseases and various ailments of living creatures. With time and attention, you can speed up a patient's healing process, enabling a person to recover a single Health Level given a night's rest. Such efforts often require a Static Mental Test, with a difficulty based on the severity and nature of the damage, equipment at your disposal and any assistance or distractions. Other uses of this talent include gaining forensic information, performing a diagnosis or identifying pharmaceuticals. Of course, with learning how to repair the body comes knowledge of how to do harm as well.

MEDITATION

This talent allows you to calm your emotions, control your mind and relax your body. Sorcerers may spend a Trait in this Ability and meditate for a short while to make up for a night's rest. This talent is also common among oriental and shamanic practitioners, who employ the trance state as a focus for their spiritual workings.

MELEE

You are skilled in the arts of armed combat. This may have been acquired through formal training or on the streets of the local slum. You can use any weapon, from beer bottles and baseball bats to swords and quarterstaffs. A character without this Ability may not gain any benefits from using weapons in armed combat, including the associated Trait bonuses.

METAPHYSICS

You have a talent for utilizing esoteric information in a practical fashion. By passing a Static Mental Test, you can identify rituals you uncover or track down the inside scoop on a local cult. The difficulty of this test is determined by how obscure the subject of your inquiry is, as well as your personal scope of understanding and background in this area. Unlike the various Lore Abilities, this skill covers more general or theoretical information applicable to a wide range of pursuits and styles. This Ability may be used to call for a retest in almost any magical working.

OCCULT

This Ability is a catch-all dealing with local folklore, arcane texts, ancient legends and other forms of supernatural facts and hearsay. This understanding of the more sinister side of the world includes knowledge of curses, rituals, *voudon*, fortune telling, magic and mysticism, and it contains much that is only speculation and fantasy. This Ability is often used with retests for Sorcery, as a skilled occultist casts spells and rituals with a greater degree of success.

PERFORMANCE

You are able to entertain others with your creativity and inspiration. The quality of your efforts may be determined by a Static Test: Physical, Social or Mental depending upon the specific medium. A particularly sensitive person can even become entranced by your use of this skill, though this requires you to defeat the other character in a Social Challenge. You should declare a specialty when learning this Ability, such as singing, dancing, acting or even exotic forms such as escape artistry or contortion.

A NOTE ON THE OCCULT ABILITY

Unlike *Occult*, specific *Lore* Abilities reflect reliable knowledge about a particular supernatural creature and its society. *Occult*, on the other hand, reveals information based as much in folklore as in reality, such as that werewolves can abide neither silver nor wolfsbane, and that vampires can die from sunlight or a stake through the heart.

It can be easy for players to forget just how little their character might know about the supernatural, and this difference between *Occult* and *Lore* does much to help remind them. In short, *Occult* is rarely as effective or precise as a specific Lore, but does give general information about a wide variety of topics.

PSYCHOLOGY

You understand how the human mind works, both at the conscious and subconscious levels. This Ability may represent formal training in schools of Freud or Skinner, or a more intuitive understanding common to many counselors and clergy. It is useful in situations where you are trying to figure out how someone is thinking, as well as getting them to think a certain way. Unlike *Subterfuge*, this skill represents more of a Mental approach than Social interaction. Sorcerers who study the path of *Mind Bending* often call of upon this Ability to aid their efforts.

SCIENCE

You have a degree of factual and practical expertise in the hard sciences. With this Ability, you to can perform experiments, fabricate items or access information that less trained individuals could not normally utilize. A Static

Mental Test is necessary for all but the most trivial uses of this skill, with the difficulty determined by the equipment and research data available, the complexity of the task and the time you can spend. You should select a particular specialty or area of study when purchasing this Ability — for example, Engineering, Physics, Biology or Chemistry. Technowizards often utilize these Traits when working their "magic."

SCROUNGE

This Ability allows you to acquire items through your connections, wits and ingenuity; it is common among those who lack the wealth to purchase the things they want or need. Material acquired through these means isn't always brand new and is rarely even exactly right for the desired application. Depending upon the nature and availability of the items sought, a Narrator may call for a Static Mental or Social Test appropriate to the means you describe in your attempt.

SECURITY

You are familiar with the ways others protect places and things. Not only can you counter physical security, such as locks, alarms and guards, but you can also determine the best way to secure items and areas. Other uses of this Ability include breaking and entering, infiltrating, safecracking and hot-wiring. However, this talent does not cover electronic measures, such as motion sensors and keyless entry systems.

Almost all applications of this skill require a Static Physical or Mental Test. The complexity of the task, the extent of the defenses, your equipment and the amount of time you can invest in the attempt influence the difficulty of this test.

SLEIGHT OF HAND

The art of prestidigitation has made magicians famous for centuries. While most sorcerers have other means to achieve these feats, common misdirection can never be counter-spelled. Most applications of this art call for a Static Physical Test, though Narrators may allow simple amusements to succeed automatically. Those who study *Conjuration* often make use of this path.

SUBTERFUGE

Subterfuge is the art of deception and intrigue, used when participating in a social setting or conversation with a subject. With this Ability, you may attempt to draw information out of a subject through trickery and careful probing. After a period of conversation on a related topic, you may propose your true question (out-of-game). For example, to determine someone's nationality, you engage them in a discussion on foreign culture. After conversation has been suitably engaged, you ask your true question and go to a Social Challenge. If you win the challenge, your subject must disclose this information, preferably by roleplaying.

Conversely, *Subterfuge* may be used to conceal certain facts or to lie without detection, negating an opponent's attempts to find things out about you. This Ability may even be used to withhold information obtained through surface scans using the Praxis of *Mentalis*.

BACKGROUNDS

Background Traits specify a wide variety of outside resources to which you have access. These Traits should be taken only when they fit the character concept, not just because they are convenient to have. You need to make sense out of your Backgrounds and integrate them into your character history.

Sorcerers get five Traits to allocate among the various Backgrounds, including Influences and Equipment.

ARCANE

Part of a your talent for magic includes the ability to slip quietly past common notice. This Background is not synonymous with invisibility. Rather, it causes people to not pay attention to you or to forget you after you have left the area. For each Trait in this Background, your opponent must bid one additional Trait on any attempts to detect or remember you. This includes pesky reporters, government agents and the werewolf you annoyed last week. Unfortunately, it also includes the friend who needs your help, the bank you used to have an account at and the person at the dry cleaners who seems to have misplaced your clothes. A character with Arcane may not also have the Background: *Prestige*, nor may you take the Flaw: *Surreal Quality*.

ARTIFACT

This Background grants you access to some form of magic item. This may have been created using the art of *Enchantment* or perhaps it is an item of True Faith. This Background could even represent a Garou fetish or chimerical treasure. You must describe the abilities and functions of the Artifact, at which point the Storyteller will assign a cost for the item. For anything other than a minor (1-2 Trait) item, you must also detail the origin of this prize in your character history. The Storyteller has a right to limit the kind of Artifacts you may possess.

DESTINY

You have been chosen by the Fates to take part in some historic future. You may be slated to accomplish some great feat, or save countless

souls, to die facing overwhelming odds in battle or perhaps even turn to the forces of evil. Your *Destiny* benefits you by allowing you to recover a number of Willpower Traits each story equal to your rating in this Background. After all, you have a destiny to fulfill, and it won't do to have you die before you make good. On the other hand, the Storyteller will make sure that you are never bored, as in the old Chinese curse: May you live in interesting times. *Caveat magus.*

FAMILIAR

You are not alone on your journey of discovery. This Background describes a mystical companion, some spirit incarnate who is willing to aid you in your endeavors. Such relationships are a two-way street, however, as the familiar also requires things in return. The type and nature of your company varies depending upon your magical heritage, from the traditional witch's black cat to the hawk-spirit of the Native American shaman.

Each Trait provides five freebie Traits, which are used to build your familiar. Attributes, Abilities, Willpower, Backgrounds, Merits and Flaws cost the same as for mortal characters. If you have access to **Laws of the Wild**, familiars may even purchase any of the Charms listed in that book. In addition, this spirit has as many Corpus Levels as you have Traits in this Background. These function as Health Levels, though the familiar does not suffer any wound penalties due to accumulated damage.

INFLUENCES

You have pull in one or more areas of mundane society. Perhaps you hold some position of power, it comes with your mundane job, or you simply have an ear to the ground. For each Influence, you must specify the nature and origin of this connection in your character history.

LIBRARY

This Background represents your access to a special collection of books pertaining to magic and the supernatural. This library provides a number of Experience Traits per chronicle equal its rating. Unlike most other Backgrounds, other members of your group may use a library. In this case, you must designate which other character is gaining the benefits from this Background.

MANA POOL

You have an additional set of Traits that you may use to power your magic. Your rating in this Background creates a pool with permanent and temporary Traits similar in function to Willpower. Rather than forfeiting an Attribute or other Trait to cast a particular spell, you may instead spend temporary Traits from this pool. The decision to substitute *Mana* Traits is made when the path is first learned. Each Trait spent on *Mana Pool* grants two Traits in the pool for use with sorcery.

You must specify the nature of this reserve in your character history, as well as the conditions under which it is refreshed. For example, you may have learned the art of Chi Kung during your studies in Asia, and you recover Traits by meditating.

MENTOR

Most sorcerers and priests receive their initial training at the hands of an older, more experienced practitioner. You were wise or lucky enough to continue this relationship even after striking out on your own. This Background represents the relative power level and availability of your teacher. A mentor is not a protector and will not solve all of your problems. However, he might be available between games for instruction or other assistance. You may gain a number of additional Experience Traits per chronicle equal to your *Mentor* rating. Any other use must be played out with a Narrator.

RESOURCES

Sorcerers can get their hands on money in a variety of ways: research funding, lottery winnings, transforming lead into gold or perhaps even a real job. This Background represents the amount of money and equipment you have available or could get your hands on in a pinch. However, if no source for these funds is apparent, you may begin to attract unwanted attention. For each *Resources* Trait, you have $500 available each month after expenses. In addition, your rating in this Background indicates the relative extent and luxury of your home and property.

OPTIONAL RULE: MENTOR TRAINING

Some Storytellers limit the number of Experience Traits you may spend during a given interval. In such situations, there is an alternate way to use this Background. Rather than providing additional Experience Traits to the mage, a Mentor allows you to spend one additional Experience Trait per month for each level in this Background. Thus, it increases the rate at which you can learn, rather than increasing your experience directly.

SANCTUARY

This is a general term for a sorcerer's haven. These locations vary greatly according to your heritage, from uptown apartments to out-of-

the-way chapels. Sanctuaries may also contain many of the bulkier ritual components that you might use, such as alchemical ovens, cauldrons or permanent circles. Each Trait in this Background suggests the level of wealth and space available to you. You may be working out of your parents' basement, have a single room in a group house, an apartment in a trendy district, or even your own house.

INFLUENCES

USING INFLUENCE

To use Influence, you should explain to the Narrator what sort of effect you wish to create with your Influence. The Narrator then decides the Trait cost, the time involved (both real and in-game) and any tests required to achieve the Influence effect. Influence Traits used this way are temporarily considered to have been expended and are not recovered until the next session. The effects of using Influence can be instantaneous and brief, or slow to manifest and permanent, depending on the nature of the manipulation and the degree of power the character wields.

The difficulty of a task is set by a Narrator, and it equals the number of Influence Traits that must be expended to accomplish the task. A given chore's difficulty can be subject to sudden change, depending on circumstance. The suggested guideline listed along with each area of Influence can change dramatically between chronicles or even between sessions. After all, you may not be the only person attempting to Influence something.

Sometimes a Narrator will require a challenge of some sort to represent the uncertainty or added difficulty involved when exercising Influence. Some uses of Influence may not actually cost Influence Traits to use, but rather require that the character simply possess a certain level of the Influence in question.

In practice, the use of Influence is never instantaneous and rarely expedient. While a character may be able to, say, condemn any building in the city, it will not be torn down that night. For sake of game flow, a Narrator may allow trivial uses of Influence to only take half an hour. Major manipulations, on the other hand, can become the center of ongoing plots requiring several sessions to bring to fruition.

The guidelines below by no means limit the number of Influence Traits that can be spent at one time or the degree of change a character may bring about. They are merely an advisory measure to help Narrators adjudicate the costs of certain actions.

Actions followed by an asterisk (*) are ones that can generally be accomplished without expending an Influence Trait.

LOANING INFLUENCE

Characters can trade Influences with each other much like exchanging possessions. These trades may be permanent or temporary. In the case of permanent trades, the old owner erases the Trait from his sheet and turns over the appropriate Influence card (if your chronicle uses these) to the new owner. The new owner then records her newly acquired Influence Trait on her character sheet. Temporary trades of Influence occur when someone is merely doing a favor or loaning her Influence to someone else. In this case, the owner does not erase the Trait, but instead makes a note that it is no longer in her possession. The holder of the Influence Trait may use it immediately or hold onto to it until she feels she needs it. However, the original owner of the Influence Trait may not regain the Trait until the current holder expends or voluntarily returns it. Some chronicles dictate that the Trait reverts to its original owner after a certain time. A good rule of thumb is to say that one month is the maximum duration of any loan of Influence. If your chronicle's sessions are scheduled less frequently than once a month, the Narrator(s) should probably expand this window of opportunity. Any exchange of Influence Traits requires the presence and assistance of a Narrator.

CONFLICTING INFLUENCES

Sometimes characters may wish to try to counteract the Influence of other characters. In such cases, it generally costs one Trait per Trait being countered. The character willing to expend the most Influence Traits (assuming she has them to spend) achieves her goal. All Traits used in this sort of conflict are considered expended.

BUREAUCRACY

The government exists not as a single entity, but as a mass of departments and organizations and independent agencies. The trick is to know which of these to contact in any given situation, and how the interaction between them can accomplish (or stall) certain tasks. A character with this Influence has some sway in one or more local, state or federal agencies. This may be anything from the Building Commission to the Parks Department to the local morgue.

Cost	Desired Effect
1	Trace utility bills*
2	Fake a birth certificate or driver's license; Disconnect a residence's utilities; Close a small road or park; Get public aid ($250)
3	Fake a death certificate, passport or green card; Close a public school for a single day; Turn a single utility on a block on or off; Shut down a minor business on a violation

| 4 | Initiate a phone tap; Initiate a department-wide investiga tion; Fake land deeds |
| 5 | Start, stop or alter a city-wide program or policy; Shut down a big business on a violation; Rezone areas; Obliter ate records of a person on a city and county level |

CHURCH

Founded before many of the world's governments, organized religions hold a vast amount of power, much of it behind the scenes. Even these spiritual institutions are not without politics and personal intrigue, and you may be able to manipulate the personal agendas of those in the hierarchy to your own ends. This Influence applies only to the mainstream faiths, such as Christianity, Judaism, Islam or Buddhism. More esoteric religions fall under the *Occult* domain. Contacts can include ministers, priests, bishops, activists, evangelists, witch-hunters, nuns, monks, laity and various church members.

Cost	Desired Effect
1	Identify most secular members of a given faith in the local area; Pass as a member of the clergy*; Peruse general church records (baptism, marriage, burial, etc.)
2	Identify higher church members; Track regular members; Suspend lay members
3	Open or close a single church; Find the average church-associated hunter; Dip into the collection plate ($250); Access to private information and archives of a church
4	Discredit or suspend high-level members; Manipulate re gional branches
5	Organize major protests; Access ancient church lore and knowledge

FINANCE

Money talks, and you are fluent in its language. You can follow audit trails, perform and verify accounting tasks, and understand such concepts as mutual fund investments, leveraged buy-outs and the like. This Influence allows you to alter financial records, arrange for loans or ride the waves of economic trends to your best advantage. In many chronicles, the number of Traits in this Background may even augment your character's income. CEOs, bankers, corporate yes-men, financiers, bank tellers, stock brokers and loan agents populate *Finance's* ranks.

Cost	Desired Effect
1	Earn money through a steady source of income; Learn about major transactions and financial events; Raise capi

tal ($1000); Learn about general economic trends*; Learn real motivations for many financial actions of others

2	Trace an unsecured small acount; Raise capital to purchase a small business (single, small store)
3	Purchase a large business (a few small branches or a single large store or service)
4	Manipulate local banking (delay deposits, some credit rating alterations); Ruin a small business
5	Control an aspect of city-wide banking (shut off ATMs, arrange a bank "holiday"); Ruin a large business; Purchase a major company

HEALTH

At heart, most sorcerers are just people, human and subject to the limitations of that mortality. Many organizations exist which research and monitor the vast spectrum of health and illness, both physical and mental. A character with this Influence has ties to the medical community, from the institutions (such as hospitals, clinics and asylums) to the people who staff them (doctors, nurses, specialists, lab workers, therapists, counselors and pharmacists).

Cost	Desired Effect
1	Access a person's health records*; fake vaccination records and the like; Use public functions of health centers at your leisure
2	Access to some medical research records; Have minor lab work done; Get a copy of a coroner's report
3	Instigate minor quarantines; Corrupt results of tests or inspections; Alter medical records
4	Acquire a body; Completely rewrite medical records; Abuse grants for personal use ($250); Have minor medical re search performed on a subject; Institute large-scale quaran tines; Shut down businesses for "health code violations"
5	Have special research projects performed; Have people institutionalized or released.

HIGH SOCIETY

There exists a clique of people which, by virtue of birth, possessions, talent or quirk of fate, holds itself above the great unwashed masses. High Society allows the character to direct and use the energies and actions of this exceptional mass of talent. Among the ranks of the elite, one can find dilettantes, the old rich, movie and music stars, artists of all sorts, wannabes, fashion models and trend-setters.

Cost	Desired Effect
1	Learn what is trendy*; Obtain "hard to get" tickets for shows; Learn about concerts, shows or plays well before they are made public
2	Track most celebrities and luminaries; Be a local voice in the entertainment field; Borrow idle cash from rich friends ($1000)
3	Crush promising careers; Hobnob well above your station*
4	Minor celebrity status
5	Get a brief appearance on a talk show that's not about to be canceled; Ruin a new club, gallery, festival or other gathering

INDUSTRY

Civilization reached its peak with the Industrial Age, when machines took over the menial labor required to run the world. From manufacturing to marketing, automobiles to toasters, technology and labor are interwoven into what is commonly referred to as the Industrial Complex. Industry is composed of union workers, foremen, engineers, contractors, construction workers and manual laborers. A character with Influence in this area can keep track of current trends, control the flow of natural resources and perhaps even affect the lab results when new products are being tested.

Cost	Desired Effect
1	Learn about industrial projects and movements*
2	Have minor projects performed; Dip into union funds or embezzle petty cash ($500); Arrange small accidents or sabotage
3	Organize minor strikes; Appropriate machinery for a short time
4	Close down a small plant; Revitalize a small plant
5	Manipulate large local industry

LEGAL

There are those who quietly tip the scales, even in the courts, law schools, law firms and justice bureaus. Inhabiting these halls are lawyers, judges, bailiffs, clerks, district attorneys, public defenders and ambulance chasers. A character with this Influence may postpone (or speed up) court dates, arrange for bail or even get minor charges dropped entirely.

Cost	Desired Effect
1	Get free representation for minor cases
2	Avoid bail for some charges; Have minor charges dropped

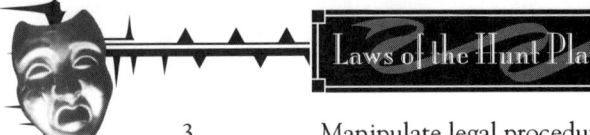

3	Manipulate legal procedures (minor wills and contracts, court dates); Access public or court funds ($250); Get representation in most court cases
4	Issue subpoenas; Tie up court cases; Have most legal charges dropped; Cancel or arrange parole
5	Close down all but the most serious investigations; Have deportation hearings held against someone

MEDIA

The media serves as the eyes and ears of the world. While few in this day and age doubt that the news is not corrupted, many would be surprised at who closes these eyes and covers these ears from time to time. The media entity is composed of station directors, editors, reporters, anchors, camera people, photographers and radio personalities, and (if the Storyteller deems it appropriate) the myth-makers of Hollywood (special effects, foley artists, cameramen, sound technicians and other technical aspects of film and television — actors, directors and writers are the province of *High Society*).

Cost	Desired Effect
1	Learn about breaking stories early*; Submit small articles (within reason);
2	Suppress (but not stop) small articles or reports; Get hold of investigative reporting information
3	Initiate news investigations and reports; Get project funding and waste it ($250); Access media production resources; Ground stories and projects
4	Broadcast fake stories (local only)

OCCULT

Most people are curious about the supernatural world and the various groups and beliefs that make up the occult subculture, but few consider it anything but a hoax, a diversion or a curiosity. This misconception could not be further from the truth. The occult community contains cult leaders and followers, alternative religious groups (such as Wicca or Santeria), charlatans, would-be occultists, antiquarians and New Agers. Some sorcerers use this to seek assistance, information or potential acolytes.

Cost	Desired Effect
1	Contact and make use of common occult groups and their practices; Know some of the more visible occult figures*
2	Know and contact some of the more visible occult figures*; Access resources for most rituals and rites

3	Know the general vicinity of certain supernatural entities (Kindred, Garou, wraiths, etc.) and possibly contact them; Can access vital or very rare material components; Milk impressionable wanna-bes for bucks ($250); Access occult tomes and writings; Research a Basic ritual
4	Research an Intermediate ritual
5	Access minor magic items; Unearth an Advanced ritual

POLICE

"To protect and serve" is the motto among the chosen enforcers of the law. These days, however, everyone can have reason to doubt the law's ability to enact justice. Perhaps they should wonder whom the law defends, whom it serves and why. The Police Influence encompasses the likes of beat cops, desk jockeys, prison guards, special divisions (such as SWAT and homicide), detectives and various clerical positions.

Cost	Desired Effect
1	Learn police procedures*; Hear police information and rumors; Avoid traffic tickets
2	Have license plates checked; Avoid minor violations (first conviction); Get "inside information"
3	Get copies of an investigation report; Have police harass, detain or hassle someone; Find bureau secrets
4	Access confiscated weaponry or contraband; Have some serious charges dropped; Start an investigation; Get money, either from the evidence room or as an appropriation ($1000)
5	Institute major investigations; Arrange setups and stings; Instigate bureau investigations; Have officers fired

POLITICS

Nothing ever gets done for straightforward reasons anymore. It's all about who knows who and what favors can get paid off in the process. In other words, it's politics as usual, and there's a whole class of people who thrive in this world of favors and policy flacks. Some of these individuals include statesmen, pollsters, activists, party members, lobbyists, candidates and politicians themselves.

Cost	Desired Effect
1	Minor lobbying; Identify the real platforms of politicians and parties*; Be in the know*
2	Meet small-time politicians; garner inside information on processes, laws and the like; Use a slush fund or fund-raiser ($1000)

3	Sway or alter political projects (local parks, renovations, small construction)
4	Enact minor legislation; Dash careers of minor politicians
5	Get your candidate into a minor office; Enact encompass-ing legislature

STREET

Disenchanted, disenfranchised and ignored by their "betters," a collective of humanity has made its own culture and lifestyle to deal with the harsh lot life has dealt out. Gang members, the homeless, street perfomers, petty criminals, prostitutes, the forgotten and subcultures that stay close to the streets all reside in the dark alleys and the slums.

Cost	Desired Effect
1	Have an ear open for the word on the street; Identify most gangs and know their turfs and habits
2	Live mostly without fear on the underside of society; Keep a contact or two in most aspects of street life; Access to small-time contraband
3	Get insight on other areas of Influence; Arrange some services from street people or gangs; Get pistols or uncommon melee weapons
4	Mobilize groups of homeless; Panhandle or hold a "collection" ($250); Get hold of shotgun, rifle or SMG; Have a word in almost all aspects of gang operations
5	Control a single medium-sized gang; Arrange impressive protests by street people

TRANSPORTATION

This world is in constant motion, its prosperity relying heavily on the fact that people and productions fly, float or roll to and from every corner of the planet. Without the means to perform this monumental task, our "small" world would become a daunting orb with large, isolated stretches. The forces that bridge these expanses include cab and bus drivers, pilots, air traffic controllers, truckers, travel firms, sea captains, conductors, border guards, airport ground crews and untold others.

Cost	Desired Effect
1	Know what goes where, when and why; Travel locally quickly and freely*
2	Track an unwary target if he uses public transportation; Arrange passage safe (or at least concealed) from mundane threats (robbery, terrorism, etc.)

3	Seriously hamper an individual's ability to travel; Avoid most supernatural dangers when traveling (such as werewolves)
4	Temporarily shut down one form of transportation locally (bus lines, ships, planes, trains, etc.); Route money your way ($500)
5	Reroute modes of travel; Smuggle with impunity

UNDERWORLD

Even in the most cosmopolitan of ages, society has found certain needs and services too questionable to accept. In every age, some organized effort has stepped in to provide for this demand, regardless of the risks. This Influence covers hitmen, the Mafia, La Cosa Nostra, Yakuza, Tong gangs, bookies, fences, launderers and the Chinatown triads.

Cost	Desired Effect
1	Locate minor contraband (knives, small-time drugs, petty gambling, scalped tickets)
2	Obtain pistols, serious drugs, stolen cars; Hire muscle to rough someone up; Fence minor loot; Prove that crime pays (and score $1000)
3	Obtain a shotgun, rifle or SMG; Arrange a minor hit; Know someone in "the family"
4	Make white-collar crime connections
5	Arrange gangland assassinations; Hire a demolition man or firebug; Supply local drug needs

UNIVERSITY

In an age when the quest for learning and knowledge begins in schools, colleges and universities, information becomes currency. This Influence represents a certain degree of control and perhaps involvement in these institutions. In this sphere of Influence, one finds the teachers, professors, deans, students of all ages and levels, Greek orders, and many young and impressionable minds.

Cost	Desired Effect
1	Know the layout and policies of local schools*; Have access to low-level university resources; Get records up to the high school level
2	Know a contact or two with useful knowledge or skills; have minor access to facilities; Fake high school records; Obtain college records

3	Call in faculty favors; Cancel a class; Fix grades; Discredit a student
4	Organize student protests and rallies; Discredit faculty members; Acquire money through a grant ($1000)
5	Falsify an undergraduate degree.

EQUIPMENT

While most supernatural beings have a wide array of powers to fall back on, mortals are often caught on the short end of the stick. To make up for this, humans often depend upon technology.

Characters may gain access to firearms and other gear in a number of ways. For each Trait in the Equipment Background, you may "acquire" one Trait of equipment each month. In addition, you can also temporarily sacrifice an appropriate Influence (*Police*, *Street*, *Underworld*) to obtain some types of equipment. Finally, you may purchase one Trait of gear for each Trait in the Background: *Resources* you are willing to spend, limited by what is legally available in your area.

HUMANITY

All humans have a fundamental wellspring of life and nature that provides a uniquely mortal perspective. Pick four Humanity Traits that represent the best aspects of your character's personality even if you keep them hidden. What is fundamentally good and right about your character, even if it's not always displayed?

OPTIONAL RULE: MILITARY INFLUENCE

In chronicles set on or near a military installation, it may be appropriate to allow characters to have some effect upon base operations. This Influence would be equivalent to a combination of *Police* and *Bureaucracy*, but limited only to military activities. Storytellers should be very careful when this Influence is called into play. Tanks and assault helicopters, even if legitimately obtained, tend to upset game balance severely.

Item	Cost	Notes
Firearms		
Light Pistol	0*	
Heavy Pistol	1	
Rifle or Shotgun	1	
Taser	1	
Automatic Weapons	2	
Munitions		
Silver Bullets	1	per twenty shots, specify weapon type
Dragon's Breath	1	per ten shots
Dynamite	1	per four sticks
Plastic Explosive	2	per kilogram
Other Weapons		
Knife	0*	
Sword/Axe	1	
Crossbow/Bow	1	
Silver Quarrels/Arrows	1	per twenty
Body Armor		
Leather Jacket	0	provides one Physical Trait
Armored Vest	1 ‡	provides three Physical Traits
Kevlar Jumpsuit	2 ‡	adds one extra Health Level
Environmental Suit	3 ‡	immunity to toxins, self-contained

Notes

Up to one free per appropriate Ability Trait, all others cost one Trait each.

These items have the Negative Physical Trait: *Bulky*.

Normal ammunition for firearms or bows has no additional cost

Item	Cost	Notes
Cameras		
35mm Camera	0*	
Video Camera	1	
Kirlian Camera	2	detects supernatural beings (with appropriate *Lore* Ability)
Surveillance Gear		
Tracking Bugs	0*	
IR Goggles	1	
Tracking Locator	2	required to be able to monitor Tracking Bugs
Spy Camera	2	requires a test to notice, based on location
Electronics		
Cellular Phone	0	
Computer	1	
Laptop	2	
Satellite Uplink	4	
Vehicles		
Motorcycle	1	
Economy Car	1	
Luxury Car	3	
Light Airplane	3	
Armored Van	4	
Helicopter	4	

HUMANITY

Humanity separates mortals from the rest of the supernatural world at large. Humanity is the mortal's connection to the fundamental forces of life. Through Humanity, people are connected to one another and to their surroundings. Therefore, characters with many Humanity Traits are very much "in touch" with themselves and their environments; individuals with little Humanity are cold and distant.

Most mortals have four Humanity Traits. Particularly caring or insightful mortals may have more, possessing up to eight Traits. Conversely, no mortal

can ever fall permanently to zero Humanity Traits. There is always a spark of humanity at the core of any mortal's being.

The modern world often derides Humanity as dangerous and worthless. Nice guys finish last, after all. Just getting by in the World of Darkness requires some degree of callousness and a willingness to do whatever is necessary to survive. Yet still, many people hold on tight to their Humanity. The habits of compassion and honor die hard. In a world gone mad with killers and manipulators, Humanity — the power of fundamental integrity — may actually be the best defense.

HUMANITY TRAITS

Benevolent, Charitable, Chivalrous, Fair, Generous, Giving, Gracious, Helpful, Honorable, Humane, Innocent, Kind, Liberal, Loyal, Merciful, Moral, Naive, Pious, Sympathetic, Warm

USING HUMANITY

Humanity Traits serve many purposes. As a measure of character and inner strength, Humanity Traits give mortals exceptional endurance when threatened.

RELIEF OF DERANGEMENTS

Early in each game, a player may expend one Humanity Trait to temporarily relieve her character of a Derangement. A Storyteller should note this expenditure of Humanity, which lasts for the duration of the evening's game. The player should ideally use this capability at the beginning of the session. It's inappropriate to suddenly decide to use Humanity to avoid a Derangement after the Derangement becomes a problem in play.

Using Humanity to fight a Derangement should be played out. Whether a character confides in a trusted friend about his constant battle to work through a Derangement, prays vociferously for strength or displays the St. Christopher medal his mother gave him on her death bed, he should perform some in-game action to demonstrate the expenditure of this very important Trait.

THREATS TO LIFE AND LIMB

Humanity Traits can also be used when a character's "fight or flight" instinct is triggered. In a survival situation, a player can spend a Humanity Trait to be up one Trait for a challenge. Alternately, the player can use the Humanity Trait in place of another Trait, drawing on reserves of inner strength to persevere. This only works in life-threatening situations.

LOSING HUMANITY

Humanity is a precious thing, and it is all too hard to hold onto while living the life of a hunter. Contact with the supernatural tends to distance a character from the benefits of everyday life.

Whenever a mortal commits a base or inhumane deed, he jeopardizes his Humanity. From torture, to certain Praxes, to the creation of a demonic pact, acts of cruelty and other immoral deeds can all lead to the erosion of a mortal's Humanity.

Depending on the number of Humanity Traits the character has, some actions may be deemed acceptable, while others are definitely depraved. A character with seven Humanity Traits might shy at breaking and entering, whereas one with only three Humanity Traits wouldn't hold back at roughing up someone for information. Whenever a situation or session concludes in which a character has committed a deed worthy of a loss of Humanity, the Storyteller should engage in a Simple Test with the player. If the player loses the test, the character loses a permanent Humanity Trait. The Storyteller should feel free to choose the Trait to be lost, making it as appropriate to the situation as possible.

At the Storyteller's discretion, characters of particularly low Humanity may be awarded Negative Traits (the Negative Social Trait of *Callous* seems quite appropriate) or even Derangements, to reflect the growing disconnection with their humane side. These Traits can be assigned even if the characters succeed in the test to avoid losing a Humanity Trait. Humans who fail a test while only possessing one remaining Humanity Trait automatically gain some sort of Negative Trait or Derangement, at the Storyteller's discretion; the fundamental connection to Humanity can never be lost, but the character will spiral into madness. No freebie Traits or Experience Traits accompany the gain of such Negative Traits or Derangements.

The following chart shows the least sin that will cause a temporary loss of Humanity in a character with the corresponding number of Humanity Traits. (For example, a character with four Humanity Traits would be horrified if he accidentally killed someone, but likely would not bat an eyelash at punching someone in the face. A person with eight Humanity Traits, on the other hand, would head straight for his father confessor for accidentally running over a pedestrian's foot.)

Remember, losing Humanity is a terrible thing. This sort of erosion of a mortal's soul profoundly affects the character's personality. Characters who lose Humanity tend to be cynical, jaded and vicious. The loss of even one Trait has a noticeable effect on long-established behavior patterns.

HIERARCHY OF SINS

Eight Humanity	Accidentally inflicting injury
Seven Humanity	Purposefully inflicting injury
Six Humanity	Theft and robbery
Five Humanity	Unreasonable destruction
Four Humanity	Accidental killing
Three Humanity	Premeditated murder
Two Humanity	Mass murder, torture
One Humanity	Gross perversion and acts of great evil

REGAINING HUMANITY

Regaining Humanity Traits is a function of how the Traits were used or lost. Humanity spent to save a loved one, counteract a fear or face a life-threatening situation is regained in time (in other words, all Traits spent this way return by the next event). Mortals in a hurry or in desperate need can also expend a Willpower Trait to replace a Humanity Trait.

Humanity Traits lost permanently can only be regained through extraordinary penance, decreed by a Storyteller and roleplayed out over a series of sessions. The character must show remorse for the actions that caused him to lose Humanity, and even then, Humanity should not be returned lightly.

Reaffirming a connection to your inner childlike innocence, performing charitable works (and not just for the possibility of regaining Humanity!) or being sympathetic to the problems of others are just some examples of the kind of behavior that might merit a gain of Humanity. Of course, the cost in Experience Traits must still be paid. The same applies to actually improving one's Humanity. The character must experience a fundamental connection to her own inner strength and to the mass of humanity around her.

Storytellers may note characters who are constantly losing and regaining Humanity Traits. If this situation becomes chronic, the Storyteller may declare that the character has become jaded, and may no longer attempt to regain Humanity Traits that have been lost permanently.

WILLPOWER

Willpower is more than just strength of personality. It is a mark of the greater power and determination within each of us. Unlike other types of Traits, Willpower Traits are not adjectives. Instead, your character has a permanent Willpower rating, which defines how many temporary Traits you may use during any given game session.

Willpower may be spent in a variety of ways. The more common uses are described below.

• Willpower allows your character to ignore the wound penalties up to and including Incapacitated for one turn. When used out of combat, this benefit extends for a full minute.

• Willpower can be used to call for a retest on any feat. This represents your determination to win regardless of your opponent or situation.

• By expending a Willpower Trait, you may retest any one Social or Mental Challenge, including most forms of magical control. In addition, your opponent may not use that power against you for the remainder of the scene. However, this does not apply to attacks, which inflict damage or target your Physical Traits.

• A Willpower Trait may be spent (as an action) to replenish all lost Attribute Traits in one category (Physical, Social or Mental). Some Storytellers extend this benefit, allowing characters to replenish Ability or Humanity Traits as well.

Once lost, Willpower is very difficult to recover. Normally, a character's Willpower pool refreshes at the start of each game session. However, Storytellers may wish to allow you to recover a temporary Willpower Trait when you perform exceptionally well relative to your Nature and character concept. This should not be a frequent occurrence, but rather a reward for outstanding roleplaying.

Mortal characters begin with one Willpower Trait.

FREEBIE TRAITS

Mortals, unlike the supernaturals around them, do not automatically get any special gifts for being mortal. Mortal characters' players, however, receive five freebie Traits, with which they may improve their characters Traits or purchase Numinae. These freebies may be expended any way the Storyteller allows.

Attribute or Ability Trait	1
Background or Influence Trait	1
Humanity Trait	2
Willpower Trait	3
Merit	Merit Trait cost
Basic Sorcery spell	3

Characters may also gain freebie Traits from Negative Attribute Traits, rather then converting them directly into positive Attribute Traits. This option does not change the normal limit of how many Negative Traits may be taken.

DERANGEMENTS

Derangements represent insanity and mental instability. You may choose to take one Derangement, if you desire, which counts as two Negative Traits. If you do choose to take a Derangement, you are limited to no more than three additional Negative Traits (since you can only take a total of five).

Under extreme pressure, the human mind tends to crack, attempting to let off steam by giving way. Such problems are represented by Derangements, which may activate under times of stress to cause mental problems for the character. Sorcerers who deal with Umbrood regularly, who are in a pressure-cooker of supernatural trouble, or who are just plain not quite all there, are just as susceptible to Derangements as any other.

You can opt to start with one Derangement. A Derangement counts as two Negative Traits, but it can be quite dangerous if you run into a few vampires while in the midst of a panic attack. Conversely, hunters under great stress may suffer from Derangements at the discretion of the Storyteller. Any hunter who loses her last permanent Humanity Trait immediately gains a Derangement, as she spirals into inhuman insanity. The final Humanity Trait is retained (as it's impossible for a human to fully lose touch with her human nature) but the Storyteller assigns an appropriate new Derangement.

Expenditure of Willpower can curb the effects of a Derangement, but the Derangements always come back to haunt the character. Only prolonged use of Willpower can stave off Derangements permanently. A character who has spent seven to 15 Willpower Traits in resisting Derangements may manage to overcome the handicap, at the Storyteller's discretion.

AMNESIA

In highly traumatic situations, you sometimes forget who and even what you are. You may simply forget the memory of a single situation, or you may forget everything about your identity, including your current mission. When events and situations that remind you of your lost memories present themselves, those memories may return, sometimes violently.

COMPULSIVE LYING

You were in New York with a friend once — the name isn't important — and you managed to convince this car dealer (he was pretty hard up to make a sale) to sell you his brand-new Dodge Viper for, like, a thousand dollars. What a great deal! He didn't even charge tax or have you go through the whole paperwork of registering it or anything. He did all that himself. Oh, you want to see the car? Well, it's in the shop right now being repainted. It was this nasty shade of lime green. You say Vipers don't come in green? Well, this one was a special edition, signed by the president of the company. What

was his name? Well, the signature wasn't very legible — you know how big businessmen are....

When you are being pressured about something, this Derangement can be triggered and you must spend Willpower not to lie outrageously.

DELUSIONAL

When things get particularly hard to deal with, you often revert to someone you can trust to do a better job than you would. Somebody efficient; somebody stalwart.

Delusional identities arise from feelings of complete hopelessness and despair, and they reflect your deepest terrors. In moments of stress or fear, your real personality will retreat, and a replacement identity (but with the same Traits, etc.), constructed from your ideas of what competence is, will take its place. This other self can be a fictional, historical or composite character.

Alternately, your delusions may take the form of misinterpretation of the situation at hand, to make it seem more comfortable and acceptable to you.

DIPSOMANIA

You are possessed by the urge to drink yourself into an absolute stupor when the going gets tough (or even mildly irritating). Such a Derangement can destroy any trust others may place in you. This weakness, should it become known, could be used very effectively against you as a weapon. If the Derangement comes over you at an event, you will immediately be affected by the Negative Mental Trait *Witless*.

Happy drunk or not, you are unsightly in this state. You stagger about, weave as you walk and say all the wrong things. You know you are stronger and more effective while drunk, however, and you turn to it as a crutch to help you out.

HEBREPHRENIA

The horror of the World of Darkness unveiled has shattered your perceptions of everything you once held as logical and real. This mental trauma has plunged you into a state of mind where you maintain you sanity by clinging to the idea that everything is going on in your head. Everyone you know is but a character in the little play world your mind has created. Those around you get pretty mad when you are rude with them, but it doesn't matter because they aren't even real. Who cares if a figment of your imagination gets annoyed, anyway?

HYPOCHONDRIA

You have noticed that when you get even the slightest bit stressed you begin to get sick. The sickness is usually just a headache or upset stomach, but sometimes it gets much worse. If, at any time during an event you become upset about anything, you will begin to think you are coming down with something. In all probability you are quite healthy, but you need some kind of excuse to get sympathy from those about you. When you begin to get "sick" from all the stress, you will effectively be down by one Physical Trait for the rest of the event or until your "attack" passes.

INTELLECTUALIZATION

You have recoiled from the horror of your situation, and you protect yourself by feeling nothing. You insulate yourself in a world of logic and intellectual vigor where emotions have no place. By isolating your incompatible needs and thoughts into separate compartments, you avoid losing control. However, the pressure inevitably mounts, and the dam eventually bursts during a stressful situation.

MANIC-DEPRESSION

You sink into deep and fitful depressions, showing no interest in anything that used to capture your imagination. You view the world as flat and gray, holding nothing of value for you. You cannot rouse yourself to do anything, though you will go along with others rather than expend the energy to resist. Conversely, occasional fits of great energy grab hold of you, and you will work for hours or even days on your projects. During this time you resist even the need to sleep as you burn up all your resources on your schemes.

MASOCHISM

Sometimes things will go wrong, dreadfully so, and deep in your heart, you know it's your fault. Since nobody else may necessarily know that it's all your fault, you have to work out a way of keeping yourself in line. Sometimes you do this by getting in harmful situations or by hanging about people and creatures who dislike you. You deserve their abuse, after all.

You even tend to injure yourself physically, but never to a degree that most people would notice. You don't want anybody to know what a terrible person you are. If a problem comes up and you get blamed, even falsely, you apologize profusely and offer yourself up to the mercy of your accuser. Even if you're not responsible for it this time, odds are it's just karma catching up with you for all of your other crimes.

MULTIPLE PERSONALITIES

You possess a number of different personalities, and you change Nature and Demeanor in times of great personal stress. Thus you behave in radically different ways at different times. Naturally this causes others to distrust you, as they're never quite sure who they're talking to. Your current personality persists until either you change personality again during a stressful situation or you expend a Willpower Trait to return to your "basic" personality.

OBSESSION

When a new person enters your life or you are faced with a dramatic situation, you can sometimes become obsessed with that person or some fetish associated with the situation. This Derangement gives you a sort of perverse ambition toward which you direct all your energy. If you are directly thwarted in your obsession, you may react violently.

OBSESSIVE-COMPULSIVE

You are obsessed with keeping track of things, maintaining exhaustive records and keeping everything in its place. Unless absolute order is maintained in your life, everything will dissolve into chaos.

FANZAISM

Since your induction to the ways and world of the supernatural, you have become completely detached. When this Derangement is at its mildest, you have some trouble with the idea of the world at large being real. You seem to be halfway out of your body, in a way.

When the Derangement is at its worst, however, things get really interesting. When thus afflicted, you realize that nothing is real. Nothing. You are nothing. Everything is unreal. You can't affect it and it can't affect you because there is nothing there. When everything seems to be going wrong, you wrap yourself up in this idea and don't come out until things are a little more to your liking.

PARANOIA

When someone threatens or stubbornly opposes you, you become convinced that the person is after you. You become obsessed with those you believe to be your enemies, and you make all kinds of mad preparations to protect yourself. During bouts of this Derangement, you trust no one and hold even your closest friends under suspicion.

PERFECTION

When nothing seems to be going right, you can become obsessed with perfection. Everything must be just so, and you use all your energy to prevent

anything from going wrong. You focus all your attention on keeping everything about you in perfect, unaltered order.

POWER-MADNESS

You can become so obsessed with power and dominance that you lose all control of yourself. When your ambitions are thwarted, you sometimes become enraged and attack those who oppose you. In general, you seek total and absolute control over everything and everyone around you.

QUIXOTISM

This Derangement is the opposite of *Panzaism*. You believe absolutely in everything you see or hear. Yes, there are faeries. That guy with all the hair, he's a werewolf. This pendant came from Atlantis. You'll be out challenging windmills to personal combat, at least metaphorically. You most likely came from a perfectly mundane background where nothing out of the ordinary happened. Now that you've been initiated into the true nature of the World of Darkness, you've taken everything to the farthest reaches of your imagination. When stress overtakes you, you are down two Mental Traits.

REGRESSION

In times of stress, when much is being demanded of you, you can become childlike, retreating to a less mature aspect of yourself. At such times you find it difficult to do anything for yourself, and without the aid of others, you are quite helpless.

SADISM

You tend to revert to cruelty when under pressure. Nothing relieves your stress like causing people pain. Physical pain isn't all you excel in, though — sometimes mental scarring can last much longer than a mere physical wound. Whenever confronted with something that profoundly bothers you, you must either spend a Willpower Trait or find some way of taking out your anger on someone immediately.

MERITS AND FLAWS

Merits and Flaws represent special advantages and disadvantages that extend beyond mundane capabilities. By taking Merits or Flaws, you mark your character as unique, with rare powers or resources beyond those available to most normal humans. Merits grant special powers and benefits, and they can only be taken by expending available Traits. Conversely, Flaws mark hindrances or special disadvantages and give you additional Traits with which to flesh out your character.

You do not have to take any Merits or Flaws, and your Storyteller may choose to limit certain ones or forbid them entirely. However, a few well-chosen Merits and Flaws can round out a character, defining why he specializes in a particular Ability or giving him notable powers.

You may start by selecting up to five Traits' worth of Flaws for your character; you gain additional freebie Traits equal to the value of the chosen Flaws. Merits, on the other hand, cost freebie Traits to acquire. If you wish (and if your Storyteller approves), you may take more than five Traits' worth of Flaws to represent a particularly disturbed or crippled character, but you cannot gain more than five freebie Traits regardless of the total number of Flaws taken. In some cases, the Storyteller may restrict the purchase of Merits and Flaws — or ban their use outright — so be sure to ask first.

Merits and Flaws are unusual advantages and disadvantages that go a long way toward creating a three-dimensional character. Many of them will be familiar because they have always been available to supernatural creatures, but there are some new ones specifically for mortal characters.

Players can only choose Merits and Flaws at character creation, and those chosen should fit in with the concept of the character. Over the course of a chronicle, and with the Storyteller's approval, a character may develop a Merit or overcome a Flaw due to something monumental that happens in a story. To do so costs double the Merit or Flaw's normal cost in Experience Traits.

APTITUDES

These Merits and Flaws deal with your abilities and natural talents.

Ability Aptitude (1 Trait Merit)

You have a natural affinity for a particular non combat-related Ability. You are two Traits up on all tests directly related to that Ability.

Ambidextrous (1 Trait Merit)

You are skilled at using both hands at once and suffer no penalties regardless of which you use. You can fight with two weapons, simply risking one additional Trait with each attack (normally, someone attacking with two weapons would risk one additional Trait for his primary hand and two additional Traits for his "off" hand). This does not grant additional attacks. Furthermore, you suffer no penalties when performing tasks with either hand, unlike other people who must risk an additional Trait to perform tasks with their "off" hand.

Pitiable (1 Trait Merit)

There is something about you that causes others to take care of you as if you were a child. Some Natures will not be affected by this Merit, and some Demeanors may pretend they are not. You need to decide what it is about you that attracts such pity, and how you feel about it. When someone has challenged you with intent to do you harm, you are one Trait up in your own defense.

Silver Tongue (1 Trait Merit)

You possess a talent for getting people to accept what you want them to believe. For a single Trait, you are two Traits up on all tests when someone is trying to determine if you are lying. This Merit does not work against supernatural "lie detectors", such as vampiric *Aura Perception* or the Gift: *Truth of Gaia*.

Daredevil (3 Trait Merit)

You are good at taking risks, and you aren't too bad at surviving them, either. You are one Trait up on any challenge in which you try something particularly dangerous. This Merit only applies to combat if you are obviously outmatched, but wade in anyway.

Natural Linguist (3 Trait Merit)

You possess a miraculous ability to understand and use languages. For each Trait of Linguistics you possess, you know learn two languages. Many sorcerers find such very useful in the course of their studies, especially as uncommon or rare texts are usually not translated.

Jack-of-All-Trades (5 Trait Merit)

You have a large pool of miscellaneous talents, skills and knowledge obtained through your extensive travels, the jobs you've held or too much time spent watching public television. You may invoke Abilities which you do not normally possess, though you must risk an additional Trait to do so. For instance, you could expend a Mental Trait to try to pick a lock with *Security*, even if you don't possess that Ability; you still need to make any associated tests (such as a further challenge to actually pick the lock) normally. Of course, you may choose to expend a Willpower Trait to attempt an unknown Ability, as usual.

Illiterate (1 Trait Flaw)

You can neither read nor write. This is especially appropriate for sorcerers who come from poor countries or from tribal backgrounds. Western sorcerers will be especially hampered by this Flaw.

Ritual Dependent (2 Trait Flaw)

You have a natural affinity for operating within a formal or ritual context. Unfortunately, this makes you ill-suited to cast spells on the spur of the moment. All applications of sorcery require some form of ceremony appropriate to your magical heritage. While you must perform these spells as if they were rituals of equivalent level, you also only need to pay for them at normal ritual cost.

Inept (5 Trait Flaw)

You are not attuned to your natural aptitudes. You start the game with no Ability Traits or Influences. Furthermore, you cannot raise any Ability or Influence above one level until you've overcome this Flaw.

AWARENESS

These Merits and Flaws deal with your physical perceptions.

Acute Sense (1 Trait Merit)

One of your senses is particularly keen. You are two Traits up on any related perception tests involving one sense (vision, hearing, touch, taste or smell).

Hard of Hearing (1 Trait Flaw)

Your hearing is defective. You are two Traits down on any hearing-related challenges. You may not take the Merit: *Acute Sense (Hearing)*.

Impaired Sight (1 Trait Flaw)

You are severely nearsighted or farsighted, and you require corrective lenses. Without them, you are one Trait down on sight-related challenges. You may not take this Flaw and the Merit: *Acute Sense (Sight)*.

One Eye (2 Trait Flaw)

You are missing one eye, determined randomly or chosen. You have no peripheral vision on your blind side, and are two Traits down on any test requiring depth perception. You may choose to cover one eye while you are playing.

Weak Sense (2 Trait Flaw)

One of your senses is defective, though not totally absent. In all challenges relating to this sense, you are automatically down two Traits. Such damage is not correctable; rather, you suffer from an incurable deficiency. This could be something like severe astigmatism, tinnitus or thick scar tissue from an old injury. Obviously, you may not have a sense that is both acute and weak.

Deaf (3 Trait Flaw)

You cannot hear sound. You must relent on all challenges related to hearing. You should get your Storyteller's approval before choosing this Flaw, as it can be difficult to roleplay.

Blind (6 Trait Flaw)

You have no vision whatsoever, and must relent on sight-related challenges. You should roleplay this Flaw to the best of your ability, but take care not to risk anyone's safety doing so (including your own).

MENTAL

Common Sense (1 Trait Merit)

You possess a certain amount of everyday wisdom and practicality. Whenever you are about to do something contrary to better judgment, a Narrator can alert you to your potential mistake. This Merit is an excellent choice for players new to the World of Darkness.

Concentration (1 Trait Merit)

You find it easy to avoid distractions. In any situation where your attention needs to be focused, you gain a free retest on any attempt to maintain your concentration.

Time Sense (1 Trait Merit)

You are always aware of the time, even when you've been sleeping or underground. You can estimate the current time to a minute or two and follow the calendar in your head with exacting precision. Furthermore, you resist any powers that disorient your time sense (such as the changeling Art of *Chronos*) with two additional Traits.

Eidetic Memory (2 Trait Merit)

You are up two Traits on all memory-related challenges, as you can remember anything you see or hear with perfect clarity. Although supernatural befuddlement can still cloud your memory, you're likely to become quite suspicious if someone draws attention to your clouded mind, simply because you're used to remembering everything clearly. At any time, you may ask a Narrator for information regarding something you wish to recall, and the Narrator is obligated to inform you appropriately (you may be required to make a Simple Test for complex or lengthy dissertations).

Iron Will (4 Trait Merit)

Once your mind is made up, nothing (short of a sledgehammer) can change it. You are highly resistant to powers that attempt to control your mind, such as the sorcery Praxis of *Mind Bending* or the vampiric Discipline of *Dominate*. Subtle illusions, emotional effects and mental trauma will still occur, as will any surface probing. Whenever magical means are used to control your mind, you may expend a Trait of Willpower to automatically resist. The Storyteller may deem that a particularly powerful foe, such as an elder vampire or spirit, requires you expend Willpower to retest only, not resist. If you do not have any remaining Willpower Traits, or if you are unaware of the attempt and thus unable to actively resist, you are still two Traits up in the challenge.

Fragile Will (1 Trait Flaw)

You possess less Willpower than most, finding it hard to maintain your self-control and composure. For a single Trait, you start with only one Willpower Trait (rather than two) during character creation. A character with this Flaw may not have either of the Merits: *Iron Will* or *Quiet Heart*.

Confused (2 Trait Flaw)

You are often confused, and the world seems to be a very disoriented and twisted place. Sometimes you are simply unable to make sense of things. You need to roleplay this behavior all the time to a small degree, but your confusion becomes especially strong whenever you are surround by excessive stimuli (such as a number of people all talking at once, or the noise in a loud

nightclub). You are two Traits down on all challenges in such situations. You may spend a Willpower Trait to override the effects of your confusion, but only for a scene.

Absent-Minded (3 Trait Flaw)

Though you don't forget things like your Abilities, you do forget names, addresses and whether you turned the iron off. In order to remember anything other than your own name, address and phone number during stressful situations, you must win a Static Mental Challenge (the Storyteller will determine the difficulty) or spend a Willpower Trait.

PHYSICAL

Double-Jointed (1 Trait Merit)

You are unusually flexible. You are one Trait up on all Physical Challenges requiring flexibility, such as squirming into a small space.

Light Sleeper (2 Trait Merit)

You can awaken instantly at any sign of trouble or danger, and you do so without any sleepiness or hesitation. While most mortals are two Traits down on all tests for a turn after awakening, you wake up automatically at anything amiss and suffer no penalties for drowsiness. You get by quite well on four hours of sleep per night, a significant advantage when you must run a ritual long into the night and go to school the next day.

Poisonous Blood (3 Trait Merit, 3 Trait Flaw)

If you take this as a Merit, for whatever reason, your blood is poisonous to vampires. Although you suffer injury normally when a vampire drinks your blood, the vampire gains no nourishment from the fluid, and he suffers one Health Level of damage for each Trait of blood he consumes. Unfortunately, vampires cannot tell that your blood is poisonous until it is ingested, so this does not protect you from initial attack, but it does mean that vampires are unlikely to feed on you again later.

If you take this as a Flaw, your blood is poisonous to *everyone*, except yourself. Getting medical treatment is a difficult proposition, surgery is often out of the question, and you certainly can't donate when the bloodmobile's in town. In addition, this may make things difficult if you must shed your blood during a ritual or offer some to the spirits (who may see a toxic offering as a gross insult).

Increased Pain Tolerance (3 Trait Merit)

Whether due to extensive training or just naturally thick skin, you are more resistant to the effects of damage than others. Treat all wound penalties as if you were one Health Level less injured than you actually are. A character with this Merit may not also take the Flaw: *Low Pain Threshold*.

Huge Size (4 Trait Merit)

You are abnormally large, possibly as much as seven feet tall or over three hundred pounds. You have one extra Health Level, allowing you to suffer more harm before you become incapacitated. Represent this Merit by wearing bulky clothes and heavy boots if you are not actually of huge size.

Long-Lived (4 Trait Merit)

This simply indicates a vastly extended life span. You are able to live 10 times the normal mortal life span. You will continue to age, albeit more slowly than other mortals. You also enjoy an enhanced resistance to disease, but cancer, AIDS or catastrophe can still kill you. Needless to say, such a life span can give you plenty of opportunities to make equally long-lived (or immortal) friends and foes. Detail how you got so lucky with your Storyteller.

Deep Sleeper (1 Trait Flaw)

When you sleep, it is very difficult to awaken you. If you are awakened unexpectedly, you are disoriented, leaving you two Traits down for all challenges during the following hour. Furthermore, the Storyteller may require you to make a Simple Test to wake up in the first place when danger or mishap threatens.

Allergic (1-4 Trait Flaw)

You have an adverse reaction to some substance that normally does not bother most people. This could be pollen, animals, certain metals (like nickel), drugs (such as aspirin), or even stranger things. At one Trait, it the reaction can be controlled with over-the-counter medicine and is fairly common (allergies to cats or ragweed, symptoms of sneezing or upset stomach). Two Traits gives you something more irritating, resulting in a rash or violent sneezing bouts and putting you at a one-Trait disadvantage; you may need to be treated with prescription medicine, which could make you groggy. Three Traits means a more unusual allergy, or a serious reaction that causes you great discomfort and leaves you at a two-Trait disadvantage if you're challenged in the middle of a reaction (allergic to penicillin; asthmatic reaction). A four-Trait allergy means either a rare substance for allergies, or a common allergy with a life-threatening reaction if not treated (certain drugs, the pollen of a rare plant; breathing difficulties, swelling, bleeding). Such a reaction causes you to suffer up to two Health Levels of damage. You must detail with the Storyteller what you're allergic to and what reaction it causes.

Disfigured (2 Trait Flaw)

A hideous disfigurement makes you ugly and easy to remember. You may never have any *Alluring*, *Gorgeous* or *Seductive* Social Traits. If your true appearance is visible, you are two Traits down on any Social Challenge (except *Intimidation*) that you initiate.

Aging (3 Trait Flaw)

You're not as young as you once were, and you're beginning to feel the weight you years. You automatically lose one of your Physical Traits, and your maximum Physical Traits are one less than other mortals. You may take Flaw once per decade above 40 years of age. This Flaw will take some effort to roleplay, so think carefully before choosing it.

One Arm (3 Trait Flaw)

You have only one arm, determined randomly or chosen at character creation. You have become used to using your remaining hand, so you suffer no off-hand penalty. You are, however, two Traits down on challenges where two hands would be required.

Deformity (3 Trait Flaw)

You have some sort of deformity — a misshapen limb, a hunchback or whatever — which affects your interactions with others and may inconvenience you physically. You are one Trait down on all tests of a physical nature, and two Traits down on all challenges related to physical appearance.

Partially Crippled (3 Trait Flaw)

Your legs are injured or otherwise prevented from working effectively. You are down three Traits in all challenges relating to movement. You may need assistance in walking, such as a pair of crutches or a wheelchair.

Potent Blood (3 Trait Flaw)

Your blood is especially nourishing and desirable to vampires. Your blood is worth twice as many Blood Traits as a normal mortal's, so a vampire who drinks one of your Blood Traits gains two instead (although you still suffer only one Health Level of damage). Vampires have names for people like you — "Slurpee," "Cornucopia" or simply "Mine!"

You cannot have the Merit: *Lifegiver* in addition to this Flaw.

Hemophilia (4 Trait Flaw)

When you are injured, you do not naturally stop bleeding. Cuts continue to bleed and bruises worsen through internal injury. Once you are physically wounded, you suffer an additional health level of damage every 10 minutes until someone helps you and makes a successful Mental Challenge (with a difficulty of six Traits) using the Medical Ability. For obvious reasons, you may not also purchase either of the Merits: *Vibrant Health* or *Increased Pain Tolerance*. Vampires who bite you will also discover that they cannot lick the wound closed for some reason.

Mute (4 Trait Flaw)

Your vocal apparatus does not function, and you cannot speak at all. You can communicate through other means, typically writing or signing. Obviously, this deficiency makes it impossible for you to call on sorcery or other powers requiring speech.

PSYCHOLOGICAL

These Merits and Flaws deal with aspects of your personality.

Code of Honor (1 Trait Merit)

You have a personal code of ethics to which you strictly adhere. You can automatically resist most temptations that would bring you into conflict with your code. When battling supernatural persuasion that would make you violate your code, you are considered to have two extra Traits in challenges. You must construct your own personal code of honor in as much detail as you can, outlining the general rules of conduct by which you abide, and this code must be approved by the Storyteller.

Higher Purpose (1 Trait Merit)

You have a goal that drives and directs you in everything. You do not concern yourself with petty matters and casual concerns because your higher purpose is everything to you. Though the purpose may sometimes force you to behave contrary to your survival instinct, it can also grant you great personal strength. You have two extra Traits in challenges that have anything to do with this higher purpose. Be sure to discuss your idea for a higher purpose with the Storyteller.

This Merit can be a common one for hunters, since they frequently hold to the lofty ideal of ridding the world of supernatural menace, but your Storyteller should not allow it to be abused.

If you have the Flaw: *Driving Goal,* you cannot take this Merit.

Home Advantage (1 Trait Merit)

You find yourself better able to function in certain situations. This may require you to be in a particular location or in the company of a specific individual. It may even come from possession of a particular item, though the object is not itself magical. This Merit grants you one additional Attribute Trait or two Ability Traits, which do not count against your maximum Trait totals. This Trait is bid and can be lost like any other.

You must detail the origin and conditions of this boon in your character history and note on your character sheet which Traits you gain.

Quiet Heart (4 Trait Merit)

Parallel to *Iron Will,* this Merit allows you to resist any attempt to control or influence your emotions. This includes the sorcery path of *Fascination,* the vampiric Discipline of *Presence* and the wraith Arcanoi of *Keening.* Attempts to read from your mind, non-directed illusions or other passive effects are not hindered by this Merit. You may spend a Willpower Trait to automatically resist a supernatural attempt to work on your emotions. For especially powerful foes, the Storyteller may deem that you may only retest when you spend Willpower. If you do not have any remaining Willpower Traits, or if you are unaware of the attempt and thus unable to actively resist, you are still two Traits up in the challenge.

Anachronism (1 Trait Flaw)

You are an older sorcerer, who has never taken the time to fully understand the wonders of the modern age. Or you could be a shaman from a culture that continues to practice ancient ways. You are one Trait down in challenges involving modern technology such as computers.

Compulsion (1 Trait Flaw)

You have a psychological compulsion that causes you a number of different problems. Your compulsion may be for cleanliness, perfection, bragging, stealing, gambling, exaggeration or just talking too much. You may temporarily avoid your compulsion for one scene by spending a Willpower Trait.

Dark Secret (1 Trait Flaw)

You have some sort of secret that, if uncovered, would embarrass you immensely and make you a pariah in your society. Perhaps you practice a Praxis forbidden by your society, you betrayed your coven, or an innocent was harmed by one of your spells. While it weighs on your mind at all times, it will only surface occasionally in stories — lest it begin to lose impact.

Intolerance (1 Trait Flaw)

You have an unreasoning dislike of a certain thing, and at the Storyteller's discretion you may have one less Trait in any challenge dealing with the object of your intolerance. It may be an animal, a class of people, a color, a situation, or just about anything at all. Some dislikes may be too trivial to be reflected here — a dislike of pomegranates or tissue paper, for instance, will have little effect on play in most chronicles. The Storyteller is the final arbiter on what you can pick to dislike.

Isolated Upbringing (1 Trait Flaw)

You were born and raised by a particularly peculiar set of parents, and you rarely ventured into the outside world. Perhaps your father was a Nephite priest who hoped to shield you from the sins of mankind and prepare you for your task as God's hammer, or maybe you were raised in a Chapter House of the Arcanum, where you spent all of your time among books. Whatever the reason, you are ill at ease in the mundane world, and you often fail to understand the customs of everyday life. You are automatically one Trait down on all Social Challenges with people from outside of your corner of reality.

Nightmares (1 Trait Flaw)

You experience horrendous nightmares every time you sleep, and memories of them haunt you during your waking hours. Sometimes the nightmares are so bad that you have one less Trait on all your challenges for the next day

(Narrator's discretion). Some of the nightmares may be so intense that you mistake them for reality.

Overconfident (1 Trait Flaw)

You have an exaggerated and unshakable opinion of your own worth, and you never hesitate to trust your abilities — even in situations where you risk defeat. Because your abilities may not be enough, such overconfidence can be very dangerous. When you do fail, you quickly find someone or something else to blame. If you are convincing enough, you can infect others with your overconfidence.

Phobia, Mild (1 Trait Flaw)

An overpowering fear of something causes you to instinctively and illogically avoid it. You must expend a Mental Trait if you wish to remain in the vicinity of the object of your fear.

Shy (1 Trait Flaw)

You are distinctly ill at ease when dealing with people, and you try to avoid social situations whenever possible. You have one less Trait on all challenges concerned with social dealings. You are also one additional Trait down on all challenges in which you are the center of attention for a large group of people (over 10). These two effects are cumulative for social dealings in which all attention is focused on you, such as making a speech.

Soft-Hearted (1 Trait Flaw)

You cannot stand to watch others suffer — not necessarily because you care about what happens to them, but simply because you dislike the intensity of emotion. If you are the direct cause of suffering and you witness it, you will experience days of nausea and nights of sleepless grief. You avoid situations where you might have to witness suffering, and you will do anything you can to protect others from it. Whenever you must witness suffering, you are one Trait down on all challenges for the remainder of the scene.

Speech Impediment (1 Trait Flaw)

You have a stammer or some other speech impediment that hampers verbal communication. You should roleplay this impediment most of the time, though not to the point of offensiveness or parody.

Addiction (1-3 Trait Flaw)

You have developed a physical or psychological dependence upon some substance or situation, believing that you need it to be able to survive. One Trait in this Flaw represents a harmless or easily obtainable substance, such as coffee or cigarettes. Two Traits indicates a craving for a more uncommon item or perhaps one that is illegal or dangerous to obtain, while three Traits in this Flaw means that you are addicted to something rare or harmful. At base cost, this need is psychological in nature and only affects your behavior. For an additional Trait, the effects are more severe, imposing a one Trait penalty on all feats until your craving is satisfied. For two Traits above the base value, the dependence has become physical. Withdrawal from this substance will leave you Wounded and in great pain for days. In this case, you will stop at nothing to get your hands on another fix, forsaking friends, loyalties and everything else in pursuit of your addiction.

Hatred (1-4 Trait Flaw)

You have an unreasoning dislike of some item or person. All interactions with the object of your hatred will be colored by this emotion and you will take any opportunity to harm what you detest. The base value of this Flaw is determined by how strong your reaction is: one Trait for disdain, two Traits for blind anger and three Traits for uncontrollable fury. In this last case, you must to spend a Willpower Trait to prevent yourself from losing control and attacking the object of your hatred. Normally, the object in question will be reasonably uncommon. Exceptionally rare targets are worth one Trait less, while very common situations are worth one extra Trait.

Amnesia (2 Trait Flaw)

You are unable to remember anything about your past, or your identity for that matter, though this does not affect your magic or your Abilities. If you want, you may take up to five Traits' worth of additional Flaws that the Storyteller will select. Rest assured, you will find out about them soon enough.

Frenzy (2 Trait Flaw)

Unlike most other individuals, you are prone to lose control of your faculties in certain circumstances. You must describe a particular condition that will bring about this condition when this Flaw is taken. This could be anything from running out of Willpower to encountering a particular type of item. If this situation occurs, you must spend a temporary Willpower Trait if you wish to avoid the frenzy. There are two possible responses when this occurs, depending upon your Nature and the source of this hysteria. A terror frenzy will force to you flee the area, while a rage frenzy causes you to attack the object of your hatred.

While in frenzy, you ignore all wound penalties down to Incapacitated. In addition, you need not bid any Social Traits when someone initiates a Social Challenge against you. However, you are incapable of initiating such challenges yourself. The state of frenzy lasts for 10 minutes or until you win a Static Willpower Test. Bonuses due to your Nature or Merits such as *True Love* or *Code of Honor* will apply to this test. A character with this Flaw may not also have the Merit: *Quiet Heart*.

Low Self-Image (2 Trait Flaw)

You lack self-confidence. You are two Traits down in situations where you don't expect to succeed (at the Narrator's discretion, though the penalty might be limited to one Trait if you help by pointing out

when this Flaw might affect you). At the Narrator's option, you may be required to expend a Willpower Trait in order to attempt things that require strong belief in yourself.

Obsession (2 Trait Flaw)

There is something that drives you onward, a person or object that you worship above all else. Whatever you seek, this compulsion causes you to ignore the bounds of reason in its pursuit. In any situation where you must choose between the object of your Obsession and another course of action, you must win a Static Mental Test to avoid going after what you value most. This effect may be ignored for one scene by spending a Willpower Trait. Characters with this Flaw may not also have a Driving Goal or Higher Purpose.

Vengeance (2 Trait Flaw)

You have a score to settle. You are obsessed with wreaking vengeance on an individual (or perhaps an entire group), and you make revenge your first priority in all situations. The need for vengeance can only be overcome by spending a Willpower Trait, and even then it subsides only temporarily.

Driving Goal (3 Trait Flaw)

You have a personal goal, which sometimes compels and directs you in startling ways. The goal is always limitless in depth, and you can never truly achieve it. It could be to eradicate all vampires, or to achieve more in magic than your big brother. Because you must work toward your goal throughout the chronicle, your single-minded devotion will get you into trouble and may jeopardize other goals. You may avoid your driving goal for one scene by spending a Mental Trait, and for one session by spending a Willpower Trait.

If you have the Merit: *Higher Purpose*, you cannot take this Flaw.

Flashbacks (3 Trait Flaw)

An event from your past still haunts you. In times of great stress, you will fall back into a specific situation (described in your character history). People around you will take on the roles of those present during that past event. This memory is not necessarily a violent or unpleasant one, though slipping back to more idyllic times can be just as dangerous in the wrong situation. Flashbacks can be very disrupting depending upon the nature of the incident. Storytellers should carefully consider whether they want to allow this Flaw in their chronicles.

Hatred (3 Trait Flaw)

You have an unreasoning hatred of a certain thing. This hate is total and largely uncontrollable. You may hate a species of animal, a class of person, a color, a situation ("*AAARRRRGGGHHH! If I have to practice this spell one more time…!*") — anything. You constantly pursue opportunities to harm the hated object or to gain power over it, so much so that your reasoning is clouded. The Storyteller may impose a Trait penalty in dealings with the object of your hatred, due to your disgust and divided attention, or he may direct you to undertake certain courses of action.

Low Pain Threshold (3 Trait Flaw)

You have never liked the thought of injury, especially your own. Your aversion to pain is such that the slightest cuts and bruises cause you to scream as if you're being butchered. While normal injuries do not cause any additional physical damage, the psychological impact of such wounds can be devastating. Treat all wound penalties down to Incapacitated as if you were one Health Level more injured than you actually are. A character with this Flaw may not also take the Merit: *Increased Pain Tolerance*.

Phobia, Severe (3 Trait Flaw)

An overpowering fear of something causes you to instinctively and illogically flee from it, even to the point of endangering yourself. You must expend a Willpower Trait if you wish to remain in the vicinity of the object of your fear.

SUPERNATURAL

These Merits and Flaws concern the way you interact with supernatural aspects of the game. Because they should be rare and unusual and can possibly change the flavor of a chronicle, the Storyteller may restrict them, or only permit one per character.

Loyalty (1 Trait Merit)

You are sworn and devoted to some group or cause. This Merit works similarly to *True Love*, but the object may be an organization or ideal.

Shivers (1 Trait Merit)

Although you can't actually see or hear ghosts, you get a creepy feeling whenever wraiths are around. Whenever a wraith enters the room, you may automatically make a Static Mental Challenge with a difficulty of six (no Traits are risked). If you succeed, you are aware of the presence of the ghost

True Love (1 Trait Merit)

You have discovered, but may have lost (at least temporarily), a true love. This love provides joy in a torrid existence. If this loved one is in mortal danger, you may use a Humanity Trait as a bonus Trait. Similarly, you may use a Humanity Trait in the place of a regular Trait during your initial bid if your true love is at risk. A Humanity Trait used in this way is gone regardless of the outcome of the challenge. Your true love may be a hindrance, and require aid (or even rescue) from time to time.

Faerie Blood (1-5 Trait Merit)

You must take the Merit: *Kinain* before you take this Merit. You possess a strong amount of faerie blood, which affords you some of the powers of the changelings. For each Trait that you place in this Merit, you may take one Merit or Flaw normally reserved for changelings. Additionally, you have one Trait of Glamour, just like a changeling, and the potential to gain more; each additional permanent Trait of Glamour costs you three Traits (Free or Experience), though you can never have more permanent Traits of Glamour than the number of Traits spent on this Merit. Although you may use your Glamour like a faerie, you can only replenish Glamour by creating art or receiving a token from a changeling. Still, you can learn the Basic Arts and Realms of faerie magic, giving you the ability to cast minor enchantments. Arts cost six Traits to learn, while Realms cost four. You also add the level of this Merit to the number of days that an enchantment lasts on you. With one Trait in this Merit, you can be enchanted for eight days at a cost of only one Glamour Trait (seven days for being kinain, plus one day for one level of *Faerie Blood*).

You can find more information about Glamour, Arts and Realms in **The Shining Host**.

Magical Item (1-3 Trait Merit)

You possess an item of some supernatural power, be it a relic, fetish, talisman or treasure. Its powers are up to the Storyteller, and you may not even be fully aware of them.

Burning Aura (2 Trait Merit)

Even if you do not have True Faith, you have the brilliant aura of a person of power. Those able to sense auras will give you a wide berth, as you seem to display potent spiritual powers. Even people who cannot detect your aura find something about you compelling. Those who deal with spirits find they are like beacons, even across the Gauntlet.

Danger Sense (2 Trait Merit)

You have a sixth sense that warns you of danger. When you are in a perilous situation where you could potentially be surprised, you have two extra seconds (for a total of four) in which to react.

Faerie Affinity (2 Trait Merit)

For some reason, changelings seem to like you. At least, they tend to hang around you more than others. On the down side, you are always considered two Traits down on resisting enchantment, making it easier for them to affect you with their arts. Further information on changelings may be found in **The Shining Host**.

Medium (2 Trait Merit)

You possess the natural affinity to sense and hear wraiths. Though you cannot see them, you feel their presence and are able to speak with them when they are in the vicinity, though they may choose not to listen to you. You may even be able to summon them to your presence through pleading and cajoling. They will not simply aid you, or give you free advice — they will always want something in return.

Soothing Voice (2 Trait Merit)

Your voice is calm and soothing, almost entrancing. You are two Traits up on any challenge that directly involves the use of your voice (be it for singing, preaching, leadership, etc.).

Totem (2-6 Trait Merit)

Characters who come from Native American or similar heritages have the option of allying themselves with a Totem spirit. The benefits and requirements for this type of service are too numerous to describe here. Players and Storytellers may draw available Totems from **Werewolf: The Apocalypse** as well as any of the various tribebooks. Plant Totems are detailed in the **Changeling Player's Guide**. Unlike most Merits, you may strengthen your link to your Totem over time, increasing its power as mentioned in **Laws of the Wild**. Your Storyteller may require you to have this before you may learn the *Totem Link* Praxis.

Ghostsight (3 Trait Merit)

You can see beyond the barrier that separates the land of the dead from the world of the living, but only with effort. By succeeding in a Static Mental Challenge with a difficulty of seven Traits, you can see wraiths and even (dimly) the lands of the Underworld, for the remainder of the scene.

Kinain (3 Trait Merit)

Though not a changeling, you have fae blood running through your veins, literally. Being kinain makes it easier for you to walk in the Dream as if you were fae yourself. While this product of your heritage may expose you to chimerical attack, it also opens you to a new and wondrous world. Although you do not necessarily have access to the powers of the fae, you are more in tune with their world, and they find it easier to affect you. Conversely, you are more likely to remember your encounters with them.

Kinain, as slightly supernatural entities, have a maximum of nine Traits in all abilities, instead of the usual human maximum of eight Traits. You are related to one of the types of faerie races, and you may even share some of their abilities. You do not necessarily have the ability to use changeling Arts (unless you have the additional Merit: *Faerie Blood*), but you are more easily accepted into Kithain society. You have only five Banality Traits, giving you a much wider opportunity to explore faerie society, as changelings are more likely to associate with you and you are less susceptible to the amnesiac effects

of the Mists. Similarly, you are easily enchanted; any changeling can enchant you by simply expending a Trait of Glamour (without the need for a token), and you remain enchanted for a full week.

If you are playing kinain in a predominantly changeling game, the Storyteller may choose to waive the cost of this Merit, to encourage play of intermediaries between human and changeling society.

More information about changelings and their capabilities can be found in **The Shining Host**.

Kinfolk (3 Trait Merit)

By some quirk of fate, you are kin to one the Changing Breeds. The Changing Blood has not stirred in you, but it has left its mark. Though you may not understand why, you are immune to the Delirium (the madness inspired by viewing a werewolf in the full rage of his Crinos form). This doesn't mean that you know sensitive secrets, or that you can wander around the shapechangers' holy sites without retribution, but you have a certain edge among them that no normal mortal can match.

As partial supernaturals, Kinfolk have a Trait maximum of nine Traits in each of the Physical, Social and Mental categories, instead of the normal mortal limit of eight Traits. All Kinfolk are considered related to one of the tribes, and they are likely to have close ties to at least one Garou of that tribe. Additionally, Kinfolk may learn Basic homid or tribe Gifts that do not require Gnosis or Rage, at a cost of six Traits (whether freebie or Experience Traits), or eight Traits for Gifts of a tribe other than the one to which you are related.

In a predominantly Garou game, the Storyteller may choose to waive the cost of this Merit, encouraging the interaction of mortal relatives with the Garou.

More information about Garou Gifts and tribes exists in **Laws of the Wild**.

Luck (3 Trait Merit)

You were born lucky, and have always found that the odds are in your favor. You gain three retests per story that you may use on any failed tests. You cannot make more than one retest on any single challenge.

Supernatural Ally (3 Trait Merit)

You are friends with some supernatural being, perhaps a werewolf or nature spirit, maybe a vampire or a wraith. While your companion may occasionally come to your aid, expect to return the favor from time to time. After all, you are friends. The Storyteller will create this companion and assign someone to play him as a Narrator character, with his own personality and goals. If you also purchase the Mentor Background, you may select this companion to fill both roles.

Symbol Independence (3 Trait Merit)

POWERFUL GHOULS

Some Storytellers may feel that limiting ghouls to Advanced Disciplines is too constraining for normal troupes. After all, since most troupes won't have many elder Kindred around, giving an Intermediate Discipline to a ghoul of a ninth-generation vampire seems like a reasonable way to keep the dichotomy between elders and neonates without adding in seventh-or sixth-generation vampire powerhouses.

If this idea appeals to you, you may wish to use the following alternate dispersion for ghoulish Discipline limitations:

Domitor of 11th or weaker generation: Basic Disciplines

Domitor of eighth to 10th generation: Intermediate Disciplines

Domitor of seventh or stronger generation: Advanced Disciplines

Ghouls should never have access to Master-level Disciplines — some powers are reserved for the elders alone.

The use of True Faith against a supernatural creature typically requires the use of a holy symbol. However, you are free from this restriction, and you may use your Faith unfettered by any such psychological or religious crutch.

Twin Link (3 Trait Merit)

You share a deep bond with another character. This may be a chosen familiar or perhaps a beloved soul mate. Your bond does not permit telepathy, but you can sense each other's strong emotions, such as fear or joy. Your companion is not just an extra pool of Traits. She must be created and played as an independent character. Given the depth of the connection, the potential repercussions to one of the pair when the other is distressed or injured should be obvious (ever hear of the Corsican Brothers?). Don't even think about what would happen if one of you were to die.

Unbondable (3 Trait Merit)

You are immune to being blood bound. No matter how much blood you drink from vampires, you will never be bound to them.

Psychic/Sorcerous Awareness (3/4 Trait Merit)

You are automatically aware whenever magic or psychic power is used within 10 feet of you. The use of Garou Gifts, vampiric Disciplines or even hedge magic causes a distinct tingle to run up your spine if you have *Sorcerous Awareness*; with *Psychic Awareness*, you notice various phenomena and certain supernatural powers that mimic psychic abilities, like vampiric

Auspex. Furthermore, you may make a Mental Challenge (with a static difficulty of eight Traits) in order to discern what effect was used and who used it (assuming that you have enough *Lore* Abilities to be able to tell a vampire Discipline from, say, a changeling Art).

Destiny (4 Trait Merit)

A great destiny lies ahead of you, though you may not yet realize it. Your destiny will become more and more apparent as the chronicle proceeds. The Storyteller will decide your destiny, though you may make suggestions. Because this Merit tends to transform a character into a main protagonist, you must have your Storyteller's permission to choose it.

Easy Consort (4 Trait Merit)

Wraiths and other spirits find it easier to possess you than other mortals. Although this Merit can be disadvantageous at times, it means that you are a natural channel for beings from the other worlds. As such, they may choose to barter with you for the favor of borrowing your body. All tests to possess you have a two-Trait bonus; furthermore, you retain full awareness of all events while your body is ridden.

Ecumenist (4 Trait Merit)

Although you are steadfast in your own faith, you recognize the workings of the Holy Spirit in other religions. Usually, when using True Faith, you must use a holy symbol from your own religious tradition. With this Merit, you see the divine spark at the core of religions beyond your own. You are able to make use of their religious icons and holy ground when confronting the supernatural.

Ghoul (5 Trait Merit)

At some point, a vampire fed you some of her potent vitae, possibly bonding you into service. Somehow you broke free, but the blood's force has granted you some of your mistress' power. Your aging has stopped, and you have the *Potence* Discipline at the Basic level of *Might*, giving you a free retest on any strength-related Physical Challenge. This Merit does not come without cost, however. You must continue to feed on vampire blood once per month, or you will regain your mortality and lose all the benefits of being a ghoul.

Ghouls, as supernatural entities, may have up to nine Traits in any category (unlike most mortals, who are limited to eight). Additionally, a ghoul may learn the vampiric Disciplines that are natural to her vampire mentor. For players with **Laws of the Night**, the ghoul begins with one Basic Discipline from her domitor's clan (in addition to the automatic level of *Potence*), and the ghoul can learn the other Basic levels of her domitor's clan Disciplines, at a cost of six Experience Traits each. Particularly powerful domitors give their ghouls the ability to learn greater Disciplines; ghoul servants sustained by a vampire of the seventh or sixth generation may learn Intermediate Disciplines (at a cost of 12 Traits each), while ghouls of vampires of lower generations may learn Advanced Disciplines (at the incredible cost of 18 Traits each).

If you are playing a mortal ghoul in a predominantly vampiric game, the Storyteller may choose to waive the cost of this Merit. After all, any vampire can simply turn you into a ghoul by feeding you one Trait of her blood.

See **Liber des Goules** and **Laws of the Night** for more complete rules.

Clear Sighted (5 Trait Merit)

You are unusually sensitive to the use of supernatural powers of illusion, trickery and disguise, and can see through them to the heart of the matter. With a successful Mental Challenge, you can see through *Unseen Presence*, *Mask of 1000 Faces*, *Blur of the Milky Eye*, *Blissful Ignorance*, *Chimerstry* and the like. When engaging multiple opponents at once, you need only risk one Mental Trait to attempt to perceive all of them; make a single test against everyone simultaneously, resolving ties as normal, but if you lose any of the challenges you only lose the one Mental Trait that you bid.

Lifegiver (5 Trait Merit)

You have a particularly strong life-force, such that you heal rapidly and even extend your healing abilities to others. Whenever you suffer non-aggravated damage, you heal it faster than the normal time. Furthermore, if you are uninjured, then anyone under your care heals at this advanced rate as well (assuming that your subject is capable of natural healing, that is).

As an aside, though, your blood is mighty tasty to vampires, and you have the added bonus of healing quickly. You automatically have the Flaw: *Potent Blood*, but you gain no additional Traits for it.

Speaker with the Dead (5 Trait Merit)

Your sight extends beyond the Shroud of the spirit world and into the lands of the dead. You see and hear the Underworld at all times; to you, life is an existence stumbling through two simultaneous half-worlds, one of solid, bright matter, the other of decaying grayish detritus. In addition, you can see and hear wraiths and other beings within the lands of the dead. Obviously, you are a target for those ghosts who wish to contact the living world, and malevolent Spectres may hound you and attempt to drive you insane. However, your intimate knowledge of the deadlands affords you the opportunity to gain *Wraith Lore* without a mentor, and you have a clear advantage when using sorcery or Psychic Phenomena that interact with the dead.

Gnosis (5-7 Trait Merit)

You must take the Merit: *Kinfolk* in order to have this Merit. In addition to your blood ties to the Garou, you have a small measure of spiritual awareness as well. You are tied to the powers of life and Gaia much like your changing cousins. You have one to three Traits of Gnosis, depending on the number of Traits spent on this Merit (one Gnosis for five Traits, two Gnosis for six Traits, and three Gnosis for seven Traits). You can use this Gnosis to use werewolf Gifts and assist in Rites, just like a Garou. Having this Merit allows you to learn a greater selection of Gifts (since you can use the ones that require Gnosis), and accords you a great deal of respect among the shapechangers. Furthermore, if a vampire attempts to Embrace you, you may make one simple test for each Trait of Gnosis that you possess. If you succeed in any of the tests, you die quickly and peacefully without becoming a vampire. If you tie any of the tests without any wins, you die slowly and painfully, but still do not become a vampire. Only if you lose all of the tests do you join the ranks of the undead.

You may not raise your Gnosis with later Experience Traits; any Gnosis that you possess during character creation is the limit of your spiritual capability, forever. However, if you expend a permanent Gnosis Trait in the course of a Gift or ritual, you may use Experience Traits to regain that Gnosis Trait later.

See **Laws of the Wild** for an in-depth explanation of Gnosis and the Gifts that it powers.

Mysterious Guardian (6 Trait Merit)

Someone or something watches over you, protecting you from harm and aiding you on random occasions. The Storyteller will decide why (and by what) you are being watched over, as well as what else having such a guardian entails.

Fist of God (7 Trait Merit)

Through natural devotion, intense training or some other mystical means, you have forged a supernatural ability to strike and injure paranormal creatures. Perhaps you've developed an incredible martial arts technique, or maybe your handgun was once blessed by an extremely devout priest. Whatever the reason, your "Witch-Hammer" strike inflicts aggravated damage against supernatural creatures. However, the Fist only functions with one particular weapon — your gun, your sword, your body, whatever. Furthermore, this Merit only functions (though it cannot be lost) if you have at least four permanent Humanity Traits.

True Faith (7 Trait Merit)

You have a deep-seated faith in and love for some higher divine power. You begin the game with one Trait of True Faith. Your belief provides you with an inner strength and comfort that continues to support you when all else fails. The effect of Faith varies from person to person, and from religion to religion. More details can be found in the Numinae section of Chapter Three.

Bard's Tongue (1 Trait Flaw)

You speak the truth, and with uncanny accuracy. This is not a talent for prophecy, but a facility for blurting out unpleasant truths at inappropriate times. Once per session, the Storyteller may approach you with a nasty truth you must spit out, and you may only swallow the urge by spending a Willpower Trait.

Offensive to Animals (1 Trait Flaw)

For some reason, animals cringe from your touch and are uneasy in your presence. Perhaps it is because you have been tainted by your dealings with the infernal or perhaps they just dislike your smell. For whatever reason, animals are jittery around you. You are one Trait down on challenges involving animals.

Echoes (1 or 3 Trait Flaw)

You carry a bit of superstition in your heart — so much so that old wives' tales come true around you. This may be something as simple as street lamps temporarily going out when you pass by (one Trait) or as dramatic as a cold wind that follows you everywhere (three Traits). This Flaw is never harmful, just annoying and perhaps disconcerting to those nearby. The Storyteller will assign a value to this Flaw based upon your description of the effect and how often it occurs.

Geas (1-5 Trait Flaw)

You are under some form of compulsion or magical prohibition. This may be voluntary or something imposed upon you by outside forces. Violating this ban may cause illness, the loss of magical ability, or even death. The Trait value of this Flaw is based upon the nature of the geas and its potential consequences.

If you accidentally violate this stricture, it may be possible to atone. Take, for example, a character with a compulsion to stop and greet every lady he passes on the street. One day, he walks by a cloaked figured running in the other direction without being able to tell whom it is. His conscience (or whoever else is watching over this geas) might forgive him if he took the next month going out of his way to help females in need. However, if you willingly violate such a prohibition, then you suffer the full consequences as described in your character history.

Cursed (1-5 Trait Flaw)

You have been cursed by someone or something with supernatural or magical powers. This curse is specific and detailed, cannot be dispelled without extreme effort and can even be life-threatening. Some examples include:

- If you pass on a secret, your betrayal will later harm you in some way. (1 Trait)

- You stutter uncontrollably when trying to say something important. (2 Traits)
- Tools break or malfunction when you attempt to use them. (3 Traits)
- You are doomed to make enemies of those whom you love. (4 Traits)
- All of your accomplishments will inevitably become somehow tainted. (5 Traits)

Surreal Quality (2 Trait Flaw)

You don't know quite what it is, but everyone seems to think you are fascinating. You find yourself the center of attention wherever you go. This quality puts you two Traits down on any challenges involving stealth or going unnoticed. In addition, a character with this Flaw may not purchase the Background: *Arcane*, nor study Praxes which allow him to go unnoticed.

Magic Susceptibility (2 Trait Flaw)

You are particularly susceptible to Thaumaturgy, hedge magic, Garou rituals and other forms of magic. You are two Traits down in challenges relating to resisting all such spells and rituals, and they have twice the normal effect on you. You may never learn to use such magics, however, as you could never prevent them from slipping out of control.

Enmity (3 Trait Flaw)

A particular group of supernaturals (vampire clan, werewolf tribe, changeling kith, wraith Guild) has an aversion to you. It may be a matter of reputation, or something from your past that has come back to haunt you. Either way, you must bid two extra Traits when initiating any Social Challenges with that type of being.

Spectre Meat (3 Trait Flaw)

While most Spectres (wraiths that have fallen into the clutches of darkness and insanity) cannot perceive the living lands, you stick out to their perceptions. Spectres can see you, and they're likely to do all sorts of nasty things to you, just out of general maliciousness. See **Oblivion** for more details about Spectres. Storytellers may disallow this Flaw if their games do not include much interaction with wraiths and Spectres.

Wyrm-Tainted (4 Trait Flaw)

For some reason, you have the stink of the Wyrm about you. This may be because you willingly serve It, or it may just be hereditary and beyond your control. In any case, Garou can often sense this about you. Most of them will kill first and ask questions later.

(Note: The degree of Wyrm-taint represented by this Flaw is too severe for a simple Rite of Cleansing to purge. As opposed to mere incidental corruption resulting from being in the vicinity of Wyrm-tainted or Wyrm-serving entities, this taint has seeped into every aspect of your character's life whether he realizes it or not.)

Bound (5 Trait Flaw)

You owe someone, and you owe him big. We're not talking about the local loanshark — this is someone with the power to make your life *very* miserable if you try to wiggle out of it. This could be a vengeful ghost, a vampire or even a demon. In exchange for some bargain, a powerful being offered you something. Now you owe him a favor, and he fully intends to collect. Work with your Storyteller to put together the details of this bargain — With whom did you bargain? What did you get, and for how long? What did you offer in return? The Storyteller is under little obligation to be merciful. Be assured that *something* will come knocking on your door some night to demand payment, with interest.

Dark Fate (5 Trait Flaw)

The powers that be have something special in store for you. However long it takes to arrive, eventually everything you have struggled for will come to nothing. The Flaw will not manifest immediately, although you may have glimpses of the future in the form of nightmares. The Storyteller will decide your fate, though you may make suggestions. You must have your Storyteller's permission to choose this Flaw. A character with this Flaw may not take the Background *Destiny*.

SOCIETY

These Merits and Flaws describe aspects of your character's interaction with normal human society and the hunter groups.

Arcane Heritage (1 Trait Merit)

Whether you have a witch in your family or a grandfather with startlingly faerie-like eyes, your particular family line is considered gifted with a touch of the supernatural by those who dabble in such things. Although this touch may draw negative attention from groups such as the Inquisition, you gain a great deal of prestige from more studious organizations such as the Arcanum.

Ecclesiastical Rank (1-3 Trait Merit)

You are a vested priest in a recognized church hierarchy (such as the Roman Catholic church), with all of the implied social benefits. Although this Merit does not grant any special supernatural power or knowledge in and of itself, you may call on your church for advice, and you are often granted some deference and leeway by people who respect your vocation. The number of Traits in this Merit determine your relative standing. One Trait would indicate a local priest, while three Traits might indicate that you are an influential bishop. Although this Merit does not automatically imply influence within the church, you can certainly ask for information or aid through normal job channels.

Reputation (2 Trait Merit)

You are well-regarded in your particular society, and are one Trait up on all challenges with other members. You should decide what it is about you that they respect. This need not be a sorcerous society; you may be well-known among antique bookdealers or musicians.

Mentor's Resentment (1 Trait Flaw)

Your mentor dislikes you and wishes you ill. If you're part of a mystical society, you may have difficulties dealing with them because your mentor has spread stories about you. On the other hand, you may be getting unwelcome overtures from his enemies.

Mistaken Identity (1 Trait Flaw)

They say everyone has a twin somewhere in the world. Well, yours is somewhere nearby. This tends to get you into trouble every now and then, entangling your friends and enemies in a comedy of errors. You must decide if your double is a well-known mundane, another sorcerer or perhaps even some other type of supernatural being.

Twisted Apprenticeship (1 Trait Flaw)

Everything you know about your magical heritage is wrong. On the other hand, perhaps you are a Solitaire who never interacted with other magical individuals before. While this does not affect your magical efforts, it does put you at a disadvantage in understanding what is going on in the mystical world. You may not begin with any *Lore* Traits, though this Flaw may be considered automatically bought off when you have purchased at least two such Traits through Experience.

Blackmailed (1-2 Trait Flaw)

Someone's got dirt on you, and he's not afraid to use it. Whether an individual or an organization holds your dirty laundry, you're stuck with the results: Your blackmailer demands your money, your cooperation or your organization's secrets. For one Trait, you suffer from a rather embarrassing secret that might cost you your job and your organizational position. For two Traits, you harbor a dangerous secret that could very well be the death of you if the blackmailer gets it out. Obviously, your antagonist is too smart to make it easy for you to kill him. You'll need to go through a good bit of clever roleplaying to overcome this Flaw.

Enemy (1-5 Trait Flaw)

Somewhere out there is an individual or group who wishes you harm. The feeling is mutual, however, and you are out to get them as much as they are after you. The value of this Flaw is dependent upon the relative strength of your adversary. A one-Trait Flaw would indicate someone of lesser power than yourself, while five Traits might mean you are in conflict with a large organization.

Guardian (1-5 Trait Flaw)

You have taken it upon yourself to protect someone, perhaps an orphaned child or aging relative. This person occasionally gets into trouble, forcing you to come to his rescue. The base value of this Flaw is determined by how competent your fosterling is. One Trait indicates a competent sorcerer, mage or some other supernatural being, while two Traits would be a skilled mortal or someone with very minor powers. Three Traits suggests a person who is barely able to take care of themselves, whereas four Traits translates into a child or other individual who cannot survive on their own. By taking an additional Trait in this Flaw, the person you are protecting is either a mundane or is not aware of your aid and you plan to keep it that way.

Dangerous Secret (2 Trait Flaw)

You are privy to some sort of highly secret information that puts your life in jeopardy. Perhaps you've discovered that the archbishop in your area is actually an infernalist, but nobody will believe you and the archbishop could easily bring the weight of the Inquisition down on you. Maybe you've found a secret government conspiracy to work with vampires, but you can't tell anyone without risking arrest and execution. Worse still, the source of your information isn't exactly reliable, and your knowledge doesn't do you any real good. You may be in a position to do something about what you've learned, but it will certainly endanger you if you take any action.

The difference between *Dark Secret* and *Dangerous Secret* relates to the material you know. A *Dark Secret* is something about you that is yours to keep (and potentially someone else's to find out). A *Dangerous Secret*, however, is something that you know that belongs to someone else, and that someone would do a lot to get the information back — even killing. It could even happen that your *Dark Secret* is someone else's *Dangerous Secret*; some twisted Storytellers do like to get creative. A single player character may not take both, though.

Notoriety (2 Trait Flaw)

Something you've done pegs you as a liability, who tend to avoid you. You have a bad reputation among your own society, and Solitaires tend to be wary of you. Perhaps too many of your friends have been died mysteriously, or maybe you just have so much zeal that you make people sick. Work with your Storyteller to determine the nature of your notoriety.

Hunted (3 Trait Flaw)

You have become the target of another hunter. Whether he seeks you because he knows of your unusual Numina or has made a false assumption about your association with the supernatural, you must be careful wherever you go, lest you fall victim to another like yourself.

OPTIONAL RULE: FRINGE POWERS

It is very rare for a sorcerer or priest to be able to learn more than one type of power. However, there are always those who find some excuse for gaining access to different types of effects. Other mortals (psychics, ghouls, Kinfolk or kinain) may ask about purchasing one or more paths of sorcery. Even some Bastet are capable of learning these arts, according to legend. Storytellers are strongly urged to limit the number of crossovers in their chronicles, but if a player is able to justify the risk to game balance, here's how it works:

Since their own powers (Disciplines, Gifts or Arts) would occupy most of their attention, any of the paths of sorcery learned by these part-time sorcerers would cost double the normal number of Experience Traits. However, in cases where a given path is particularly appropriate to a character's heritage, this penalty may be reduced to paying only one additional Experience Trait per level of the effect. For example, a Garou Kinfolk might be able to learn the paths of *Shapeshifting* or *Totem Link* at only a slightly increased cost, while all other Praxes would cost double. A character may learn at most two paths in this manner.

Alternatively, the sorcerer may wish to concentrate on her magical studies, only picking up the occasional Gift or Discipline. Sorcerer-ghouls may select one Discipline to be purchased in this manner, while sorcerer-Kinfolk are limited to the Gifts of their breed (Homid). In this case, you must pay one additional Experience Trait per Basic effect, plus two more for each Intermediate power. Advanced Gifts and Disciplines always cost double.

SORCERY

Regardless of how strong your ties are to the rest of humanity, your ability to work magic also sets you apart. There are two modes of sorcery covered in these rules.

• Hedge Wizards are the most common practitioners of sorcery, covering mystical societies from Kabbalism to Aboriginal. The Praxes available to these character also cover the broadest range of powers, limited only by your interests and experience.

• Priests rely upon True Faith and the paths of *Theurgy*, matching their spiritual strength against supernatural lore. The focus here is not personal knowledge, but rather reliance upon the divine. Those who chose this option are limited to those paths taught within their ecclesiastical framework.

STARTING PATHS

The spells and rituals of sorcery are grouped together by common function and intent. These paths are referred to as either Praxes or Viae depending upon your chosen mode of practice. Either way, you begin the game with five Basic spells selected from the preferred paths of your heritage.

Sorcerers must learn each path in order, first mastering all the Basic effects before any Intermediate arts may be purchased. You must also know at least one spell of the appropriate level before acquiring any rituals at that level of complexity. Thus a Hedge Wizard must already have at least one Intermediate spell of a Praxis before learning any Intermediate rites for that path. However, the special rituals available to Priests are an exception to this rule. These rites may be learned at any time, as long as your True Faith rating is high enough.

MORTAL TRAIT LIMITS

Trait Category	Maximum Traits
Attribute Traits	8 (9 for partially Awakened mortals)
Willpower Traits	3
Humanity Traits	8
Faith Traits	8
Influence Traits	Total of Physical, Social and Mental Traits

SPARK OF LIFE

Having described your character in terms of game mechanics, it is now time to come full circle. The first task in creating a character was coming up with a character concept. This rough sketch outlines her personality, strengths and weaknesses. Now it is time to finish that portrait in greater detail. This additional information is necessary to change the character from a collection of statistics into someone you will portray. It is important to remember that while game mechanics are an important part of this system, the essence of the game is roleplaying.

USING EXPERIENCE

Once a character earns Experience Traits, these Traits may be spent to purchase new Traits or to improve existing ones.

- **New Attribute Trait** — One Experience Trait.
- **New Ability Trait** — One Experience Trait.
- **New Humanity Trait** — Two Experience Traits.
- **New Willpower Trait** — Three Experience Traits.
- **New Influence Trait** — Three Experience Traits.
- **New Faith Trait** — Only at Storyteller discretion.
- **New Sorcery Spell** — Three Experience Traits for a Basic-level spell, six for an Intermediate, nine for an Advanced, 12 for Master-level.
- **New Sorcery Ritual** — Two Experience Traits for Basic, four for Intermediate rites, seven for Advanced, 10 for Master-level.
- **New Stigmas (Dauntain only)** — Dauntain characters gain Stigmas at the Storyteller's discretion. Generally, a new Stigma arises when the Dauntain gains an additional Trait of permanent Banality.
- **New Agenda (Dauntain only)** — Three Experience Traits for a Basic Agenda, six for an Intermediate Agenda and nine for an Advanced Agenda.
- **Remove Negative Trait** — Two Experience Traits per trait to be removed.
- **Purchase Merit** — Twice the Merit's Trait cost, with Storyteller approval.
- **Remove Flaw** — Twice the Flaw's Trait value, with Storyteller approval.

HISTORY

No person is an island. Each character touches many lives and goes through different experiences before she enters the game. When creating a character, you must take some time to document her past, telling the story of her life before she comes on stage.

In addition, a good character history enables the Storyteller to work your character into the chronicle more intimately, granting her a greater role in the unfolding drama of the game. Great detail is not necessary. One or two pages can describe your character's life, her introduction to

the supernatural world, friends and family, even what she does when she is not out saving the world.

EXPERIENCE

We learn by doing. Learning from mistakes is just as important (if not more so) as studying one's successes. As such, all characters learn and grow through the process of experience.

By participating in games, you gain Experience Traits for your character, which may then be expended to improve his capabilities. In general, you gain one Experience Trait for each game session in which you take part; the Storyteller may award additional Traits for exceptional roleplaying, if your character does something particularly courageous or if he learns something significant. However, a character should never gain more than three or four Experience Traits from any one session of play.

TRAIT MAXIMUMS

Humans have their limits. Although humans improve with experience, there are maximum limits to which any human may aspire. As a result, the following table shows the maximum number of Traits a hunter may possess in any given category. For instance, a normal mortal may not possess more than eight Traits in any given Attribute category; thus, you cannot buy additional Physical Traits when you have eight Physical Traits, though you might still be able to improve your Mental Traits.

Some humans manage to expand their limits beyond normal capabilities, if only slightly. Any partially Awakened hunter has a higher maximum for Attribute Traits, as indicated. Partially Awakened hunters include ghouls, kinain, Kinfolk, sorcerers and those with an Intermediate level of any Numina.

SAMPLE CHARACTER CREATION

Sarah is interested in joining up with the local chronicle and needs a character. She's new to live-action, but she's very eager to learn. Her Storyteller, Susan, tells her about the current chronicle's dynamics, and asks Sarah what kinds of characters she likes to read about in books (which might give some ideas about what kind of character she could play). Sarah mentions that she likes stories about people with magic, but not the stereotypical hoary old wizard. Susan thinks that Sarah would make an excellent sorcerer, and the two sit down to the business of character creation.

Sarah decides that her character is new to her powers and the world around her, a teenager who's experimenting and finding she has a talent for these gifts. She's unaware of the more hidden supernatural world for now. Susan likes the idea — it sounds like a fresh perspective on the World of Darkness. Looking over the Archetypes, Sarah chooses Judge for her Nature and Visionary for her Demeanor. The character is young, but has a strong inner sense of right and wrong. Sarah decides Gwyneth's always looking for the good in a situation or person, since the world hasn't taught her differently yet. Now also seems like a good time to name this character. Sarah thinks a bit; having just seen "Shakespeare in Love", she likes the name Gwyneth. For the last name, she opens the newspaper — the full name becomes Gwyneth Williams.

Now Sarah chooses Traits for Gwyneth. She prioritizes the categories — Mental, Physical and Social — thinking that Gwyneth is clever but a little shy. For Mental Traits, Sarah chooses *Clever, Creative, Knowledgeable, Shrewd* and *Reflective*. As she looks over the Trait lists, she notices *Divination* listed under *Intuitive*. That sounds like something she wants, so she adds *Intuitive*. For Physical Traits, Sarah wants Gwyneth to be graceful and light on her feet, not built like a football player, so she chooses *Athletic, Dexterous, Graceful* and *Quick*. Recalling that she thought Gwyneth might not be extremely outgoing, Sarah looks for Traits that reflect Gwyneth as being the sort of person that people like, once they get to know her — *Alluring, Friendly* and *Expressive*. Sarah's starting to get a picture in her head about the sort of person Gwyneth is, what sorts of things she's likely to know or magic she'd be drawn to.

Now it's time for Sarah to choose Gwyneth's abilities. She immediately picks *Enigmas* and *Linguistics (French)*, but there's so many that look interesting she's not sure what should come next. Susan reminds Sarah that she'll have some freebie points coming to her, which she could put to use in Abilities. Sarah then decides that Gwyneth's still in school, and gives her a level of *Computer*, to reflect that Gwyneth is very much a child of the modern world.

For Backgrounds, Susan suggests that here might be a good place to start fleshing Gwyneth's current situation out. Sarah agrees and starts alloting Traits. The first Trait lands in *Influence: High Society* — Gwyneth hears all manner of gossip around the high school, and knows something about the current dynamics around town. One Trait goes toward *Mana*, giving Sarah two Traits of mystical energy that Gwyneth can use to power her spells when burning Attributes or Willpower would be too risky. Sarah's not quite sure how Gwyneth gets her *Mana*, but Susan tells her to think on it for the next game. The third Trait goes into *Resources*; Gwyneth is living at home, has a part-time job and a piggy bank, so her needs are taken care of. The last two Traits go into *Sanctuary*, and Sarah tells Susan about the old gardening shed at the back of the property that Gwyneth uses for performing rituals and building her talismans. Susan smiles, seeing some interesting hooks for stories.

For sorcery style, Sarah looks over the magical societies, but none of them quite mesh with what she has in mind. The Fenians sound interesting, but Susan warns that there are currently no changelings in the game, which could leave Gwyneth without allies for a while. Finally, Sarah asks if Gwyneth could be a Solitaire, which Susan thinks would work fine. She asks Sarah what sort of magic has Gwyneth been learning all this while, and Sarah reads the hedge paths for inspiration. She remembers *Divination* from choosing her Attributes, and starts Gwyneth's spellbook with *Query* and *Hidden Meaning*. This is followed by the Basic level of *Enchantment* and *Assessment* from *Healing*. For the final spell, Sarah thinks it might be fun to play with the weather like wizards and witches were said to do, and picks up *Touch the Air* from the path of *Weathercraft*.

Gwyneth comes into play with four Humanity Traits (*Helpful, Innocent, Kind, Warm*) and one Willpower Trait. Sarah also takes two Negative Traits — *Delicate* and *Shy* — deciding that Gwyneth isn't exactly a social butterfly, and that she's not likely to get back up if she gets knocked down. She now has two Traits to put where she pleases, which she will in a minute.

Merits and Flaws come next. Sarah takes *Twisted Apprenticeship*, thinking that Gwyneth's learned all her magic from books and a few things she's made up, and has no idea about this larger world of magic or the other people in it. Susan thinks that it will make for some great roleplaying when Gwyneth encounters her first wizards. As it's Sarah's first roleplaying experience, Susan suggests that she take the Merit: *Common Sense*, which will allow Susan to occasionally give Sarah a hand while she learns the game and story. Sarah agrees and marks it down.

Now comes the fun part — spending freebies! Sarah has seven to throw around (from her two Negative Traits and the five Free Traits everyone gets). Immediately, she picks up more Abilities — *Crafts, Investigation* and *Occult*. She decides that Gwyneth is a little more "human" than four Traits, so Sarah picks up *Helpful*, leaving her with two last Traits. She puts one Trait into the Background: *Library*, saying that Gwyneth has a few magical texts and her own grimoire. The last Trait goes for the Merit: *Arcane Heritage*. Sarah likes the notion of someone in Gwyneth's respectable family being a potential black sheep who might have started her down the path of "ruin," although she says that Gwyneth has no idea which person it could be.

Sarah asks Susan if it could be an unknown, something for Gwyneth to learn later, and Susan agrees, smirking a little at the possibilities.

Traits finished, Sarah thinks about Gwyneth in more abstract terms — how she dresses, how she talks, how she works her magic. Susan approves her choices, and points out the things that Sarah will need to think about while creating her history. With the nuts and bolts finished, Sarah prepares Gwyneth's history for their first big step into a much larger world.

Chapter Three: Hedge Paths and Theurgy

Do not quench your inspiration and your imagination;
Do not become the slave of your model.
—Vincent Van Gogh

There are as many faces to magic as there are cultures throughout history. Though the names and means of practice may change, the fundamental structure remains the same. Rather than representing a particular paradigm or heritage, the powers and effects described in this chapter may be found in a thousand different forms across the world.

SORCERY

praxis ('prak ses) n. [pl. praxes] 1: the exercise of an art, science or skill; 2: practical application of rules, as distinguished from the theoretical; 3: accepted or ritual practice, custom or behavior.

— Graham's New Collegiate Dictionary

There are many paths of sorcery. Each follows a set course of study, delving further into the mysteries of one particular art. There are two types of powers found in each Praxis: spells, which are cast directly, and rituals, which must be performed according to time-honored traditions.

Spells happen quickly, with Basic effects taking but a single action. Intermediate powers require one additional turn of prior concentration, whereas Advanced applications can take a minute or more to cast. However, the sorcerer may reduce the time requirement for any spell to a single action by spending a temporary Willpower Trait.

Rituals take significantly longer to perform and require extensive props or a carefully prepared site. Basic rites may be performed in about a minute, and the material components can usually be carried in a pocket or purse. Intermediate ceremonies take between 10 to 15 minutes before their effects are felt, and Advanced workings require an hour or more, depending upon the specific circumstances and desired results. Each sorcerer's personal style determines the specific format of the working, from the formal liturgies of *Theurgy* to the dances and chants of tribal shamans to the inscribed circles and tools of high hermetic workings.

A number of spells can have their affects extended if they are performed as full rituals. For a sorcerer to work a spell as a full ritual, she needs greater preparation and performance. Time requirements for such rituals may be considered the same as regular rituals, although she may not spend Willpower to reduce her spell to a single action.

COUNTERSPELLS

All sorcerers have the ability to resist hostile forces. When you witness (or are affected by) another spell, you may bid a Mental Trait in an attempt to counter the offensive rote. This may take the form of a Static Test or it may be used when defending against a challenge. However, because you are working to deny the power in question, you are considered to have relented to the original challenge if your attempt fails. In addition, you may only attempt to counter powers you understand, such as powers covered by an appropriate *Lore* Ability.

This does not affect vampiric Disciplines (except *Thaumaturgy*), Garou Gifts or wraithly Arcanoi. A sorcerer may attempt to counter cantrips if the changeling has called upon the Wyrd or the sorcerer is enchanted.

UNWEAVING

Though counterspells only work against powers while they are being cast, you may also attempt to disrupt existing magical effects when you stumble across them later. Unweaving takes the same amount of time as a ritual of the same level as the effect (Basic, Intermediate, Advanced) you are attempting to dismantle. You must also pass a Static Mental Test, its difficulty determined by the relative strength (vampiric generation, Garou rank, etc.) of the original caster and the familiarity you have with the effect. The restrictions on counterspells apply to Unweaving.

TECHNOWIZARDS

Magic comes in many guises. Some who practice its ways even deny that there is anything supernatural about what they are doing. New Age science has opened the door to technological wonders that the common man would not believe: cameras that photograph the aura, machines that transfer life energy from one individual to another, even sonic projectors capable of instilling specific emotions in a target.

Technowizards will never admit to being sorcerers. In fact, many scoff at their mystical counterparts, chiding them for clinging to obsolete ways of thought. But whether you believe your power comes from mystical symbols or from scientific breakthroughs, the results are the same. Characters who rely upon technology are created using the same rules as traditional sorcerers; however, the manifestations of their power are very different.

The techno-magical devices used by these wizards come in two forms. Portable instruments are roughly equivalent to spells, whereas stationary installations are comparable to rituals, with the same time requirements and conditions of use. This alternate application does not affect the costs, levels or the associated game mechanics for these powers, only their physical form.

ALCHEMY

This art deals with the creation of substances that provide special benefits or enhance the recipient's inherent qualities. Unlike the Praxis of *Enchantment*, this path does not grant magical powers beyond the potential of the being. *Alchemical* creations normally affect only living beings, including Garou and changelings. Rumors of *Alchemical* substances that can affect vampires circulate now and again, but no one's offered any substantial proof.

Alchemical products come in many forms: potions that take effect when consumed; pastelike salves, which must be applied to the target; perfume worn to give off a scent or incense, either in solid form or as a liquid applied to something else to be burned. A card must be prepared for each dose, describing its effects and listing its physical form. Once used, that dose is gone. Each potion, no matter what form it has been worked into, also has a shelf life based on its level. If the substance has not been used by the end of that time period, it is considered expired. Advanced-level elixirs are said to produce some rather unpleasant effects if they're consumed after the "sell by" date.

OOPS...

Sorcerers, as much as many hate to admit it, are human. Sometimes they screw up. And when they do, it can get messy, especially if the mistake was in the middle of casting a spell or working a ritual.

Storytellers and Narrators should feel free to come up with creative results for botched spells and rituals. A player who continually insists on dodging the required time for ritual-working should find his rituals giving him some mighty interesting returns on his character's poor efforts. Such failures need not be immediately evident. A botched *Alchemical* potion may look fine but turn out to be glue. An *Enchantment* talisman has the effect opposite that intended. A person caught with a botched *Fascination* spell becomes murderously obsessed with his target. And any botch involving the spirit world should be unpleasant at best. In short, sorcery is not for wimps. It comes with risks, and the general sentiment among long-time practitioners is that anyone who can't take the heat should stay out of the kitchen.

Sorcerers often take their powers for granted, believing themselves to be above mere mortals by their power, and they can get full of themselves because of it. Reminding your sorcerer now and again that the universe does not revolve around him should keep him nicely humble.

Each level of mastery automatically provides an understanding of how to brew poisons and healing tonics as well as elixirs that grant temporary Attribute Traits. Additional formulae are learned individually, with the same experience cost as rituals of the equivalent level. The recipes listed below are just a sample of the hundreds of alchemical creations possible. The sorcerer must research these other applications, presenting them for Storyteller approval before bringing them into game.

BASIC

Healing potions are common throughout history, providing a handy remedy when the sorcerer is not around. Though most tonics come in potion form, alternate versions are known to exist, such as salves that are applied directly to a wound. Either variant restores one Health Level of normal damage per dose, and a given character may only receive one dose per hour.

Alchemy also teaches the creation of poisons that are usually undetectable to mundane senses, though certain forms of perception would reveal them (such as vampiric or Garou *Heightened Senses* or changeling treasures). Normally, these come in potion form, inflicting one Health Level of damage when consumed. Alternatively, the substance could be prepared as a salve that may be applied to an edged weapon (sword, dagger or arrow). In this case, the poison inflicts one additional wound the first time the weapon is successfully used.

CAVEAT MAGUS

Most sorcerers take care with how they throw their powers around, and with good reason. The centuries-long Burning Times and events such as the witchcraft trials at Salem Village warned many a would-be wizard about showing off in front of the "mundanes." The Inquisition, though it may harbor Theurgists in its ranks, keeps a close eye on those sorcerers who practice the "black arts," and the lady is still for burning if she trucks with otherworldly powers. Nosy neighbors, government agencies and star-struck groupies can also make life interesting in the Chinese sense of the word. Not a few sorcerers have decided to police their own to prevent outside forces getting interested in them as a whole. An inexperienced teenager who doesn't know better is one thing, but someone acting maliciously and with full knowledge needs to be spanked.

This doesn't necessarily mean that a sorcerer is any safer around supernatural creatures. Many of the spells listed here, if used against a supernatural, would be considered hostile, no matter the sorcerer's intent. A wizard who sprays *Hellfire* around in the wrong part of town may find himself with a number of angry vampires on his tail, and a magician who makes a habit of imprisoning nature spirits into his homemade fetishes could get a surprise visit from six very large, very hairy and very angry Garou. Vampires have centuries to wait out a pesky magician, werewolves can make sure there's just enough of an offending wizard to bury in a plastic baggie, changelings can call on a power that transcends mortal understanding, and half the time you can't hit ghosts because they're not there. All make lousy enemies.

In short, behave, or don't have the gall to look surprised when the elder vampire you just insulted rips your throat out for it.

Finally, *Alchemical* elixirs may enhance a person's natural aptitudes. Basic versions grant the user two Attribute Traits that last for the remainder of the current scene (or until used). These Traits must be assigned during the brewing process and may only modify one Attribute category (Physical, Social or Mental). A character may benefit from only one of these elixirs at a time, and only one such boost may be applied within a one-hour span.

Basic *Alchemical* formulae take one hour to prepare and last for one week before losing their potency. Some additional recipes available at this level include:

• Blood of the Snake —Part of learning to brew poisons is learning to make the antidotes. This anodyne reduces the damage from any mundane poison (e.g., cyanide, spider venom) by half (round down). Thus, a toxin that normally inflicts three wounds would only cause a single Health Level of damage. These benefits last for the remainder of the game session if the antidote is taken before the poison. When used after the fact, this affects only a single dose. In addition, the antidote must be applied during the same scene in which the poison took effect. Blood of the Snake cannot affect Advanced-level *Alchemical* poisons, although it may have the normal effect against Basic preparations and reduce normal damage from an Intermediate poison.

• Nectar of Restoration — Since complex formulae can take a long time to prepare, alchemists have developed the means to sustain themselves over many sleepless nights. This draught restores all personal Attribute Traits in one category (Physical, Mental, Social), specified when the dose is created.

• Philter of Longing — Love potions have put coins in sorcerers' pockets for centuries. This is not the only passion that can be instilled, however; some have found fear or loyalty to be equally useful. Prepared as either perfume or incense, each dose evokes one specific emotion (chosen during creation) for a single scene. These effects may be avoided if the target wins a Static Mental Test.

INTERMEDIATE

This level allows the alchemist to create more potent brews. Intermediate tonics restore two Health Levels of normal damage or mend a single aggravated wound, whereas poisons inflict equivalent injuries. In addition, you may now brew venoms that paralyze someone for a scene or send him into a deep sleep for up to an hour.

The benefits provided by Intermediate elixirs are also more significant, granting the user three Attribute Traits which last for the remainder of the game session (or until used). A character may only benefit from this or any other elixir once per night, and the bonus cannot be combined with any other magical form of Attribute enhancement within the same category (Physical, Mental, Social).

Intermediate *Alchemical* works take one full day to formulate and lose their efficacy after one month. Some recipes at this level include:

• Blood of Valor — Many a warrior has wished for that one last burst of strength needed to finish a battle. *Alchemy* is only too happy to provide them that gift. This potion enables the user to ignore all wound penalties for a single scene. Alternately, a version may be created which simply reduces wound penalties by one level (Bruised counts as Healthy, Wounded counts as Bruised); this variant lasts for the remainder of the game session.

• Essence of the Judge — By applying this salve to her ears, the subject gains the ability to know when someone is lying to her. Alternately, this formula may be prepared as eye drops, allowing the user to tell if written text is fact or mere opinion. Either version requires a Static Mental Test for each statement you wish to verify. This effect lasts for a single scene.

• Philter of Passion — As with the Philter of Longing, this brew causes its target to feel a specific emotion, but the feelings are more intense and the effects last for one hour. Unlike the previous level, this passion may only be averted by the expenditure of a Willpower Trait.

ADVANCED

As your mastery increases, you are able to bring about amazing changes in a target. Your healing tonics can now restore all normal injuries over the course of an hour, including up to two aggravated wounds. Sleeping potions that drop victims into an enchanted slumber lasting for a week or more are possible. Poisons are also more dangerous, requiring the target to win a stamina-based Physical Challenge to even remain standing; those characters who win the challenege suffer one aggravated wound. Those who lose suffer enough aggravated damage to drop them to Incapacitated.

Finally, incredible enhancements to a person's body and mind are possible, granting up to four normal Attribute Traits or a single Trait that cannot be lost. Either benefit lasts for the remainder of the game session. As with lesser versions, the specific Traits must be specified when the elixir is made and cannot be combined with any other form of magical Attribute increase.

Advanced *Alchemical* preparations require one week of dedicated effort and last up to one year before becoming inert. There are few standard Advanced formulae, but many alchemists have found some remarkable creations (with Storyteller approval). Some known examples include:

• Blood of the Messenger — This formula is usually found as a potion allowing a character to speak and understand any language. A salve variant allows the user to select one of the following applications: By applying the salve to the eyes, the user can read any written language. By applying it to the ears, the character may understand any spoken words. Finally, by coating the tongue, the recipient may be understood by any listener. Each of the above uses lasts for one hour.

• Essence of Inner Strength — Some alchemists have uncovered the means of storing personal energy within a substance and recalling it in times of need. For every two temporary Willpower Traits spent during the final hour of brewing, the preparation affords one such Trait. This is one of the few ways to raise a character's temporary Willpower Traits

above her permanent rating. Rumors hint at other formulae that create draughts of Gnosis or Glamour, though these potions are subject to the Storyteller's approval. In any event, if the alchemist is not capable of donating this energy personally, a volunteer must be present during the creation. The effects end with the scene.

MASTER

These creations are the stuff of legends — flying ointment, Love Potion #9, complete cure-all or instant death poison. Your tonics can now increase a person's Traits well beyond their normal maximum, granting up to six Attribute Traits for the remainder of the game session. Again, these benefits may not be combined with any other magical form of Attribute increase.

Master-level *Alchemical* creations are said to last indefinitely, although not many have been willing to test the theory with the musty old bottles found in the back of an alchemist's pantry. These concoctions require one month of isolation to prepare, however. You may not engage in any other downtime activity, and your character must remain out-of-game for any stories which occur during this time.

In addition, some whisper that a Master of *Alchemy* is capable of learning the secrets of life itself….

Homunculus

This formula allows the alchemist to construct an artificial life form. These creations are fashioned in the shape of small animals, anything from a mouse or spider up to the size of a small dog. The homunculus may even be given wings, gills or similar movement-related capabilities. Each homunculus has eight Attribute Traits, though these are not broken up by category. Any ties or overbids are resolved using the entire set of Traits.

Though the creature's intelligence is no more than that of a well-trained monkey, it is capable of understanding reasonably detailed instructions. In addition, the homunculus may communicate short phrases or simple images to its creator through a limited form of telepathy.

Homunculi have the same Health Levels as humans and suffer damage in the same way. Once created, this servant lives for one year (or until destroyed).

RITUALS

Shaping the Elements (Basic)

This Praxis may be employed for other purposes than creating potions. By winning a Physical Test, you may change the physical shape of an object, sculpting it as if it were clay. Particularly complex or intricate changes may also require one or more Traits in *Crafts*. Once your remolding is complete, the changes are permanent. Most objects can only stand up to three remoldings before falling apart from stress.

There are separate versions of this ritual for each elemental or material form: stone, glass, metal, vegetable matter (wood, cloth, grains), living plants, even ice or water.

Destroying the Elements (Basic)

Similar to the previous procedure, this ritual allows you to destroy up to one pound of matter for each success you gain in a Static Mental Test. By spending a temporary Willpower Trait, you may even unmake fetishes or, provided that you have at least two Traits in an appropriate *Lore* (and you can expect to make some very unpleasant enemies in the process).

As with the previous working, separate versions are required for each different type of material.

Enhance Craftsmanship (Intermediate)

This rite allows you to enhance the mundane qualities of an object. For example, you could enchant a mirror to never crack, forge a blade whose edge will never dull or craft a bow which would never break a string. Though the items prepared using these rituals are not inherently magical, those sorcerers skilled in *Alchemy* will be able to detect these enhancements by winning a Simple Test.

Transformation of the Vile Body (Advanced)

This rite must be performed on a willing target: She literally becomes a factory for poisons and corrosive substances. The subject's kiss becomes fatal, and her bodily fluids inflict aggravated wounds. Even metals and stone will be corroded by extended contact with her blood. As a side effect, the host becomes immune to all toxins. This condition lasts until the next dawn.

COILING

Modern sorcerers have developed spells to interact with and control technology, including electronic devices such as radios, computers and even most modern appliances. Simple machinery and mechanical instruments of a non-electronic nature may not be affected through this path.

Sorcerers who practice *Coiling* are not technowizards — that is a distinction of practices, not semantics. Technowizards prefer to work their "magic" through devices of science, usually of their own creation, and disdain the idea of magic altogether. Coilers are sorcerers through and through.

BASIC

Malfunction

By spending a Mental Trait, you may cause one nearby electronic device to shut down. This power may be used on contemporary automobiles (which have electronic control systems), forcing them to stall. The effects of this power continue for one turn (10 seconds), after which the device can be turned back on. Anyone looking at the device will find nothing out of the ordinary.

Electronic Control

In addition to turning electronic systems on and off at a distance, you are able to operate such equipment at range. Though an electronic device can be made to perform any of its normal functions, it cannot do anything beyond its design. Thus, a telephone may be made to dial a particular number but not to emit a hypersonic burst of noise. Each success on an Extended Static Mental Test lets you issue one command during the scene. If the device in question is sufficiently complex, a Narrator may require you to possess an appropriate Ability to operate it.

INTERMEDIATE

Jamming

This spell allows you to set up a field that disrupts electronic communications in your immediate area. By spending a temporary Willpower Trait, you may also prevent any electronic devices from functioning. This effect covers a 10-foot radius for each Mental Trait you have and lasts for one scene. If a technowizard wishes to use an apparatus whose mundane equivalent is blocked, he must first defeat you in a Mental Challenge.

Data Tap

At this level, your awareness of the technological world has progressed to the point at which you may tap into the electronic information around you. By winning a Mental Challenge, you may "see" television transmissions, "hear" radio broadcasts or "feel" the electrical flow through a device. This spell also allows you to read information directly from computer media, such as floppy disks or CD-ROMs. Each use of this power allows you to monitor a single source for one scene.

ADVANCED

CyberLink

Your relationship with electronic devices has grown beyond your role as an external operator. By spending a Mental Trait, you may directly interface with a single device or network, controlling this system as if it were part of your own body. You may even override programmed security features by making a Mental Challenge. If another character attempts to take control of this system while you are linked to it, your adversary must first defeat you in a Mental Challenge. Once established, your link to the device lasts for up to one scene. If you perform this spell as a full ritual, you may sustain your connection for as long as you remain awake.

MASTER

Implant

Whereas lesser spells allow you to control devices as an external agent, this potent effect enables you to physically merge with a machine. By spending a Physical Trait and winning a Mental Challenge, you may embed any one hand-held device within your body. Once the device is implanted, you may perform any of its normal functions as if they were part of your natural body. For example, an embedded telephone would allow you to send and receive calls simply by thinking about it. Likewise, an implanted calculator would enable you to do complex calculations "in your head." You may never have more implants than your permanent Willpower Rating.

This melding lasts up to one hour for each Mental Trait you have, after which point you must remove the device or suffer two aggravated wounds.

CONJURATION

This Praxis allows the sorcerer to manipulate objects much as a stage performer does. Unlike simple misdirection, reality *is* being altered right under the observer's nose. Any objects you wish to affect with these arts must be prepared in advance according to the style of magic practiced, such as consecrating a blade to the Goddess or hypnotizing a human subject. Because of the necessary preparation time, this Praxis is ineffective in combat. While you may prepare objects for conjuration, you cannot claim to have the spell "lying in wait" in a corner.

Unless otherwise specified, any use of this Praxis requires a Static Mental Test.

BASIC

Tip the Scales

At the simplest level, you are able to levitate or move small hand-held objects weighing up to one pound for each Mental Trait you have. Precision applications, such as opening a lock, require you to win a Static Mental Test. The force generated by this spell is not enough to cause damage or even resist another character's efforts to stop it.

Thin Air

This spell allows you to make small life-forms or other hand-held items (up to 5 pounds for each Mental Trait you possess) invisible. By spending an appropriate Mental Trait, you may even teleport the object to any hidden location within 10 feet of its original location.

Alternatively, you may cause one apparently solid object to pass through another. This includes the classic sawing-in-half trick as well as more subtle applications. Neither item is harmed by this traversal, and the objects may remain co-located for up to one minute for each Mental Trait you spend.

INTERMEDIATE

Call to Hand

You can summon, move or levitate a living creature of less than half an average human's mass. You may also perform the same trick with inanimate

objects of approximately steamer-trunk size. Not only can you shuffle these objects about, you may also cause them to disappear from one location and reappear in another. Both the origin and destination of this spell must be within line-of-sight. The maximum range of this effect is 50 feet.

From the Hat

This art allows you to snatch large or complex inanimate objects, such as a bottle of wine, a sword or a boom box, from the air. The object must be prepared beforehand and may be no larger than a chair.

ADVANCED

Presto

Dramatic efforts are now possible for the conjurer. You may levitate large items (roughly car-sized) or up to three human-sized creatures, moving them anywhere within line-of-sight, to a maximum range of 100 feet. Living things may be affected with this spell, though only if they do not consciously resist.

MASTER

Hidden Pockets

As your control over matter and space reaches its peak, you are able to fashion extra-dimensional pockets around you. These spaces exist outside of normal reality, accessible only to their creator. However, this spell does not grant you unlimited capacity — each object squirreled away weighs about half as much as it normally would. Thus, if you were carrying a large book in one of these spaces, it would seem as if you had a paperback in your coat pocket. Each use of this spell pushes a single hand-held object outside reality. This object may remain there for up to one month, though you may return it to hand simply by taking an action to reach for it. Living creatures may not be stored in this way.

RITUALS

Setting the Stage (Basic)

This common ritual prepares an item to be the target of a *Conjuration* spell. This attunement has two effects. First, it allows for a free retest when casting any spells along this path that involve the object. In addition, *Presto* may be performed in a single action if the target of that Advanced spell has been prepared in this manner. After an item has been conjured, it must be reset before it can be summoned again.

Reaching Out (Intermediate)

Similar to the Intermediate spell *Call to Hand*, this ritual allows the caster to retrieve an attuned object from any well-known location, regardless of how far away it is. This process can be reversed by spending a temporary Willpower Trait, sending one small object to a well-known location anywhere in the world. In either case, you must be able to hold the item in one hand, and the remote location must be prepared using the Basic ritual: *Setting the Stage*.

Leverage (Advanced)

This ritual extends the powers of *Presto*, allowing you to levitate or move any single object. You may also affect a living target (even if he is unwilling) by winning a Mental Challenge versus your opponent's Physical Traits.

CONVEYANCE

Whereas *Conjuration* deals with the relocation of objects, this path allows the sorcerer (or other willing targets) to move quickly from place to place. This includes both direct flight and teleportation. The nature and manifestation of these effects must be specified when this path is learned. Some practitioners employ a vehicle, such as a broom or flying carpet, and others use more flashy means, including the infamous "puff of smoke."

Unless otherwise specified, any use of this path requires a Static Mental Test.

BASIC

Short Hop

The first level in this art allows you to move anywhere within your immediate area in a single turn, up to 10 feet away for each Mental Trait you possess. You may only travel to a location that you could normally reach: Jumping or teleporting across a room is valid, but appearing inside a locked room is not.

Secret Portal

This spell allows a character to walk through any single material barrier, such as a door or wall. If someone else is the beneficiary of this effect, she must pass a Static Mental or Physical Test or be disoriented for a full turn after the crossing.

If this rite is performed on a barrier that only exists in game (say a curtain that represents a steel door), then the player simple steps through when the spell is cast. On the other hand, if the barrier is real and there is already a scene taking place in the target location, the action there is put on hold while you move out-of-game to the destination. Once you arrive, you must describe your arrival to any players there.

INTERMEDIATE

Gift of Wings

This spell allows you to fly at a significant speed, covering distances of up to a mile in a few minutes. Once set in motion, the destination is fixed; you cannot change your mind after the journey has begun. Some vehicle or other means of transport (such as a broom or flying carpet) is necessary to manifest this effect.

Safe Journey

Similar to the previous spell, this application extends both your capacity and the distance you can travel. This flight is quite fast and can cover a distance of up to 100 miles in just an hour or two. It costs one Mental Trait to cast this spell, plus an extra Trait for each additional person (or equivalent cargo) you wish to bring along.

ADVANCED

Stepping Out

Whereas the preceding spells move an individual through space, this effect bypasses standard motion and teleports the caster (or one other willing individual) directly to her destination. Travel takes only a minute. If the destination is not within line-of-sight, then it must be well known and within one mile for each Mental Trait you possess. This transport ignores any physical obstructions along the way, though magical barriers or wards will prevent the effect.

Upon arriving at your destination, you must undergo an Extended Simple Test. Each consecutive failure on this test leaves you off balance and unable to function for one turn. A temporary Willpower Trait may be spent before the initial test to prevent this disorientation.

MASTER

Going Home

An enhanced version of *Stepping Out*, this effect allows you to teleport to or from any well-known location, regardless of how far away it is. You may even bring (or send) additional people, even if you do not go. This latter option costs one Mental Trait per person and only willing targets may be affected. If this spell is performed as a ritual, you may bring others to where you are, though the same costs and limitations apply. In this case, your targets must either be in a known location or else carrying a specific token that you have prepared in advance for this purpose.

As with *Stepping Out*, those people who travel in the blink of an eye suffer the risk of becoming disoriented upon arrival.

RITUALS

Walking the Clouds (Intermediate)

This dramatic rite allows the sorcerer and her companions to travel high into the air, up to the level of the clouds. By spending a temporary Willpower Trait, you may then traverse great distances and reach any point on the globe within a day. As with similar flights, the destination is fixed once the journey begins. The sorcerer may bring along one additional person for each success on an Extended Static Mental Test.

Going Home (Advanced)

An enhanced version of *Stepping Out*, this rite enables the caster to teleport multiple people to or from any well-known location. The ritual costs one Mental Trait per person when it is performed and only willing targets may be affected. If the caster is not present at the origin point, she must have some personal link to the targets. As with the spell, you must either spend a temporary Willpower Trait or perform an Extended Simple Test to determine if you are disoriented upon arrival.

CURSING

This Praxis has caused more than one sorcerer to be burned at the stake, for it allows you to use magic to bring harm to your opponents. All curses require a Mental or Social Challenge, which may not be negated with Willpower. A sorcerer may only bestow one curse upon a given individual at a time, though you always have the option to override any prior use of this path. Other sorcerers skilled in this Praxis may attempt to break an existing curse, as long as their knowledge equals or exceeds that of the original caster. This process uses the normal rules for Unweaving.

Because of the nature of these effects, you may be required to forfeit a temporary Humanity Trait if a Narrator feels that these powers are being used carelessly or maliciously. Cursing also requires that the exact words be noted for the benefit of the Storyteller, who will determine what results the curse has in accordance with the story.

BASIC

Mishap

You may hex someone with a minor inconvenience, such as causing him to drop an object or to say something inappropriate, for example. You may even cause a target to have a small accident, such as tripping and spraining an ankle (one Health Level of normal damage). The curse may be brought about immediately if the circumstances are right at the time of casting; otherwise, the effect will manifest sometime during the current game session.

Falling Out

This spell allows you to promote the effects of *Mishap* to all members of a small group. The targets must be directly linked in some way: two lovers, all the living children of an individual, everyone who participated in a specific attack on the caster, etc. The specific manifestation of the effects may not be the same for each victim, but there will be a common thread among all the victims' misfortunes.

INTERMEDIATE

Misfortune

At this level, you may cause calamities with lasting consequences. For example, your curse could ruin a friendship, cause a target's house to burn down, or have someone charged with a crime he did not commit. You may even bring about direct injury — two Health Levels of normal damage or one aggravated wound — in the form of a lasting illness or random mishap, such as getting hit by a stray bullet. Again, the specific nature of the curse will determine how quickly it comes into effect, though most such afflictions will manifest before the end of the current story.

ADVANCED

Great Curse

You may now inflict a long-term debilitating illness (permanently lose two Attribute Traits or gain up to two Negative Traits) upon your target. This may be the result of a heart attack or stroke, the loss of a limb or an emotional breakdown. Alternately, the curse may invoke a terrible disaster, such as a member of the victim's immediate family being murdered. If you intend the subject to die, you must also spend a temporary Willpower Trait before the challenge is resolved. As with all Advanced sorcery, you must spend a full minute preparing: In this case, you build up anger and malice toward your subject. The Storyteller may choose to waive this premeditation if the curse is directed at someone immediately threatening your life.

DEATH CURSES

Some of the most terrifying applications of this art include curses cast at the moment of death. If the Storyteller wishes to allow this option, you may cast any single curse that you already know, but it will have a much broader scope of effect. This curse may only be cast upon an enemy, either one directly involved in your death or one that you have been fighting with for a long time.

For each permanent Humanity Trait you have, increase the duration of the curse by one level: the remainder of the chronicle, one year, 10 years, the lifetime of the target, etc. In addition, permanent Willpower Traits may be used to increase the number of people affected: the target's immediate family, all of his descendants or living relatives, even members of the victim's extended family (clan, tribe or kith). This potent bane is subject to Storyteller approval and may be removable after the target makes amends, usually through extraordinary means.

MASTER

Hand of Fate

The most directed application of this Praxis is the ability to tip the scales of destiny in one direction or the other. By defeating a character in a Mental Challenge (versus his Social Traits), you may force him to lose all ties for the next hour. If your target has a power allowing him to win all ties, the effects cancel each other out and tests are resolved normally.

RITUALS

Anathema (Basic)

Magical societies often use this rite to brand members who have violated their tenets. This may be a physical mark that manifests in certain conditions (such as a deep red scar that appears in the palm during the waning moon) or a more spiritual brand, visible in the aura or causing other sorcerers and supernatural creatures to be uneasy around the target (e.g., Garou may find that she "smells funny"). Once set in place, the mark is permanent until removed. As a side effect of the branding, the target may never Unweave this effect herself.

Voodoo Doll (Intermediate)

By spending a Willpower Trait and defeating your target in a Mental Challenge, you are able to create a sympathetic bond between that individual and an appropriate representation. Any actions performed on the replica will have the equivalent effects on the target; this includes control over physical movements as well as inflicting sympathetic damage. The link lasts for the duration of the ritual, though the subject may ignore its effects for one minute by spending a temporary Willpower Trait.

Tainted Heritage (Advanced)

This rite allows the sorcerer to taint her target, passing on the effects of *Inconvenience* to others with whom she comes into contact. The scope of the taint must be specified when the curse is cast; it may apply to the target's family or everyone he speaks to in the next month. Alternately, a *Misfortune* may be called down upon a small group, similar to the effects of *Falling Out*.

Seven Plagues (Advanced)

This potent rite is used when simply directing your wrath against an individual is just not sufficient. Once the rite is set in motion, a series of maladies (each equivalent to *Misfortune*) will rain down upon an entire area or large group. As with other the powers of this Praxis, the sorcerer may only hint at the results; the specific manifestations are determined by the Storyteller. To determine the severity of the effect, the sorcerer must engage in an Extended Static Willpower Test, each success calling forth one additional blight.

DAIMONIS

Believing themselves secure in their powers, mortals have long sought to command the forces of the otherworld. Also known as *Daimonic Summoning*, this Praxis deals with the nebulous powers of the Deep Umbra. This is the most dangerous form of magic possible, for the creatures being courted extend beyond the limits of human understanding. Some sorcerers claim that every god, demon or angel ever conceived has some otherworldly incarnation. As with most arts, the style and mode of this practice varies with the tradition — a Kabbalist works differently than an American Satanist, and one does not attempt to call an angel with the rite used for an African devil. However, one thing is certain — commerce with creatures so alien to human existence always comes at a high price.

No sorcerer with half a brain performs these spells lightly or carelessly. This sort of summoning demands plenty of ritual tools, days of preparation and all senses working on full thrusters when — or if — the summoned creature appears. A sorcerer needs to be clever, strong-willed and lucky if she's going to truck with Umbrood — there are reasons why the gods do not walk the earth, and the Storyteller is under no obligation to be merciful. Depending on the creature that arrives, the Storyteller may allow it to win on all ties or even shrug off certain spells.

Daimonis is concerned only with Umbrood. The path of *Spirit Calling* handles incarnations of nature and the elements, and the Restless Dead are the province of *Necromancy*. For rules regarding spirit creation and combat, see Chapter Four or **Laws of the Wild**.

BASIC

Summoning

You may summon a single Umbrood, such as one of the infernal host, a demon baron, an angel, even a Celestine if you get *very* lucky. However, you cannot control what it will do once it arrives. Casting this spell requires an Extended Mental Challenge.

Dismissal

This simple spell allows you to protect yourself from the forces you summon. By winning a Social Challenge, you may force a summoned Umbrood to leave the immediate area for the remainder of the scene. If you take the time to enact a full ritual, you may extend the duration to an entire day. This spell may even be used to attempt to exorcise a hostile spirit that has taken possession of another individual (this has no effects on wraiths using *Puppetry* or who are skinriding). You may not cast such a spell on yourself.

INTERMEDIATE

Lesser Pact

You are now able to force certain behavior in lesser beings or negotiate a temporary truce with greater entities. If you succeed in a Mental Challenge, you may require a minor Umbrood to perform one action. If the task assigned would take more than an hour to complete, you must also spend a temporary Willpower Trait once the challenge is resolved.

Alternately, a successful Social Challenge (and plenty of roleplaying) will render any otherworldly being non-hostile. The spirit will not harm you or those under your protection for the remainder of the scene, though any other action is fair game.

Dolor

This spell allows you to direct your wrath against spirits who displease you. For each success on an Extended Mental Challenge, you may inflict one aggravated wound. Willpower may not be used to resist this effect, though it does allow for a retest. This power may be used on any being that originated somewhere other than the physical world.

ADVANCED

Truce

A greater form of *Dismissal*, this spell can be used to terminate your relations with a particular spirit. This effect only prevents the creature from coming within sight of you or affecting you directly. Alternately, you may choose to protect some other individual or object. The application requires a temporary Willpower Trait and lasts for the remainder of the current storyline. *Truce* may not be used to end demonic pacts.

MASTER

True Binding

Beyond mere control over lesser Umbrood, this potent spell allows you to attempt direct mastery over any being you are capable of summoning. You must know the appropriate *Summon* spell before attempting to control a specific individual, though your target need not be one that you personally summoned.

This spell requires an Extended Mental or Social Challenge (Storyteller's choice). However, unlike normal Extended Challenges, both sides continue accumulating successes until there is a clear winner. The first player to gain a number of successes equal to his opponent's current Willpower Rating wins the overall challenge.

The terms and conditions of this binding must be specified before the spell is cast. They may be as specific as requiring a single action of arbitrary difficulty or as open-ended as serving the victor until released. However, if the binding lasts for more than one month, the captive may reattempt the challenge. If the captive is successful, the tables are turned

and the servant becomes the master. This gambit may occur at any point during a game session, though only one attempt is allowed per month.

It should go without saying that only a fool would attempt to make an Umbrood into a pet. The sorcerer would do well to remember that his captive will, at some point, go free and is likely to savor his revenge in the way that only immortals can.

RITUALS

Lesser Daimonic Ward (Basic)

This simple rite allows you to guard an area or person from trespass by certain types of spirits. Any ephemeral beings that wish to enter (or affect) the subject of the ward must first defeat you in a Mental Challenge. Alternatively, you may reverse the protection, creating a mystical prison that holds a spirit within the specified boundary.

This protection lasts as long as you are present to support it. However, by spending a Willpower Trait, you may empower the ward for the remainder of the game session, even if you leave the area.

This rite protects only against angelic or demonic Umbrood spirits.

Greater Daimonic Ward (Intermediate)

This is an enhanced version of the previous rite, which must be learned first. Any spirit (of the appropriate type) wishing to cross the boundary must spend a Willpower Trait to do so. Even then, the spirit will suffer one aggravated wound per crossing. This protection lasts as long as the components of the ritual (sprinkled salt, iron shavings, carved runes, etc.) remain undisturbed.

Summon Daimonic Being (Basic, Intermediate, Advanced)

This rite places a call into the otherworld, summoning a specific being whose name you know or just any one of a certain type. Completion of the spell puts forth the evocation, but you must win a Social Challenge against the spirit in order to force it to respond.

The Basic version of this ritual calls only lesser demons and minor angelic beings, whereas the Intermediate form allows you to summon greater demons and the more powerful angelic hosts. Some sorcerers claim to know an Advanced version that calls upon the demon lords and cherubim, but few sensible folk would take such risks.

DIVINATION

The art of fortune telling has long been a mainstay of sorcery, from Tarot cards and tea leaves to rune casting and the I Ching. The specific set of tools or method used will depend upon your chosen style and is subject to Storyteller approval. Unless otherwise stated, all uses of this Praxis require a Static Mental Test.

Looking into the future can be problematic in many chronicles. Storytellers should feel free to tailor the format and content of information gained as needed to preserve the story plot. A Narrator or Storyteller must be present during the use of this Praxis, and she will determine the exact nature of the information given out.

BASIC

Query

At this level, you may gain answers to simple yes-or-no questions. As with all applications of this art, the trick is knowing which questions to ask. You may ask up to three questions about any specific topic during a given scene, though each requires a separate Static Mental Test. In general, information about the present or near future (a few hours) only may be gained.

Hidden Meaning

This spell may be cast any time you are studying a written text or listening to someone speak. By winning a Mental Challenge, you are able to "read between the lines" and get the basic gist of what is being said. You will be able to determine whether the writer (or speaker) believes what is being expressed as well as how much is opinion versus fact.

ON VISIONS

Nothing is ever simple, and this is especially true for *Divination*. Storytellers should consider how they hand out information gained during a divination with regard to the storyline and the recipients. Divinations are rarely clear — they show possibilities, circumstances and a few red herrings.

Examples:

Good: "You cast the I Ching, and the sticks fall into an unusual pattern. It mentions betrayal, and an upsetting of the careful order of things. A second toss suggests strength will appear when least expected."

Bad: "The I Ching says Jacob's going to betray the order, and Lynn's going to kick over the anthill at the same time, but don't worry, you're going to be the hero in all this."

Divination is about suggestions, possibilities, how things might be, and as such, is subject to interpretation, mistakes and even something that just doesn't happen. Don't hand out facts on a silver platter — there's no fun in that. On the other hand, you can get a lot of mileage out of an ominous card appearing in a spread or pulling out a blank rune from the pouch.

Even if you do not know the language in question, you will gain a general sense of the tone and content of the work, though no other details will be available.

INTERMEDIATE

Attunement

This spell allows you to draw general information about your surroundings. If you pass a Static Mental Test, you may gather basic impressions about the local area: the presence (but not location) of other supernatural beings, the rough population of the region, disturbances (supernatural, physical), current social dynamics, etc. Hard facts (names, dates, phone numbers, etc.) may not be gained through this power. Any use of this spell requires the presence of a Narrator, who will decide exactly what information is obtained.

Secret Whispers

Your powers of information-gathering have become reflex, allowing you to size up an individual even if you have never met her before. You must engage your target in conversation for at least five minutes and have her touch something of yours (i.e., a handshake, a Tarot card) before attempting to cast *Secret Whispers*. An Extended Static Mental Test will determine how much you discover. As always, your information comes in flashes and glimpses, with no hard facts.

This power may only be used on a given individual once per game session.

ADVANCED

True Visions

By now, you have mastered the art of pulling information out of thin air. You can read details about the subject of inquiry, gaining one piece of information for each success on an Extended Static Mental Test. This may be a name, a date or even a brief vision related to the question or subject at hand. These inquiries may be spread out over the course of a scene, though once you fail a test, you may not seek information on this topic for the remainder of the game session. You must spend at least five minutes with your chosen *Divination* medium, concentrating on the subject and speaking to no one, before beginning the test.

Time also imposes less of a limit in your visions. However, the farther ahead you go, the more significant the events need to be and the vaguer the vision in return. Thus, you could tell that the subject of your inquiry would meet someone within the next six months, and a serious accident or a marriage could be predicted years in advance. The events must have far-reaching consequences for you to be able to see them in the tapestry of fate.

MASTER

Pulse of the World

This is a more potent version of *Attunement* and is always considered active once it is learned. A Narrator may come up to you at any time and provide you with hints about events occurring both within the chronicle and elsewhere across the globe. This awareness may even take the form of prophetic visions of the future, though again, details are subject to change without notice. It may manifest while you are staring into the depths of a cup of tea, creating art or making crafts, even in the middle of conversation with friends (which can be disconcerting to people watching you).

It is important to remember that this power is an intuitive or subconscious ability. If you're lucky, the power may manifest largely in dreams, but more often it will follow your waking hours. Constantly catching snatches of events without context and being psychically assaulted by the resonances of Third World massacres can take their toll on your body and mind.

Successes	Information Gained
1	Target's first name, general area he is from
2	Nature, occupation, supernatural or not
3	First and last name, age
4	Abilities, glimpses of powers
5+	Intimate information(Derangements, Merits and Flaws)

RITUALS

Dowsing (Basic)

This common rite allows you to determine the approximate location of a nearby person or object. This takes the form of a subconscious tug leading you to what you seek. In the case of a specific target, you must either know the subject intimately or have some item closely associated with the individual. Alternately, you may locate the nearest member of a group, such as a source of fresh water or a particular type of plant. If you are unable to locate your target within an hour, the effect fades. In addition, if your concentration is interrupted for more than a turn, you will lose track of your quarry and must begin again. Maintaining your focus under these conditions requires a Mental Challenge (or a temporary Willpower Trait). You must recast the ritual with each new target. You may not use *Dowsing* to track supernatural creatures or things.

Tracking (Basic)

Similar to the previous ritual (*Dowsing*), this rite allows you to follow an individual's movements even after he leaves your presence. You must either have personally interacted with your target during the scene in which you cast this ritual or you must possess some physical link to him (a lock of hair, blood, etc.) as a focus.

By passing a Static Mental Test (difficulty equal to your target's number of Mental Traits), you are able to follow another character at a distance of up to one mile for each Mental Trait you have. If your quarry moves beyond this range, you must win another Static Mental Test to regain the trail. If he is able to remain out of range for at least an hour, he has successfully eluded your pursuit. In this case, you must again come within line-of-sight before you may attempt to track him again.

Past Impressions (Basic)

Though the far future and remote areas are still beyond the range of your vision, recent local events are open to your scrutiny. Make a Static Mental Test to determine what recently happened in an area. Superficial events do not leave impressions for more than an hour, but violent or emotionally charged incidents may linger for days, weeks, even years if they are powerful enough.

These visions come across as disjointed flashes or hazy dreamlike images. Few details are available, but you can make out the general situation. For example, you could tell that two people were having an argument, perhaps even hear snippets of what was said. However, though you could see that someone had been shot, you would not be able to determine the extent of the injury or what type of gun was used.

Insight (Intermediate)

As your ability to tap into unseen sources improves, you may begin to answer more complex questions. *Insight* allows you to perform a standard reading using whatever tools are your stock in trade. Details of the future will be vague and uncertain, though simple cause-and-effect relationships will be revealed. The difficulty of the test is determined by your relationship to the subject of your inquiry. The closer you are to your target, the more difficult it is to keep your answers unbiased. You may now also query through time, though only events within the current chronicle (no more than six months in the future or two years in the past) can be seen.

Omen of Fate (Advanced)

This ritual allows you to read aspects of an individual's fate, including the ones described in the Background: *Destiny* or the Flaw: *Dark Fate*. If cast at the beginning of a game session, *Omen of Fate* may reveal impending dangers or moments of transition that warrant close attention. You must pass a Mental Challenge and have something belonging to the target, such as a piece of clothing, blood, hair or a treasured item like a wedding ring, in your possession.

Scrying (Basic, Intermediate, Advanced)

This rite enables you to peer across space (and occasionally time), looking in on a specific person or location. The Basic version allows you to view current events within a quarter mile of your immediate location. The Intermediate application extends your range of perception to anywhere within a 20-mile radius and up to a month past, and the Advanced form enables you to see any physical site. A well-known location will be seen and heard clearly, whereas those places less familiar to the caster will provide fuzzier perceptions.

Two in-game mechanics may be used to simulate this power. If you are able to reach the location where a desired scene is taking place, you may watch the action as an out-of-game observer. If this is not feasible, a Narrator must be called in to inform you of what you see. Some form of focus, such as a bowl of water, a mirror or a crystal ball, is required to use this ritual. No one but the sorcerer will see anything in the focus, and the people being observed will not be aware of it.

ENCHANTMENT

The counterpart to *Alchemy*, this path deals with the creation of magical items. These artifacts take many forms, from rings and amulets to enchanted weapons and cloaks. Templates for creating other artifacts are also available. These additional procedures have the same experience cost as rituals of equivalent level.

The particular style of the creations will depend upon your character's heritage, and anything you create may normally be used only by members of your particular magical tradition (an African shaman cannot use a Scottish witch's creation). You may, however, design an item specifically for another character. Such dedicated talismans may only be used by the creator and the intended recipient and do not require any sort of test to activate.

There are two requirements for creating a talisman. First, the sorcerer must specify the effect she is creating. Second, she must specify the condition under which the talisman works (i.e., when the moon is full, when blood is wiped across it, the user must sing while using it). Without both, the creation fails.

All uses of this path require a Static Mental Test to see if the creation process was successful. The Storyteller may opt to make this a blind test with the outcome only revealed the first time you attempt to use the item.

BASIC

At the lowest level, you may create simple magical tokens. Each token may be activated only once and the effects typically last for a single scene. These items take one day to prepare and will hold their power for up to a week before the enchantment fades. Some common tokens include:

• Fate's Blessing — This simple favor grants the user three retests during the course of a single game session. No more than one of these retests may be used during any given set of tests. The creation could be a string of beads that must be rubbed to activate the magic or a cake that must be shared with someone else.

• Minor Amulets — Native shamans have long known how to distill the essence of the great beasts, gaining the powers inherent in their nature. The strength of the buffalo, the grace of the cougar or the vision of the eagle can all be called upon by shamans wise in these ways. Amulets grant the user two Attribute or Ability Traits that last for an hour (or until used). A character may only benefit from one of these Amulets at a time and the Traits gained must be specified when the item is created. The token may be a medicine wheel carried in a pocket or on a necklace or a feather harvested from a particular bird and worn in the hair.

• A silver toe ring that causes the wearer to dance beautifully (*Performance: Dance* x 3), as long as she goes barefoot.

• A pen that translates chicken-scratch writing into calligraphy when the pen is dipped in ink made from violets.

INTERMEDIATE

More complex workings allow you to extend the durability of your creations. Rather than having only a single use, these items may be used once per game session for each temporary Willpower Trait you spend during the final hour of their manufacture. The scope of these items is still the same, however, providing Basic effects, Merits (up to three Traits in value), or something of your own creation for one scene.

These charms take an entire week to create, during which time the sorcerer may do nothing other than eat, sleep and work. The items remain enchanted one month for every two Mental Traits you have.

• Lesser Wards — These talismans duplicate the effects of the various Lesser Ward rituals found in other Praxes. Each of these patterns must be learned separately, though there is no additional experience cost to create a talisman if you already know the ritual form. Once activated, the benefits apply for the remainder of the current scene.

Spirit and Creature wards function slightly differently than their equivalent rituals. Rather than requiring a Mental Challenge to enter a protected area, the creature must win a Static Physical Test, or the spirit must win a Static Mental Test (difficulty equal to the sorcerer's Mental Traits at the time of creation). Each attempt to touch the protected individual requires a separate test, and if the attacker fails, he may not try again for the remainder of the scene.

• Major Amulets — Similar to the Minor Amulets of the previous level, these items grant the wearer one Attribute or Ability Trait that may not be permanently lost. This benefit lasts for the entire scene in which the amulet is activated. As with similar gains, the specific Traits are specified when the item is created and cannot be combined with any other form of enhancement within the same category. Pearl earrings that grant an extra Social Trait if washed in wine and rubbed with velvet before wearing, or shoes that confer a single *Stealth* Ability when filled with grave dirt are good examples of Major Amulets.

• A golden locket that shows a picture of any relative or friend of the sorcerer after a rose petal is placed inside it.

• A silver basin that will allow water collected in it under full moonlight by the target's mother to wash away a flesh scar for a single game session.

ADVANCED

Though similar in format to the Intermediate level, both the scope and utility of Advanced creations are increased. Each Mental Trait spent during the final hour of its creation allows an item to be used once a night.

These objects require a month of dedicated effort to fashion properly. No other activity is possible during this period. If the creation test is successful, the sorcerer must determine the desired life span of the item. She may opt to spend a temporary Willpower Trait, which will empower the newly forged artifact for one full month, or a permanent Trait, resulting in a lasting creation. If she fails the Static Mental Test, the item may still function, though it will crumble to dust after its powers are used once.

• Greater Wards — Similar to the Intermediate version, these talismans duplicate the protection granted by the various Greater Wards of other Praxes. However, the benefits apply only as long as the ward is worn. Such items are usually pieces of jewelry or clothing and have an activation condition (i.e., a necklace that wards against a specific demon so long as the target doesn't come in contact with flies).

In the case of Spirit and Creature wards, the banned creature must spend a temporary Willpower Trait to touch the protected individual. Even then, the creature or spirit still suffers the harmful effects of the ward whenever it comes into contact with the wearer. In addition, ranged attacks or supernatural powers require a Static Mental Test to target the bearer of the ward.

• Potent Amulets — In addition to granting the wearer one permanent Attribute or Ability Trait, this charm allows the recipient to throw the Bomb in tests or challenges involving the appropriate Trait. These benefits are considered always in effect and may not be combined with other forms of Attribute enhancement. Examples include a tattoo, made with enchanted inks, that grants an extra Social Trait if placed over the heart or a golden torque that grants a Physical Trait if dipped in freshly spilled blood before each full moon.

• Menial Golems — Servants are always handy to have around. This rite allows you to enchant a statue, animating it in a limited fashion. Though capable of simple functions such as digging, cleaning or moving

objects around, these servants have almost no intelligence of their own. They may follow simple orders, nothing more complex than a three-year-old child could understand. Menial servants possess no Attribute or Ability Traits, no Willpower and two Health Levels. If they take more than two levels of damage, they crumble to dust. Because they are not alive, these automatons require no food or rest, nor do they need to breathe. The animated brooms from *The Sorcerer's Apprentice* are good examples of menial golems.

MASTER

More potent and versatile than Advanced charms, creations at this level require one month of isolation to prepare. Your character must remain out-of-play and undisturbed for the entire duration of the working or all time spent to that point is wasted. These are often creations of legend — a harp that plays by itself if strung with human hair, a cloak that confers invisibility when stitched with silver thread, or a salve that removes disfiguring flesh scars.

These artifacts are almost unlimited in their scope. Master-level powers may be employed once per game for each Mental Attribute you spend during the final hour of creation. Alternately, you may fashion talismans which bestow any Intermediate effects at will. Some specific creations available at this level include:

• Superior Golems — Whereas the Menial Golems described above are incapable of independent thought or action, the servitors created at this level have a much greater capacity for direction. You may issue moderately complex orders, anything a 10-year-old child could understand. These servants will then attempt to carry out those commands, dealing with situations as they arise.

Each servitor is fashioned with 10 Attribute Traits, though these are not broken up by category. Any ties or overbids are resolved using the entire set of Traits. Superior Golems have two Ability Traits and four Health Levels, do not need to eat or sleep and may ignore all wound penalties.

• A book that will translate anything written into it into the caster's native language if the pages are first sprinkled with paper ash.

• A breadbox that always has a fresh loaf of bread in it, so long as three slices from the last loaf are left inside.

RITUALS

Eldritch Mark (Basic)

This simple rite brands an object or location with the signature of the caster, much like a craftsman signs his work. Though the sigil is invisible to mundane eyes, any sorcerer or supernatural being will be able to detect it after a moment's examination. Once cast, the mark is permanent until removed.

Enhance Craftsmanship (Intermediate)

This rite allows you to enhance the mundane qualities of an object. For example, you could enchant a mirror to never crack, forge a blade whose edge will never dull or craft a bow which would never break a string. Though the items prepared using these rituals are not inherently magical, those sorcerers skilled in *Alchemy* will be able to detect these enhancements by winning a Simple Test.

FASCINATION

Many sorcerers earn a good living using this Praxis, brewing the common love-spells of unrequited suitors and forging more potent chains of dominion over political rivals. This art skirts the border between the light and the dark, bending the will of the people affected to the desires of the caster. Bewitchment takes many forms, from the subtle attraction one person has toward another to the feelings of fealty or submission that turn people into playthings. Though legend exaggerates the powers of this art, most spells do not need to last forever to achieve their effects. Beware, though — such things do come with their downsides. An individual with extra charisma may find herself the recipient of unwanted attention. An entrapped woman might start to obsess over her "beloved," and everyone knows that hell hath no fury....

Supernatural creatures are well aware of powers that affect emotions, and they may make a Willpower test to ignore you for one scene. In addition, the vampiric power of *Presence*, the Garou Gift: *Rollover* or the changeling Art: *Sovereign* may be unaffected by certain levels of this path.

As with all forms of sorcery, you must specify the magical style you employ to bring about these effects. Most styles involve some form of binding or sympathetic magic.

BASIC

Entrancement

The simplest form of allure is friendship. This spell evokes that emotion, toward either the sorcerer or some other individual. Though this does not allow you to command the target like a puppet, he will at least be open to reasonable suggestions and be polite to you. This power requires a Social Challenge and lasts for a single scene. If you attack the target, insult him or otherwise treat him rudely, the enchantment fades. Vampires with *Majesty*, Garou with *Rollover* and changelings using *Grandeur* are not affected.

Awe

This spell creates an aura of attraction and respect around you, influencing everyone you encounter. By spending an appropriate Social Trait, you

gain a free retest on any Social Challenge for the remainder of the scene. The benefit does not apply to any sort of intimidation or fear-based powers and drops immediately if you exhibit any violent behavior. Vampires with *Majesty*, Garou with *Rollover* and changelings using *Grandeur* are not affected.

INTERMEDIATE

Voice of Passion

You are able to instill any single emotion in a character. For example, you could force an individual to feel uncontrollable fear, extreme exhaustion or intense lust. This is normally done through your voice.

Though you may dictate a target's feelings, how he responds to them is another matter. Thus, if you invoke terror in your opponent, he may choose to run away, freeze in place or even cower in a corner. He would not be able to attack, however, as that is not an appropriate response. A Narrator has final say over which actions are allowable, taking into account the victim's Nature.

The duration of this effect is determined by an Extended Social Challenge. One success evokes these feelings for a scene, whereas two successes increase the duration to an hour. Three or more successes cause this emotion to manifest for the remainder of the game session, though the target may spend a temporary Willpower Trait to ignore the effects for a single scene.

ADVANCED

Glory

Your mere presence is enough to cause heads to turn and hearts to race. This spell surrounds you with an aura of grandeur and majesty that make it difficult for others to act in a hostile fashion near you. Anyone within 30 feet of you who can see you is affected and must defeat you in a Social Challenge or spend a Willpower Trait before initiating an aggressive or hostile action. If a would-be opponent fails in this challenge, he may not attempt to circumvent this spell again for the remainder of the game session. Vampires with *Majesty*, Garou with *Rollover* and changelings using *Grandeur* who encounter *Glory* have both effects cancel. In other words, a vampire's *Majesty* and a sorcerer's *Glory* cancel each other out and both characters interact normally.

Once you cast this spell, you should hold your arms out to the sides to let other players know about this effect. These benefits apply for the remainder of the current scene, though the spell immediately fades if you take any hostile actions.

MASTER

Captive Heart

This potent rite binds an unlucky victim, body and soul, to the regent. The thrall gains the Negative Social Trait *Submissive* x 2, though only the regent may call upon it.

While this binding is in place, the regent may force the thrall to perform any single action by defeating him in a Social Challenge. Of course, given the Negative Traits in the regent's favor, this rarely proceeds to a test. The effects are similar to a vampiric blood bond.

Once cast, the bond remains in place until one of the pair dies, though the caster may specify a set of circumstances which will release this compulsion. This may be as simple as the sorcerer or regent speaking the words "You are free" or it may last as long as the regent (or thrall) possesses a particular item. The Storyteller has final say over the boundaries of the bond and what termination conditions may be set.

A NOTE

The regent's player should take the thrall's player's feelings into consideration when commanding him. Being degraded, abused and humiliated, even in game, isn't fun for anyone, and only an asshole would trample another person's feelings deliberately. The Storyteller has every right to deny this spell in game or to revoke a bond if the regent's player is getting out of control or the thrall's player is suffering. This is supposed to be fun for *everyone*.

RITUALS

The sorcerer is not the only person who can benefit from this path. She may choose to grant the advantages to another character. In this case, the recipient must either be present when the ritual is performed or must contribute some personal token to the working.

These rituals also require some connection to the person being controlled. This may come from a close personal item (ring, lock of hair, etc.) belonging to the target or some other form of intimate connection. Of course, if the character is present for the working, that will do nicely.

The term "thrall" is used to denote the target of one of these rituals, and the title "regent" refers to the sorcerer or her client, as appropriate.

Confession (Basic)

You are able to evoke trust in others. By defeating an individual in a Social Challenge, you are able to get her to tell you the truth about any topic. This ritual can extend beyond simple conversation, with one secret or confidence being revealed for each success on an Extended test. This is not an information dump, however — the regent must continue to encourage her target with expressions of sympathy or interest.

Tales of Inspiration (Basic)

Fascination is not always used to control others. This ritual enables you to boost your compatriots' morale in times of need. By taking the time to tell an inspiring story, you may instill a sense of inner strength in the people around you. For each appropriate Social Trait spent, one allied character may gain a single temporary Willpower Trait during the upcoming scene. The story should be relevant to the impending events and must be roleplayed for this ability to work.

Siren's Song (Intermediate)

You are able to hypnotize others with your voice or presence, drawing them to you or some other point of focus — another individual, an object or even a location.

The initial attraction is felt as soon as you begin the ritual. Anyone within earshot will feel drawn to you if he fails a Static Social Test. However, the full effects are not felt until the rite is complete.

Once someone has been observing you for 10 minutes, he becomes entranced. While in this state, he will do nothing but watch and listen as long as the ritual continues. Anyone affected will relent on any challenge during this time, though the effect is broken if the target is injured. This effect cannot be recorded or sent over the phone.

Regency (Advanced)

More than just affection, this rite instills a hopeless attraction in the target. He will wish to be close to and help the regent in any way that he can. This does not result in slavery, though the thrall will be willing to do almost any "favor" for his regent. Depending upon the circumstances, the thrall may spend a Willpower Trait to ignore this compulsion for a single scene, though only if he were asked to perform some action that would violate his basic Nature. If there is an emergency or his regent is attacked, the thrall's first instinct will be to save her. Self-sacrifice is not uncommon, especially if the thrall has been well treated and the bond has been in effect for some time.

Though *Regency* initially lasts only one month, the effects of multiple successive compulsions extend the duration. Each later casting must take place as the prior effect starts to fade (within a few days). The second application of this bond lasts for six months, and the next lasts for a year. If the target is bound a fourth time to the same regent, the bond endures as long as the thrall is alive; should he die, his regent becomes a Fetter. The only way to negate this compulsion is to avoid the regent completely for the duration of each summoning or to destroy the means by which the thrall is being drawn (although this is only temporary). This will be difficult — and require continual expenditures of Willpower — as the bond draws the thrall to his regent like a moth to the flame.

HEALING

This Praxis covers the treatment and care of living creatures, from small animals to humans. Like other paths, the specific style of practice must be specified when this art is learned. Some common examples include acupuncture, laying on hands or naturopathic herbalism. Unless otherwise specified, any applications of this Praxis require physical contact with your patient (you may need to win a Physical Challenge to get your hands on an unwilling target), and difficult workings may require an Extended Mental Test. In addition, a character may only benefit from this path once per scene. This path cannot heal aggravated wounds.

BASIC

Assessment

You begin as a healer by learning to diagnose your patient. Make a Static Mental Test to determine the general state of a creature's health (how many Health Levels of damage it is currently suffering), including the presence of any illnesses or injuries. You may even be able to pick up on certain Physical Flaws, gaining one such detail for each success on an Extended Simple Test. In addition, sorcerers with an appropriate *Lore* are able to determine what type of creature a given subject is: mortal, shapeshifter, changeling, vampire, mummy, etc. If the sorcerer does not possess the necessary *Lore*, she will certainly notice something odd about her patient but might not understand why the pallid person talking to her is registering to her senses as dead.

Soothing Touch

Once you know how to evaluate a patient, you start to learn how to treat minor aches and pains. At this level, you may cure stun damage completely and heal normal damage down to Bruised. In addition, you may help an Incapacitated character regain consciousness, though the actual injuries remain. When applied to a mortal character who is Mortally Wounded, this power will stabilize the injury, preventing the person from slipping further toward death.

INTERMEDIATE

Still Mind

Sorcerers who study this path learn how to treat the mind as well as the body. This spell allows you to free a target from the liabilities of one Derangement for the remainder of the game session. By winning a Mental

Challenge, you may alleviate any natural or magically induced insanity, including the effects of the *MindBending* Praxis or the *Shadows* spell: *Touch of Darkness*. In the case of Derangements created by the vampiric Discipline of *Dementation*, the healer must spend a Mental Trait to make the spell effective. If the sorcerer loses the challenge, she must (at Storyteller discretion) make a second Mental Challenge. If she loses again, *Dementation* reaches out and slaps her with its diseased touch, and she gains one Derangement for the rest of the game session.

Alternatively, the sorcerer may attempt to bring another character out of frenzy by winning a Social Challenge. If you are successful, your target immediately returns to normal and will not frenzy again for the remainder of the scene. Unlike other applications of this Praxis, *Still Mind* may be cast at range.

In any case, if you fail in your attempt, you may not use this power again on the same individual for the remainder of the current storyline.

Deep Cure

You are now capable of treating more severe injuries, restoring up to two Health Levels of normal damage even if your target is Incapacitated. However, subsequent attempts to repair a single wound provide no additional benefit.

If cast as a proper ritual, you are able to reduce the long-term recovery times for major injuries or illnesses. Even life-threatening diseases and injuries are not beyond your care, though some cures may take hours or even days to effect.

ADVANCED

Deep Healing

There is little beyond the scope of your healing abilities now. Normal applications of this power allow you to restore up to three Health Levels of normal damage or a single aggravated wound. However, like previous spells on this path, multiple attempts to repair the same injuries will have no additional effect.

MASTER

Touch of Life

At the Master level, nothing is beyond your healing abilities. You may regenerate nerves, repair internal organs or even cause seemingly incurable illnesses to go into remission, although it takes an immense amount of time and energy. You must be treating the patient for a full month and may take no other actions during that time. If you stop before the time is up, all the previous effort is considered wasted and you must start again.

If a patient is at Incapacitated, you may repair all outstanding injuries with an Extended Mental Challenge for each level until you fail. Your talents even extend beyond that, however. If your target is below Incapacitated, you may return her to Wounded, regardless of how much damage she has suffered. If the person has died or been Embraced, you may not attempt to heal her — this Praxis is reserved for the living.

RITUALS

Healing Sleep (Basic)

This rite places a willing or unconscious target into a deep sleep, healing one normal wound for each success on an Extended Static Mental Test. Normal injuries require the subject to remain out-of-game for one hour per Health Level restored, and aggravated wounds may only be healed between game sessions.

Purify the Blood (Basic)

This simple rite cleanses a target of all foreign substances (pollutants, poisons and drugs), including *Alchemical* creations. It has no effect on supernatural conditions such as a vampiric blood bond, nor will it remove vampire blood if the subject is ghouled. Whereas lesser toxins are removed automatically, potent venoms, Advanced *Alchemical* poisons and viral infections require the subject to pass a Static Physical Test. This cleansing is often very painful, because the subject's body rids itself of toxins through sweating, vomiting or toxic tears.

Rise and Shine (Basic)

This simple rite allows you to awaken another character, regardless of how deeply she is sleeping. Waking someone from magically induced sleep requires that you pass a Static Mental Test, equivalent in difficulty to Unweaving.

Tone of the Mind (Basic)

Similar to *Assessment*, this rite allows you to determine the psychological state of your patient. Make a Extended Static Mental Test to detect any Derangements or mind-affecting Flaws (such as *Nightmares* or *Phobia*). This will also determine if someone is asleep, drugged or simply knocked unconscious.

Restore Psyche (Intermediate)

A more durable version of *Still Mind*, this curative rite drastically increases the duration of the spell's effects. Any foreign condition, even conditions caused through supernatural means, may be healed permanently. This also applies to Beast or Path Traits that have been gained during the current story. For cases in which a target's insanity is caused by a Flaw or is an inherent aspect of his character type, the recipient must still spend the appropriate Experience to buy off this condition; otherwise, it will return at the rise of the next full moon.

HELLFIRE

This Praxis deals with summoning destructive energies, either in direct elemental form or manifested through the environment. The sorcerer who controls these powers often commands a great deal of respect, suspicion and fear. There's a good chance that people will suspect her of trucking with the infernal if she throws around such power. Because *Hellfire* is extremely showy and not particularly subtle, the sorcerer tends to get a lot of unpleasant attention. At best, she may suspected of arson by the police. At worst, she'll make a lot of supernatural enemies; vampires and the Inquisition in particular make a habit of tracking those mortals who exhibit such a power.

Unless otherwise stated, the flames created through this Praxis are mystical in origin but behave as normal flame unless otherwise specified. They may be extinguished through normal means (water, fire extinguishers); someone wishing to stop-drop-and-roll to put out flaming clothing must win a Simple Test to see if his efforts have put out the fire. Vampires may need to test for frenzy. *Hellfire* flame causes aggravated damage. It's also worth noting that *Hellfire*, especially the ritual forms, requires the same preparation as any other path. If you intend to use this Praxis in combat, better plan ahead.

BASIC

Spark

Unlike the more powerful applications of this Praxis, this simple spell calls forth natural flame, which may be used to ignite flammable objects. This could be as controlled as lighting a candle or as random as setting fire to a trash heap. Objects less obviously flammable may require a Static Mental Test.

Flamebolt

More direct uses of this path allow you to hurl bolts of fire from your fingertips. By defeating your opponent in a Mental Challenge (against his Physical Traits), you may inflict one Health Level of aggravated damage. These flames are mystical in origin but behave like normal fire.

INTERMEDIATE

Engulf

Summoning greater energy, you can now surround a target in flames. If you win a Mental Challenge against your target's Physical Traits, you may inflict two aggravated wounds.

Firewall

This defensive spell creates a barrier of mystical fire. Anyone attempting to pass through this curtain automatically suffers one aggravated wound. In addition, the character must win a Physical Challenge (difficulty equal to half your current Mental Traits) or suffer a second such wound during the crossing.

You have the option to form this barrier into either a dome (10-foot radius) or a flat wall (up to five feet in length for each Mental Trait you possess). Either application lasts for a single scene or until you leave the area.

ADVANCED

Firestorm

This potent spell allows you to affect multiple opponents. You may expend two Mental Traits to blanket an area with flame, inflicting one aggravated wound on each person within a 10-foot radius around a target point. The targets may attempt to dodge the effect — if they see it coming. Unfortunately, such power is indiscriminate; unless your allies are standing beside you (and that means close enough to embrace), they'll be toasted too, unless they have some means of mystical protection from flame.

MASTER

Inferno

By (figuratively) opening the gates of Hell, you are able to call down a huge conflagration of mystical fire. This blaze fills a region up to 10 feet in radius for each Mental Trait you have, causing two aggravated wounds to everyone within the blast area. The caster is immune to this effect.

In addition, you may shield one other person for each Mental Trait you spend. These allies must be within line-of-sight to receive this benefit and all must be declared when the spell is cast.

RITUALS

Bladefire (Intermediate)

This simple rite attunes a weapon (usually a sword or dagger) to the spells of this Praxis. By spending a Mental Trait, you may surround the weapon with mystical fire, which inflicts aggravated wounds whenever the weapon strikes. Once activated, this effect lasts for the remainder of the scene. If the caster attempts to pass the weapon to someone else, the flames immediately go out.

Fire Ward (Intermediate)

This rite allows a specific individual to partially withstand the effects of this Praxis and similar powers as well as any sort of natural flames.

Fire Ward grants a free retest against fire-based damage for the remainder of the game session. The target may spend a stamina-related Physical Trait to completely ignore one Health Level of damage. You may not cast this ritual on yourself.

RELATED RITES

Whereas the normal spells and rituals of this Praxis concentrate on summoning mystical fire, these effects branch out to include other destructive forces. Priests who learn the *Theurgic* version of this path (*Via Ignis*) do not have access to these additional powers.

Each of these rites has Basic, Intermediate and Advanced versions, which must be learned in order. The Basic version inflicts one Health Level of normal damage, whereas the Intermediate rites cause one such wound for each minute a victim is within the area of effect. Advanced rituals cause tremendous damage, inflicting one aggravated wound per turn until the victim escapes or dies. These rituals typically last for one scene.

Rust

The forces of entropy are invoked with this rite. The sorcerer must expend a Mental Trait and win an Extended Mental Test. If she is successful, any ferrous metal object (up to five pounds per win) on the target disintegrates. Precious metals, such as silver or gold, are not affected; iron, steel, aluminum and most alloys are susceptible. Technowizards and Thal'hun in particular despise this effect and the sorcerers who practice it.

Earthquake

This rite causes the earth to buckle, rocking the ground in a 20-foot radius (win a Simple Test to stay on your feet). A more potent version causes the earth to crack open and swallow your target and any others unfortunate enough to be in range, leaving victims to dig themselves out (which requires a Physical Challenge).

Tanglewoods

By channeling magical forces through vegetable matter (living or dead), the sorcerer can cause plants to animate and attack anyone in the area. Trees will batter people with their branches, and vines will coil around the victims, entrapping or choking them. Any characters trapped in this manner may attempt to escape by winning a Physical Challenge.

Drowning Tide

This ritual may only be cast on a large body of liquid (no smaller than an Olympic-size swimming pool). A sudden undertow or wave drags the target under and forces water into his lungs. Those victims who need to breathe may attempt to hold their breath by winning a Simple Test; if they fail, they take one level of normal damage per turn underwater. After the target reaches Incapacitated, she begins to drown and will die within 10 minutes if she is not freed. She may make a Physical Challenge to attempt to free herself.

ILLUSION

This Praxis enables you to control others' perceptions to a greater or lesser degree. Legends of sorcerers with cloaks of invisibility or shoes of silence have been stock in trade for centuries and were no doubt fueled by this art. Some say this Praxis was developed during the Burning Times to allow sorcerers an escape from the witch-hunters' torches.

This art affects only people's perceptions, be the people living or unliving. Some sorcerers have made attempts to create spells that render one invisible to electronic devices, but such wisdom has proved elusive. Most believe this is caused by the fast pace of technological advancement — the devices that one learns to cloak against are soon rendered obsolete, and with them go the spells. A very old wizard might know how to cloak himself against the enormous still cameras of the early 20th century, but how likely is he to encounter one now?

BASIC

Lesser Veil

This simple spell allows you to turn unwanted eyes away from yourself. By remaining motionless, you may blend into your surroundings and escape the notice of the people nearby. If you move, other characters may be able to detect your presence by winning a Static Mental Test. If you speak, the spell is broken. When using this power, you must cross your arms in front of you to indicate to other players that their characters are not aware of you. The vampiric Discipline of *Auspex* or Garou *Heightened Senses* may detect you if you move or otherwise give your presence away.

Facade

As your control over illusions becomes more directed, you may now alter the details of your appearance completely. However, your basic body structure remains the same, so height and mass may only be changed by a small amount. Inanimate objects may also be masked, thus allowing a broom to appear to be a sword. Of course, this phantom blade will be very dull and prone to breakage if the sorcerer is foolish enough to use it in combat.

The sorcerer may cover one sense for each success on an Extended Static Mental Test. Thus, a purely visual illusion would require only an initial success, whereas one that affects all senses would need five such successes.

If you are attempting to duplicate the appearance of another individual or unique object, you must spend a Mental Trait and win on a Mental Challenge. Losing the challenge indicates that the likeness is incomplete, and those characters familiar with the object or person who win a Mental Challenge may see through your illusion.

Normally, only the caster may benefit from this illusion. If you wish to mask another individual or object, you must spend an additional

Mental Trait. This spell lasts for the remainder of the game session or until the illusion is dropped.

INTERMEDIATE

Greater Veil

A more enhanced version of the Basic power, this spell enables you to remain invisible at all times. Moving around no longer renders you vulnerable to detection. Any form of Physical Challenge enables those characters present to detect you automatically. Once the effect has dropped, you must recast the spell from scratch.

Phantasm

With *Phantasm* (not to be confused with the Arcanos of the same name) you may create a detailed illusion with a life of its own. This apparition normally lasts for a single scene, though you may extend the duration for the remainder of the game session by spending a temporary Willpower Trait.

Success on a Static Mental Test allows you to cause the illusion to respond to its environment or even to move on its own. Each reaction requires a separate test. However, if you fail three of these tests within a single scene, the spell automatically fades.

Alternately, you may program the *Phantasm* to follow a set routine. Each minute or two of animation requires you to spend one appropriate Mental Trait, with the expenditure of a Willpower Trait causing this projection to loop for the rest of the night.

ADVANCED

True Mask

Whereas *Facade* allows you to change your physical appearance, this rite extends the masquerade to cover other forms of magical detection. This includes the vampiric Discipline of *Auspex*, a wraith's inherent *Lifesight* or the Garou Gift: *Scent of the True Form*. This ritual costs one Mental Trait for each detail you wish to change: personality, emotional state, species, whether the target is living or undead, etc.

Once set in place, this mask lasts for one day, though a permanent Willpower Trait may be spent to extend these effects indefinitely.

MASTER

Phantom Killer

At this level your creations do not merely deceive the senses — they can directly affect other characters as if they were real. As with *Facade*, you must achieve enough successes on an Extended Static Mental Test to cover all the senses appropriate to the illusion. Thus, a faux fire would require a minimum of visual, auditory and tactile elements to be believable. This illusion affects one person for each Mental Trait the sorcerer expends when casting it, though all present may be included by spending a temporary Willpower Trait.

These phantoms may inflict one Health Level of normal damage each turn and are normally stationary. You may animate the illusion as described in the previous spell, though any complex motion requires your complete attention. Thus, a wall of steel or fire would be sustained automatically, but a ravaging beast would need constant supervision. Damage caused by static illusions may be soaked if the target passes a Static Physical Test. If you are controlling the phantom directly, such attacks require a Mental Challenge against your target's Physical Traits.

In either case, any damage suffered by the caster immediately causes the illusion to fade.

RITUALS

Backdrop (Basic, Intermediate, Advanced)

Similar to *Facade* or *Phantasm*, this ritual allows you to alter the appearance of an area up to 10 feet in radius for each Mental Trait you possess. Whereas the Basic settings are static and unchanging, the Intermediate version is capable of being animated as described above. The Advanced version of this rite even fools magical perceptions (at Storyteller discretion, the target may make a Mental Challenge to penetrate the illusion). This illusion lasts normally lasts for one day. If you spend a permanent Willpower Trait, the projection will remain as long as the area is undisturbed.

LIFE STEALING

Often used as a form of punishment, this art allows you to drain the very life and spirit from a being. Whereas the lesser effects are merely harmful to the target, the higher-level applications may be used to your benefit or to help some other willing recipient. Sorcerers who employ this Praxis must be clear in their intentions, for feeding off the life force of others has been known to taint the soul. Careless use of these powers may require you to forfeit a temporary Humanity Trait, whereas more malicious applications may result in a permanent loss.

Put simply, this is a nasty art. Like *Hellfire*, those sorcerers who make use of this power are often accused of trucking with the infernal and can command a great deal of fear-driven respect. Unlike *Hellfire*, though, this art can be used subtly in many unpleasant ways. In older times, those victims withering under continued *Life Stealing* attacks were often treated as victims of vampires. Certain applications of this power have no effect on vampires, Risen or materialized wraiths — one cannot steal what is not there.

BASIC

Sapping the Will

This art allows you to dampen an opponent's will. If you can defeat your target in a Mental Challenge, you may prevent him from spending any Willpower for the rest of the scene. Alternately, your opponent may forfeit a Willpower Trait, which may not be recovered for the remainder of the game session.

Weakening the Body

By winning a Mental Challenge against the victim's Physical Traits, you can temporarily drain two of his Physical Traits. This may be turned into an Extended Challenge in the normal manner. By spending a Willpower point, you may instead choose to inflict one Health Level of normal damage for each success on the Extended test. However, you may not take your opponent below Wounded. This spell has no effect on vampires or Risen, and the effects last only for the duration of the scene.

INTERMEDIATE

Stealing the Breath

This power allows you to drain the life force from a target and use it to heal yourself. For each success on an Extended Mental Challenge against the victim's Physical Traits, you may drain one Physical Trait from your opponent and use it to restore one Health Level of normal damage. The Extended Challenge ends when you lose a test, regardless of how much damage is healed, or when you heal all damage. If performed as a full ritual, this effect may be used to heal a companion. The lost Physical Traits are gone for the remainder of the game session and will return at the beginning of the next game. This spell has no effect on vampires or Risen.

Draining the Body

Similar to the previous effect, this spell allows you to steal an Attribute Trait from your target and gain it yourself. You must enter into a Mental Challenge with your opponent, although he may defend with whatever category he chooses. If your challenge is successful, you gain whatever Trait your opponent used in defense. This Trait is considered yours for the remainder of the game session. It will return to your opponent at the beginning of the next game. If you lose the challenge, the spell fails and you lose the Trait you bid. This spell has no effect on vampires or Risen.

ADVANCED

Theft of Power

This forbidden spell allows you to steal mystical energy (such as *Mana* Traits, Gnosis or Glamour) from a target, transferring it to yourself. You must have either the innate potential for that sort of power (due to being Kinfolk or kinain, for example) or have at least two Traits in the appropriate *Lore*. Even then, if you have no way to spend this energy, the act has little more effect than spite. If your target has no other Traits to drain, you may opt to drain Willpower, using these Traits to replenish your own reserve. You may not take more than your maximum Trait capacity.

Each use of this spell requires a Willpower Challenge against your target's permanent Trait rating (*Mana*, Gnosis, Glamour or Willpower). If you are successful, you may steal one Trait of the appropriate type plus one additional Trait for each Mental Trait you spend. You may transfer only as many Traits as the target has remaining. A Kinfolk or kinain may not raise their Gnosis or Glamour ratings above their normal maximums with this spell. Once the pool is full to maximum, the rest is considered spillover and vanishes.

Your victim may not replenish these lost Traits for the remainder of the game session, and you hold onto your prize until the Traits are used or you go to sleep.

MASTER

Vacant Mind

This spell literally rips information from the mind of your victim. Each success on an Extended Mental Challenge allows you to remove one Ability Trait (or other specific memory) from your target, transferring it to yourself. These Traits last for the remainder of the game session, at which point they revert to the original owner. However, if this spell is performed as a proper ritual, the effects are permanent.

RITUALS

Salting the Earth (Basic)

This ritual is one of pure spite, preventing a target from healing through any normal means. The duration of this ban is determined by a Static Mental Test.

Though this rite does not normally prevent magical forms of healing or supernatural regeneration, these will not function during the scene in which the ritual is performed. At the Storyteller's discretion, you lose a temporary Humanity Trait, with more to follow as she deems appropriate.

Erosion (Advanced)

This vicious rite duplicates the effects of *Weakening the Body*, except that any Attribute losses sustained are permanent. Any wounds received through *Erosion* are aggravated. Vampires and Risen are not affected by this rite. Lose a temporary Humanity Trait when you use this rite.

Drinking the Soul (Master)

The most sinister application of this dark Praxis, *Drinking the Soul* allows you to permanently drain the living essence of a being, using it to enhance your own powers. The procedure involved is similar to *Theft of Power*, though it may be used to steal Attribute Traits as well. Unfortunately, this rite only works against individuals who have a higher Trait total than yourself in the relevant area.

If you target the victim's power (*Mana*, Gnosis, Glamour, etc.), you may permanently gain a single Trait of the stolen type. Alternately, you may transfer one Attribute Trait for every two the victim has above your own (round down). Thus, if your target has five more Mental Traits than you do, you would gain two.

The victim's soul is consumed during the course of the rite. The merciful thing at this point would be to let the body die as well. However, you do have the option to leave your victim an empty husk, open to possession by wandering spirits. There is no justification for such malice — lose one *permanent* Humanity Trait for such an action, more if the Storyteller deems it appropriate. Vampires and Risen are not affected, and this rite does not produce a wraith.

Successes	Duration
1	Current scene
2	One hour
3	Current session
4	One month
5+	Current storyline

MENTALIS

This Praxis deals with common forms of mental communication and control. It enables you to reach into the mind of a target (willing or otherwise), observing what is there or altering the fabric of his thoughts. Sorcerers skilled in this art may detect its use by other characters, but likewise, those characters skilled in similar applications (vampiric *Auspex* or Numinae like *Telepathy*) may be aware of unwanted visitors in their minds. *Mentalis* takes a great deal of concentration, and a sorcerer using most applications may not take any other actions. She can talk, but her sentences will most likely be disjointed and confused. If she is attacked or distracted, the mental contact is broken. Some have identified sorcerers using this art simply by their intense expressions of concentration.

BASIC

Surface Thoughts

This passive spell allows you to scan the outer thoughts and emotions of your subject. It requires a Static Mental Test and may be used to determine if someone is deliberately lying. By focusing beyond emotional impressions (and winning a Mental Challenge), you are able to listen to an individual's stream of consciousness. Such mind-reading can be confusing — stream of consciousness is literally a river of thoughts, with random sparks and flashes rather than straight facts. The target may, at Storyteller discretion, make a Mental Challenge to detect an unwanted presence (especially vampires with *Auspex* or those sorcerers with appropriate Numinae).

Mindspeak

Beyond mere perception, you may now touch your target's mind, enabling two-way communication. Images and complex concepts may not be sent, and all conversations must take place in a common language. Though a Mental Challenge permits your words to be received by an unwilling target, it does not force the recipient to respond.

You may speak at any distance within line of sight, though your subject must be within arm's reach if you are not looking at him. Alternately, you may connect to anyone you know well (up to one mile away) by spending a Mental Trait.

Characters using this power should hold two fingers to the side of their foreheads to indicate that their conversation may not be overheard.

INTERMEDIATE

Word of Command

This power allows you to issue a brief command contained in a single word or phrase. For the benefit of anyone listening in, this directive may be inserted into a sentence. However, any additional commentary has no effect on the command or its interpretation. By spending an appropriate Mental Trait, the caster may opt to apply this control telepathically. However, even this application may still be overheard by other mentalists, as described above.

This spell requires either a Social or Mental Challenge against your target's Social Traits and the command may not require more than one scene (10 minutes) to complete. Some example orders are "Stop right there," "Be silent," "Go home" or even "Sleep." The command may not be obviously harmful to the subject, nor may it violate his basic Nature.

You may not attempt this effect on a vampire of 10th or lesser generation.

Deep Probe

Moving beyond the surface, you may now delve into an individual's memories and beliefs. Personal knowledge can be accessed, even information which the subject has forgotten. In such a case, you have the option to restore these memories to your subject or leave them blocked. Normally, your target is aware of any such probe. However, by bidding an additional Mental Trait, you may attempt to slip in without being noticed; this requires a Static Mental Test rather than the normal Mental Challenge. If your target is aware of your presence, she may make a Willpower Challenge to force you out. Opening blocked memories will take a month of out-of-game time (or more if the Storyteller deems it necessary) during which neither the target nor the sorcerer may do anything but work on the memories.

ADVANCED

Implant Thought

Similar to hypnosis, this potent spell enables you to introduce suggestions and beliefs into your target's subconscious. The simplest applications duplicate the effects of *Word of Command* but postpone the activation of the directive or altered memory for up to one month. You must specify a trigger event or situation that will activate this implanted thought. In addition, for each success on an Extended Mental Challenge, you may set one additional condition that will trigger the same command.

You may choose to insert a belief or memory (up to one scene in length) into your opponent. Your target must treat this idea as if he came to that conclusion or experienced the event himself. These may be entirely new fabrications or they may replace existing recollections. This latter application is permanent, though later evidence could cause him to revise his opinions.

You may not attempt this effect on a vampire of 10th or lesser generation or better. Vampires skilled in *Dominate* may also discover and destroy your creation with a successful Mental Challenge if they possess at least Intermediate *Dominate*.

MASTER

Mind Link

This spell creates a deep bond with another character, allowing you to freely pass thoughts back and forth and share knowledge. You may not pass on images this way, nor may you go probing in your partner's mind. This spell may be cast on someone who is unconscious or in torpor by passing a Static Willpower Test (difficulty 5).

RITUALS

Dream Walking (Basic, Intermediate, Advanced)

These rituals allow you to enter, and possibly affect, the dreams of your target. Whereas the Basic version of this rite only permits you to observe what is occurring within the person's head, the Intermediate form allows you to join in his dreams as an active participant. Some sorcerers speak of an Advanced variant of this rite that grants the caster control over her target's dreamscape, directing events as if she were scripting a movie.

Shared Visions (Intermediate)

This rite, called "Slide Show" by some rather flippant sorcerers, allows snapshot images to be passed between the sorcerer and his target. The images are truly like vacation pictures — occasionally out of focus, turned the wrong way or just plain bad. There is no movement involved, and this is not an upload/download rite — the human brain was not meant to function in that fashion.

Mind Ward (Intermediate)

This common rite shields the mind of one individual (usually the caster) from external control. This protection applies to direct forms of mind control (typically a Mental Challenge). It even protects against attempts to read or probe the mind, whether the subject is aware of them or not. Once cast, the subject gains a free retest against the relevant forms of mental attack or invasion for the remainder of the game session. Be aware, however, that vampires who are of the ninth or lower generation and skilled in *Dominate* may be able to bypass this ward.

Conditioning (Advanced)

With this potent ritual, you may rework another character's personality. You may implant memories, change fundamental beliefs, even alter the subject's Demeanor.

This rite must be performed consecutively over three nights, each segment requiring a separate Mental Challenge. These tests are usually performed blind, without the caster being aware of the final result. If even one of the three challenges is not successful, the conditioning fades after one week. Otherwise, the effects are permanent.

You may not attempt this effect on a vampire of the 10th generation or lower. Vampires skilled in the higher levels of *Dominate* may uproot your *Conditioning* with a successful Mental Challenge and a spent Willpower Trait.

Telepathic Net (Master)

This useful rite allows you to set up a network of telepathic communication among no more than four willing individuals. The effects duplicate the Basic spell: *Mindspeak*. Distance limitations require that the individuals be in the same city, and they must all speak the same language. They may not pass images among them, nor may they perform deep mind probes. All who wish to share this link must be present when the ritual is cast. This effect lasts for the remainder of the game session,

though the link may be continued indefinitely if each person spends a permanent Willpower Trait.

MINDBENDING

This dark Praxis moves beyond the scope of mere communication or mental influence and instead allows you to play upon the weaknesses that pervade your opponent's subconscious. Those sorcerers in league with darker powers usually study this art, though some other disturbed individuals have been known to possess it. Unlike *Mentalis*, this art can lead a person to violate his Nature or harm himself, depending on the effect and the instability instilled. Any use of this power requires you to defeat your opponent in a Mental or Social Challenge. Repeated uses of this power may also cause you to lose Humanity at your Narrator's discretion.

BASIC

Pushing Buttons

This power allows you to bring certain psychological imbalances to the fore, activating certain psychological and Mental Flaws (such as *Nightmares* or *Hatred*) or provoking a Derangement. You may also invoke frenzy in any creature susceptible to that state. Finally, you may elect to draw out the weaknesses inherent in a character's personality or intellect. If your target has an appropriate Negative Social or Mental Trait twice or more, you may force him to experience that limitation to a greater extent. If your target suffers from none of these limitations, he must act out his archetypal Nature, temporarily ignoring his Demeanor. Any application of this power lasts for one scene.

Psychosis

You are able to use your influence to inflict some unbalance upon your target. You may bestow a Psychological or Mental Flaw (chosen randomly by the Narrator) for the duration of a scene.

INTERMEDIATE

Confusion

This spell shrouds a target's mind, scrambling his thoughts and rendering coherent action very difficult. Each success on an Extended Mental or Social Challenge allows you to bestow two of the following Negative Traits upon your opponent: *Dull*, *Forgetful*, *Oblivious* or *Witless*. These effects last for the remainder of the scene.

Mind Wipe

Beyond merely muddying the intellectual waters, you are able to drain knowledge directly from the mind of your target. There are two applications of this spell, each of which requires a Mental Challenge. You may not perform both on a single target.

First, you may permanently block any single memory from your opponent's mind. This could be anything from his name to the fact that he is married. You may even remove one entire scene that occurred earlier in the chronicle. The victim will eventually be able to relearn this information, though not for the remainder of the game session.

Alternately, you may block access to one Praxis for a scene or a specific Ability, spell or ritual for the remainder of the game session. Though these powers and Traits are not removed, the target may not call upon them for the duration of the effect.

ADVANCED

Dementia

This dangerous spell allows you to shake an opponent's sanity. By figuratively crawling inside a person's mind, you may implant up to seven Traits" worth of psychological Flaws and Negative Traits for a scene or half that many (round down) for the remainder of the game session. This act is almost as unsettling to the caster as it is to the target, requiring you to forfeit a temporary Humanity Trait regardless of the spell's success.

MASTER

Destroying the Will

This dark spell targets a person's psychological foundation. By defeating your opponent in a Willpower Challenge, you may reduce his permanent Willpower rating by one. Though this Trait may eventually be bought back with experience, the target may never purchase any beyond that. His confidence is shattered and it will take years for him to recover. If the subject loses his last Willpower Trait, he dies. This spell may be performed against an individual no more than once per storyline.

By the way, lose one permanent Humanity Trait for the callous act if it succeeds, more if your Storyteller decides you should. Lose a temporary Humanity Trait if the spell fails.

RITUALS

Penitence (Basic)

You are able to evoke feelings of guilt and remorse in people, leading them to make amends for their sins. Whether these transgressions are real or imagined is of little consequence. This ritual preys upon the smallest doubt, blowing it entirely out of proportion. By defeating your target in a Social Challenge, you may convince him to "do the right thing," finding some way to make up for whatever wrongdoings he might have committed. You have no control over what form the act of contrition will take.

Breaking the Mind (Advanced)

Similar to the *Mentalis* ritual: *Conditioning*, this rite instead targets an individual's emotional stability. By successfully casting this ritual over three consecutive nights, you may instill the effects of *Psychosis* or *Confusion* for the remainder of the current storyline. It will take a master psychologist to heal the damage to the mind. Lose a temporary Humanity Trait for the act.

NECROMANCY

Similar to the Praxes of *Spirit Calling* or *Summoning*, this path allows you to control the spirits of the dead, including wraiths and Spectres. Wise necromancers know that the Restless Dead, ghosts in common parlance, make very bad enemies and use this ability with care. In some cultures, dealing with the dead in such a fashion is akin to black magic, and a necromancer who does not take care may find herself in a great deal of trouble. A complete description of the Underworld and the Restless Dead may be found in **Oblivion**.

Necromancy does not affect Risen. Those wraiths who have managed to climb back into their bodies no longer belong to the world of the Restless Dead and are more akin to vampires than wraiths for the purposes of this Praxis.

BASIC

Deathsight

Focusing upon your awareness of death, you can cast your vision into the Shadowlands. You will see everything, including any nearby wraiths and Spectres, as if you were present. They will not be aware of your presence, although a wraith using *Lifesight* may become aware of your inordinate concentration. You must have the Merit: *Medium* to converse with any ghosts at this level.

Forbiddance

There is a reason that wraiths are called the Restless Dead. Sorcerers who study this path quickly learn that the dead do not like to be disturbed by the living. This spell allows you to hold a wraith or Spectre at bay. If you defeat your opponent in a Social Challenge, he may not approach you as long as you remain passive. Slow movement or quiet conversation will not disrupt this effect, though initiating any other challenge will immediately cancel the spell.

INTERMEDIATE

Death's Call

This spell allows you to summon one of the Restless Dead, drawing him to you. Wraiths called through this spell must be in the nearby Shadowlands. In addition, you must know your target's name or have some direct link to the individual, such as a Fetter. This effect requires a Social Challenge and the victim must remain for at least one full minute once called. You may speak with the ghost in question as if you had the Merit: *Medium*, but the effects only last while your target is in your presence.

If performed as a full ritual, this spell calls a wraith or Spectre to your presence from anywhere in the Shadowlands. This effect does not convey any special movement abilities, so it may take some time for your target to arrive. Wraiths who have Transcended or fallen into Oblivion are beyond this effect, as are wraiths who have no Fetters.

Compulsion

By defeating a wraith in a Mental Challenge, you may require her to perform one action. Though this task may be almost anything, it may not take more than one scene (10 minutes) to complete. Alternately, a successful Social Challenge will render the target non-hostile for one hour. She may not harm you or other targets you designate (you must be specific — spirit of the law is just a bad joke), though any other action is fair game.

ADVANCED

Soul Bind

This terrible power allows you to snatch a wraith or Spectre from the Shadowlands, trapping it in a specially prepared prison. You must defeat your target in a Mental Challenge, though no test is required to set the soul free once you have trapped it.

While imprisoned, the wraith is aware of its condition but is under no obligation to do as you bid. Each night, the wraith may call for a Mental or Willpower Challenge against your remaining (not total) number of Traits. If it defeats you, it is released from the prison. Most spirits never forgive or forget this type of binding — once free, they may act as they see fit, and ghosts make lousy enemies.

It takes one week of dedicated effort to prepare this prison, which may only be used once. The prison is rendered useless with the release of the prisoner, and you must construct a new one. Wraiths who suffer Harrowings while imprisoned will snap back to their prisons instead of their Fetters.

MASTER

Crossing Styx

This powerful spell allows you to cross from the world of the living into the Shadowlands, in effect becoming one of the Restless Dead. You retain your normal Attributes and Abilities, as well as your skills in Sorcery. In place of Health Levels, you have Corpus Levels equal to your permanent Willpower rating. You do not gain Pathos or Angst, you cannot be Harrowed for Corpus loss, nor do any Shadow-specific powers work on you. When you cross the Shroud, your body is left behind and becomes your only Fetter. While in this state, you may be affected by any *Necromancy* spells, and Arcanoi affect you as if you were a ghost. If you lose all your Corpus Levels, you will be violently ejected from the Shadowlands back to the living world. No one seems to know what happens to sorcerers whose bodies are killed or destroyed while the soul is sojourning in the deadlands.

This effect lasts for the remainder of the game session, though you may extend it for one additional day for each temporary Humanity Trait you spend. While in the Underworld, you must indicate your alternate location to other players with the appropriate hand signal.

RITUALS

Revisit Demise (Basic)

This ritual allows you to look back at one subject's moment of death. *Revisit Demise* will only work on a freshly dead corpse, although some sorcerers claim success with vampires and Risen. Each success on an Extended Static Mental Test reveals one important detail of that event. This information will always be from the perspective of the deceased and probably patchy at best.

Seance (Basic)

This rite duplicates the Basic spell: *Deathsight*, conferring the benefits to all participants for as long as the ritual is maintained. It also allows wraiths to be felt and heard across the Shroud, even if they do not know the *Embody* Arcanos.

Lesser Ward (Basic)

There are three versions of this rite, each of which protects an area (or individual) from trespass by wraiths and Spectres. Any such beings who wish to enter a protected area or otherwise affect the recipient of the ward must first defeat you in a Mental Challenge. This protection lasts as long as you are present to support it. By spending a Willpower Trait, you may empower the ward for the remainder of the game session, even if you leave the area.

Greater Ward (Intermediate)

These are enhanced versions of the previous rites, which must be learned first. Any ghost wishing to cross the boundary must spend a Willpower Trait to do so. Even then, the creature will suffer one Corpus Level of damage per crossing. This protection lasts as long as the components of the ritual remain undisturbed.

Animate Corpse (Advanced)

Common among some of the older religions, these rites allow you to animate a recently dead corpse. Those zombies created using this ritual remain animate until the next new moon.

Once created, the zombie follows the orders of its creator, though complex or detailed commands are beyond its understanding. The automaton may not move quickly, run or swim, nor can it speak more than a few one-syllable words. The corpse is considered to have as many Physical (*Tireless*) Traits and Social (*Intimidating*) Traits as the caster has permanent Willpower Traits. In addition, it has as many Health Levels as the caster has Mental Traits and suffers no wound penalties from accumulated damage. The animate corpse has no Mental Traits of its own and is immune to all Mental and Social Challenges.

SHADOWS

This Praxis concerns itself with manipulation of the elemental form of darkness, tangible shadows. Darkness does not always imply evil; those sorcerers closely allied with the spirit world also practice this art. Just as day and night must balance each other, so too is darkness as potent as light. Even so, people who display this power are often suspected of infernal workings.

BASIC

Fading Light

This spell allows you to call darkness into an area, emphasizing any shadows that are already there. Lights dim and edges shift unpredictably. The disorientation caused by this spell is equivalent to the Negative Mental Trait *Oblivious*. In addition, characters within this region gain a free retest on any challenge involving stealth. You must specify the center of this spell when it is cast. Most often, the spell covers a fixed area affecting everything within a 10-foot radius.

This spell may not be cast in direct sunlight or other brightly-lit areas and the effects last for one scene.

Shadow Cloak

By drawing darkness around yourself, you can mask your presence when standing in shadows. For each success on an Extended Static Mental Test, you may cloak one additional person or medium-sized object (short sword, backpack, chair). Some form of natural shadow must be present.

A cloaked character is undetectable as long as you remain still and silent. However, anyone with *Heightened Senses* will have a chance to detect you (Static Mental Test) if you move. If you speak, the cloak is wasted. If you leave the shadowed area or initiate any form of physical attack, all benefits are immediately lost.

INTERMEDIATE

Cover of Darkness

This potent effect covers an area in a cloud of darkness impenetrable to mortal eyes or even the various forms of *Heightened* Senses. In addition, sound and smell are muffled and all but useless. The caster (or a Narrator) should describe this effect to anyone observing it, as it is quite unnatural and nothing like normal shadow.

The cloud covers a 10-foot radius around a target point, doubling in size for each success on an Extended Static Mental Test. The sorcerer must maintain concentration for the duration of this effect, engaging in nothing more than slow movement or minor conversation. However, if you spend an appropriate Mental Trait, this effect can be sustained on its own. In this case, the cloud lasts for the remainder of the scene, even if the caster leaves the area.

Shackles of the Abyss

You are now able to create chains of physical darkness. These bindings reach out from some nearby shadow and ensnare your opponent, preventing him from moving or escaping. This requires a Mental Challenge against your target's Physical Traits. If you are successful, the victim may not move or use any magical powers for the remainder of the scene. Bright light, whether artificial or natural, will dispel this effect.

ADVANCED

Touch of Darkness

By defeating your opponent in a Mental Challenge, you may wrap his mind in darkness and give him the Negative Traits *Dull* and *Confused* . Alternately, you may let the shadows play, instilling one Storyteller-chosen Derangement in your victim. Either effect lasts for the remainder of the game session.

MASTER

Shadow Form

Your understanding of darkness and light now allows you to become as intangible as a shadow. Though this power does render you invulnerable to physical attacks, you are likewise unable to affect the world around you. It costs one Physical Trait to shift into an immaterial state and another to return to normal. If you run out of Traits while in shadow form, you are trapped in that form until the next sunrise.

SHAPESHIFTING

Native shamans long ago discovered how to shift their own bodies in much the same way that they affect external reality, and this Praxis is still in use today by shamans and witches of primitive cultures. Some Kinfolk and kinain also practice the art to keep up with their cousins. *Shapeshifting* allows you to transform your physical self, from simple cosmetic alterations to completely changing shape. However, taking on the form of an animal has its own consequences. Though you may gain all normal attributes of the creature in question, you also acquire some of the animal's wild nature. Storytellers should pay close attention to how long a sorcerer remains in non-human form or how frequently she shifts. Over time, you may find yourself less and less connected to humanity as your baser instincts rise to the surface. Forms exclusive to supernatural creatures may not be duplicated, such as a Garou's Crinos form or the vampiric *Horrid Form*.

Shifting shape takes one full turn to accomplish *after* the spell verbal or ritual has been completed.

BASIC

Seeming

This spell allows you to change the details of your appearance. Cosmetic differences, such as varying your eye or hair color, require only a Simple Test. Significant alterations like modifying your facial features or skin tone require you to spend an appropriate Physical Trait. In general, you may effect any change that could be made with street makeup. However, because your bone structure and mannerisms remain constant, anyone intimately familiar with you can recognize you by passing a Static Mental Test. *Seeming* lasts until you next sleep or you choose to dispel it.

Doppelganger

A more dramatic form of *Seeming*, this effect allows you to take on a completely different appearance. You may change your height and mass by a noticeable amount or even switch genders. Each of these alterations requires the expenditure of an appropriate Physical Trait. This change lasts for one week or until you drop the effect.

Another application of this spell grants you one additional appearance-related Social Trait, either positive or negative, for each success on an Extended Simple Test. These bonus Traits last for the remainder of the game session or until used and may not be combined with any other form of Attribute increase.

Initially, you may select one alternate visage. Any additional masks you wish to wear require you to pass a Simple Test. However, if you are attempting to duplicate the image of another individual, you must pass a Static Physical Test.

When using this effect, you should find some way to indicate to other players that you look different, such as wearing different clothes or makeup, changing mannerisms, or wearing a card bearing your description pinned prominently to your shirt. If anyone asks if you are the same individual, simply inform him that you do not look anything like your normal character.

INTERMEDIATE

Second Form

You are now able to leave your human frame behind completely. By spending an appropriate Trait, you may take on the shape of any creature found in nature between half and double your normal size. You must describe a specific category of shapes that you are capable of assuming. This could be one particular type of creature, like any bird or reptile. Alternately, you may select a fixed list of enumerated creatures, one for each Trait of *Animal Ken*. Extinct or mythical creatures, such as dinosaurs or dragons, may not be copied with this art.

In either case, you may select up to three additional appropriate Attribute Traits each time you shift. In addition, by taking one or more Negative Traits in your new form, you may select corresponding positive Traits. However, any Traits lost in previous forms may not be regained or replaced for the remainder of the game session. However, if any of these three Traits are lost while you are in your alternate form, they may not be regained for the remainder of the game session.

EXAMPLE OF PLAY: ENHANCED TRAITS

Jenine uses *Second Form* to become a house cat, granting herself the extra Traits *Agile*, *Graceful* and *Observant*. During the scene, she loses a Static Test in which she bid *Graceful*. Later in the game session, she uses the same spell to become a panther. She may only claim two additional Traits because she lost one earlier. This time her intent is more aggressive, so she selects *Ferocious* and *Wiry*. She also takes the Negative Traits *Bestial* x 2 and *Tactless*, enabling her to select the additional Traits *Tough*, *Intimidating* and *Alert*.

If the form possesses other inherent capabilities, such as wings or the ability to breathe water, you gain these as well. However, venoms and similar biological weapons may not be duplicated. Thus, though a bear-form would include claws that inflict aggravated damage, taking the shape of a cobra would not make you poisonous.

There is a danger associated with taking on a shape not your own. If you remain in animal form for more hours than you have Mental Traits, you risk forgetting your human side. To retain your sense of self, you must pass a Static Mental Test. If you fail, your human personality begins to fade, replaced by the beast's mind. Each time this happens, you lose one permanent Humanity Trait as more and more of the wild permeates your soul.

Should you need to take on any alternate pattern for an extended period of time, you may spend a temporary Willpower Trait each day to hold onto your identity. Once you run out of Willpower, your consciousness slips beyond reach, and you assume the animal shape and mind permanently.

Change Self

This spell allows you to undergo significant physical transformations. Rather than changing your entire form, you may make functional alterations. *Change Self* enables you to grow claws that inflict aggravated wounds, enhance the strength of your legs to leap great distances, sprout wings that enable to you fly (at normal walking speed) or gills that let you breathe water. Each such change requires the expenditure of a Physical Trait and the effects last for up to an hour. However, if this spell is performed as a ritual, you may sustain these alterations for a full day. The Storyteller has final approval on any intended alterations.

A ritual casting will also allow you to enhance your natural body, granting yourself three extra Physical, Social (Appearance) or Mental (Perception) Traits or one additional Health Level. These Traits last for the remainder of the game session or until used.

ADVANCED

1000 Forms

As your mastery of shapes increases, you may take on the shape of any natural creature from one as small as a mouse to something as large as an elephant. This must be a creature you have personally seen.

In addition, each time you take on a new form, *1000 Forms* allows you to refresh your pool of bonus Traits. In the example above, Jenine would be able to gain the full three Traits with *1000 Forms*, regardless of how many she had lost in previous forms.

MASTER

True Shifting

With this art, you are able to leave behind the living kingdoms and take on the form of any object you can think of. The size limitations at the previous level still apply, however, so you could not shrink to microscopic size or grow to a hundred feet tall.

Any solid shape may be assumed at will. In addition, by spending a temporary Willpower Trait, you may shift into a fluid state, taking on the form of water or wind or smoke. In this latter case, only magical attacks would be able to harm you. However, moving around of your own volition requires you to spend an appropriate Mental Trait at the beginning of each scene during which you wish to move. Otherwise, you must let the wind, current or other natural forces move you.

SHAPESHIFTING MERITS AND FLAWS

Only sorcerers who purchase the *Shapeshifting* path may select these advantages and limitations. However, they may be chosen after character creation if the Praxis is learned during the chronicle.

Common Visage (1 Trait Flaw)

Whenever you change shape, some identifying mark will be common to each form. This may be a shock of white hair or the fact that your eyes consistently come out golden. This limitation may be inherent in the source or style of your magic, or it may simply be due to inexperience. In either case, you must detail the reason for this Flaw in your character history.

Floral Kingdom (1 Trait Merit)

Normally, you are restricted to animal forms when selecting your possible shapes. This Merit allows you to bypass this rule and select a plant form. The same size limitations still apply, however. Thus, you could become a small hedge or sapling but not a mushroom or giant redwood. In addition, though the range of options is extended, the number of alternate forms remains the same. Bear in mind that plants have a much different perspective on the world, and you're in just as much danger of losing your humanity as a plant as you are an animal.

Restricted Range (2 Trait Flaw)

This Flaw limits the forms you can take. *Restricted Range* is common among Kinfolk or kinain, who can often only take forms related to their breed or kith. As a Garou Kinfolk, for example, you may grow claws using *Change Self*, and *Second Form* would permit a standard non-Crinos shape, gaining the normal Trait benefits as per **Laws of the Wild**. However, you could not grow gills or take on the form of a hawk.

Each new form grants you six freebie Traits that may be used to purchase additional Attribute Traits or Merits appropriate to your new shape. You may also gain up to six more Traits by taking Flaws or Negative Traits as appropriate. It is wise to consult with a Narrator before doing anything particularly bizarre, however, as certain forms may be disruptive to game balance.

RITUALS

Transform Other (Basic, Intermediate, Advanced)

Whereas the normal arts of this path allow you to transform only yourself, these rituals permit such effects to be applied to others. Each version of the ritual is learned independently, and all require the sorcerer to win a Mental Challenge against her opponent's Physical Traits.

The Basic version of this ritual duplicates the effects of *Seeming*, whereas the Intermediate form extends the effect to those changes described under the spells: *Doppelganger* and *Change Self*. Either application lasts for one day, though spending a Willpower Trait extends the duration indefinitely.

With the Advanced version of this rite, equivalent to *Second Form*, you are able to transform another individual into an animal. However, your target may not be changed into a form that cannot survive in the immediate environment. Thus, if you wish to transform someone into a fish, she must already be in or near a body of water. This change is permanent, though a willing target may return to human form by spending a temporary Willpower Trait. Of course, all the dangers inherent in taking an animal form still apply, including potential loss of personality.

SPIRIT CALLING

Whereas most of us live out our lives in the physical world, most sorcerers are at least aware that other layers of reality exist. This Praxis concerns itself with the inhabitants of the Middle Umbra, including elementals and nature spirits. Wraiths and Spectres are handled through the path of *Necromancy*, and the various otherworldly beings (demons and angels) are the province of *Daimonis*.

This Praxis is often followed by tribal cultures familiar with the necessary means to appease the spirits and show them respect. Umbrood do not think like humans, and communicating with them can be a chore even in the best of circumstances. As noted in *Daimonis*, there's a reason why these creatures don't walk the earth, for which experienced sorcerers are profoundly thankful. Umbrood make bad enemies, and it doesn't take much to offend them. Behave yourself if you invite them in.

For rules regarding spirit stats and combat, see Chapter Four or **Laws of the Wild**.

BASIC

Spirit Speech

This spell enables you to perceive and communicate with all types of spirits, regardless of their origin. You may speak to them if you wish, though they are under no obligation to reply. This ability is automatic once learned, though you must have an appropriate *Lore* to identify the spirit in question.

Banish

Before extending your powers any further, it is prudent to learn how to protect yourself from spiritual forces. By winning a Social Challenge, you may force any nature spirit or elemental to leave your immediate area. You must declare whether the target is banished from that specific location or the prohibition is against approaching you personally.

The duration of this compulsion is determined by an Extended Social Challenge.

Successes	Duration
1	Current scene
2	One hour
3	Current session
4	One month
5+	Current chronicle

INTERMEDIATE

Summon Spirit

You are now able to place a call into the Umbra, requesting either a specific spirit whose name you know or just any one of a certain type of Umbrood. Whereas the completion of the spell puts forth the summons, forcing the spirit to respond requires a Social Challenge.

Normally, this spell only calls forth lesser spirits, such as Gafflings and weak elementals. By performing it as a ritual, you may summon more powerful beings: Jagglings, preceptors, greater elementals or even Totem avatars. Of course, what the spirit does once it arrives is another matter entirely.

Spirit Wrack

You are now able to direct your wrath against spirits who displease you. For each success on an Extended Mental Challenge, you may inflict one aggravated wound upon an inhabitant of the Middle Umbra. Alternately, by winning a Social Challenge, you may force a spirit to perform any one service. However, if the task assigned would take more than an hour to complete, you must also spend a temporary Willpower Trait once the challenge is resolved.

ADVANCED

Nimbus

You are well-respected among the Umbrood, though whether that respect comes about due to fear or friendship is up to you. This spell allows you to take advantage of that reputation, surrounding yourself with an aura that shines like a beacon in the Umbra. This glow is visible to all inhabitants of the Umbra, regardless of their plane of origin. However, its effects are *felt* only by the inhabitants of the Middle Umbra

Any spirits who wish to engage in any aggressive or hostile actions in your presence must first defeat you in a Mental or Social Challenge. If a would-be opponent fails this test, he is bound by this effect for the remainder of the game session. Consider it a form of *Majesty* for the Umbrood. Your aura lasts for one scene, though it immediately fades if you perform any hostile actions. Certain Umbrood, such as totems and Celestines, may cancel this out by their own presence.

MASTER

Spirit Walk

As your understanding of the spirit world reaches its peak, you are able to bridge the Gauntlet, stepping from the physical plane into the Middle Umbra. Your normal characteristics (Attributes, Abilities, Sorcery, etc.) do not change — you are still mortal, just existing on a different level of reality.

While in the Umbra, you must indicate your alternate location to other players by holding one arm across your body. In chronicles with multiple forms of spirit interaction, you might also want to specify which level of the Periphery you have chosen. Remember, you're on the spirits' home turf, so mind your manners.

RITUALS

Opening the Door (Basic)

The first step toward truly understanding the spirit world is to open yourself to its influence. Though hazardous, this is an important part of your training. *Opening the Door* allows a nature spirit with the *Possession* Charm to gain free control over you. This bypasses any normal tests, delaying them until you wish to try to evict the spirit. While using this ritual, you are automatically considered attuned to the effect.

Window in the Curtain (Basic)

This ritual allows you to look through the Gauntlet, making the Penumbra visible to everyone in the area. However, this awareness works both ways. Though you may see and hear any activity within the Periphery, any spirits present may observe you as well. Once cast, this effect lasts for the remainder of the scene.

Lesser Spirit Ward (Basic)

This simple rite allows you to guard an area or person from trespass by certain types of spirits. Any inhabitants of the Middle Umbra who wish to enter the protected area or affect the subject of the ward must first defeat you in a Mental Challenge.

This protection lasts as long as you are present to support it. However, by spending a Willpower Trait, you may empower the ward for the remainder of the game session.

Greater Spirit Ward (Intermediate)

This is an enhanced version of the previous rite, which must be learned first. Any elemental or nature spirit wishing to cross this boundary must spend a Willpower Trait to do so. Even then, the spirit will suffer one Health Level (or two Corpus Levels) of damage per crossing. The ward lasts as long as the components of the ritual (sprinkled salt or iron shavings, carved runes, etc.) remain undisturbed.

SUMMONING

This Praxis enables you to summon and control other living things, from small animals to supernatural creatures. However, these arts have no effect on incorporeal beings or spirits. Those entities are the province of *Daimonis*, *Necromancy* and *Spirit Calling*. Also, be aware that there are very few defensive applications of this path; thus, you must be very careful about what you summon. Magical creatures — vampires, werecreatures, changelings — may counterattack with their own abilities unless a Ward or some other outside force prevents them. This Praxis, then, is best worked with lots of help nearby.

BASIC

Beckoning

You begin your training by learning to summon and control animals, starting with small ones — lizards, bats, birds, rats, etc. You must win a Mental Challenge to call the beast. Three such animals will answer your summons if you're successful.

Come Hither

Higher mammals (chimpanzees, dolphins, cats, wolves, apes, dogs, etc.) may be summoned and controlled at this level. You must win a Mental Challenge to summon anything to you. This spell calls two creatures per casting.

INTERMEDIATE

Beastmaster

A more advanced form of the Basic spell *Beckoning*, this effect allows you to summon and control any animal found in nature. This includes intelligent creatures, even normal humans. You must win a Mental Challenge to call the creature to you and a Social Challenge to compel it to obey you for one scene. Obviously, if either challenge is muffed, things are going to be unpleasant. If you wish to summon a specific human, you must have a personal effect of hers (handkerchief, jewelry, etc.) and add it to your working. Only one creature may be summoned at a time.

Servant's Bell

Minor supernatural beings — ghouls, revenants, Kinfolk, familiars, fomori, kinain, etc. — may be summoned. You must win a Mental Challenge to call the subject to you, and you must have a personal item if you have a specific target in mind. Only one person may be summoned at a time.

ADVANCED

Call by Name

A more refined application of *Summoning* allows you to summon any creature, human or not, that you know personally. This call will be heard regardless of the distance between you and your target, though a Social Challenge is required if the subject is unwilling. However, because this spell does not bestow any special movement capabilities, it may be some time before the summoned individual arrives. In addition, if the subject is not entirely mundane, he will be aware that this compulsion is external.

The standard mechanism for using this power is to select an out-of-game envoy to carry your summons. This person (often a Narrator) will also handle the challenge, if one is required. While this message is being carried, you must remain in place. so that the target will be able to find you. *Call by Name* can take quite a lot of time, especially if the target needs to be tracked down in order for the summons to be delivered. Players are therefore advised not to use this power frivolously.

MASTER

Geas

Similar to the *Necromancy* spell: *Compulsion*, this power allows you to command any specific behavior from an individual. There are two forms of *Geasa*: quests and bans. Quests require the target to perform a specific action — only once or every time a set condition occurs — and bans prohibit certain behavior. Either form may also carry with it a punishment, the conditions of which are specified when the spell is cast.

To lay a *Geas* upon someone, you must first defeat her in both a Mental and Social Challenge. You may choose the specific terms and conditions before the challenges or after, though this has no effect other than to warn the target of your intent. A *Geas* normally lasts up to one month, though the target is released sooner if the termination conditions are met. However, the binding remains in place indefinitely if the *Geas* is laid in ritual form.

RITUALS

Asking Nature (Basic)

A more specific version of *Beckoning*, this rite allows you to control any plants in the immediate area. Tall grass or bushes might part, and trees could drop fruit or move their branches out of the way. Any simple action within reason may be performed. Each command involves a Static Mental Test, though large-scale or complex activity might also require the expenditure of an appropriate Mental Trait.

Vermin Swarm (Basic)

Also similar to *Beckoning*, this rite summons a swarm of normal insects to fly and crawl through the area in an endless wave. Any other character wishing to remain in the region must pass a Static Physical or Mental Test or flee the scene in disgust. Even then, everyone in the area except the caster must bid an additional Trait on any feat for the remainder of the scene. Though this will compensate for the distraction of dozens of minor stings, nips and bites, most feel it is hardly worth the effort.

Summon Creature (Intermediate)

A general form of the Advanced power: *Call by Name*, this rite forms the heart of its Praxis. There are many variants, each of which allows you to summon one specific type of being (as listed above). For each appropriate Social Trait spent, one random individual of the specified type will be summoned. However, like the spell, this rite does not grant the creature any special powers of movement. Thus, if the nearest bear, for example, is a long distance away, it may take a while to get to you.

TOTEM LINK

This Praxis allows a sorcerer, most commonly a Kinfolk or shaman, to enhance her bond with her chosen totem. Unlike the Gifts granted to the Garou, these powers come purely from the study and dedication of the sorcerer. Only shamans or characters with the Merit: *Totem* may study this path.

BASIC

Opening the Senses

This simple spell allows you to attune your senses to match your chosen totem's senses, gaining the extra perceptions inherent to that species. Thus, a follower of Hawk may be able to see a mouse from a mile away, and a student of Lynx could see in near darkness. The senses of plants are more subtle but just as powerful. A sorcerer who has dedicated herself to Oak might be able to sense upcoming weather or seismic disturbances. When this path is learned, you should consult with a Storyteller to determine exactly what sorts of perceptions you acquire.

Totem Gift

This spell grants you one physical characteristic of your chosen totem, similar to the *Shapeshifting* spell: *Change Self*. Aquatic totems would allow you to breathe underwater; predators might grant claws. Consult with your Storyteller if you are uncertain about the benefits that might be gained from a particular totem.

INTERMEDIATE

Adaptation

As you become more in tune with the essence and lifestyle of your spirit guide, this rite allows you to survive comfortably in any environment that your totem calls home. A shaman dedicated to Orca would not suffer from prolonged exposure to or consumption of seawater, whereas a student of Wendigo would be comfortable in bitter arctic cold. This protection lasts one day for each temporary Willpower Trait spent, and these Traits may not be regained until you have had time to recuperate in a more hospitable setting.

Wisdom of the Spirit

Similar to *Adaptation*, this spell allows you to tap into the knowledge and teaching of your totem. The specific knowledge gained depends upon the nature of your spirit guide. Each success on an Extended Static Mental Test provides you with one relevant piece of information in the form of Narrator clues.

ADVANCED

Form of the Beast

This spell is equivalent to the *Shapeshifting* spell: *Second Form*, though only shapes and features appropriate to your totem may be selected. Because of your close association with this spirit, you do not risk any loss of personality, no matter how long you remain in your altered shape. In addition, you may assume this totem form even if it represents an extinct or mythical beast. You must spend a full turn in transformation.

MASTER

Intervention

You may petition your patron spirit for aid in times of great need. After spending a temporary Willpower Trait, you may undertake an Extended Simple Test to determine how much help will arrive. The specific form of this assistance is up to the Storyteller, though it will always be appropriate to your totem. Thus, a follower of Dolphin lost at sea may be found by a local pod, whereas a student of Rabbit might come across a warm, safe shelter in the wilderness. However, neither Rabbit nor Dolphin could be called upon to attack your enemies — it's just not appropriate to the totem's nature. On the

other hand, Rat or Wasp might be more than happy to summon a related swarm for that very purpose.

RITUALS

Food of the Land (Basic)

This simple rite allows you (or any other students of the same totem) to draw nourishment from the food of your chosen guide. Thus, a follower of Deer could eat grass, and a disciple of Oak could survive on only sunlight and water. Though this ritual does provide full sustenance as if you had eaten regular food, you may only rely upon it for as many days as you have Physical Traits. After that, more typical (human) fare must be obtained.

Hibernation (Intermediate, Advanced)

Most animals have an innate knack for self-preservation, allowing them to find shelter and rest when they have been injured. Followers of this Praxis may acquire both the instincts and the power to make them manifest. The Intermediate application is the same as the *Healing* ritual: *Healing Sleep*, though you may only perform it upon yourself.

The Advanced form allows you to drop yourself into a deep slumber, remaining in this state up to one week for each success on an Extended Static Physical Test. During this period, you do not need to eat or worry about fresh air. You also gain all the benefits of *Adaptation*. Once you awaken, however, you are likely to be hungry, thirsty and cranky.

WARDING

Magic has many purposes, not the least of which is the continued survival of the practitioner. Many say that the best offense is a good defense, and sorcerers who follow this Praxis are likely to agree.

Warding is entirely passive. It may not be counterspelled, though it is subject to normal Unweaving. In addition, affected characters may not spend Willpower to ignore any effects of this Praxis, though a Willpower Trait would permit a retest in any challenge.

BASIC

Halting the Approach

The first thing you learn on this path is how to keep someone away. By defeating your opponent in a Social or Mental Challenge, you may prevent her from approaching you, as long as you concentrate. Though you may slowly move about or even carry on light conversation, any other magical endeavor or active challenge will cause the spell to fade. In addition, if you lose the initial challenge, you may not cast this spell against the same opponent for the remainder of the scene.

Glancing Blow

This spell allows you to protect yourself against physical attacks, both magical and mundane. For the remainder of the current scene, you gain a free retest when defending against any Physical Challenge. If you are attacked before this protection is in place, you may still gain its benefits by spending an appropriate Mental Trait, but the application only lasts for the current turn.

INTERMEDIATE

Neutral Guard

This is a more potent form of *Halting the Approach*. The effects are the same, but the protection extends to a 10-foot radius. Anyone outside this circle must defeat you in a Mental or Social Challenge before approaching or initiating any form of attack against you. Opponents within this area must win the test or be immediately forced outside the perimeter. In either case, if a hostile character fails this test, he may not attempt to breach your sanctuary for the remainder of the scene.

Allied or neutral individuals within this radius are likewise protected from any external assault. However, if one of these other characters performs any violent actions, she is immediately forced outside the protection. Any such behavior on your part automatically cancels the entire effect.

Force Shield

Force Shield allows you to merge your current Mental and Physical Trait pools when passively defending against physical attacks. The combined total is used for resolving ties or overbid attempts, and either type of Trait may be bid for defense. Under no circumstances does this effect apply toward initiating any offensive challenge or counterattack.

Alternately, by spending an appropriate Mental Trait, you may bestow this protection upon another character. This adds your current Mental Traits to her Physical total for defense purposes. However, only the target's Traits may be bid in defense. This benefit is immediately lost if the recipient engages in any form of offensive Physical Challenge.

Either application of this spell lasts for the remainder of the current scene.

ADVANCED

Barrier

Similar in effect to the Intermediate spell: *Neutral Guard*, this spell completely seals an area against intrusion. Anyone attempting to cross the prescribed boundary must first pass both a Static Mental and Physical Test against your total (not current) Mental Traits. You may opt to attune others to this barrier, allowing them to cross at will. This requires an appropriate Mental Trait for each such individual and may occur while the ritual is being cast or afterwards, when the newcomer arrives. Of course, you may pass through this wall as often as you like.

Once cast, *Force Barrier* remains in effect for up to an hour. However, a temporary Willpower Trait will extend this duration for the remainder of the game session.

MASTER

Sanctuary

The ultimate defensive application, this spell renders you or your chosen target completely invulnerable to harm. You may not be targeted by hostile spells or powers and may completely ignore any physical attacks. However, while this spell is active, you may only slowly walk around and converse with people. You may not initiate any challenges or Static Tests (other than perception-based tests), nor may you use any form of magic against the environment or other characters. This protection lasts for up to an hour. However, if cast as a proper ritual, *Sanctuary* may last for as long as a month or extend to protect everyone within a 20' radius.

RITUALS

Sleeping Sentinel (Basic)

This ritual is commonly used to guard a person's home or sanctuary against intrusion. During the rite, you must describe a boundary around a particular area. Anyone crossing this perimeter during the next 24 hours will leave an imprint that you are able to detect. Players who breach this defense must inform you out-of-game (either in person or by leaving a note at the scene) that they were in the area. Though mundanes have no awareness of the silent alarm, most supernatural beings will know that something has happened. How much they can figure out (and what they do about it) will largely depend upon their understanding of sorcery and the reasons for their trespass.

Hidden Glen (Basic)

This simple ritual guards an area from magical surveillance, including the Praxis of *Divination* or the vampiric Discipline of *Auspex*. Mundane observation is not prohibited, though anyone trying to spy on the area must bid an extra Trait on any such attempt.

Once cast, this effect lasts for the remainder of the scene.

Lesser Power Ward (Basic)

Lesser Power Ward protects an area, person or object from various types of magical effects by granting a free retest when defending against these powers. In addition, any attacker must bid an extra Trait when attempting to harm the subject of the ward.

There are separate versions of this ritual for each type of supernatural power: sorcery (including *Theurgy*), Psychic powers, vampiric Disciplines, shapeshifter Gifts, wraithly Arcanoi, fae Arts, spirit Charms or even the rotes of True Magick. Any sorcerer may learn the rite that protects against the

Praxes of sorcery, though other versions require you to possess the appropriate *Lore* Ability.

Greater Power Ward (Intermediate)

This is a more potent form of the previous rite, the appropriate version of which must be learned first. Anyone attempting to use the proscribed powers must spend a temporary Willpower Trait before initiating any associated test. This version lasts for the remainder of the game session. However, if the ward is cast on an object or area, it remains in effect as long as the ritual markings are undisturbed.

Bastion (Advanced)

Similar in style and effect to the spell: *Force Barrier*, this ritual is often used to protect a sorcerer's home or sanctuary. Any would-be intruder must pass a Static Willpower Test against your permanent Willpower rating before attempting to pass this boundary. Even then, a hostile intruder must spend one appropriate Mental Trait each minute he is inside.

The conditions and requirements are the same as the Advanced spell, though the effects of this rite last indefinitely.

WEATHERCRAFT

One of the main purposes of magic throughout history has been to gain control over the environment. There is no better example than the power to summon the elemental forces of nature. From the rain dances of the Native Americans to the weather-witches of medieval times, this Praxis has been both a blessing and a weapon for those sorcerers who study it.

BASIC

Touch the Air

At the simplest level, *Weathercraft* allows you to summon gentle gusts of wind. Though it is not strong enough to cause damage, this breeze can shift light objects around or even extinguish small fires. However, if you wish to accomplish something out of the ordinary, such as driving away a swarm of insects, you must first pass a Static Mental Test.

Lightning Strike

This dramatic effect calls lightning down from the sky, striking any single target within line of sight. By winning a Mental Challenge against your opponent's Physical Traits, you may inflict one Health Level of aggravated damage.

This spell may only be cast during an actual storm, though the storm's origin — magical or otherwise — is immaterial.

INTERMEDIATE

Gust of Wind

You are now able to direct powerful gusts of wind against your opponent. This will prevent someone from moving in a particular direction or even knock him to the ground. In the latter case, the target suffers a normal wound and must pass a Static Physical Test to stand up again.

Either application requires a Mental Challenge against the subject's Physical Traits. Like *Lightning Strike*, this spell may only be cast when the surrounding weather conditions are appropriate.

Clap of Thunder

This is one of the few applications of this Praxis that can be invoked independent of the local environs. When casting this spell, you must clap your hands together forcefully, though the resulting sound is entirely out of proportion for such a simple act.

There are two applications of this spell. First, you may direct it at an individual, inflicting one Health Level of stun damage for each success on an Extended Mental Challenge. Your opponent may resist using either Physical or Mental Traits.

Alternately, by spending a temporary Willpower Trait, you may release the thunder into the general area (20-foot radius). This automatically deafens everyone in the vicinity for a single turn. In addition, the affected characters must pass a Simple Physical Test, its difficulty equal to your Mental Traits. If a character loses this challenge, he is stunned and may only defend passively for the remainder of the scene. In the case of a tie, this effect lasts for one minute. However, should your foe win this test, he becomes immune to *Clap of Thunder* for the remainder of the scene.

ADVANCED

Lightning Storm

This level allows you to affect multiple opponents. For each Mental Trait bid, you may target one specific person or object with the Basic spell: *Lightning Strike*. Alternately, you may cover an area of up to a 10-foot radius with ball lightning. This costs one temporary Willpower Trait, and each person in the area must make a Static Physical Test. The difficulty is equal to your current Mental Traits; anyone who fails suffers an aggravated wound.

MASTER

Open the Sky

Though significant changes in the local weather patterns require ritual efforts, you are able at the Master level to break those patterns temporarily. This spell allows you to call any weather system into the immediate area, up to a 20-foot radius for each Mental Trait you possess. Hail, blizzard, even hurricane-force winds are all possible for a brief duration. The environmental changes begin when you start the spell and reach the desired results as you finish casting. The full extent of this change is subject to Narrator approval, but assume that you can duplicate any Basic or Intermediate effects from this Praxis for the remainder of the scene.

RITUALS

Eye of the Hurricane (Basic)

This defensive rite allows you to protect an area from inclement weather, including other applications of the Praxis. If another sorcerer wishes to cast those spells (or create equivalent effects) within the region, she must defeat you in a Mental Challenge. You may insulate an area of up to a 10-foot radius for each Mental Trait you have, and the effect lasts for the remainder of the scene or as long as you maintain the ritual.

Elemental Ward (Intermediate)

Similar to other warding rituals, there are multiple versions of this effect, each guarding against one particular element: fire, wind, water, wood, metal, stone, etc.

The rite may be cast upon a person or object, granting the individual a free retest when resisting the appropriate type of effect. In addition, by spending an appropriate Attribute Trait, you may ignore up one Health Level of elemental damage. However, this only applies to non-magical situations. Thus, an individual protected by a *Fire Ward* would be able to walk with impunity though a burning building (spending one Physical Trait per minute) but would only gain a retest against a *Flame Bolt* from the *Hellfire* Praxis.

Once cast, *Elemental Ward* lasts for the remainder of the game session, though a temporary Willpower Trait may be used to protect an inanimate object indefinitely.

Parting the River (Basic, Intermediate, Advanced)

These rites, which must be learned in sequence, allow you to control the currents of a body of water, causing them to flow in any desired manner. Alternately, you may alter the depth of a pool or even cause a river to part, allowing people to cross. The level of the ritual determines the size of the body of water that can be controlled as well as the extent of the effect.

The Basic version can only lower a small pond or part a minor stream, whereas the Intermediate form could control a mid-sized lake or deeper river. The Advanced applications of this rite permit major tributaries or even ocean tides to be affected. More drastic alterations shorten the duration of the effect. A slight change in current, therefore, might last for hours or days, but reversing a river or parting a sea would last for minutes at most.

Storm Calling (Basic, Intermediate, Advanced)

Three versions of this ritual exist, and they must be learned in sequence. Though the intent of each is to summon abnormal weather patterns, the extent of the effect varies with the ritual level.

Basic rites permit minor changes, like summoning a thick fog or creating a light shower, that affect the immediate area for a single scene. Intermediate rituals can blanket a city with these effects for an hour or cause more drastic changes in a limited area for a scene.

Advanced *Storm Calling* can affect an entire region with drought or a cold snap for up to a week or park a hurricane over the city for a day. In general, the more drastic alterations have shorter durations than less obtrusive effects. You may even summon a small tornado with this rite, though the twister will touch only one or two places before dissipating.

Earthquake (Basic, Intermediate, Advanced)

These rituals are identical to the *Hellfire* rituals of the same name and level.

Whirlpool (Basic, Intermediate, Advanced)

These rituals are identical to the *Hellfire* rituals of the same name and level.

THEURGY

When members of the Society of Leopold possess any Numinae beyond True Faith, they refer to them as the art of *Theurgy*. To its advocates, *Theurgy* is merely another manner of invoking the aid of Heaven, a sanctioned variant of magic. To its detractors, it is still magic, and thus it is evil. Theurgic rituals are performed in a Christian manner, invoking the name(s) of God, the Savior, Mary or various saints and angels.

Theurgists have different names for each Numina, which are referred to as ways. Most of these forms of *Theurgy* are functionally equivalent to the other Numinae previously listed.

VIA IGNIS, THE WAY OF HOLY FIRE

The Inquisition calls upon God's fire to punish the wicked, summoning searing flames to light its way in darkness and burn the faithless.

The *Via Ignis* is functionally similar to *Pyrokinesis* (see **Laws of the Hunt**), and the rules for that Numina should be used, with a few changes kept in mind:

• The *Via Ignis* is limited to touch range and to objects that the Inquisitor holds. The Inquisitor can cause his own hands to be wreathed in flame or he can make a weapon burst into flames. Missile weapons cannot carry the Holy Flame; the Inquisitor must strike in hand-to-hand combat, such as *Brawl* attacks.

• *Via Ignis*, when used in combat, adds one *Burning* Trait at the Basic level, a second *Burning* Trait at the Intermediate level and a total of three *Burning* Traits at the Advanced level.

• The Inquisitor must learn separate rituals to affect types of weapons with *Via Ignis*. Thus, casting *Holy Fire* over a sword requires a different ritual than does invoking *Holy Fire* around one's fist. Each of these rituals is considered Basic.

• *God's Fire* allows the Inquisitor to inflict aggravated damage when using the Basic levels of the path. The Intermediate levels inflict one health level of aggravated damage in addition to any damage from the weapon. The Advanced level scores an amazing two health levels of aggravated damage in addition to the weapon's normal damage.

Theurgic Way	Equivalent Numina
Via Ignis, the Way of Holy Fire	(see text)
Via Medicamenti, the Way of Remedy	Healing
Via Genoriam, the Dark Path	Spirit Calling
Via Necromantiae, Necromancy	Necromancy
Via Oraculi, the Way of Prophecy	Divination

Chapter Four: Rules, Systems and Drama

TIME

The clock ticks inexorably onward, especially in live-action games. Time that passes in the real world also generally passes in play, so once the sun has set, night can be dangerous for the unwary sorcerer.

To distinguish specific events in the game, **Mind's Eye Theatre** calls on certain conventions. Some events require that time effectively be halted in the game while Narrators or Storytellers resolve issues. Other actions require that the game jump from a particular game time to a different section of game time. As long as the Narrators and Storytellers keep track of continuity and make sure that the players are aware of any discrepancies, the game will flow smoothly.

TURNS

When characters start getting involved in complex and detailed actions that involve many challenges, it's time to start using turns. A turn lasts anywhere from three to 15 seconds of game time. In any given turn, each character may take one action (although some special powers allow characters to act more than once in a turn). Some actions, like repairing a piece of delicate equipment or working an Advanced spell, take multiple turns to

complete. Other actions, like speaking a short sentence, do not use up a character's turn at all. Once everyone has taken an action, play proceeds to the next game turn.

In some cases, a character's action may be interrupted or the character will be forced to respond to events before he takes his normal action. In such a case, the character can defend himself, but taking any other action — counterattacking, running away, activating a special power — uses up his available action for the turn. Thus, if a character intends to punch an enemy but someone else attacks him first and he decides to punch back, he uses up his action immediately when counterattacking and can't strike his original target later in the turn (unless some special ability gives him extra actions).

If a power affects a character for up to 15 seconds, it is assumed to work for one turn when turn-based time is in effect. In normal roleplaying, such powers simply work for their allotted periods of time.

CHALLENGES

Any time an in-game outcome is in doubt or when an event cannot be handled through pure roleplaying, a challenge is required. Challenges resolve fights, unreliable powers and instances in which a player wishes to attempt a task for which the character is suited but the player is not.

INITIAL BID

The challenge begins when a player declares the use of a particular Trait associated with an action or condition. The defender must either relent or bid a Trait in order to respond.

The Traits used in the challenge should correspond to the type of test involved. That is, a player should use Physical Traits if her character is attacking with a rapier and Social Traits when attempting to convince another character of something. In most cases, both parties will use the same type of Traits. Experienced players may allow for a little more flexibility, but this flexibility should only be allowed with the consent of all parties involved.

Once the Traits are bid, the players proceed to a test. If the defender relents, she does not risk a Trait but automatically suffers the effects described by the terms of the challenge. Similarly, if the defender does not have an appropriate Trait, she must automatically relent, losing the challenge immediately. If both parties bid sufficient Traits, they proceed to a test, in which the winner achieves his goals and the loser suffers the effects, temporarily losing the Trait he bid.

TESTING

Once players risk Traits to attempt a challenge, they proceed to a test. Tests determine a random outcome, influenced by the characters' capabilities. The parties involved play Rock-Paper-Scissors to resolve the outcome. In such a challenge, either one party will win or the participants will tie.

If one player wins, the loser suffers the conditions of the test (gets stabbed, is convinced of a lie, etc.) and temporarily loses the Trait he bid. In the case of a tie, check the total number of Traits each participant has; the player whose character still has the most Traits wins the challenge. Remember to use the current number of Traits, as a character who has suffered several recent losses will have temporarily lost some Traits. Flaws or special circumstances also lower the number of Traits available to a character; use the adjusted total Traits to resolve the tie.

You may lie about the number of Traits you possess in a tie, though you may only declare fewer Traits than you actually have. Doing so allows you to conceal your true capabilities, but remember that you risk losing the challenge if you don't use enough Traits.

The challenger always declares Traits first in resolving a tie. If both players declare the same number of Traits, the defender wins, but both parties lose the Traits they bid.

 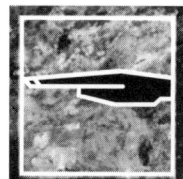 

ROCK-PAPER-SCISSORS

If, for some strange reason, you are unfamiliar with the game of Rock-Paper-Scissors, you might want to consider re-examining your childhood. To play, you choose one of three hand signs to indicate a selection: Rock is a closed fist, Scissors is a hand with the first two fingers extended and spread apart and Paper is a flat and open hand. Compare your symbol with your opponent's to determine the victor. Rock crushes Scissors, Scissors cut Paper and Paper covers Rock. Identical signs indicate a tie.

ADJUDICATION

When the result of a challenge is in doubt, call on the services of a Narrator for assistance. It's best to remain in character while looking for a Narrator. Try not to interrupt the flow of the game. Since time marches inexorably onward, it's bad form to hold up a scene for 15 minutes while looking for a Narrator to get a concrete ruling. Often, it's simpler just to go with the story and let improvisation guide the way.

When a character fails a particular Mental or Social Test, she generally can't attempt the same test against the same person or thing for at least five minutes (and time spent arguing with a Narrator doesn't count). Some powers specify differently, but assume that this rule holds true if not otherwise noted. Thus, someone who tries to use *Security* to pick a lock but fails the Static Mental Challenge must wait for five minutes before trying to lift the object again. Similarly, if a sorcerer attempts to convince someone to help him (with a Social Challenge) but fails, the sorcerer must wait for five minutes before attempting to convince the person again in the same way.

COMPLICATIONS

Naturally, quite a few additional situations can complicate matters during a challenge. Although the flow of the story is always important, some fairly common adjuncts to the normal challenge procedure follow.

NEGATIVE TRAITS

If you have deduced an opponent's Negative Trait, you may bid that Trait in addition to your own. This means that your opponent must risk an additional Trait before the test. If you are wrong about your opponent's Negative Trait, you must risk an additional Trait of your own. You may work as many Negative Traits as desired into your test, but be careful, because you must cover your bets if your opponent doesn't have the Traits you call.

If an additional Trait is not available, you may still test, but if you win, your opponent does not lose the Trait he risked. If multiple Negative Traits are brought into play and you cannot match them, your opponent gains that many bonus Traits in the event of a tie, making resolution in his favor much more likely.

OVERBIDDING

Overbidding allows a supremely experienced and competent hunter to crush more feeble prey. After all, Kabbalist scholar with his eight Mental Traits should far outmatch a department store clerk with three. Overbidding lets a confident character recoup an initial loss to a less powerful opponent.

Using Overbids

Once you've resolved a test, the loser has the option of calling for an overbid. In order to do so, the loser must risk an additional Trait. Then, both parties reveal their number of Traits, starting with the player who called for the overbid. If the initial loser has at least twice as many Traits as his opponent, then he may make a new challenge, the results of which supersede the previous challenge.

Should your overbid fail, you still lose the challenge and you also lose the additional Trait risked. If the overbid is successful, the overbidder loses the Trait he risked in the first challenge but not the Trait for the overbid, whereas the opponent loses the Trait he bid initially. Additionally, a successful overbid turns the tables on the initial challenge, and the results of the overbid count instead. Note that an overbid can only be called immediately after losing a challenge. You cannot lose a challenge, spend an hour continuing play, then call for an overbid to reverse the previous effects.

STATIC CHALLENGES

A Static Challenge involves only one player, who tests against a Narrator or the Storyteller. Static Challenges come into play when a character tries to use his Abilities to affect some object or event. A researcher uses a Static Mental Challenge in conjunction with the *Linguistics* Ability, for instance, to interpret a book written in a strange language, and a Static Physical Challenge with the *Security* Ability might be required to bypass an electronic lock. The difficulty of the challenge is a set number of Traits to which the character compares his Trait total in the case of a tie. You can overbid normally in a Static Challenge, but the Narrator may call for an overbid if a particularly recalcitrant object resists your efforts.

In some cases, a Storyteller may simply leave a note on an object, detailing its Traits in case of a common test. This note should have the effective number of Traits associated with the object and a comment about any required Abilities.

Use of some special powers may require a Static Challenge. In this case, the player is not necessarily testing against an object or event but rather is making a test to see if he can successfully activate the power at all.

EXTENDED CHALLENGES AND TESTS

These tests work no differently than the Static Tests or challenges they are based on. These are not only to see if you can activate your power but also to see how well it works. Some powers may be satisfied with a single success, whereas others grant greater rewards when you acquire more successes.

Put simply, you play Rock-Paper-Scissors until you lose. In the case of Extended Static Tests, you keep bidding against the difficulty number set by the Narrator. For Extended Challenges, you must keep bidding Traits if you want to continue the challenge.

SIMPLE TESTS

A Simple Test is a challenge in which no Traits are risked. Generally, the player makes a quick Rock-Paper-Scissors test (which succeeds if the character wins or ties) against another individual. Some Simple Tests require a win (no ties) to succeed; these exceptions are noted in the specific rules.

RETESTS

Certain Traits grant retests. A retest allows the player to ignore the first results of a challenge and test again for a new result. Retests are most commonly gained through the use of Abilities. In general, expending an Ability Trait in an appropriate situation allows one retest.

Multiple retests can be made on a given challenge, but only if they come from different sources. Thus, it's legal to retest a *Firearms* challenge once with the *Firearms* Ability and then again with the Merit: *Luck*, but two levels of *Firearms* could not be used to gain multiple retests on the same challenge.

Retests can be canceled by an opponent who is able to match the conditions of the retest. For example, if a player uses *Melee* to retest when striking with a sword, the opponent can also expend a level of *Melee* (provided he has that Ability, of course) in order to cancel the retest and force the attacker to accept the results of the original test. Alternately, the opponent could wait to see if the retest succeeds, then call for an additional retest with his own *Melee* Ability. This tactic holds the Ability in reserve but risks losing on the successive retest if the attacker succeeds on his first retest.

RELENTING

At any point before the test, either player may acquiesce and accept defeat in the challenge. Though you automatically lose the challenge, you do not lose the Trait you risked. If the challenge is not particularly important (or if you think that losing would be fun to roleplay), relenting enables you to save your Traits as well as make the game run more smoothly.

BONUS TRAITS

Weapons and some special abilities can give a character the edge in a test. You add the bonus Traits to your total number of Traits to determine ties when using a special Ability. Thus, if you have the Merit: *Ability Aptitude (Computers)*, you have two additional Traits when determining the results of ties in that area.

ORDER OF CHALLENGES

Since multiple challenges may be happening simultaneously in any given fight, the Narrator will need to know who attacks first and acts last. The system for determining this order is quite simple. Each person involved in a given game turn checks the number of current Traits appropriate to the action being attempted. Thus, a character trying to stake a vampire would use Physical Traits to determine speed, whereas a character casting a spell would probably use Mental Traits, even if the spell only requires a Static Mental Challenge. If an action does not require any sort of Trait challenge, then it occurs last in the turn. Characters with equal numbers of Traits should be assumed to act simultaneously, although for resolution purposes the Narrator will need to simply choose one to act first.

Sometimes, a character with a high number of Traits will attack a character with fewer Traits who will decide to strike back. In this case, the character with fewer Traits resolves his action in the same test with the faster character, but in doing so, he loses the ability to take any other aggressive action for the turn — he uses up his one action with the counterattack.

HEALTH

Mortals are fragile. Sorcerers may brag about their magic skill, but they get sick, they can be shot, and most importantly, they can die. A healthy respect for both life and death go along with being breakable. Health Levels track the amount of damage that a character sustains and represent the penalties and problems of injury.

A character begins Healthy, but various effects — combat, hostile magic, bad luck — cause injury. In general, most combat challenges result in one Health Level of damage, though some particularly vicious attacks inflict more. When the character sustains one level of damage, move to the next level on the Health Level chart. Thus, a Healthy character who suffers a level of damage becomes Bruised, and another level of damage would cause the character to become Wounded. All penalties from injury are cumulative. Thus, a Wounded character suffers the penalties of being Bruised as well.

• **Bruised** — A Bruised character has only suffered a small amount of injury. At this level, the character is possibly scraped up a bit, or he may be suffering from a flesh wound or two. A Bruised character suffers slightly from injury and fatigue and must risk an additional Trait in any challenge. Thus, entering any challenge — even defending — requires the expenditure of at least two Traits.

• **Wounded** — At this level of injury, the character suffers from fairly significant damage. The character may have a couple of nasty bullet wounds, substantial burns or blunt trauma. A Wounded character automatically loses all ties, regardless of Traits; if the character has a power that normally allows him to win all ties, then ties are resolved normally by Traits. Worse still, if the character has fewer Traits than his opponent, his enemy gets a free additional test. This additional test is not a retest but an actual extra action (although powers which grant multiple actions do not multiply this follow-up challenge — it's one test and one test only).

• **Incapacitated** — An Incapacitated character is out of the picture. He may be suffering from major internal injuries, or perhaps he's been horribly mauled by the claws of an enemy. An Incapacitated character is completely unconscious for 10 minutes after receiving the incapacitating injury, and he cannot move or enter challenges even after regaining consciousness. An Incapacitated character can do little more than speak quietly. Without some sort of supernatural aid, the character can do nothing else until at least one Health Level has healed.

• **Mortally Wounded** — Bleeding profusely and suffering from shock, a Mortally Wounded individual has little time left. Mortally Wounded characters do not regain consciousness normally. Instead, the character loses a Physical Trait every 10 minutes. Once the character runs out of Physical Traits, he dies. Only the assistance of someone with the *Medicine* Ability can halt this inexorable loss, and the character will not even begin to heal unless he is treated by magic or full hospital resources.

HEALING

Unlike their supernatural foes, mortals heal slowly, and they may suffer debilitating and lasting effects from injuries. Although some types of magic speed healing, mortals generally need bed rest or even hospital care to survive the effects of serious injury.

Some powers, such as the werewolf Gift: *Mother's Touch* or the vampiric Discipline of *Obeah*, heal wounds instantly. Obviously, these powers are of great assistance to mortals. Other capabilities, such as the Sorcery path of *Healing*, simply accelerate the speed of natural recovery. Either way, the mortal will definitely wish to avail himself of whatever services are available in healing quickly.

RECOVERY

With proper care and rest, it takes one day to heal from Bruised to Healthy, a week to heal from Wounded to Bruised and a month to heal from Incapacitated to Wounded. Characters heal from Mortally Wounded at the Storyteller's discretion, and they will recover with a new Negative Physical Trait (such as *Decrepit*, *Delicate*, *Lame* or *Sickly*). A mortal must heal through each level of injury separately; a Wounded character needs to spend a week healing to Bruised and then another day healing to Healthy.

Characters recover from wounds between sessions or stories. If a magical power (such as the Sorcery path of *Healing*) is used to speed recovery, the character heals at the next faster rate — thus, a Wounded character would heal to Bruised in a day with accelerated healing. A Bruised character heals after 10 minutes of rest if accelerated healing is used. (Note: Accelerated healing methods are not cumulative. An Incapacitated character treated by someone with *Healing* and the *Medicine* Ability heals no faster than if just one or the other was used.)

ILLNESS

Mortals, frail creatures that they are, must cope with the possibilities of disease and infection. It's difficult to cast a ritual properly when you're sneezing through your verbals because of the flu. Disease is fairly incidental to play, but it can provide a new and looming threat for mortals.

DISEASES

Characters generally catch diseases through exposure to tainted material and unsanitary conditions. Add to this a wizard who has been burning the midnight oil too long and is physically run down, and the likelihood of picking something up increases.

Mortal characters should only need to worry about disease if the Story-teller decides to make an issue of it. There are no hard-and-fast rules for getting sick; a Storyteller might have each player make a Static Physical Challenge to avoid disease after wandering through a particularly nasty and refuse-strewn location or after coming into contact with virulent foes. (Animated rotting corpses, diseased monstrosities and leprous street dwellers are all staples of horror fiction, after all.)

Once a character is diseased, the Storyteller should determine the disease's severity. Minor diseases like colds are nothing more than a nuisance, but more serious afflictions can threaten a magician's life.

Mild Diseases

A mild disease is uncomfortable but not completely incapacitating. Mild diseases typically cause the character to suffer from the Negative Traits of *Sickly*, *Repugnant* and *Oblivious*. Mild diseases last for about a week, although a skilled healer can rid the character of the symptoms in a day (by using *Healing* or *Medicine*). Mild diseases might include a nasty cold, a sinus infection or a mild flu.

Serious Diseases

Serious diseases carry the risk of permanent damage, but they are usually surmountable with rest and some medication. A sorcerer suffering from a serious disease may well be completely incapacitated by the symptoms, and he is likely to have a great deal of difficulty even with everyday activities. Serious diseases afflict a character with the same Negative Traits as mild diseases, and they cause the character to lose one health level while suffering from the disease. Thus, a normal mortal suffering from a serious disease is automatically at least Bruised for the duration of the disease. Serious diseases generally last for a month, though a skilled healer can clear up the symptoms with a week of care and rest. A serious disease left untreated — that is, if the character survives without the assistance of a skilled healer — generally leaves the character with a Negative Physical Trait such as *Lame* or *Decrepit*, though some may cause scarring that makes the character *Repugnant*. Furthermore, a character who suffers from a serious disease and remains untreated must win or tie a Simple Test to avoid death. Pneumonia, measles and malaria are examples of serious diseases.

Deadly Diseases

Deadly diseases are generally fatal if untreated, and they may even kill a character who has medical assistance. Deadly diseases are completely incapacitating; a sorcerer suffering from a deadly disease cannot enter challenges at all for the duration of the disease. Without medical assistance, characters with deadly diseases recover only at the Storyteller's discretion. Characters who are treated with magical remedies or medical assistance might recover after a full month of rest and care. In either case, a Simple Test is required for each month in which the character suffers from the disease; if the test is tied or failed, the character dies. Deadly diseases include typhoid fever, hepatitis and Ebola Zaire.

THE UMBRA

No other setting in the World of Darkness provides as much raw potential as the Umbra. Beyond the thin veils that contain the physical world lie countless spiritual realms waiting to be explored. Those who have studied such things agree that that the Umbra consists of three main levels:

• *The Middle Umbra* is what most people think about when they refer to the spirit world. Here emotions, rather than thoughts, provide the raw substance for creation. This level is a second home to the Garou and other Changing Breeds as well as an infinite variety of elementals and nature spirits.

• *The Lower Umbra*, also known as the Dark Umbra or the Underworld, is the realm of the dead. Apart from a few who study the ways of the departed, few sorcerers have any knowledge of this realm. Fewer still have ventured into it and returned, for the Restless Dead do not appreciate being disturbed by the living.

• *The High Umbra*, often called the Plane of Constructs or the Dreamlands, is a place where thought and imagination take solid form. Some claim that it is possible to meet the incarnations of certain concepts, such as colors or sounds, and that the beings here converse in terms beyond mortal understanding.

THE GAUNTLET

In times long past, Earth existed as a multi-layered quilt, with passage between the various worlds free for the taking. As fear and disbelief solidified reality, the worlds of thought and spirit were pushed farther away. This barrier of doubt and denial that separates physical reality from the various Umbral realms is known as the Gauntlet (or the Shroud when referring to the Underworld).

This barrier has a rating from one to ten, indicating the relative separation between the physical and spiritual worlds. This rating is used as the difficulty number for any spells dealing with the Umbra or the spirits. In areas where science and disbelief are strongest, the Gauntlet is thicker and requires more effort to penetrate; this could include research labs or shopping malls. Conversely, places where nature has free rein, where ghosts and spirits are inclined to gather or where magic is worked on a regular basis often have thinner walls. These could be sacred groves and glades, undeveloped woodlands, sanctums or graveyards.

GAUNTLET RATINGS

Area	Gauntlet
Science lab	9
Inner city	8
Shopping mall	8
Most places	7
Rural countryside	6
Deep wilderness	5
Graveyard at midnight	4

THE PERIPHERY

Beyond the Gauntlet is a layer known as the Periphery. It is the mystical counterpart to the physical world, a shadow realm where the physical and spiritual worlds reflect each other. Each level of the Umbra has a different term for this layer.

THE PENUMBRA

Just as the Middle Umbra is the most common destination for most spiritual travelers, the Penumbra is the most frequented aspect of the Periphery. The reflection that the physical world leaves here is usually connected with the feelings and ideals of a particular place. Thus a park frequented by happy children would be warm and lush, whereas a similar place visited only by lonely senior citizens would seem cold and empty. The manifestations can take on even more severe differences, depending upon the spiritual effect of the area. The aforementioned Umbral park would closely follow the layout of its real-world counterpart, but a toxic waste dump would appear as a foul pit inhabited by Bane spirits. The thinner the Gauntlet, the more closely the physical and spiritual worlds resemble each other.

THE SHADOWLANDS

This dark realm is most often what Necromancers see. Here the Restless Dead continue their existence and keep track of the activities of the living. Whereas the Penumbra reflects the current essence of a place, the Shadowlands hold visions of what was. Long after a monument or building has disappeared from the mortal world, its image and memory remains in the Shadowlands. The Shroud not only shields this world from mortal sight but also clouds much of the mortal world from wraithly eyes. Wraiths, with some effort, can peer through this Shroud to watch the world left behind, drawn by the light of life that mortals unconsciously radiate. Unfortunately, Spectres can also see across this barrier and often prowl the Shadowlands looking for the flickering black light of Oblivion in potential prey.

THE ASTRAL PLANE

More a state of consciousness than a separate existence, this is where the High Umbra touches the material world. Because of its nature, the Gauntlet is much easier to see through here than in other parts of the Periphery. Beings who use *Astral Projection* are able to view the physical world, though such impressions are often somewhat hazy or out of focus. Likewise, mortals, even mundanes, sometimes find themselves wandering this realm as they dream.

THE NEAR UMBRA

Though most sorcerers never move beyond the Periphery, some chronicles may have scenes that take place farther away from the physical world. The Near Umbra is not a single place. Rather, it is composed of numerous Shard Realms and pocket Domains.

These various spirit realms are too diverse to go into here. For more detailed descriptions of these locations and their inhabitants, consult the White Wolf books **Axis Mundi: The Book of Spirits**, **Umbra: The Velvet Shadow**, **The Book of Madness**, **Werewolf: The Apocalypse** and **Wraith: The Oblivion** as well as the **MET** systems for these games.

THE DEEP UMBRA

Far from the Tellurian, well beyond the vast reaches of the Near Umbra, lie unknown worlds. Little is understood about these worlds, for none who venture into them return unchanged. Those explorers who have ventured in, however, are very glad for the Gauntlet's protection, claiming it is less for keeping mortals *out* and more for keeping the spirits *in*.

SPIRITS

Sorcerers, at some point in their careers, meet up with spirits, whether through chance encounters or more deliberately due to the Praxes practiced. Some sorcerers may request aid and assistance from them, while others order and force them to obey on threat of punishment. Shamans invoke nature spirits, while the high hermetics call on angels and demons. However such meetings occur, the wise sorcerer learns how to deal with the otherwordly in some fashion, and preferably in a manner that allows him to survive the encounter.

TYPES OF SPIRITS

Spirits rarely look human, unless it becomes necessary to deal with the person talking to them. A raccoon-spirit may look like the "perfect" raccoon, or it may choose to alter its coloring or size for its own purposes. A spirit that frequently traffics in emotions like hate or lust may decide to materialize as a lecherous old man or something with a more mythical bent. Many sorcerous invocations that call upon spirits to appear request that the spirit appear "in a form not terrifying or to give harm"; how the spirit chooses to honor that request, if it does, is up to the Storyteller.

There are numerous types of spirits, even if they don't fit neatly into the various categories — from the jinni of the Middle East to the rainforest-spirits of South America to the kachina of the American Southwest. The Storyteller is encouraged to make up spirits and corresponding powers if she needs something particular.

GAFFLINGS AND JAGGLINGS

These are considered the most common of spirits, and the sort that often become familiars. While not particularly powerful in their own right, they are often extensions of greater powers. Banes are also found among these types. Gafflings are considered the weakest of spirits. Jagglings are slightly more powerful and the most numerous, the sort that most sorcerers are likely to meet.

THE INCARNA

Incarna are considered the servants of the totem spirits, and often command a great number of Jagglings and Gafflings. Not a few have their own places in the Umbra, and are of considerable age, granting them power and Abilities in plenty.

TOTEM SPIRITS

Certain Incarna are called totems — these are the spirit-founders of animals, plants and even other natural things such as certain stones. Shamans and other sorcerers who come from tribes where the old ways are honored are likely to encounter such spirits. They are considered quite powerful, and thus deserving of a great deal of respect.

THE CELESTINES

Above the level of the Incarna are the Celestines — powerful and eternal spirits that embody fundamental forces in the universe. Celestines are the least "normal" appearing of the spirits. They assume abstract forms and communicate in strange ways. These entities are so transcendent and distant that it is difficult to describe them in simple terms. Gaia is considered to be a Celestine.

SPIRIT CREATION TABLE

Note: The number of points each spirit type has is in the table below this one.

Cost	Power
1	Per two points to spend on Willpower, Rage, or Gnosis.
1	Per point of Power.
1	Per point of an Ability.
2	Per Charm possessed.
2	Spirit has one Renown among other spirits.

SPIRIT COMBAT

When a spirit attacks, it does so by making a Willpower Challenge against the target's Physical Traits. If successful, a spirit can make a Rage Challenge against the target's Gnosis and do a second level of damage (aggravated this time) if it succeeds. Spirits defend using their Willpower against Physical Challenges and Gnosis against Mental or Social Challenges. Damage is marked off against a spirit's Power Pool; Spirits do not bid with Trait disadvantages once injured.

When a spirit is reduced to zero Power, it dissipates into the Umbra for a number of hours equal to 20 minus its Gnosis (minimum of five hours), after which it reforms somewhere in the Umbra with one Power Trait and with some unpleasant ideas for the one who gave it a hard time.

GAFFLING

These are the smallest and weakest of all spirits.

Creation Points: 7

Negative Traits: 5 maximum

Power Pool: 7 maximum

Charms: *Airt Sense* only and at no cost

Rage: 5 maximum

Willpower: 5 maximum

Gnosis: 5 maximum

Abilities: 5 Maximum

JAGGLING

These are the most common spirits in the Umbra.

Creation Points: 25

Negative Traits: Maximum of 5

Power Pool: 10 maximum

Charms: Any up to 5

Rage: 7 maximum

Willpower: 7 maximum

Gnosis: 7 maximum

Abilities: 10 maximum; maximum of 5 Traits per Ability

INCARNA

These are the more powerful servants of totem spirits.

Creation Points: 40

Negative Traits: Maximum of 5

Power Pool: 20 maximum

Charms: Any up to 7

Rage: 8 maximum

Willpower: 8 maximum

Gnosis: 8 maximum

Abilities: 15 maximum; maximum level 6

TOTEM SPIRIT

All totem avatars come from these very powerful spirits.

Creation Points: 50

Negative Traits: maximum of 5

Power Pool: 30 maximum

Charms: 10 maximum

Rage: 10 maximum

Willpower: 10 maximum

Gnosis: 10 maximum

Abilities: 20 maximum; maximum level 7

CELESTINES

These are the most powerful spirits; Gaia and Luna are Celestines.

Creation Points: Unlimited (minimum 50)

Negative Traits: No more than five

Power Pool: Unlimited

Charms: Any

Rage: No maximum

Willpower: No maximum

Gnosis: No maximum

Abilities: Whatever you think they need at whatever level.

Storyteller Note: Celestines are beings of deific power, and no character should be able to make a Celestine even work up a sweat. If a character takes a swing at a Celestine to the point you need to consider the spirit's stats, it's time to power down your chronicle.

CHARMS

Charms are spirit powers. They often require a challenge of some sort in order to be activated. Any spirit can buy Charms during character creation. Unless stated otherwise, a Charm lasts for one scene.

Acquisition

Power Cost: Variable

This Charm allows a spirit to take an inanimate object into the Umbra. Once it is in the Umbra, the spirit can use the item, play with it and move it around until the end of the scene, when it returns ("How did my keys get behind the refrigerator?") to the real world. Items up to the size of a thick wallet cost one Power Trait, while ones up to hat sized cost two, and larger items up to the size of a suitcase cost three.

Affinity Attack

Power Cost: 2/attack

This is a catch-all attack ability. It is a one-Health-Level attack associated in some way with the spirit's affinity. For example, a fire-spirit will have a fire-based attack, though it's up to the Narrator to work out the details (hurled fireballs or gouts of liquid flame are possible applications, etc.).

Affinity Defense

Power Cost: 1

This is a catch-all defense ability. The defense must be associated with the spirit's affinity. For example, an air spirit may cause a wall of swirling wind to protect it against an incoming attack. It is up to the Storyteller to define the type of defense for each spirit. This Charm absorbs one level of damage each turn.

Affinity Sense

Power Cost: 2

This enables a spirit to sense things in both the Umbra and on Earth that are appropriate to its affinity. For example, the *Affinity Sense* of a tree-spirit might be *Forest Sense*, which would enable it to detect the changes made to an area around a forest, or to sense intruders in a wooded region.

Affinity Ward

Power Cost: Variable, +1/challenge

This enables a spirit to designate an area of the Umbra that is protected from other spirits of the ward's specific affinity. The area is usually circular in shape, and is about the size of a single room (10' diameter). The initial Power cost of this Charm is the number of Power Traits the spirit wishes to invest in protection. These Traits are the difficulty against which a Static Rage Challenge must be made by any spirit attempting to enter the area. These invested Traits are lost when the Ward is abandoned.

Agony

Power Cost: 6

This Charm doubles all wound penalties on a single target for one combat round.

Airt Sense

Power Cost: 1

This Charm enables a spirit to determine the best path through the Umbra to a given destination, and can help the spirit find hidden places in the spirit realm.

Appear

Power Cost: 3, +1/minute

This Charm allows a spirit to be seen and heard in the real world, but not touched or harmed. Furthermore, it may not touch or harm any on Earth.

Break Boundary

Power Cost: 1 (more can be added at Narrator discretion)

Static Gnosis Challenge made against a lock or other security feature opens it without causing damage to the boundary. Difficulty is Narrator's discretion.

Break Reality

Power Cost: 2–10

The spirit can disrupt the reality of a substance, and thereby modify its Umbral form, through a Static Gnosis Challenge (difficulty is Narrator discretion). This can be anything from putting a door in a wall (in the

Umbra), to turning a house upside down. The cost is determined by the extent of the attempted change and how clever the idea is. If the Static Gnosis Challenge is lost, the spirit will lose one Gnosis, so most spirits with this Charm are restrained in its use. Some Spirits have the *Break Reality* Charm only for specific areas associated with their affinity.

Calcify

Power Cost: 2/target

This Charm is possessed only by Weaver-spirits. It allows a spirit to bind a target to the Pattern Web by making a Willpower Challenge against the target's Rage. Each successful attack subtracts one Physical Trait from the target until there are none left and the target is encased in the Web. To free the prisoner, others must do damage to the Web equal to the number of Physical Traits lost by the target.

Call for Aid

Power Cost: 5

This Charm allows the spirit to call for help from other spirits of the same affinity. The spirit must succeed in a Static Gnosis Challenge (against seven Traits); any other spirits in the vicinity must respond for at least one turn.

Cleanse the Blight

Power Cost: 10

This Charm purges spiritual corruption in the spirit's vicinity.

Disorient

Power Cost: 2

This Charm is possessed only by Wyldings. The spirit may totally alter how others perceive the local landscape (up to and including obscuring the four cardinal directions) with a successful Gnosis Challenge against the local Gauntlet rating (minimum of six). When affected by *Disorient* during gameplay, a character must succeed in a Mental Challenge against the spirit or head off in the direction the spirit wishes.

Dream Journey

Power Cost: 10/visit

This enables a spirit to enter a person's dream and use Gnosis Challenges against the target's Mental Traits so as to change the nature of the dream. This Charm can be used for comforting, communicating dark portents and dream omens, or just walking through someone else's dream. The target must succeed in a Simple Test when she awakens in order to remember the dream.

Healing

Power Cost: variable

This is the ability to heal beings in the Umbra. Normal wounds can be healed at a rate of one wound per Power Trait. Aggravated wounds can be healed at a rate of one wound per two Power Traits. Anything living (Garou, spirits, humans…) can be healed with this Charm.

Informational Link

Power Cost: 3

This power enables a spirit to connect into the "cosmic switchboard" and gain information about virtually any subject. A Static Gnosis Challenge, the difficulty of which is equal to the complexity or specialty of the information sought, determines the level of detail of the information gained.

Intangibility

Power Cost: 4, +1/minute

This Charm protects a spirit from all attacks. A spirit can be seen and heard, but not touched or harmed when *Intangibility* is active. While intangible, a spirit cannot be affected by mental attacks, but can be tricked by outside influences into lowering its guard.

The spirit cannot simultaneously use the Charm: *Reform* with *Intangibility*.

Materialize

Power Cost: Variable

A spirit with this Charm may materialize and affect the physical world, assuming its Gnosis equals or exceeds the Gauntlet in the area. When it materializes, the spirit must spend Power to create a physical shape and to give itself bodily Traits. However, a spirit still uses its Gnosis for all Social and Mental Challenges. Power costs for creating a physical form are as follows:

Power Cost Trait

1   Per one Physical Trait.

1   For each level of an Ability that requires physical action.

1   For Basic Health Levels (as per human).

1   Per Health Level above that (each extra one also increases size).

1   For natural weaponry (teeth, claws, etc.) that will do aggravated damage.

Spirits are not limited in their potential Traits. A spirit may stay materialized as long as it desires, but may not enter an area with a Gauntlet higher than its Gnosis. Spirits may not regain Power while materialized (without the use of certain Charms). If a materialized spirit's Health Levels are reduced to zero, it dissipates into the Umbra as normal. Aggravated damage suffered by a materialized spirit is removed from both its Health and Power.

Spirits rarely escape a sojourn on Earth unscathed, and circumstances must be dire for a spirit to use this Charm.

Mindspeak

Power Cost: 1/scene

This enables a spirit to speak directly with the mind of someone nearby, even if he is not in the Umbra or cannot understand spirits.

Obscure

Power Cost: 1/scene

This surrounds a spirit in an obscuring cloud or fog that keeps it from being recognized or identified. This fog cannot be penetrated by eyesight alone.

Possess Animal

Power Cost: Three, +1/scene

This enables a spirit to possess an animal if it wins a Gnosis Challenge against the Gnosis of the animal's spirit. The animal is then controlled by the possessing spirit until the animal is slain, the spirit runs out of Power or someone banishes the spirit (as with *Rite of Cleansing*). This Charm is usually the first step in creating a Wyrm–infested animal. Some demons also enjoy possessing animals.

Possession

Power Cost: 3 +2/command

The spirit engages in a Gnosis Challenge against the target's Mental Traits. After that, a Social Challenge is required every time the spirit tries to command the target's body to move or perform specific actions. During a *Possession*, the spirit can use some of its Charms and Abilities through the host (Storyteller discretion). The target can spend a Willpower Trait to repel any attempt to use *Possession*.

Possess Tech

Power Cost: 1

The spirit controls one item of technology and can operate it as a human might. Of course, Gnosis Challenges may be required for the spirit to figure the item out; very few spirits are computer-literate or certified mechanics.

Reform

Power Cost: 10

This Charm allows a spirit to dissipate and reform somewhere else in the Umbra, usually far away from its enemies.

Shapeshift

Power Cost: 5

This enables a spirit to change its size, shape, color or appearance. A shapeshifting spirit may look like anything it desires, but does not gain the Abilities or Traits of the new shape.

Spirit Static

Power Cost: 10

This Charm increases the strength of the Gauntlet by one in a particular place until it is sidestepped through a number of times equal to the enhanced level. The local Gauntlet rating then returns to normal.

Steal Gnosis/Mana

Power Cost: 1/attempt

This enables a spirit to attempt to drain Gnosis (which can be converted to Power on a one-for-one basis), Rage or Willpower. The attacking spirit must win a Gnosis Challenge against the target (who bids Social or Mental Traits) or spirit that is the target of this Charm. If the attack is successful, the target loses a point of Willpower or *Mana* at the attacker's discretion. The spirit must announce beforehand which Trait it is attempting to steal.

Garou and spirits can also submit to this Charm voluntarily in order to replenish a spirit.

Umbraquake

Power Cost: 5/10 foot area, 10/level of damage

The spirit can shake the Umbra in a confined area. Those standing are thrown to the ground and everyone in the affected area automatically takes a Health Level of damage.

SPIRITS OF THE DEAD

Wraiths are something entirely different from the spirits described above. They are not creations of the Umbra, but human souls who either refused to travel on to the next world or who were prevented due to a variety of reasons. Wraiths are best described in and created with the help of **Oblivion**.

THE DIVINE AND INFERNAL

Sorcerers have been wanting to deal with angels and demons since Biblical times, and it still holds true today. For many sorcerers, such as hermetics, these may be the spirits they are most likely to come in contact with. In a way, they are the totem avatars for the Divine and the Infernal Forces of the universe. For Storytellers, creating these creatures without falling into stereotypes can be a challenge. The suggestions listed here are just that — suggestions.

It is wise to keep an ear out to listen for player rumblings when including such beings in a chronicle. If a player with strong religious belief is genuinely offended by something, listen to the complaint and try to find a solution. Trampling real-life beliefs for the sake of a chronicle is in very poor taste.

Angels have a number of different forms depending on what religion one follows. Muslim angels are said to be associated with fire, with colorful wings and occasionally not looking particularly human, while Judeo-Christian angels are described as majestic and near-perfect in their appearance. However, angels may choose to alter their appearances for their own reasons, or vary them according to the people around them. In demeanor and nature, angels are representatives of God, and as such, they should carry themselves as servants of the Divine. That does not always mean "nice" — justice can be harsh. Likewise, they are under no obligation to help out if a sorcerer should get too full of himself. It should go without saying that an angel can pull out True Faith when necessary.

• For the "average" angel, the stats given for Incarna make a good start. Chances are she's a messenger or servant for a higher power, although she's likely no slouch herself.

• Archangels (such as Michael who commands the militant angels, or Gabriel the messenger) are on par with Celestines — amazingly powerful and no character should prove a challenge to them. Should a character take a swing at one to the point you need to think about its stats, something is seriously wrong.

Demons are both far less concerned with niceties and very much concerned about human perceptions of them. After all, demons thrive on fear, horror and revulsion, and this is in short supply if mortals aren't bothered by the visage before them. According to theology, some demons began as angels, but followed Satan during his rebellion and fell with him. Others rose through the ages in response to human beliefs. While some demons delight in shocking mortals and do so by appearing in the most grotesque guises imagineable (particularly useful with would-be infernalists to test their resolve), others find subtler forms more to their liking. A demon may choose to appear as his fallen angel self, with sullied wings and a face that spiritually reflects the utter void within, or perhaps as a grotesquely large rat. Many have forms that are useful for walking among mortals, although imperfect in some fashion, such as the faintest miasma wafting behind them, slit pupils or clawlike fingernails. As servants of the Infernal, these creatures are predators, pushers and grotesqueries, interested only in end results that will guarantee them sustenance, whether that is fear or a fallen mortal soul.

• Lesser demons are somewhere between Jagglings and Incarna. They are primarily servants of greater powers, meant as messengers and go-betweens, or to raise some amount of mischief.

• Full-fledged demons, such as Mephistopheles from *Faust*, are on level with the Incarna or totem spirits. They personify deadly sins or foul emotions such as lust, hatred or pain, but usually pursue their own agendas in addition to any commands from their superiors.

• Demon lords and the creatures said to dwell beyond the barriers of the Deep Umbra are off the scale in many regards. Such creatures have minds and visages that mortals simply cannot fathom, and they usually prefer to work through avatars. If a demon lord is threatening to make an appearance in the chronicle, it's time to re-evaluate the game's direction.

Once materialized, both angels and demons will require Attributes, Abilities, Health Levels — in short, the things that come with a physical body. However, there are very few limits to avatars of the Divine or Infernal, and the Storyteller is welcome to make them as tough as necessary to get their jobs done. If Charms seem inappropriate, borrow from Disciplines or Praxes, or create your own systems for your specific needs.

TRUE FAITH

True Faith is belief in a power, entity, consciousness — or sometimes even a purpose — that is greater than one's self. True Faith is not limited to any particular religion; anyone of any belief can have it. This sort of deep-seated faith is extremely rare, and it is not necessarily limited to mortals, though it is even more infrequent among vampires and other supernatural entities. Only people of unquestionable character — the truly compassionate, caring, selfless and courageous — have even a chance of exhibiting True Faith.

True Faith must be purchased as a Merit, which gives a starting character one Faith Trait. Faith is a powerful tool for a hunter because it has many practical uses against the supernatural.

True Faith gives its wielder the power to accomplish miracles. It is based on a strong belief in a specific deity or religion on whom the character may call to strengthen his will. It is not the character who is turning evil away but his force of belief. Thus, the miraculous powers of Faith best serve the ideals of the individual's beliefs instead of his personal motivations. When belief intersects with need, the possessor of True Faith exhibits the full power of religious conviction.

People who possess True Faith do not have to be saccharine in demeanor; they must only practice their ethics. Most involve kindness, fairness, helpfulness and a strong sense of right and wrong. In general, True Faith promotes a strong sense of community and selflessness. Still, it is not unheard of for bearers of Faith to also evidence prejudice or even ruthless devotion to their cause.

Most games will see little or no use of Faith. An average mortal is lucky to possess one Trait in Faith; the considerably-above-average mortal is extraordinary to possess three. A Faith of five Traits indicates a true saint. An individual's Faith is obvious in her mannerisms and bearing after even a few minutes of casual conversation, as it is the wellspring of the her lifestyle. Very few people possess the conviction to think and act according to the precepts of Faith at all times, so living examples of True Faith are rare indeed.

IMPROVING TRUE FAITH: BY THE NUMBERS

Some Storytellers may find the task of constantly monitoring the Faithful onerous or burdensome; certainly, in a game of dozens of people, including multiple hunters with True Faith, deciding when each of them improves in Faith can be a trying exercise.

In such circumstances, the Storyteller is advised to simply keep a running tally of "Faith Improvement." In each session in which a given character upholds the tenets of his Faith, award one Faith Improvement Trait. Once the accumulated Faith Improvement Traits equal 10 times the character's total number of regular Faith Traits, remove all of the Improvement Traits and grant an additional Faith Trait. Conversely, if the character undertakes activities that run counter to her Faith, remove all of the Faith Improvement Traits immediately.

This system makes it a fairly simple matter to track characters' Faith and to allow them to slowly improve their True Faith. Similarly, the Storyteller can vary the multiple in order to make it easier or more difficult to improve Faith, though 10 times the character's Faith rating is recommended for most long-running games. (Just make sure that all characters use the same multiplier, in the interests of fairness.) Additionally, using this system means that characters of great Faith take longer to improve and have less room for error (since one misstep sets them back at the beginning of the long road of improvement). Of course, Inquisitors will find it easier to use Experience Traits to improve their Faith — which is just fine for these scions of the Church.

STRENGTHENING FAITH

Advancement in one's True Faith rating must be earned before it can be purchased, and Faith's effects (other than those stated below) are largely the Storyteller's option. Only constant dedication to and sacrifice for one's beliefs merit advancement in Faith. Similarly, as Faith is so strongly tied to these beliefs, the powers of Faith often follow the patterns of the believer — the miracles of a Christian may well be different from those of a Buddhist or Taoist. Ultimately, Faith is its own end. One does not pursue Faith to gain the power of miracles but rather gathers these powers as a byproduct of wholehearted devotion to the tenets of Faith.

REGAINING FAITH

Lost or spent Faith Traits are difficult to regain because they are so meaningful. The character must undergo a spiritual or religious experience, such as participation in a mass or a confession. The character needs to reaffirm the strength of his spiritual commitment. Simply going through the motions of ritual isn't enough; the character must plumb profound personal insights in order to strengthen his Faith once again. This introspection is a good opportunity for roleplaying as the player explores the depth of the character's Faith. Similarly, the Storyteller can rule that a deeply moving experience — participating in a cathartic confession and affirmation session with colleagues, witnessing to new converts, meditating and praying intensely at a retreat — may bestow the strength of Faith once more.

CRISIS OF FAITH

Any time a character loses a challenge in which she uses True Faith, she is left questioning her Faith. She is down one Trait on all Social Challenges for the remainder of the session, and she may not invoke her Faith until the Storyteller rules that she has resolved the crisis. At the very least, the character should spend half an hour praying in a place of solitude away from the concerns of the mundane world (that is, out of play). Similarly, experiences that reaffirm Faith (as noted previously) may serve to renew the character's convictions.

HOLY SYMBOLS

A holy symbol is an object used to represent the influence of the deity invoked by those characters with True Faith. Most wielders of True Faith channel that Faith through their holy symbols, raising them up to ward off evil or holding them in prayer. Crucifixes are commonly associated with True Faith, but the faithful of other religions may use prayer wheels, mandalas, statuettes or other iconic trappings. The Faith symbolized by an object empowers the holder.

When wielded by someone with True Faith, a holy symbol of the appropriate religion grants additional Traits and some defensive capabilities. The wielder must call out, "In the name of ____," (or a similarly appropriate paean) when channeling his Faith through a symbol. The bearer of the holy symbol gains the additional Social Trait *Intimidating* when using a holy symbol to repel the undead or ward against other supernatural effects. The holy symbol also gains the Physical Traits *Burning* and *Searing* and inflicts one level of aggravated damage if used to physically strike a supernatural creature. Furthermore, when blessed by a priest of the appropriate faith (who must expend a Humanity Trait to empower the blessing), the holy symbol gains the additional Physical Trait of *Blinding*, *Branding*, *Cleansing*, *Purging* or *Purifying*.

RELICS

Relics are belongings or pieces of saints' bodies that have somehow been preserved and imbued with holy energy over the centuries. True relics, as opposed to frauds passed off by con-men, are rare, though even a fake relic can gain power if enough people believe in its sanctity. Indeed, although there are enough "splinters of the True Cross" to make up a small forest, one clergyman noted that this abundance is yet another miracle!

Relics can be as large as an altar or as small as a splinter of bone; however, physical size is no measure of the relic's true power. Any container that houses a relic is known as a reliquary. Reliquaries are designed to protect their contents, though they often have decorative forms as well as functional designs. Most relics are too fragile to be moved and are therefore rendered useless to most hunters. Relics may, however, possess as many holy Traits as the Storyteller wishes to suit the story. A sliver from the True Cross would probably wield a maximum of five Traits, whereas Saint Aloysius Gonzaga's alms bowl might only possess one or two. A supernatural entity touched by a relic may suffer one level of aggravated damage for each holy Trait possessed by the relic in question, although the Storyteller may rule that a particular relic does not affect certain individuals. Because a relic can inflict large amounts of damage, it is recommended that no relic in play possess more than three Traits. A relic's holy Traits are never lost unless the relic itself is somehow defiled or damaged.

At the Storyteller's discretion, certain relics might possess miraculous powers in addition to their natural holiness. These relics should have a special card indicating the abilities available to a user with the appropriate True Faith. In general, using such rare abilities calls on the Faith of the wielder but grants special benefits beyond the reach of "normal" miracles. Truly potent relics possess powers that always function. A sip from the Holy Grail might cure all ills for anyone, and St. Vitus' heel could grant the additional Physical Traits *Nimble* and *Graceful* to someone who expends a Trait of Faith (since St. Vitus was the patron of epileptics and of dance).

HOLY GROUND

Holy Ground is a place of sanctity where the faithful congregate and perform the rituals of their religion. A Storyteller may establish certain areas within the chronicle's setting as Holy Ground. These locations carry their own Faith, and they bolster the Faith of others through the long dedication of the devoted. Ultimately, the Faith itself is more important than its outward forms; mysterious, secluded locations where many faithful gather often will possess a more powerful Faith than impressive, exorbitant locales that cater to marginally devoted laypersons.

Being present on Holy Ground will allow a character who already has True Faith to boost her own Faith by the site's Faith rating. A cathedral attended by hypocrites may have no Faith at all, whereas a hill by a deep pond where a dedicated congregation has met twice a week for the last 30 years may have a Faith of two or three. Sites of great devotion like the Vatican could possess five or even six Faith Traits. When a person with True Faith stands on such Holy Ground, she adds the site's Faith Traits to her own total, allowing for greater miracles.

Holy Ground is not something that should be common or created as an emergency escape. It should be established at the beginning of the game for those who would know of its existence and left anonymous for those who would not. As Holy Ground rarely surfaces in public, visible locations, it may take some effort to discover a site of true reverence. However, Holy Ground is not limited to Christian sites; holy places might also include sacred groves, synagogues, mosques or sites of pilgrimages (such as Canterbury, Jerusalem or Mecca).

When a site is activated by a possessor of True Faith, no vampire may travel across the site (unless invited in) without spending either Mental Traits equal to the site's Faith rating or a single Willpower Trait. Even then, the location's Faith Traits add to the total for the faithful when warding off any sort of supernatural creature. If a user of True Faith successfully wards against a paranormal entity while on Holy Ground of the appropriate religion, the creature must immediately leave the site — only the expenditure of a Willpower Trait allows the character to remain — traveling up to 50 feet away or staying away for 10 minutes (whichever comes first).

USES OF FAITH

ONE TRAIT OF FAITH

Regaining Willpower

For every hour of meditation and prayer that you sit alone communicating with no one, you either gain one additional temporary Willpower Trait that lasts 12 hours or you regain one Willpower Trait previously lost.

A mortal possessing three Traits of Faith would be required to spend three hours in meditation, prayer or reflection in order to re-acquire three Willpower Traits. Conversely, a mortal possessing one Trait of Faith would only be able to concentrate for one hour because of the limit to his practice and his dedication, so he could acquire or restore only one Willpower Trait in any given 24-hour period.

In the case of a long game (one lasting over consecutive nights or a regular chronicle game), these meditation hours may take place during the day or when the game is not in session, as long as the 24-hour time limit is observed. In a short four- to six-hour game, the Storyteller may feel free to shorten the meditation periods required, as long as she keeps in mind that Willpower Traits are not easily regained and should not be tossed around carelessly.

Repel Vampires

By brandishing a holy symbol, speaking the phrase, "In the name of ___" and engaging in a Social Challenge, you may drive off vampires. If you win the challenge, the vampire must flee the scene. Even if you lose, the vampire must back off a few feet and cower before taking action. The vampire may not initiate any actions — whether using Traits or activating Disciplines — for the entire turn after the use of Faith (although she may defend normally). A vampire may only resist this use of Faith by attempting to overbid with Willpower; if the vampire has twice as many Willpower Traits as you have, she remains unaffected. Of course, all vampires attempting to overbid like this must declare their Willpower Traits first, before you, and the ones who fail automatically lose the challenge, fleeing the scene and losing the Willpower Traits risked.

You may engage in as many simultaneous Social Challenges as you have Faith Traits if there is more than one creature to be repelled. In this case, you make one challenge against all of the targeted characters; the outcome is determined as described previously. For example, if a hunter with two Faith Traits engages two vampires and attempts to repel them, she makes a single test against both vampires. If the hunter throws Scissors while one vampire throws Rock and the other Paper, the first vampire would recoil, stunned, and the second vampire would flee the scene.

Infernalists and servants of demonic evil suffer even more from True Faith. Such agents of dark powers automatically flee, regardless of the results of the Social Challenge. Of course, there is no way to distinguish such results from the normal flight of other creatures.

Creatures who are able to remain in the presence of the mortal may use Disciplines, Gifts or ranged weapons against her if they desire. Of course, they risk further uses of Faith from the dangerous hunter.

Substitute for Willpower

Willpower and Faith are complementary energies in a character's personality. Willpower is a belief in your own capabilities, whereas Faith is reliance on a power greater than yourself. A Faith Trait may substitute for a Willpower Trait in any circumstance which calls for Willpower. Of course, the reverse does not hold — Willpower is insufficient to power Faith. Furthermore, this substitution is only possible when you are out of Willpower Traits.

TWO TRAITS OF FAITH

Holy Resistance

With sufficient Faith, you are defended by Heaven against the powers of the supernatural. By expending one Trait of Faith, you are rendered immune to the mind-influencing powers of various creatures. The vampiric Discipline of *Dominate* simply does not affect you, nor would the wraithly Arcanos of *Puppetry*. However, you can still be affected by powers that influence emotions; you have no special resistance to *Presence*. You only resist powers that directly attempt to control you in this fashion. This resistance lasts for the duration of the scene, and it is only effective against the power that it is specifically used to defend against — you cannot simply expend a Faith Trait and declare immunity to *Dominate*; you must spend the Trait after a vampire uses the *Dominate* Discipline on you, at which point you are rendered immune to that particular vampire's use of *Dominate* for the rest of the scene.

Faith Healing

By spending a Trait of Faith, you may heal one Health Level of damage to a person whom you find worthy of saving. You must engage in a Simple Test in order to successfully heal the target; failure indicates that the target is not healed and the Faith Trait is expended; success or a tie heals the subject.

THREE TRAITS OF FAITH

Pacify

By spending a Trait of Faith and entering into a Social Challenge, you may quell the Beast within a supernatural creature. Doing so will bring a vampire or werewolf out of a frenzy or calm a creature who is agitated. If a character with True Faith uses this power on a werewolf who is not in frenzy, the werewolf cannot spend any Rage Traits for the remainder of the scene.

FOUR TRAITS OF FAITH

Holy Invulnerability

Your power of Faith is so strong that you are completely immune to the mental influences of any of the supernatural, as long as you call on the divine for protection. By expending a Faith Trait, you render yourself completely immune to any use of a mind- or emotion-influencing power for the remainder of the scene. Thus, if a vampire uses the *Presence* Discipline on you, you need only spend a Faith Trait to be rendered immune to all of that vampire's uses of *Presence* for the rest of the scene. This invulnerability is fully effective against powers that manipulate emotions in addition to direct mind-controlling powers; thus, you have a defense against the wraithly Arcanos of *Keening* in addition to *Puppetry*, and you can defend against vampiric *Presence* as well as *Dominate*.

FIVE TRAITS OF FAITH

Blessing

You may leave lasting and potent blessings on objects or people. The most common use of this aspect of True Faith is in the creation of holy symbols or weapons.

To create a blessed item, you must spend a Faith Trait and spend half an hour with the item in prayer. You may bestow one of the following Bonus Traits upon the item: *Burning, Searing, Blinding, Branding, Purging, Cleansing* and *Purifying*. To injure a target in combat, the wielder of the holy item may bid its Trait in the Physical Challenge. If he succeeds, he deals one Health Level of aggravated damage to the supernatural creature just by touching it with the item. If he fails, the item loses its blessing. Bidding a normal Physical Trait means that the weapon is being used as a normal weapon and causes normal damage.

Using a blessed holy symbol in repelling creatures adds the Trait of *Intimidating* to the wielder's Social Challenge, so any character who tries to resist fleeing must bid two Traits.

Blessing another person is a very ceremonial event, and the blessing gives that person one retest that may be used up in any single challenge.

Only one blessing can be conferred per session, and it should not be done casually. An item or person can only have one blessing on it at a time.

SIX TRAITS OF FAITH

Miracle

The strongest tool in the hands of the faithful is the power of miracles. Performing a miracle requires the permanent expenditure of a Faith Trait, and a Static Social Challenge of difficulty determined by a Storyteller or Narrator. A Narrator must be present for this application of True Faith.

Nearly anything within the framework of your religion can be accomplished; curing a person of AIDS, creating Holy Ground, changing someone's Nature, resisting a supernatural power, bringing a vampire to Golconda, causing a wraith to achieve Transcendence, ignoring a source of damage or cleansing someone of Wyrm-taint are all possibilities, depending on the nature of your Faith.

Such miracles are not performed lightly, and they can be profound experiences to those characters who witness them.

DEMONIC PACTS

Just one question, ambassador — what do you want?
— Morden, *Babylon 5*

There will always be folks who are so anxious to scramble up the magic-ladder that they'll try anything, even bartering with the infernal. Maybe they're too proud or rebellious to undergo the discipline of study, or maybe they don't care about the consequences.

Every culture and magical society has its fallen, from the Satanists of Judeo-Christian tradition to the Twenty Thousand Demon Hosts of the Far East to the mad science of technowizards. Even primitive and tribal cultures have theirs — not all spirits are good, and the foul Nhanga of Africa, the Kys'Tayaa of the Pacific islands, the corpse-eaters of Thailand and the Sahara, and the witches of Native American culture bear murderous witness to their activities. However it's done, the end result is the same: the sorcerer bargains for power and the demon offers it in return for service.

Pacts don't start with soul-selling — that comes later. Like pushers, demons offer hints and tastes, the first free hit, as it were. It's enough to encourage the sorcerer to come back, and, like a destructive addiction, the sorcerer finds he wants more. It takes more service, greater acts of perversion, but each hit sends the warlock on a bigger rush until he decides he wants it all and mortgages his soul. With each step on the path, he gains more of what he wants — magical power, rituals and spells without study — but he also gains more demonic marks from his patron. These could be wings, gills, poisonous sweat, even toxic farts or inhuman features.

On the upside, a pact can grant some impressive powers for little work. The magician enjoys some newfound attention, especially from the opposite sex (the forbidden does have that attraction), has a cool otherworldly tutor, wild friends and a new perspective.

The downside — it's much bigger than it looks. The magician's powers are not truly his own but only loaners, a hollow reflection of what the magician could truly accomplish on his own. His life and soul are no longer his own, and he'll be alone when the bill comes due. Demons make less than desirable friends and even worse enemies. When the end comes, the best the magician can hope for is eternity as a servitor in some demon lord's household. Most go screaming to their deaths in the full knowledge that tortures beyond imagination await them.

THE ROAD OF THE INFERNALIST

There are those sorcerers who sign demonic pacts for a leg-up in the magic race, and then there are people who have willingly and gladly consigned themselves to the dark powers forever. Sorcerers who worship and serve the infernal hosts are called infernalists.

Theirs is a road that should not be walked by player characters. Infernalist characters can run out of control in a flash, and they're not pleasant people to have around. At heart, they are completely amoral, selfish and destructive. They are the predators, and all the world is their prey. Con men and pushers without peer, they can destroy a game without a second thought. This is *not* something to aspire to and should never be portrayed as a desirable or acceptable course of action. To do so negates the montrousness of the people who accept the power and the beings that bestow it. The dark servitors are best left as tightly controlled Storyteller characters and antagonists.

Infernalist characters are created no differently than any other sorcerer would be. They can come from any walk of life and any class; demons are not usually picky about who chooses them as long as they understand who's the master. Some may even be ghouls, Kinfolk or kinain, seeking to gain the power they have been denied by their half-blood. All have the Flaws: *Dark Fate* (to reflect what will be waiting for them at the end of their road) and *Geas* (to reflect the necessary service they owe their masters). Many often have strange Flaws and Negative Mental Traits because of demonic interference (such as a wizard with the Flaw: *One Eye*, a legacy of some punishment or as part of his bargain). They may have a great deal invested in Backgrounds, especially *Mentor* or *Familiar*. Some may even bear True Faith from their intense devotion to their patrons; this is especially common among shamans. Infernalists have no more than two Humanity Traits — frankly, the dirty work required by most demons doesn't do much to improve the condition of one's soul. Many also develop markings from trucking with the infernal, such as strange cravings (raw meat, drugs or inedible substances), physical changes (premature graying, odd-colored eyes, allergies, scars) or derangements.

Luckily for the rest of us, infernalists do have their disadvantages as well. True Faith afflicts them, they stink abominably of the Wyrm, they radiate the black light of Oblivion like beacons, and many have Banality ratings that could make Dauntain jealous. Sensitive individuals and many animals also find their presence unpleasant, if not downright uncomfortable, and will avoid them like the plague.

Infernalist powers are beyond the scope of this book. Most warlocks often practice regular Praxes like *Hellfire*, *Daimonis* and *Fascination*, but often the infernal ones offer their servants tutelage in other paths of power. Descriptions of dark sorcery and demonic investments can be found in **The Book of Madness** and **The Guide to the Sabbat**.

As antagonists, infernalists should not be played as stereotypical black-caped, cackling maniacs. These are predators, looking for converts or victims, and they understand the values of patience and subtlety. They will lie, they will steal, they will manipulate and they will kill without remorse. Even the masters of intrigue — the vampires — have been their victims. The worst enemy is one who looks indistinguishable from the people around him, and the best infernalists can appear urbane, seductive or innocent. Some excellent examples include *Faust's* Mephistopheles, *Babylon 5's* Mr. Morden and the infamous Jodi Blake of **Mage**.

WORKING THE CRAFT

Slender fingers, bare of any adornment, guided the match among the forest of candles, touching the flame to each cold wick. Dancing light filled the chamber, reflecting off the silver bowl and the athame's blade. Ellyn looked over each tool one last time, laying a crystal paperweight etched with a Star of David on the open grimoire to ensure that the pages stayed in place. She frowned — something was missing. Then she remembered and carefully poured a handful of precious frankincense nuggets into the burner. Spicy-sweet smoke drifted from the top of the burner, spreading fragrance like a cloud. The spirits she often spoke with seemed to appreciate such trappings, and it lent an appropriate air of formality to the place.

Satisfied, Ellyn stepped to the circle and picked up her chalice....

Too many players have a tendency to reduce magic to challenges and tests and forget that they're actually characters working spells and rituals. Hedge wizardry and *Theurgy* don't just drop out of the sky, and they certainly aren't worked with a few rounds of Rock-Paper-Scissors. Take some time to think about these rituals and spells before you start slinging them around.

For starters, hedge wizards are not calling on internal gifts of power. They are practicing learned formulae that enable them to tap into the hidden energies, and those energies don't just materialize without preparation. Each sorcerer learns in a different way, and, as was noted earlier in the setting material, there are many different ways to learn the magic. A Balamob shaman drapes herself in a specially prepared leopard skin to shift shape, a Fenian puts on an heirloom torc and spins in a circle while chanting in Gaelic, and a child Solitaire wears the cat costume her mother made her for Halloween.

Secondly, different spells will do different things. This can't be overemphasized, especially when dealing with Umbrood and spirits. The spells that call on angels have requirements that demons may find abhorrent and vice versa. Throw out the wrong thing and you may have a snake-spirit visiting when you really wanted to call a raccoon-spirit, or worse, an infernal tempter when you were trying to summon an angel's presence.

Lastly, preparation adds a lot to game atmosphere and gives the Storytellers stuff to hang their plots on. An untrained wizard's attempt to use his master's grimoire, a la "Sorcerer's Apprentice", can add some interesting elements to a game. What of a *voudoun* mambo being ridden by a loa while her stunned Fenian colleague watches? Or a Kabbalist trying to tell a female Thal'hun that she can't watch him working his magic? Suppose a Theurgist decides to show his cynical investigator partner that there truly are stranger things in this world than are dreamt of in all his philosophy?

PLAYING RESPONSIBLY

Magic is one of those words that makes a lot of people twitchy. Some twitch out of fear, some out of ignorance, some out of prejudice. Others take the game a little too seriously and frighten mundanes — and their fellow players — with their actions.

Running a ritual can be great for game atmosphere, and the image of a sorcerer standing in a warding circle with his grimoire in hand is classic. Be aware, however, that some people may find your actions disturbing or frightening, and they may not be interested in hearing explanations. If you must take such things under consideration, then be considerate and don't force the issue. Get back to storytelling and describe what you're doing to the Storyteller; have fun with descriptions, and see if you can work a little magic of your own for your Storyteller.

Remember also that certain items and elements of magic can be very dangerous and are best left to description. Magicians have eaten poisons, bled themselves, lit fires and sacrificed animals to work their spells — such things are not for general consumption. Use the sense you were given and consult your Storyteller about questionable elements before you bring them in.

Repeat after me, folks — it's just a game.

Magic has, from time immemorial, been something strange, something of the otherworld, to wonder at or fear. It has a long, rich heritage stretching back to the augurs of Babylon and threading through human history. It has turned the tides of battle, reduced proud men to beggars, ignited firestorms of horror and figured in some of the most remarkable stories. Reducing a hermetic spell to sitting out of game and making a couple of tests does such heritage a disservice.

HOW TO THROW A RITUAL

Ritual may be formalized, but we're not giving you directions here. There's no fun in playing a glorified game of Simon Says. Besides, what works for a shaman is not going to work for a Solitaire who's been reading Norse mythology.

A sorcerer's rituals are the result of intense study, based on her understanding of magic and her magic style. Think about how your magician works her magic, what she gravitates toward and what sort of tools she uses. Does she practice *voudoun* and use ecstatic dance to get the attention of the spirits or does she prefer creating music with multilayered harmonies on a dedicated keyboard?

It can be fun to create rituals and verbals for spells, not to mention that it adds in-game atmosphere. Give it a try and see what you come up with.

TOOLS OF THE TRADE

Sorcerers come in all shapes, and so do their tools. An Albertine Theurgist, a Wiccan priestess, and an houngan all may use a chalice, but the Albertine may use a church's communion chalice, the Wiccan a ceramic goblet made by a friend, and the houngan a wooden bowl he carved himself. Such tools are often necessary for casting of certain rituals, such as the rites of *Daimonis* or *Theurgy*.

Tools can spark stories too. What if the chalice you need is a vampire elder's prized possession? What happens if you drop the heirloom sword you use, and you knock some of the jewels out of the hilt? Even hunting for herbs can be problematic — you need belladonna, and the requirements for proper harvesting say you must harvest in the nude at night with a certain knife. What happens if the search takes you onto a vampire's hunting grounds, a Garou sept's caern, or your neighbor's backyard? What if you're a Solitaire practicing out of your parents' basement, and you need to smuggle some ingredients past them? Nobody ever said this stuff was easy....

At the Storyteller's discretion, really good items (such as a specially created dance or a handmade offering) could reduce the caster's difficulty during tests or allow her to win on ties.

• **Alchemical laboratory** — Required for the working of *Alchemy*, the lab is a complex collection of tubes, beakers, burners, books, charts, tables, ingredients and containers. Maybe everything's precisely arranged and neatly organized, or maybe it's a haphazard mess with an order apparent only to the alchemist.

• **Blood and other bodily fluids** — As vampires will tell you, there is power in blood, and it can be used to seal pacts, as a means for sympathetic workings or to attract spirits with certain appetites. Tears, saliva and semen — for their basic elements or their connection to human life — may also be called for.

• **Bones, skin and other remnants** — Bones, like blood, are considered quite powerful and may be carved into other items, ground into powder or snapped during a curse. Skin protects its "wearer," and it may also be prepared and worn by others to pass along the protection. Some shamans use animal skin (once the animal is finished with it) for shapeshifting, to grant themselves the power of the animal. Human hair, tears, excrement or fingernail clippings are often required ritual components, whereas shamans and other primitive sorcerers use animal hides, horns, hooves or feathers (after thanking the animal for their use).

• **Books** — From hermetic grimoires to a Book of Shadows to the Torah and Bible, books hold a special place in most magical workings, whether for study, meditation, spells or reflection. In most Western magical traditions, a magician can be required to know how to read and write.

• **Cards, dice, straws, lots** — The cornerstone of *Divination*, these are often required for its working.

• **Celestial alignments** — Some sorcerers keep an eye on the heavens, timing certain workings based on the dance of the stars and planets, working rituals of mystery when the moon is full or casting hostile spells when Mars is in the sky.

• **Circles and other shapes** — The sacred circle is found all over the world and in many sorcerers' milieux, whether they dance in the round or draw it on the ground as a ward. Rings also symbolize wholeness and infinity. Crosses, pentacles, squares and triangles represent different qualities and may be used by Theurgists and hermetics alike.

• **Cups, chalices, other vessels** —A golden chalice filled with communion wine, the traditional witch's cauldron, a gourd filled with seeds — all are symbols of wisdom, creation and the feminine element.

• **Dance and gestures** — Besides being fun, dance combines exercise, emotion and art into a powerful mix that often pleases spirits. Primal societies still use ecstatic dance, whereas more "civilized" folk have reduced their dances to mystic gestures.

• **Drugs and Poisons** — To transcend mortal perceptions, some sorcerers use drugs or poisons, hoping the shock to the system will bring visions. From peyote to woad or even the wine of communion, magicians have drunk, smoked, eaten or smeared themselves with all manner of concoctions. Some even allow spiders, snakes or bees to sting them.

Remember, Mind's Eye rules strictly forbid using real drugs or alcohol in a game.

• **Elements** — What could be more powerful than nature? Earth, fire, air and water have been used and called upon since time immemorial to bring connections with the natural world. Related materials can be ash, wood, metal or ice.

• **Group rites** — A group can focus more spiritual energy than a single magician ever could. This could be an Inquisition Theurgist leading his fellows in communion or the frenzied orgiastic rites found in tribal cultures. This takes a bit of showmanship on the part of the magician, but the results can be spectacular.

• **Herbs and roots** — Like the elements, plants hold a bit of life within themselves as well as special properties of their own. Brews, salves, wines, potions, powders and paints can all be created with roots and herbs, and sorcerers eat, drink, smoke or paint themselves with them in order to gain their effects.

- **Household tools** — Brooms, sickles, scissors, mirrors, pens and hourglasses are just some of the common items found around the house that have long magical pedigrees. More modern equipment, such as pagers, blenders and stoves, is starting to find its way into such distinguished company. Most such tools are used with their normal functions (sweeping, reflecting, timekeeping) extending into mystical uses.

- **Machines** — The Thal'hun and Techno wizards have long recognized the efficacy of mystically created machines, and such devices can be pretty darn effective. Keyboards that can create intense harmonies beyond the ear's capacity or cameras that can photograph the spirit are just some of the potential inventions.

- **Sex** — There's no denying that sex is a powerful tool to create, to attract and to bind energies. Its connections are intimate, it breaks down barriers and inhibitions and it can drive people to madness or vision. Some societies use it in orgies, others deny it through abstinence, some use complex Tantric rites, and darker powers scream for mutilation.

- **Symbols** — Crosses and crucifixes, the Mogen David, hermetic symbols, runes, hex signs, mandalas, spirals, knotwork and other complex designs often embody some magical or spiritual truth and fix it to a place or an object.

- **Voice** — A chant, a song, a prayer or a wail — every magic carries some spoken invocation that brings the magician's thoughts and wishes into the open where spirit ears can hear. Few magics can work without a verbal component, and some (like *Cursing*) rely on the voice.

- **Wands and staves** — Masculine imagery aside, a wand or staff extends the magician's reach and makes an effective guide for his will. Some magicians use their staves to scratch out mystic symbols on the ground. Wands and staves can be created from almost any substance (wood, stone, bone or glass are just a few), and some wizards create wands from pool cues, violin bows or teachers' rods.

- **Weapons** — Like the wand, the weapon is an extension of the sorcerer's reach, carrying mystic force past his hand and to his target. Some gods prefer a particular weapon (Thor's hammer, the bows of Artemis and Apollo, the archangel Michael's sword), and the priests who call upon a certain god's aid often use their patron's chosen weapon.

Remember, Mind's Eye rules forbid anything that even vaguely resembles a weapon. Use item cards instead.

- **Written inscriptions** — Scientists and sorcerers will both tell you that language is the greatest magic of all. From the bards and Druids of ancient Celtic times to hermetic sorcerers to witches, all agree that writing channels magic by changing thought into a physical form. Runes, hieroglyphs, hand-writing — however it is done, the setting of thought into a more lasting form (or, by contrast, destroying it) is undeniably powerful.

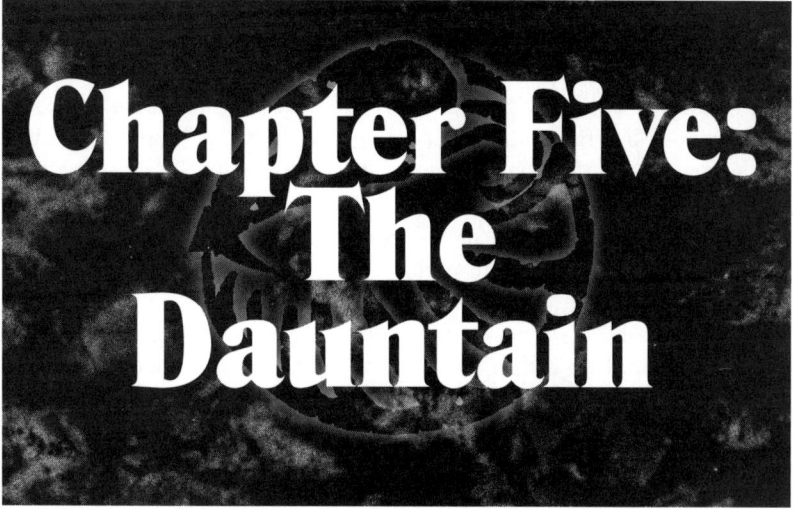

Chapter Five: The Dauntain

Perhaps the strangest of hunters, Dauntain are not mortals at all. Rather, they are changelings who have succumbed to the lure of Banality; whether seeking reason and stasis for power, vengeance or protection, they embrace mundanity and forever alter their faerie natures in the process. Some actively hunt changelings, whereas others carry Banality as a byproduct of their actions. They are one and all dangerous in the extreme to the Kithain, as their very presence destroys the creativity and Glamour that feeds changeling existence.

Some Dauntain actually take up the hunter mantle and seek out supernatural creatures to destroy, but they are more commonly forces of reason and mundanity. Indeed, many Dauntain actively deny the existence of the supernatural, destroying the power of dreams through their disbelief. Those Dauntain who call upon their faerie powers are dangerous, for they have potent magics in addition to their powers of Banality. To changelings, though, the worst are those who actively deny their fae existence; such disbelief literally tears the Dreaming (the world of faeries) apart.

Changelings become Dauntain through a variety of different methods known as Dooms. Each Doom corresponds to a particular Banal fate. It is widely believed that Dauntain are beyond hope, yet some changelings believe that Dauntain can be redeemed if they are turned away from their Banal paths. Such a task is horribly dangerous, though, as the rescuing fae are subjected to the full force of the Dauntain's Banality. An attempt of this nature would certainly be the focus of an epic saga.

Advantage: Dauntain are changelings, not mortals. As such, they are built according to the rules presented in **The Shining Host**. Dauntain characters accordingly begin with seven primary, five secondary and three tertiary Attribute Traits. Further, they begin with five Ability Traits, three changeling Arts, five Realms (if applicable) and five changeling Backgrounds. Since they are still fae, Dauntain choose a changeling Kith as usual and gain its usual Birthrights and Frailties. Dauntain have Glamour and Willpower as determined by their changeling forms and start with seven Banality Traits. Lastly, the Dauntain have special powers of Banality; they gain one Stigma and three Agendas.

Disadvantage: Dauntain are subject to all of the typical weaknesses and restrictions of changelings. Furthermore, some changelings make a point of hunting Dauntain and destroying them, specifically trying to remove the dangerous Banality of the Doomed. Because of their strong Banality, Dauntain are also constantly in danger of becoming permanently Undone and losing whatever faerie powers they might have. Because they are created as changelings and not as mortal hunters, Dauntain do not automatically gain any Free Traits, nor do they have Humanity Traits.

ORIGINS

The material for this chapter comes from the **Changeling** supplement **The Autumn People** and the Mind's Eye Theatre book **The Shining Host**. It is not necessary to own either of these books to play a Dauntain, but players may find inspiration and some other useful information in both.

LOST

The Lost are those changelings who fail to understand their faerie natures or reject their heritage. These dangerous Doomed see the changeling world as a hallucination or flight of insanity, and often try to convince others of this viewpoint as earnestly as they try to convince themselves.

Most of the Lost are not aware of the powers at their disposal, and the ones who do possess Arts use them without conscious knowledge of what they are doing. Many possess the *Kenning* Ability, able to see chimerical things even if they don't believe in them. It is up to the Storyteller to determine if a particular Lost fae possesses Arts and Agendas; some of the Lost have no control over their powers.

Those Lost who do have fae seemings have the features of their kith but appear sickly and gaunt. The further they distance themselves from their connection to the Dreaming, the more sickly they appear.

The Lost can sometimes be educated and brought into changeling society, but often they have no early instruction after the transformation into

one of the kinain and thus cloak themselves in comfortable mundanity. Some Lost seek out changelings and attempt to "cure" them, as a sort of twisted revenge for the "madness" inflicted in the form of the Dreaming.

CURSED

Kithain who have so lost themselves in their vengeance that they cannot think of anything else become the Cursed. Once he swears the Oath of Vengeance, the changeling dedicates his existence to a vendetta fueled by black hate and rage. The Cursed will stop at nothing to achieve their goals of vengeance, attempting to destroy any obstacles in their paths.

The Cursed still retain full use of their cantrips in their pursuit of vengeance. Cantrips are generally used only to achieve their goal or remove obstacles in their path. Indeed, the Cursed no longer take pleasure from Glamour; to them, Glamour and Banality serve equally as tools in the thirst for revenge.

The seemings of the Cursed reflect the anger that has consumed them. Lines become sharper, and auras of palpable violence surround them. Their most frightening aspect is often their eyes, which reveal the fires of their hatred.

Cursed can only be saved through epic quests. As the Cursed have brought about their own Dooms with the power of an Oath, release comes only if the Cursed somehow manage to circumvent the Oath and achieve reconciliation. Since Oathbreaking is a dangerous and Banal act itself, the Cursed are caught in a dangerous and almost inescapable trap.

BLACK MAGICIANS

Black Magicians are fae concerned with the accumulation of power for its own sake. This quest for power and dominance leads the magician to seek out antithetical forces in an attempt to master the very powers that could destroy him.

Black Magicians make extensive use of cantrips; the power of Glamour is just as useful to these Dauntain as the threat of Banality. Indeed, sinister tales whisper that some Black Magicians are capable of augmenting their cantrips through the infusion of Banality. Fortunately, such tales remain unfounded.

The seeming of a Black Magician takes on sinister tones, becoming chilling and somber. The Black Magician burns with a cold flame of greed.

These Dauntain can only be saved if they are turned from the path of greed and self-destruction. Naturally, few who master such dangerous powers desire rescue, and a Black Magician may turn the full force of his Banality against his would-be rescuers simply to protect his perceived power.

NIHILISTS

Lassitude and depression mark Nihilists. These changelings have completely given up on existence, seeing nothing but loss and pain in life. Greed for Glamour makes them dangerous, however, as it is the only source of comfort for these self-defeated Dauntain.

Cantrips require the use of precious Glamour, and many Nihilists are unconsciously reticent to cast them because of this. When a Nihilist does use a cantrip, he often does so to avoid notice.

A contagious aura of despair surrounds the Nihilist, and her fae seeming becomes smaller as she shrinks from the world. Nihilists' fae seemings also fade and become indistinct, causing other Kithain to overlook them.

Obviously, only hope can restore a Nihilist. A Nihilist must be convinced of her own self-worth and of the necessity of action before Banality's grip can be broken.

APOSTATES

Fae who have taken the concept of the necessity of Winter to the extreme sometimes see Banality as the Kithain's only hope. Apostates therefore embrace Banality as the force that will shield the Kithain through the coming ages of darkness. Glamour is seen as a threat; without it, there can be no destructive Winter, and so Apostates seek to destroy or nullify sources of Glamour. Apostates try to convince others of this point of view with a religious fervor.

Apostates still use cantrips, but they bend the magic to suit their own needs. Ironically, cantrips are often used to destroy sources of Glamour.

The fae seemings of Apostates seem charged with nervous energy. Like the Cursed, the eyes of an Apostate are telling; they express the madness and hurt of the Apostate's spirit. The voile (chimerical clothing) of an Apostate often appears tattered and neglected as well.

Convincing an Apostate of the true value of Glamour is her sole means of salvation; Apostates can only return to their former faerie existence by recognizing the need for dreams.

TYPHOIDS

Through no fault of her own, the Typhoid has been infected with Banality. The Typhoid spreads the infection without realizing it and is terribly dangerous because she is not even aware of the contagion.

Typhoids very frequently do not remember that they have the ability to use Glamour, let alone cast cantrips. It is not that they are truly incapable, but the Banality infection often grounds them in mundanity and thus severs them from the wonder of their being.

Typhoids are not easily recognizable by specific changes in their seemings. The alterations are subtle but often give some hint about what is infecting the individual fae.

Typhoids are best rescued by severing them from their connection to Banality. Since a Typhoid usually has only one or two sources of Banality, it is often a fairly simple matter to identify the problem. Cutting the Typhoid off is more difficult, since most Typhoids aren't willing to give up their addictive habits.

DAUNTAIN POWERS

The Dauntain, the hunters of changelings, have their own special powers; as supernatural creatures themselves, they often use changeling magic. However, they also draw on the dark powers of Banality. Dauntain often possess Stigmas, which are permanent marks of Banality on their fae miens. Additionally, Dauntain use Agendas, which function as cantrips fueled by Banality.

STIGMAS

Stigmas represent the Dauntain's ties to Banality. They largely represent the Dauntain's ability to dull the Glamour of people around them. These powers mute the Dauntain's fae soul, extending their touch even to the character's fae mien. Because the changeling appears so mundane, she is two Traits up on any challenge to defend against a *Kenning* attempt. Many Stigmas are unconscious, passive powers, always affecting the world around the Dauntain.

A Storyteller has the option of giving any Dauntain whose permanent Banality reaches nine a second Stigma, though it should be done with caution, as these Advantages are quite powerful. Stigmas are quite individualized, but some of the more common are listed here to give you ideas for creating your own. All Stigmas act as Chimerical (as opposed to Wyrd) effects unless noted.

CONVERSION

Some Dauntain possess the ability to transform other Kithain's Glamour directly into Banality. In order to accomplish this end, the Dauntain engages in a Simple Test with his target. In the case of a tie, he compares his permanent Banality to his target's permanent Glamour. If the Dauntain is successful, the target has one point of temporary Glamour changed into a Trait of temporary Banality.

DISBELIEF

Through the strength of their disbelief, many Dauntain are able to weaken the very substance of the Dreaming, eroding Glamoured effects and chimera. This Stigma comes into effect automatically when the Dauntain encounters these phenomena. A Simple Test is performed before any Glamour-related challenge can be performed on the Dauntain (ties, again, compare the Dauntain's permanent Banality to the changeling's permanent Glamour). Furthermore, the changeling is automatically two Traits down if the power he plans to use is Wyrd. If the Dauntain is successful, he is entitled to an automatic retest against the changeling's upcoming challenge.

Animate chimera who encounter a Dauntain with this Stigma must perform a similar test, and they suffer one Health Level of Chimerical damage if they fail.

The Dauntain may choose to inhibit a changeling or chimera further by spending a Willpower Trait and engaging in a second test. This follow-up test inflicts an additional Chimerical Health Level of damage if the Dauntain is successful.

ERASURE

This power is similar to Ravaging but does not require knowledge of its target. By touching a person, a Dauntain with this Stigma may choose to engage in a Simple Test to remove Glamour from a person or changeling. No initial Trait is bid, and ties are broken by pitting the Dauntain's number of permanent Banality Traits against the victim's permanent Glamour. If she wins, the Dauntain may strip a Trait of temporary Glamour from her target and gain a Trait of temporary Banality.

HATRED

The power of the Dauntain's hate is so strong that he may now attempt to weaken one of the fae directly. Just by focusing his energy on the changeling (and spending a Mental Trait), the Dauntain removes a Trait of temporary Glamour from the changeling automatically. This action requires complete concentration and occupies the Dauntain's full attention for the entire turn.

IRON WARD

The Dauntain's connection to Banality has increased the her resistance to cold iron, usually the bane of all fae. A Dauntain with this Stigma is allowed to attempt to turn damage suffered from cold iron weapons from aggravated to normal by winning a Simple Test for each wound inflicted. Thus, a Dauntain who suffered two Health Levels of damage would be required to win two Simple Tests in order to receive two normal wounds instead of two aggravated wounds.

NUMB

A surprising number of Nihilists exhibit this specific Stigma or something similar. *Numb* is the power to cut off a person's sense of emotional attachment. The power is similar to *Conversion* in that it turns a Trait into temporary Banality, but *Numb* is an unconscious power. On first meeting the Dauntain, a fae must engage him in a Simple Test (ties comparing the changeling's Glamour to the Dauntain's Banality). If the fae loses, she must lose a temporary Willpower Trait for the evening. Furthermore, she gains an additional Trait of temporary Banality. An individual changeling may be affected by this power only once per game session.

AGENDAS

Agendas are the Dauntain powers that loosely resemble the Kithain's cantrips. Though Agendas require the same number of Experience Traits to purchase as Cantrips, they are slightly easier to use than cantrips. Instead of performing a Bunk, Dauntain are required to spend Glamour to cast their magic, because of the intrinsically boring nature of the Agendas.

One very interesting note about Agendas and cantrips is that their use can often be the Dauntain's one best chance for salvation. Each time a Dauntain wishes to use an Agenda or cantrip, she must spend a point of Banality on top of any Glamour requirements. Note that this does not remove temporary Banality in the normal sense. A Dauntain has a Banality Pool equal to his permanent Banality, which may be replaced through a form of Epiphany called Tedium. By using unusual powers, the Dauntain is allowing a spark of magic back into her life.

Many Agendas' effects are not particularly concrete, and they require the target to roleplay out the results. Agendas are often quite subtle. Though they do not produce the spectacular effects of Arts like *Ensnare* or *Prometheus' Fist*, their effects on a game can be just as significant if, for example, you have 10 changelings walking around a party doing nothing but discussing the most recent episode of *Friends*.

BURNOUT

Many Dauntain exhibit the ability to sap people's will and turn their thoughts to the most boring activities. If their usual boring manner is not enough to do the trick, the Dauntain can use *Burnout* to help them along.

BASIC
Mindblock

The Dauntain makes his target unable to think about any one topic of the Dauntain's choice. A troll may be made to avoid thinking about duty or the chamberlain to forget the schedule for a court session.

The Dauntain must win a Social Challenge against his target for this power to succeed. If he is successful, his victim is not able to think about one topic of the caster's choice for 15 minutes of game play.

Type: Chimerical

Heartbind

Very similar to *Mindblock* in focus, *Heartbind* allows you to make a target unable to feel one positive emotion. Truly deep emotions, such as those caused by the Merit: *True Love*, are much harder to affect but still susceptible.

A Social Challenge is once again required for this power to succeed. A fae with *True Love* (if you are attempting to make the target not feel love) or another such strong and pure emotion, puts the Dauntain at a great disadvantage. She is automatically three Traits down in such a challenge. This effect lasts 15 minutes, just like *Mindblock*.

Type: Chimerical

INTERMEDIATE

Acquisition

The target of this Agenda will become obsessed with collecting a specific type of object for the duration of the effect. The thing to be acquired will be something trivial and relatively mundane ("I must have every hair scrunchie in this city, now!").

Once again, the Dauntain must engage the target in a Social Challenge, but in this case, the effect lasts for the remainder of the game session. The victim must spend a Willpower Trait to concentrate on anything other than his obsession, and even so, the concentration lasts for only 10 minutes.

Type: Chimerical

ADVANCED

Geek Out

At this level of power, the Dauntain may force a person or changeling to replace the subject most dear to her heart with some new, trivial and mundane hobby.

If the Dauntain succeeds in winning a Social Challenge against his victim, the victim gains the Negative Social Trait *Dull* x 2 and must engage a Narrator in a Static Challenge each day in order to break away from the new pastime. For each complete week spent under the effect of this Agenda, a fae gains one temporary Banality Trait.

Type: Chimerical

STULTIFY

As opposed to *Burnout*, which affects emotions and passions, the Agenda of *Stultify* dulls or changes the way in which a person perceives the world. The master of *Stultify* is very frequently the "efficiency expert," highly skilled at picking apart an organization and ferreting out those people who aren't "pulling their weight."

BASIC

Dull Impulse

After winning a Mental Challenge against his target, the Dauntain can make a person perform a dull task repeatedly for 15 minutes. Oven cleaning or restocking the shelves of a local convenience store are examples of the type of thing one might do if affected by this Agenda.

Type: Chimerical

Proselytize

If the Dauntain wins a Mental Challenge against his target, the victim performs as if she were suffering the effects of *Dull Impulse*. Furthermore, the victim attempts to recruit people to join her in her task. If the victim is able to convince anyone to join her, the Dauntain gains a temporary Banality Trait.

Type: Chimerical

INTERMEDIATE

Procedural Addiction

This Agenda allows the Dauntain to make a person care more about how she does something than what she does. The target, if she loses a Mental Challenge, examines one action in such a way that, for the remainder of the evening, it will take twice as long to perform that action as it normally would.

Type: Chimerical

ADVANCED

Micro-Management

Similar to *Procedural Addiction*, Micro-Management is broader in both scope and duration. The Dauntain makes a Mental Challenge against her target; if she wins, the victim finds himself creating procedures for everything he does over the course of the evening. The affected person attempts to teach everybody around him the new procedures, and he insists on having things done his way. On top of all else, the affected person acquires the Negative Mental Trait *Oblivious* and the Negative Social Trait *Dull* for the rest of the session.

Type: Chimerical

WEBCRAFT

Conformity is one of Banality's greatest weapons. Some Dauntain are able to tap into the forces of conformity — called the Weaver by the Garou — in an attempt to make others go along with their worldviews. To this end, the Dauntain try to bind everything in the lifeless web of the Weaver.

BASIC

Weave Web

This Agenda allows the caster to strengthen an inanimate object by making it a perfect example of its Platonic Ideal. The substance gains two Traits in all challenges, regardless of whether these challenges are defensive or offensive. Just like Weapon Traits, these Traits may not be bid but are used for the purpose of determining ties.

Type: Wyrd

Overwhelming Wincing

Through the use of this Agenda, the caster becomes so painfully dull that everyone around him winces and is overcome by a debilitating headache. One person (of the Dauntain's choice) is particularly affected; she must enter into a Mental Challenge with the Dauntain. If the victim loses, she is two Traits down for the next 10 minutes and will be hard-pressed to do anything other than cringe in pain. For each additional Banality Trait spent, the Dauntain may affect one extra person.

Type: Chimerical

INTERMEDIATE

Warp Will

In order to use this Agenda, the Dauntain must publicly perform some boring action and spend a Trait of temporary Banality. All people within 10 paces of the character are affected, and they must make a Static Challenge versus a Narrator (difficulty equal to the Dauntain's current Banality). Those characters who lose the challenge lose either a temporary Willpower or temporary Banality Trait for the remainder of the evening (the Dauntain must state which Trait he is trying to affect when he uses the power). This Agenda may only affect a character once per evening.

Type: Chimerical

ADVANCED

Wend Your Way

The caster is able to perform one task in such a way that it becomes so complicated that most people will lose interest in the process and not even be able to figure out what the task is. Watching the grass grow is easier, and far more fun, than trying to figure out what the Dauntain is doing. Any character wishing to initiate a challenge related to the caster's activity must win a Mental Challenge — before making any other tests — in order to take the action at all.

Type: Chimerical

Chapter Six: Mummies – The Reborn

For some, the promise of life eternal is fulfilled — the continuation of identity, true life without loss, youth renewed. Empowered by ancient spells, these favored few die and live again, retaking their former bodies and retaining their memories. The Reborn thus have eternity to learn, teach and grow. Without the curse of vampirism, they enjoy the fruits of life; returning to their corpses after each death, they share the knowledge of the dead. Foremost among the Reborn are the ones created with the Egyptian Spell of Life. These are the true mummies, preserved and returned from the gates of the netherworld.

A mummy travels through an endless cycle of death and rebirth. The Spell of Life tethers the soul and allows it to travel the Underworld, eventually returning to its mortal home, revitalizing the body to live again. So empowered with life and knowledge ascendant, the mummies are often wise mystics, powerful allies — and dedicated foes.

The term "mummy" can be a bit of a misnomer. Though the 42 faithful followers of Horus, called the Shemsu-Heru, are invariably Egyptian and therefore suffered the funerary rituals of the Spell of Life, the Great Rite itself takes many forms. Different factions of Reborn do exist, and it is possible to be Reborn without benefit of the blessings of Horus and Isis. Other Reborn — the priests of ancient Central American civilizations, the preserved lords of Babylon and Sumeria, the Greek and later scholars who achieved immortality through alchemy and spells — claim many of the same benefits and powers. Still, the Great Rite is associated first and foremost with Horus and his following.

With age and experience come lassitude and detachment. As a result of their great age, most Reborn remain hidden from the affairs of other creatures. Though their powers make them formidable adversaries and their knowledge allows them to recognize the presence of vampires, werewolves and other such beings, the mummies have their own subtle wars to fight. Woe betide the supernatural entity whose agenda crosses a mummy's, though: The Reborn do not hesitate to hunt down and destroy those unfortunates who interfere with their plans.

ORIGINS

This section was based on **World of Darkness: Mummy, Second Edition**. It is not necessary to own this book to play a mummy, but you may find some useful background material to help you build your character.

LIFE ETERNAL

The process of life, death and rebirth for the mummy is a cyclical one. Upon the first, mortal death, the supplicant receives some form of spell — generally a variant of the so-called "Great Rite" but occasionally an elixir or other specialized application — which draws the soul back to the body. Then, at some indeterminate point (perhaps immediately, perhaps several weeks or months later), the subject rises again for a second life.

Once among the ranks of the Reborn, the immortal pursues a normal life punctuated by cycles of death. Decades or even a century are not out of the question for each new life, after which the soul descends into the Underworld for a time to revitalize its energies. Once the soul has gathered enough spiritual energy to return to life, the body is restored to youth, health and vigor and the mummy lives once more.

Each life of a mummy is just like a normal existence. The mummy remembers his name and identity (at least, to some degree) and has the opportunity to indulge in all of the normal pursuits of life — study, pleasure, procreation, work, hunting....

Once the mummy is dead, his soul travels to the Underworld like one of the Restless. Within the Underworld, the mummy has the opportunity to travel to a spiritual land to wait for rebirth — most Egyptian mummies follow the Ferryman Anubis to Amenti, the Dark Kingdom of Sand, but other Reborn travel to exotic Far Shores, guided by their own Ferrymen. Some mummies choose not to languish within the shadowy kingdoms of their kind and instead travel through the Shadowlands. By engaging in great deeds and working with other souls, these mummies may garner the energies necessary

to be born again. The mummy's soul resembles a wraith while it is in the Underworld, but the mummy retains his own abilities instead of gaining the powers of ghosts — a curious exchange that has led more than one antagonistic apparition to a Harrowing.

A mummy's body and soul always remain inviolate. Reduced to ashes, the body will eventually re-form as it is repaired by the soul; torn to spiritual flinders, the soul hovers in some barely aware state in the farthest corners of the Tempest, husbanding its strength until it can return. For the mummy, there is no escape, ever.

MUMMY CHARACTERS

As immortals with hundreds or thousands of years of experience, mummies are powerful and cunning adversaries. Their strengths lie not in terrifying powers or great physical prowess, though; rather, mummies are creatures of long years, wisdom and subtle magic. As a result, mummies generally do not have spectacular supernatural capabilities but are instead possessed of a great deal of knowledge accumulated over the ages.

MUMMY TYPES

Although the stereotype of the funerary Egyptian mummy is firmly planted in the minds of horror movie watchers everywhere, there are as many types of Reborn as there are different cultures to spawn them. For game purposes, it's simplest to separate them into four basic categories: Shemsu-Heru, Ishmaelites, Cabiri and "the Others."

SHEMSU-HERU

Five thousand years ago, the brothers Osiris and Set fought for control of Egypt. Turned into creatures of darkness, the brothers slaked their thirst upon the people of the land and fought for rulership until Osiris triumphed over his brother and sent him into the lands beyond Egypt. Set swore that, were he banished to the darkness, that darkness would become all-powerful. He seems to have been correct — he returned, slaying Osiris and bringing forth his own brood of vampires, the Followers of Set. Only through the power of the Great Rite was Osiris avenged: His son Horus died and rose again as a mummy. Determined to claim vengeance for his father's death, Horus assembled followers (the Cult of Isis) and carefully chose the most loyal, noble and knowledgeable of his subjects to join him as Reborn. Those followers who stood with him in his crusade formed the Shemsu-heru.

When Horus first assembled the Reborn to stand against the armies of Set, he laid down certain strictures and called upon them all to uphold the balance of Maat against vampires and others who would twist the darkness to their own aims. The faithful among Horus's followers upheld this code through many lifetimes, fighting against the Followers of Set, protecting the balance of the cosmos, disdaining vampires and those who would traffic with foul powers. As the Shemsu-heru are perhaps the most active and most prominent of mummies, they are the image against which other Reborn are often compared.

UNWRAPPING THE MUMMY

STEP ONE: INSPIRATION

— Choose mummy type
— Choose Concept, Nature and Demeanor

STEP TWO: ATTRIBUTES

— Prioritize the three categories: Physical, Social, Mental (7/5/3)
— Choose Physical Traits
— Choose Social Traits
— Choose Mental Traits

STEP THREE: ADVANTAGES

— Choose nine Abilities
— Record Basic *Necromancy* Hekau path
— Choose three Basic Hekau paths
— Choose three Backgrounds or Influences

STEP FOUR: FINISHING TOUCHES

— Record Virtue Traits (7)
Record Ba Traits (5)
Record Ka Traits (5)
Record Sekhem Traits (3)
Record Humanity Traits (5)
Record Willpower Traits (3)
Choose Negative Traits, if any
Purchase Merits and Flaws, if any
Spend Free Traits (10)
Select Hekau spells (One per level of Hekau)

STEP FIVE: SPARK OF LIFE

In the modern age, there remain only 42 Shemsu-heru (not including Horus himself). They are largely faithful to the will of Horus, and as such they are dedicated opponents of vampires and infernal servants. The Shemsu-heru are the mummies most likely to go to Amenti, the Dark Kingdom of Sand, during their time in the Underworld. They still call upon one another and upon their patron, Horus, for assistance and information — and, indeed, Horus's zeal in his most current incarnation leads him to call together the Shemsu-heru, following a vision that he saw during his time in the Shadowlands.

The Shemsu-heru trace their lineage far into the past and to a rigorous selection process by the Cult of Isis, and they often proclaim themselves the greatest and only "true" Reborn. Their loyalty to Horus binds them together as no other group of mummies; they number more than any other group and trade information and assistance more regularly than other mummies (except, perhaps, among some of the ancients of the Central American cultures — but little is known of such mummies, even by other Reborn).

Shemsu-heru fit many stereotypes of mummies, so they are fairly straightforward to play. Should a mummy show up in a chronicle, the Shemsu-heru are the standard by which the character will be judged. They make excellent adversaries (especially for vampires with long-range plots) and intriguing (if rare) characters — though it is unlikely in the extreme that more than one would ever be found in a given locality. Players of such mummies must be certain to properly portray the attitudes of Horus and the tenets of his Code — at least publicly.

THE ISHMAELITES

When Horus issued his decrees and began his crusade against the Accursed, some questioned his wisdom and will. Unwilling to spend eternity waging a war not their own, these mummies chose to forge their own destiny. The first, Ishmael, traded harsh and bitter words with Horus before he was banished from the ranks of the Shemsu-heru and from Egypt. Others soon followed; similarly banished, they spread across the world, finding their own places in immortality and taking Ishmael's name as their symbol of separation.

In the latter days of Egypt's time as an empire, when it fell under Roman sway, other mummies were made who were not counted among the Shemsu-heru. Indeed, the Cult of Isis itself was infiltrated and corrupted to perform the Great Rite upon many candidates without regard to the harsh regimen of selection practiced in the past. Only when Horus himself awoke and intervened did this practice change. Even so, many mummies had been made for whom there was no account, and they too often left Egypt to pursue their own fortunes, so they are also counted among the Ishmaelites. It is not known how many were truly created, only that the Great Rite was indeed performed several times over the centuries while Horus slept in the Underworld.

Ishmaelite characters are generally Egyptian in concept, just like the Shemsu-heru, but they have more independence. Indeed, some (such as those mummies created in the later days of Egypt) know little of Horus or the other Reborn.

THE CABIRI

In the sixth century B.C. a new form of the Great Rite surfaced, this time passed to a Greek magician by an individual claiming to be an Egyptian mummy named Cabirus. The magician recorded the Great Rite and returned home to Thessalonica, there to spread his works. These *Secret Writings of Cabirus* went on to become the basis for mystery cults over the years — each time, a copy of the writings would surface and a new mummy would eventually be created, at which time the writings would mysteriously disappear and the cult would crumble. For over 2000 years, this cycle continued, a new mummy surfacing every two centuries or so.

Horus himself hunted down what was believed to be the last copy of the *Secret Writings* during the Renaissance, destroying it in accordance with his own Code. Even so, at least a handful of new Cabiri have surfaced since then. The exact number of Cabiri remains unknown at this time, but they all follow a pattern of Greek magics as handed down from the interpretive *Secret Writings*.

A Cabirus character is suitable for a Reborn outside Egyptian culture. Created during the Dark Ages and in various parts of Europe, each Cabirus mummy has a unique perspective on eternal life, often quite divorced from the views of Horus. These mummies could conceivably be created anew even in the modern age, though such a character would be exceedingly rare.

THE OTHERS

When the Shemsu-heru speak of mummies, they speak only of themselves and of mummies created by the Egyptian Great Rite. They do not mention the Reborn of other cultures, those people who sought and found eternal life in days before Egypt's splendor.

In the West, mummies come from Peru and Mexico, from the ancient and vanished cultures of South and Central America. These mummies often held positions as priest-kings, but now, weary of their thousands of years, they find comfortable niches in as advisors and mystics in their homelands — not so different from the old ways. In the Far East, the arts of China and Japan yield ancients to whom the secrets of immortality come through rigorous study and exercise. These immortals confound even the other Reborn; some never die at all but instead exist in a permanent harmonious balance of life.

THE CODE OF HORUS

Before leaving Egypt, Horus issued a set of commandments to the various mummies of the sands. Though some follow the commandments to the letter, they are often widely interpreted, because each mummy brings millennia of personal experience to each stricture. Among the mummies of Egypt, one can usually trace the distinction between Shemsu-heru and Ishmaelite to some section of the Code.

I.   I am Horus, your Father, the First-Among-Reborn. Heed my words always.

Obviously, mummies aside from the Shemsu-heru pay this credo little heed. Even the loyal among Horus's brood have been known to conveniently interpret or twist his words from time to time.

II.   Combat the minions of Apophis, in all their different forms, at all times, for they are the opponents of Maat.

Most mummies uphold some sort of respect for balance, if not in the form of Egypt's Maat. Still, the millennia can wear thin, and Reborn often find better ways to spend the centuries than to engage in perpetual warfare. Some among the Reborn continue to fight in the struggle against chaos, but this is more of a personal choice than one born of any loyalty.

III.   Consort not with the Accursed, for they are of the brood of Apophis.

Obviously, vampires vex Horus greatly, particularly the Setites — after all, Set did kill his father, Osiris. Most mummies view Horus' single-minded crusade as rather ridiculous. Besides, the immortal vampires are the only other company that a mummy can consistently keep over centuries of successive lives. However, most mummies are still wary of Cainites, even if they do not fight them — vampires have a way of drawing others into their labyrinthine plots.

IV.   Acknowledge your kinship in Maat with one another: Never shall one of the Shemsu-heru turn away another in need.

Though the 42 Shemsu-heru still pay some homage to this law, most mummies devote their lives to their own pleasures and agendas after a few centuries. As a result, the typical Reborn has better things to do than pursue the needs of another mummy (as evidenced by the Ishmaelites and their abandonment of Horus's crusade). Still, when there are only a handful of other people in the world like you, kinship is dear.

V.   Let not a mortal worship you, for the time of gods is past, nor let the mortal populace learn of our existence.

Cultism is mostly gone from the societies of the Reborn, except in the most remote and primitive areas of the globe. Mortal cults and worshippers do not directly provide any sort of real sustenance or profound spiritual aid to mummies; consequently, they are not terribly important pursuits.

VI.   Seek not to create others like us.

The Cabiri frustrate Horus to no end, as do the others among the Reborn. Few truly understand Horus' motives in this proclamation; very few mummies could ever invoke the Spell of Life, and much of its working has been lost to time — in general, the birth of a new Reborn is at the hands of some particularly talented and dedicated mortal seeker. Perhaps this commandment is meant to avoid the creation of any more flawed abominations like the Children of Apophis.

Regardless of origin, the Others are troubling indeed to the Shemsu-heru. The mummies of Egypt would ignore these scattered exceptions, but time and fate have a way of drawing the ancients together. So it is that most of the mummies of Egypt are cautiously aware of the Others' existence—though they know little else.

For players, the Others are exotic and unusual in the extreme. An ancient from the height of the Inca empire would be as radically different from the Shemsu-heru as a Taoist immortal of Japan. The only thing that can be said concretely of them is that they, too, share the blessings and curses of life eternal. Should one appear in a chronicle, it is highly unlikely that he would reveal his true nature or conversely that it would ever be discerned correctly by any observer. Storytellers making use of the Others are encouraged to gift them with unpredictable magics and treasures, as they hail from cultures far different from the Egyptian norms described here.

MUMMY TRAITS

A mummy character selects Physical, Social and Mental Traits and Ability Traits just like any other character. Use the adjectives and descriptions from any of the **Mind's Eye Theatre** books, but remember that certain type-specific Traits — such as *Primal Urge* from **Laws of the Wild** or *Kenning* from **The Shining Host** — are not usable by mummies. Similarly, the Reborn may purchase Merits and Flaws as described in several other **Mind's Eye Theatre** books, as long as they are generally applicable (a mummy could have the *Clear Sighted* Merit, for instance, but the vampiric Merit: *Efficient Digestion* would be pointless).

Additionally, mummies are measured by the strength of their souls. Though a mummy can and does die periodically, the energies of the soul continue. As the mummy exists in the Underworld, the soul recharges, eventually allowing the body to re-form and granting life anew. The mummy's additional Traits are Virtue Traits, which describe the mummy's ability to resist the lassitude of the centuries, and Soul Traits, detailing the power of the mummy's soul and magical abilities.

VIRTUE TRAITS

Mummies have three Virtue Traits: Memory, Integrity and Joy. Each Virtue is used to resist the pull of the centuries upon the mummy. As a mummy grows out of touch with her former humanity, she loses any connection to thought and emotion. Only the strongest convictions can drive a mummy to continue after countless centuries of existence.

Each of the three Virtues is rated simply in terms of Traits, much like Willpower. A mummy can have from one to five permanent and temporary Traits in each Virtue. Temporary Traits are expended when a mummy makes an effort to rely upon the Virtue; the mummy taxes the limits of his Memory,

the strength of his Joy or the conscience of his Integrity. Permanent Traits are lost if the mummy suffers a lapse of Virtue — if the mummy utterly fails to remember a past life, gives in to the temptations of Apophis or succumbs to bleak lassitude and despondency.

CHILDREN OF APOPHIS

Horus's eternal minions, the Shemsu-heru, proved difficult for Set to counter. With their unremitting hostility, unusual magic and inevitable resurrections, they could plague the Followers of Set forever. To take care of the problem, Set cast about for ways to create mummies of his own.

Using a stolen ritual extracted from the Cult of Isis, Set's priests turned seven victims into mummies. However, the version of the Great Rite captured by Set was corrupted. Dark spirits came at the call of the rite, joining with the souls of the victims and twisting their physical forms. The rite succeeded, but each victim became a horribly monstrous creature, deformed, malevolent and completely insane.

There are only seven of these so-called Bane Mummies in existence, and no more have ever been created — they have proven too difficult for Set to control effectively. Bane Mummies are not suitable for play but can make terrifying adversaries. Tutu the Doubly Evil, Hemhemti the Roarer, Amam the Devourer, Qetu the Evil-Doer, Hau-hra of the Backward Face, Saatet-ta, Darkener of the Earth, and Kharebutu the Fourfold Fiend are the names of the Children of Apophis, and their powers, temperaments and visages tend to match their given names. In addition to the plethora of mummy powers, the Children of Apophis generally evidence one or two unusual abilities or deformities, such as a horribly distended jaw capable of biting through anything (in the case of Amam the Devourer).

In addition to Virtue Traits, mummies track their ties to their lost lives through Humanity Traits. Just like mortals, mummies possess some vestige of Humanity — however, since the mummy is no longer truly mortal, that humanity is nothing more than a reflection, a tie to a lost existence formerly defined (instead of casually interrupted) by death. Thus, although a mummy chooses Humanity Traits just like a mortal character, these Traits are not ever used; they simply track a mummy's slide into depravity or ennui.

MUMMY FREE TRAIT AND EXPERIENCE TRAIT COSTS

Attribute or Ability Trait	One Free or Experience Trait
Remove Negative Trait	Two Experience Traits
Influence or Background Trait	One Free or Experience Trait
Virtue or Soul Trait	Two Free or Experience Traits
Basic Hekau Path	Three Free or Experience Traits
Intermediate Hekau Path	Six Experience Traits
Advanced Hekau Path	Nine Experience Traits
New Hekau Ritual	Two, four or six Experience Traits (forBasic, Intermediate, or Advanced)
New Object/Animal True Name	One Experience Trait
Humanity Trait	Awarded only at Storyteller's discretion
Purchase Merit or Remove Flaw	Cost of Merit/Flaw in Free Traits or twice its cost in Experience Traits

New mummy characters get one Trait in each Virtue for free and may spread seven more Traits among the Virtues. They also begin play with five Humanity Traits.

Virtue Tests

In certain circumstances, a Storyteller or Narrator may call for a test of Virtue. Such a Virtue Test is a Static Challenge, with a difficulty dependent upon the Virtue in question (see the individual Virtue descriptions, following). The player of the mummy makes a single test with the Storyteller, risking the particular Virtue. In general, a particular mummy character should not have to make more than three Virtue tests total in any given session; more than that is likely to rapidly reduce the mummy to unplayability.

Success in a Virtue Test represents the inner strength of the mummy — the character sorts through thousands of years to recall a lost love or a dire foe, stands up against the temptation of an easy and pleasurable life in order to pursue duty instead or realizes that hope remains even in the World of Darkness.

MUMMY TRAIT MAXIMUMS

Blessed with immortality and the potential to spend centuries accumulating skills and wisdom, it's not out of the question for a mummy to possess unlimited Traits. Possible, yes. Recommended, no.

Mummy Trait maximums ideally should be based on the age of the mummy in question. A Reborn created within the last century should not have the potential for as much power as one of Horus' original band from 5000 years ago — mummies, like vampires, are aware that with age comes power. It takes time to learn powerful Hekau or skill with crafts. Below are some suggested Trait maximums, although Storytellers may adjust these as their chronicles demand.

Mummy's Age	Trait Max.	Willpower Max.
5000 years+	20	9
2000 years	18	8
1000 years	16	7
500 years	13	5
200 years	11	4
100 years or less	10	4

Failure indicates a lapse in Virtue. When a player fails a Virtue Test, the mummy character suffers from certain debilitations, as denoted in the appropriate Virtue description.

Upon failing a Virtue test, a player may call for a single retest by risking a Virtue Trait. If the player wins the retest, the Virtue Trait is temporarily lost; the mummy taxes her inner reserves and may succumb to weakness more easily later, but she remains true for the time being. If the retest fails, the Virtue Trait risked is lost *permanently*, and the mummy character immediately gains a Derangement chosen by the Storyteller (most often associated in some twisted form with the failed Virtue).

Humanity

Overwhelmed by the centuries, a mummy can all too easily succumb to black irrationality and insanity. The mummy must fight to translate her ageless existence into terms comprehensible by her once-human perceptions. This is the mummy's struggle for Humanity, the need to have a framework with which to understand the universe.

Mummies can have up to 10 Humanity Traits and can lose them just as described on the Humanity Trait chart in Chapter Two, but they never actually use Humanity — the Traits simply track a mummy's ability to keep her eternal life in some sort of perspective. Should a mummy ever permanently run out of Humanity Traits, she succumbs to mindless monstrosity, her sanity and reason overthrown by the weight of the years, and turns into nothing more than a killing machine — such characters are no longer suitable for play. Note that mummies do not normally test for Humanity loss in the same fashion as mortals; instead of making Simple Tests to check for Humanity loss, mummies undergo tests of the Integrity Virtue, as described below.

A mummy's Humanity also defines how well she identifies with and interacts with mortals and humans. When interacting with normal humans (except in challenges of intimidation), the mummy may never bid more Social Traits than twice her Humanity Trait total, including bonus Traits. Thus, an inhuman mummy is much more likely to fail challenges against mortals while attempting to influence or persuade them, as the mortals sense the detachment and sociopathic nature of the mummy.

Memory

The Memory Virtue Traits represent a mummy's ability to recall and sort information from past lives. For a creature with 5000 years of existence, the past is never as fresh as yesterday. The difficulty of drawing out subtle information is immense. A stranger could be an old enemy or a simple lookalike. A buried hoard could have been dug up and moved, or it just might not be where the mummy remembers putting it a century before. The number of Traits in this Virtue represents the strength of the mummy's recall — with several Traits, the mummy is better able to sort through the myriad facts and minutiae of the millennia.

Tests of Memory are required when a mummy must dig through the archives of thousands of years of experience in order to remember something of importance. Remembering the face of a lost love, the location of an important tomb or the nature of an ancient ritual can all call for a test of this sort. The Static difficulty of a Memory test is usually three Traits, but it can be higher if the Narrator or Storyteller decides that the mummy is fighting to remember a particularly convoluted and unpleasant piece of information.

A failed Memory test causes the mummy to suffer from the permanent Negative Trait *Forgetful* or *Oblivious* (at the player's discretion). These Traits are cumulative, should the player fail several tests. They can be removed normally through experience and play.

Integrity

With the strength of conviction comes the ability to perform duties for eternity. Though many mummies began as soldiers in Horus' war, they found their own causes and beliefs to support over the passing years. Integrity measures the strength of a mummy's dedication to his causes and beliefs. When faced with a moral dilemma, the mummy must rise to the occasion, treading the difficult path even though it would be easier to let time cover all tracks. As the saying goes, who we are is best defined by what do when nobody's watching.

An Integrity test is called for when the mummy slips into vice or decadence — either by failing to uphold his own code or by being lured into callousness or uncaring deeds. Moral choices are always difficult, but for a mummy, they are the only compass against existence as an unending, mindless abomination. The Static difficulty of the test is usually three Traits, but it can be higher for particularly heinous deeds.

Note that a test of Integrity is not necessary if the mummy is already particularly inhumane; a mummy with only two remaining Humanity Traits, for example, probably needn't make an Integrity test for simply killing someone, as the character has already done far, far worse. Such a monster would need to perform truly demented acts to call for Integrity tests and lose his last few Humanity Traits (use the Humanity loss table in Chapter Two for guidelines).

A failed Integrity test causes the character to immediately lose one permanent Humanity Trait.

Joy

How can the pleasures of life continue to sustain one after everything has been experienced? When the world has changed into a morass of miscellaneous color, noise and technology, what joy comes from a meaningless existence devoid of place? A mummy must cling to the smallest shreds of hope, to the events that remind her of her human days. The Joy Virtue represents the spark of inner contentment that wells forth when the mummy has need for hope, compassion or happiness.

A Virtue Test of Joy may be called for whenever the mummy discovers something terrible about the world to which she has awakened ("Hundreds of children die of starvation each year, but no government does anything about it.") or when she has the opportunity to experience — or fail to experience — a moment of something astoundingly fresh and new ("These are how we tell our stories now — movies."). The Static difficulty of the test is usually three Traits, but it can be higher for a particularly devastating piece of news.

A failed Joy test inflicts the character with the permanent Negative Trait *Callous* or *Condescending* (at the player's discretion). These Traits are cumulative with failed tests. They can be removed normally with play and experience.

SOUL TRAITS

The mummy's soul consists of many parts. The Egyptians believed that the soul contained no less than 11 distinct parts; other Reborn have similar divisions of spiritual energy. As a result, all mummy characters have particular Soul Traits, measuring their strengths of spirit. The Soul Traits, just like Willpower and Virtue Traits, are simply measured with Trait values, without the use of particular adjectives.

All Reborn possess three Soul Traits: Ba, the ghostly soul that floats through the Underworld during times of death; Ka, the guardian spirit that watches over the body (*khat*) while it is dead; and Sekhem, the aura, the wellspring of magical power. Mummy characters may possess anywhere from one to 10 Traits in each category.

Ba

The Ba is the soul which most closely resembles a ghost or wraith. When a mummy dies, the Ba is released from the body to travel the Underworld for a time, there to gather energies until it can revitalize the corpse.

There is no "permanent" Ba Trait record; all mummies can track anywhere from no Ba energy to 10 Traits' worth. This Ba energy can only be reclaimed in the spirit worlds; the mummy's Ba soul must be in the Underworld to gather new Ba Traits.

Ba Traits are spent as the mummy runs out of life-force; every few years of life (two or three for a fast-paced lifestyle, up to 20 or more for a monastic and ascetic lifestyle) the mummy automatically loses one Ba Trait. When the mummy runs out of Ba (and all mummies can sense the depletion of their Ba energy), the body dies once more, freeing the soul to gather more energy in the Underworld. Mummies can also heal injury with Ba energy. In general, one Ba Trait heals one Health Level of damage to a mummy. Certain forms of magic may call upon the Ba as well.

While dead, a mummy's Ba soul wanders the Underworld in a form much like a wraith. Usually, the mummy slowly accrues new Ba Traits, which can be used to rebuild the body and live again. However, some mummies undertake great deeds in the land of spirits, the better to revitalize their souls. In the Underworld, a mummy can gain Ba Traits by engaging in a powerful quest (like diving into the Tempest in search of a ghostly artifact), seeking out hidden knowledge that re-energizes the soul (by conversing with several Ferrymen, for instance, or traveling to the Far Shores), working for a powerful spirit who rewards the mummy with energy (protecting the ferry of Ra as it crosses the sky each day) or by finding a wellspring of natural power (at a werewolf sacred site or the like). In no case should a mummy regain more than one Ba Trait per game session, though; the soul must spend some time in the Shadowlands before returning to life.

Other Reborn have Ba Traits, but use different terms for them. Cabiri, for instance, use the Greek term Psyche. Still, the function of the soul remains the same.

Ka

When the body dies, the soul flees to the Underworld. However, legends abound of the mummy's curse, of the disasters and death that plague those explorers who would dare to disturb the resting corpse. These legends are true: While the mummy's Ba travels the Shadowlands, the spiritual double, the guardian Ka, waits and watches over the body.

The Ka is normally prominent only while the mummy is dead. It is usually invisible, but under certain circumstances it can materialize to perform a brief task. Generally, the Ka looks just like the mummy's body did in life, and it waits like a watchdog near the body — it does not have the mummy's consciousness but rather is more of an automaton, an ever-vigilant guardian snippet of spirit energy. Normally it can only travel within about 500 feet of the mummy's body and exists only in the Shadowlands, where it is unhindered by walls or obstacles (except for magical barriers that ward against ghosts and wraiths).

By expending Ka Traits, the Ka spirit may temporarily interact with the physical world. One Trait allows the Ka spirit to manifest as a ghostly form; this allows it to speak, though its range of expression is limited, as the mummy's true intelligence lies with the Ba. Such manifestation lasts for one scene.

While manifested, an additional Ka Trait can be expended to corporealize, allowing the Ka spirit to become solid; in this form, it has the mummy's normal Physical Traits (not affected by amulets or other spells that would be affecting the mummy's actual body), and it is unaffected by any attacks except ones that would inflict aggravated damage on supernaturals (like vampiric claws) or powers specifically designed to affect wraiths. Injury inflicted on the Ka simply causes it to lose Ka Traits; once the spirit runs out of Ka Traits, it is disrupted. As long as the Ka remains corporeal, it may use physical objects normally; special *Ushabti* objects (see "Hekau") also manifest with the Ka. Such corporealization lasts for a scene unless the Ka is prematurely disrupted by damage.

Though the Ka normally cannot travel more than a short distance from the body, the expenditure of a Ka Trait allows the spirit to travel for a full day and night away from the remains of the body (or the heart, if the body is dismembered). Should the spirit still be away from the body at the next sunset, another Ka Trait must be expended or the Ka discorporates.

The Ka spirit must be present at the location of the heart or its remains if the Ba is to revitalize the corpse. This has no actual cost, but only one Ba Trait may be transferred from Ba to Ka to body each turn, and this requires the full attention of the Ka.

Ka Traits are replenished naturally at a rate of one Trait per session. Also, the Ba may exchange a Ba Trait for a Ka Trait (though the reverse is not true). Finally, followers and admirers in the lands of the living can make sacrifices to the mummy, and the Ka can gain strength from this memory and devotion; a truly caring supplicant may leave offerings of jewelry, art or food near the tomb or body of the mummy and, by expending a Willpower Trait, empower the Ka with an additional Ka Trait (such a sacrifice may only be made once per session by any given individual).

Among Cabiri, the term for the Ka is the Eidolon, the image of the dead (not to be confused with the Trait from **Oblivion**).

Sekhem

Through the aura, the luminous sheen of spirit through which body and soul contact the universe, the Reborn are capable of magical feats. Egyptians term their magics Hekau, though Cabiri refer to their spells as Theourgia, but all Reborn power their feats through Sekhem.

Reborn have up to 10 Sekhem Traits. Unlike Ka and Ba Traits, Sekhem Traits are tracked differently for temporary and permanent Traits. Permanent Sekhem Traits represent the mummy's potential for shaping magical forces; an experienced magician can store and harness more forces than an uneducated peasant. Temporary Sekhem Traits are expended to cast spells and represent the magical energy "on hand" for the mummy.

Sekhem is regained through rest and meditation. A Reborn character automatically regains one temporary Sekhem Trait, up to her permanent total maximum, at the beginning of each new session. The player may also opt to expend *Meditation* Ability Traits at this time; each Trait expended allows a Simple Test (win or tie) to gain back an additional temporary Sekhem Trait. Some magical items can also hold Sekhem, and these may be drawn upon to refuel the Reborn as well.

Among Cabiri, Sekhem is called Pneuma, the animating force.

BACKGROUNDS

Owing to their extended life cycles, the Reborn often accumulate objects and contacts of great wonder. As a result, mummies are not limited solely to possession of Influences, although they can and do manage Influence just like other characters, as described in **Laws of the Hunt** or other **Mind's Eye Theatre** books (subject to the limit of total Influence not exceeding total Attribute Traits, of course).

In addition, mummies can possess the special Backgrounds of *Arcane*, *Artifact*, *Contacts*, *Journal*, *Mentor*, *Resources*, *Retainers* and *Tomb*, as described below. Each Background has a maximum value of five Traits.

Arcane

Eyes are naturally averted from you. People with cameras tend to miss you. Paperwork disappears from notice, and you become lost in the red tape.

Your *Arcane* Traits measure a quasi-mystical ability to disappear from notice. Although you are not actually invisible, people tend not to notice you, to forget you and to fail to keep accurate records of you.

In game terms, your *Arcane* Traits may be temporarily expended to allow for retests on challenges in which someone tries to notice or investigate you. Thus, if you are sneaking around a museum at night, you can use *Arcane* to see if the guard overlooks your presence; you could also use *Arcane* to find out if your traffic ticket got lost in the wheels of bureaucracy. Your *Arcane* Traits, once expended, return at the next game session. Note that you can consciously dampen your *Arcane* if you wish, so that you can be found.

Artifact

You possess an object of power, a device more than a simple talisman or amulet. This object is probably something that you've gathered from one of your past lives; very likely, it has powers that you cannot duplicate yourself.

The Traits placed in the *Artifact* Background represent the strength of a particular magical item in your possession. Like a werewolf fetish, the powers of the object depend upon the number of Traits invested. A one-Trait *Artifact* may be a simple blanket that always allows you to get a good night's sleep, whereas a five-Trait *Artifact* could be an enchanted crypt that rejuvenates your *khat* and channels power to your Ka for defense. The exact nature of the *Artifact* is subject to the Storyteller's approval; in general, see the types of devices that can be made with the *Enchantment* sorcery path and equate the Traits in this Background to levels in the path (so a one-Trait *Artifact* is roughly equivalent to a Basic-level *Enchantment* talisman). However, *Artifacts* are generally self-fueled and as such are reusable.

Contacts

You know people. These people happen to be in the know, too. For favors or money, you can get them to talk, to tell you secrets and to dig up dirt.

By expending a Trait of *Contacts*, your character may gather rumors and information, as described by a Storyteller. Each Trait expended allows you to gather information from an area of Influence as if you possessed the appropriate levels of Influence, so spending three *Contact* Traits could get you information (only) equivalent to three levels of *Industry* Influence, for example. Not all Traits need be expended at once or in the same category. The advantage of this Background lies in the contacts' ability to shift Influence categories — a contact can gain different types of information each month. All expended *Contacts* Traits return at the start of the next session.

This Background is also appropriate to characters in other games, if desired.

Journal

You've kept a record of your past lives. Though it may be difficult to remember events that happened 5000 years ago, you can rely on your writings to refresh your memory. You may only have a few hastily scribbled scraps, or perhaps you've kept extensive libraries. Either way, this journal is a bulwark against fading memory.

When forced to make a test of Memory, you may expend a temporary *Journal* Trait to gain one retest which does not risk your Memory Traits. You cannot use more than one retest with your *Journal* on any given Memory test, but you can use extra *Journal* Traits on successive tests. You can still risk your Memory Traits for an additional retest, as desired. Your *Journal* Traits refresh each game session — although your notes may not help you all the time, they are always there. However, since you must actually keep your writings in some form, they could conceivably be stolen or destroyed.

Mentor

Someone with knowledge and power looks out for you. Though you may have to do favors for this mentor and he may not tell you everything, you can usually rely on your mentor for some sort of aid or assistance when matters are beyond your ken.

By expending temporary *Mentor* Traits, you may call upon your teacher and advisor for assistance. You must roleplay out seeking contact with your *Mentor* — if your teacher is in Singapore without a phone, communication may be difficult. When contacted, the *Mentor* can do one of many different things:

• One *Mentor* Trait allows you to gather information from a specific *Lore* at one level above the level you currently know, so if you have *Vampire Lore* x 2, your mentor can tell you some choice bits of *Vampire Lore* x 3 for one game session.

• Two *Mentor* Traits can be swapped for one level of any Influence, one level of *Resources* or for one *Contact* — in this case, you draw upon your advisor's experience and material assistance.

• Two *Mentor* Traits can be used to try to learn a new power at the Basic level.

• Three *Mentor* Traits enable you to call upon your mentor to instruct you in the ways of an Intermediate power.

• Four *Mentor* Traits let you petition for assistance in learning an Advanced power.

• Five *Mentor* Traits allow you to ask your mentor to aid you in unearthing a Master-class power that you don't know, subject to your normal ability to learn it.

Once you have called upon your *Mentor* for aid, you must make a Simple Test. If you win, you gain the aid requested, subject to Storyteller approval. If you tie, your mentor aids you but requests some service in return. If you fail,

your mentor requires a service of you first and only then grants you aid. Once *Mentor* Traits are expended, your mentor has listened to your pleas, and the Traits only refresh at the next game session.

This Background can be appropriate to characters of other games and genres.

Resources

You have access to liquid capital and spending money. You also have some solid resources that you can use when times are tight. Unlike the use of *Finance*, these *Resources* are always readily available and come to you automatically due to your investments, jobs and holdings.

Your number of *Resources* Traits determines the amount of money and capital that you can secure. By expending temporary *Resources* Traits (which return at the next game session), you can draw upon your regular income, as shown in the accompanying table. If you expend permanent *Resources*, you can divest yourself of holdings, allowing access to ten times the amount shown on the table. However, the limits of what you can buy are always adjudicated by the Storyteller. Truly powerful uses of *Resources* are best left to downtimes and moderation between game sessions.

Resources is well-suited to other character types as well.

RESOURCE ALLOCATION

No Traits: Poverty. Income $200. Get roommates. Bus pass.

One Trait: Small savings and holdings; income $500. Have apartment, cheap means of transportation.

Two Traits: Modest savings and holdings; income $1,000. Have condo and motorcycle or modest car.

Three Traits: Significant savings and holdings; income $3,000. Own house, car.

Four Traits: Large savings and holdings. Income $10,000. Own large house or some small properties, two vehicles, some luxuries and unusual items.

Five Traits: Rich. Income $30,000. Own estate and grounds, multiple small properties, several vehicles, arts and treasures, luxury items.

Retainers

On your payroll are several loyal and competent (not necessarily simultaneously) staff. They aid you in your living and work and will defend your holdings and person if necessary. Your retainers watch over your plans when you can't be present and advance your cause to your specifications.

Each Trait placed in this Background represents one retainer. A retainer character generally does not show up in play; rather, the retainer manages the character's assets, protects the house, watches over research projects and so on. Retainers can also be sent to perform duties and tasks. In general, retainers do not form a private army; they are more like waitstaff, although a retainer could be a house security guard or valet. *Retainers* Traits can be assigned to various duties during or between games:

• A retainer can be assigned to watch over a particular location. Generally, this means that if someone takes the liberty of breaking into your house, the retainers there will attempt to stop the intruder. In this case, the retainers are treated as normal humans, run by Narrators.

• A retainer can be used to manage your assets and perform tasks. Retainers tied up in this fashion allow you to manage more Influence than normal; they add to the number of Attribute Traits that you possess for purposes of counting your total Influences. Each retainer directed in this fashion adds one to your maximum Influence Traits. If retainers are later lost, killed or reassigned, the excess Influence Traits are lost, starting with the highest levels of Influence held.

• A retainer can perform other menial functions, as allowed by the Storyteller. You can get someone else to pick up your character's drycleaning or order the pizza.

Retainers are not always completely loyal or competent, but they are generally solid in the character's support. You should work up a reason why the retainers work for you — do you pay them, or have you promised them secrets of occult power? Do they love you, or just do what you tell them in return for drugs? Your Storyteller may arrange to strip you of your retainers if you do not keep them adequately supplied with whatever they demand for obedience.

This Background can be appropriate for characters of other games.

Tomb

You've made funerary arrangements in advance. You know that your body must be protected, so you've set aside secret property with the means to hold your *khat* until you are reborn after your next death.

Your *Tomb* rating shows how much protection you can expect while your body lies dead (assuming that your corpse makes it to the tomb). Each Trait in your *Tomb* Background can be applied to a particular benefit; these benefits must be assigned when the *Tomb* is first purchased during character creation:

• A *Tomb* Trait spent toward preservation means that the tomb is well-stocked with refrigeration, bandages, sterile environments and other artifices to keep your *khat* from decaying. Each Trait assigned to preservation lengthens the amount of time between lost Health Levels due to decomposition —

with one preservation Trait, your dead body loses only one Health Level every two sessions; for two Traits, this extends to every three sessions; and so on.

• A *Tomb* Trait spent on traps and wards keeps out intruders. When someone attempts to violate your *Tomb*, the intruder must make one Static Mental Challenge (difficulty of your normal Mental Traits) for each Trait placed as a trap. *Security* can be used as a retest in this case. Alternately, the Storyteller may run a short session, forcing the player to overcome your traps and wards through cunning and roleplaying.

• A *Tomb* Trait spent on power means that your tomb rests in a place of mystical energy. This causes you to rejuvenate spiritual power more quickly. For each Trait spent on power, you get one Simple Test per game session while your body is dead; each test that you win or tie allows you to gain one Ba or Ka Trait (your choice).

Again, if you do not make sufficient provisions to keep track of your *Tomb*, the Storyteller may reduce its effectiveness or remove it entirely.

MUMMY STATUS

With only 42 Shemsu-heru and perhaps only a few hundred mummies worldwide, the pecking order and hierarchy of mummy society is at once fierce and loose. Immortals with disparate agendas have no need for social status games, but only other similar creatures can truly judge one's standing.

Mummy characters do not normally have mummy status. However, Mummy Status Traits may be purchased as a Background or awarded for exceptional deeds. This Status is then useful in many social situations:

• Mummy Status Traits may be added to social interactions with other mummies, bolstering the Reborn's total Social Traits.

• A holder of Mummy Status may temporarily gift someone else with Mummy Status. The gifter loses the Trait, but the recipient gains it. This gives the recipient some standing and importance in mummy society, so that other mummies are more likely to pay attention to the character. This is one of the few ways to recognize a mortal, vampire or other individual as a valuable ally. A loaned Trait like this can be revoked by the original giver at any time.

• Among mummies, orders and testimony are perceived according to Mummy Status. A mummy of no Status will not be believed if he accuses a holder of great Mummy Status of some heinous deed, whereas a holder of great Status (such as Horus) can issue orders and expect other mummies to obey.

Mummy Status Traits include *Divine, Even-Handed, Faithful, Inspiring, Judicious, Sagacious* and *Temperate*. Additional Traits can be made or assigned at need by Storytellers.

HEALTH LEVELS AND CORPUS

While living, mummies die just like regular mortals. A mummy hit by a truck probably separates his Ba and spends a decade in the Underworld.

Mummies use the same Health Level track as mortals. In addition, the mummy has two Health Levels past Mortally Wounded — count these both as Dead boxes. Once the mummy is dead, further injury can strike through the Dead boxes. The Dead Health Levels have no effect upon the game (except perhaps to show that the mummy's body is in a particular state of disarray), but the mummy must heal these levels with Ba energy before rising again (see "Death and Rebirth"). Health Levels for mummies regenerate just like mortals' levels; normal time and healing, as well as magical tricks, can revitalize a still-living body, as long as the mummy still has Ba energy. The only difference is that, having died before, the mummy's spiritual attachment to the body is slightly weaker than normal, and as a result, each time a mummy loses a Physical Trait due to deterioration at the Mortally Wounded Health Level, the player must make a Simple Test — a loss indicates that the mummy dies immediately.

While dead, the mummy uses Corpus Levels to track the strength of her Ba. The Ba can be injured normally by wraiths and other denizens of the Underworld; such injury does not affect the mummy's Ba Traits at all but is simply registered as Corpus damage (the mummy has Corpus Traits just like any other wraith). A mummy's Corpus rejuvenates naturally with time; each session, one Corpus Level of non-aggravated damage heals automatically, and the expenditure of a Ba Trait instantly heals all Corpus Levels of non-aggravated damage (aggravated damage heals at the rate of one Corpus Level per Ba Trait expended). A mummy's Ba can also Slumber like a wraith; this takes the Ba spirit out of play for a session but allows the player to expend Physical Traits in order to heal one level of non-aggravated damage per Trait. Even if totally discorporated (destroyed of all Corpus Levels), the Ba does not enter a Harrowing like a wraith — rather, it hovers in the Tempest, unaware, invisible and barely existent, to re-form near a Ferryman (generally Anubis, in the case of Egyptian mummies) a century later. Of course, such Withering does annihilate a mummy sufficiently to remove the character from play because of the time involved in regenerating.

DEATH AND REBIRTH

While alive, the mummy interacts with the living world in a form just like other mortals, able to eat, sleep and enjoy the passing of days and nights. While dead, though, the mummy travels the endless byways of the dead realm.

The Ba spirit of a mummy can visit any of the parts of Underworld accessible to wraiths; mummies can, should they so desire, visit the Far

Shores, the Tempest, the Labyrinth or any of the myriad places of death aside from the Shadowlands itself (the Ba does not interact with the living world; the Ka serves as interface between the sunlit lands and the Ba). Most mummies, of course, choose to wait in the relative safety of one of the hidden Dark Kingdoms (like Amenti) where they can rejuvenate in peace, but this is not true for all.

In the Underworld, the mummy's Ba possesses all of the normal Traits that the body has in life, so the mummy can use Abilities and Attributes normally (Hekau — magical spells — are sometimes changed in effect; see the individual Hekau descriptions). Furthermore, Ba spirits are immune to many wraithly Arcanoi; the powers of *Castigate*, *Embody* and *Puppetry* have no use to a Ba spirit and cannot affect it. Similarly, a Ba spirit is not a true wraith and thus cannot learn Arcanoi.

SHADOWS AND KHAIBIT

While dead, the mummy's soul resembles a wraith, but unlike the Restless, the mummy's dark passions and emotions are not blocked and channeled into a Shadow. Instead, the mummy's personality is fully integrated, and thus the Reborn does not suffer the interactions of Shadow and Psyche common to wraiths. Still, the dark parts of the Reborn's nature are sometimes called the khaibit, for it is possible for a mummy to succumb to Shadow; a mummy who loses all of his Humanity Traits becomes an unfeeling, monstrous thing much like a Spectre. Such creatures are also called khaibits by other mummies.

REBUILDING THE BODY

Once the Ba spirit has accrued enough energy (in the form of Ba Traits), it can begin the process of restoring the physical body. To do so, the Ba must pass energy into the Ka spirit, which then revitalizes the corpse. Each Ba Trait expended in this fashion heals one Health Level of damage to the corpse. Even scattered ashes are brought together, re-knit and repaired in this fashion. Once the corpse is completely restored to full health, the mummy is reborn (as long as he has at least one Ba Trait remaining).

A mummy's body can and does decay like any other corpse, so a Ba spirit generally amasses a large amount of energy and then heals the body all at once instead of trying to restore the body bit by bit — an unfinished and unpreserved *khat* probably should lose one Health Level per session to represent this decay. However, a mummy can invest a Trait of Ba energy into his body specifically to prevent decay; in this case, the body suffers no degeneration for a full year.

RISING ANEW

Upon successful Rebirth, the mummy must face the prospect of another long span in the living lands. Furthermore, the journeys in the Underworld are often confusing and shadowy, and they have a way of blurring the memories of the mummy. Thus, the mummy must immediately make two Virtue Tests upon rising, both with a difficulty of three Traits.

First, the mummy must make a Joy Virtue Test. Success indicates that the mummy keeps the resolve to continue in yet another life as part of the endless sequence of years. Failure means that the mummy is emotionally unable to cope with the stresses of another life and loses one permanent Joy Trait. A retest may be made as normal, but a failed retest then indicates that the mummy also gains a Derangement chosen by the Storyteller.

Next, the mummy must clear her mind and try to recall the pieces of her lives and where she resides in the present. This calls for a Memory Virtue Test. Success indicates that the mummy remembers enough to continue without hindrance. Failure causes the mummy to lose one permanent level from every Ability that exceeds her number of Memory Traits — so a mummy with three Memory Traits but *Crafts* x 5 would lose one level of the *Crafts* Ability. A retest may be made normally, but failing the retest then indicates that the mummy loses a level from *every* Ability, not just from those Abilities in excess of the number of Memory Traits possessed.

HEKAU

The ancients possessed incredible secrets of control over the elements, over the forces of nature and over great spiritual mysteries. No wonder, then, that those who undergo the Great Rite carry with them a measure of that power; indeed, the very process of becoming a mummy — discovering the means or showing enough promise to be chosen — demands a measure of erudition.

For the Reborn, the secrets of magic are hoarded carefully and channeled through the power of Sekhem. Each magician learns to control his own vital energies, to act as a conduit for universal forces that in turn create wondrous effects. Even those Reborn of other cultures show some such prowess, though their paths of magical mastery often diverge from the Hekau most commonly used by the mummies of Egypt.

Each mummy character possesses a Basic level of the *Necromancy* Hekau (not to be confused with the vampiric Discipline of the same name) — this represents the minimum competency in training and preparedness imbued through the process of becoming a mummy or learned immediately upon the next life. Furthermore, all Reborn claim at least some magical knowledge, handed down through their contacts and studies of various lives. Indeed, some once possessed vast stores of lore now lost to their past lives.

KEEPING MUMMIES IN CHECK

Since mummies always come back from death, what's to stop a mummy character from always wreaking vengeance upon his foes and trying over and over again to defeat his adversaries until he succeeds?

In theory, nothing.

In practice, though, a mummy is bound by the normal constraints of time and difficulty. A mummy's body can be damaged to the point of near destruction, making it very difficult to rise again; if the body is watched and constantly damaged, the Ka must be sent to fetch aid and recover the body before rebirth is possible. The Ba spirit can also be trapped by magics that bind wraiths. Additionally, gathering Ba energy takes time, and the Ba spirit can be blasted into Withering, which can keep the mummy from having any effect upon either world for some time.

In short, don't hesitate to punish players who abuse mummy characters by taking reckless risks. Such characters can easily be removed from the chronicle with the explanation that it will take too long for the mummy to recover to ever re-enter the game.

Hekau paths function in a fashion similar to the sorcery of mortals. However, mummies use Sekhem, not Humanity, to power most of their magics. A few spells require the use of other spiritual energies, such as Ba or Ka. Unless otherwise noted, Hekau spells are cast just like mortal sorcery, but with the differences noted here; thus, a mummy casting an Advanced *Celestial* spell must spend 45 minutes on the ritual and expend the Sekhem indicated in the spell description.

For Egyptian mummies, the forms of Hekau described here are appropriate. Other Reborn, though, may have special abilities appropriate to their individual cultures. In such cases, the Storyteller can simulate those abilities by using sorcery, with the changes of using Sekhem instead of Humanity. Thus, a Cabirus Reborn in Germany, A.D. 1200, might use *Summoning* and *Warding* but know nothing of *Ushabti*.

ALCHEMY

Mummy *Alchemy* functions much like mortal *Alchemy*. Most elixirs require some sort of special ingredients or expenditures in addition to the usual time and Sekhem costs. Mummy characters should buy levels of *Alchemy* just like the path described in Chapter Three, but they use different forms of potions imbued with their own Sekhem, as described below. Alternately, Reborn of non-Egyptian heritage may use potion formulae more commonly known to sorcerers. The *Alchemical* solutions of mummies do require a test for creation, just like other potions; failure indicates a noxious concoction without any magical effects, although this may not be immediately apparent (only test for success when the elixir is actually used, so that success or failure is not known until then).

Finished *Alchemical* formulae are known as preparations. Since they function on living bodies, they generally have no effect on spirits or the undead unless specifically noted. A finished preparation can take the form of a potion (a liquid that is drunk), a salve (a cream that is applied to a surface), or an essence (a gas that is inhaled).

When a preparation is used on an unwilling subject who is aware of the nature of the item, a challenge is required — the subject pits his Physical Traits against the alchemist's Mental Traits. If the alchemist wins, her preparation is too strong for the subject to resist and takes full effect; if the subject wins, he successfully resists the effects of the preparation. Note that this test is not made if the subject willingly takes the preparation, even if he does not actually know what it is; it is possible to trick someone into drinking a poison without resisting, for instance.

Drink of Seven Days' Rest (First Basic)

Cost: None

This elixir refreshes you immediately, as if you had a full night's good rest. All fatigue is removed. This also heals a drinker who suffers from one Health Level of damage (but no more).

Potion of Resilience (First Basic)

Cost: None

Upon drinking this elixir, you gain an immediate resistance to pain. All wound penalties are treated as one level less severe. Thus, a Bruised character suffers no injury, a Wounded character only takes penalties from the Bruised Health Level, and so on. This applies even in the case of a character with multiples of a particular Health Level. A character with two Bruised Health Levels suffers no wound penalties after imbibing this potion. The effects last for the duration of the scene.

Simple Elixirs (First Basic)

Cost: None

A *Simple Elixir* is a formula that creates a potion or salve improving a subject's capabilities. Use of a *Simple Elixir* grants a the user one additional Attribute Trait for the duration of the scene. Each type of Attribute Trait has a different formula, so there are different spells for *Tireless* potions as opposed to *Resilient*, for *Patient* instead of *Calm* and so on. You may only gain one bonus to each Attribute Trait category at a time, so if you already have a bonus to your Physical Traits, you cannot drink another *Simple Elixir* to get more; only the best bonus applies at any given time.

Simple Philtres (First Basic)

Cost: None

Simple Philtres function to induce emotions in given subjects. Each type of philtre formula imbues one specific emotion — lust, hope, anger, etc. In game terms, a *Simple Philtre*, when drunk, gives the drinker one particular Negative Attribute Trait, as chosen by the maker of the potion.

Simple Poisons (First Basic)

Cost: None

Though some mummies study mundane toxicology, a skilled alchemist can make magically deadly poisons. A *Simple Poison* can be a potion (which takes effect when drunk), or a salve (which is placed on a weapon). The use of a *Simple Poison* causes the victim to immediately suffer one Health Level of non-aggravated damage; this damage can be healed normally. A *Simple Poison* has only one use.

Simple Tonics (First Basic)

Cost: None

Whereas poisons injure, tonics heal. A *Simple Tonic*, whether drunk as a potion or rubbed on as a salve, restores one Health Level to the subject. This works even on aggravated wounds but only affects those with natural healing processes — vampires cannot benefit from this preparation.

Perfume of Longing (Second Basic)

Cost: None

Always made as an essence, this fine mist acts as an aphrodisiac — modern scientists would attribute its effects to pheromones. This allows you to claim the additional Social Traits *Alluring* and *Beguiling* in Social Challenges involving attractiveness. This preparation remains in effect for the duration of the scene.

Blood of the Snake (Second Basic)

Cost: None

As a potion, this preparation is drunk as an antidote or preventative; as a salve, it is rubbed onto poisoned wounds. It negates the effects of poisons. Any poison normally inflicting only one Health Level of damage is completely nullified by this preparation. Poisons inflicting more damage have their effects reduced by one level, to a maximum of two Health Levels of damage; poisons that normally slay instantly instead inflict three Health Levels of damage. If taken preventatively, this preparation lasts for a scene or until used.

Complex Elixirs (First Intermediate)

Cost: One Sekhem Trait

Complex Elixirs add Traits just like *Simple Elixirs* but add two levels of the appropriate Trait — *Cunning* x 2 or *Genial* x 2, for instance.

Complex Philtres (First Intermediate)

Cost: One Sekhem Trait

Like *Simple Philtres*, *Complex Philtres* inflict Negative Traits upon victims; each such preparation inflicts two levels of the appropriate Negative Trait.

Complex Poisons (First Intermediate)

Cost: One Sekhem Trait

A *Complex Poison* is administered just like a *Simple Poison*, but scores two Health Levels of damage.

Complex Tonics (First Intermediate)

Cost: One Sekhem Trait

A *Complex Tonic* restores two lost Health Levels to a subject but is otherwise identical to a *Simple Tonic*.

Eyes of the Ka (First Intermediate)

Cost: One Sekhem Trait

Only made as a salve, this preparation allows you to see and hear the Shadowlands. Thus prepared, you can interact with wraiths and recognize the geography of the nearby layer of the Dark Umbra. See **Oblivion** for more details about the Shadowlands.

One Hundred Thousand Tongues (First Intermediate)

Cost: None

A deceptively simple preparation, this allows you to understand any language. You must apply the preparation to your mouth to be understood, and to your ears to comprehend. Its effects last for one scene.

The Tears of Isis (First Intermediate)

Cost: Two Sekhem Traits per Trait invested

This is one of the few known methods of definitively storing Sekhem energy. Creation of this potion allows you to invest Sekhem into the formula so that it holds energy for later use. Every two Traits of Sekhem invested in the potion upon its creation cause the potion to hold one Sekhem Trait for later. Sekhem gained in this fashion disappears at the end of the scene if unused. The artificial boost in Sekhem granted by this potion is not cumulative; only one such formula can be in effect at a time in any given scene.

Potion of Valor (First Intermediate)

Cost: None

A more advanced form of the *Potion of Resilience*, this grants you the ability to ignore two levels of wound penalties, so you only suffer from the effects of injury once you reach the Incapacitated Health Level (and even then, you only take the penalties of being Bruised). You also gain an additional Incapacitated Health Level. This potion lasts for the duration of the scene; if the additional Health Level has been used when the potion's effects wear off, the damage is immediately applied against the next Health Level (in most cases, Mortally Wounded). Thus, it is wise to heal injuries before this potion wears off.

Potion of the Separable Ka (Second Intermediate)

Cost: Two Sekhem Traits

Upon drinking this potion, you enter a trancelike state and your consciousness invisibly slips from your body. Despite the name, your Ka does not actually separate from your body; rather, you gain the ability to travel astrally, witnessing events and moving freely while your body is comatose. This potion lasts for one scene, during which time you may freely move about and watch various events, though your body lies dormant and you remain unaware of events transpiring around it (though you can be pretty sure that something's wrong if your consciousness is suddenly plunged into the Underworld as a riven Ba-spirit).

Potent Elixirs (Advanced)

Cost: Two Sekhem Traits

As per *Simple Elixirs*, but these potions grant three levels of one Attribute Trait.

Potent Philtres (Advanced)

Cost: Two Sekhem Traits

As per *Simple Philtres*, but these potions grant three levels of one Negative Attribute Trait.

Potent Poisons (Advanced)

Cost: Three Sekhem Traits

If unresisted, a *Potent Poison* automatically slays the victim. Remember, already dead subjects (like vampires) are unaffected by these preparations. *Potent Poisons* generally cause a few seconds of agonized writhing before the victim collapses and dies in a twisted and horror-stricken heap; due to the utterly horrific effects, the use of *Potent Poisons* (even by someone other than the creator) generally requires an Integrity Virtue Test on the part of the creating mummy.

Potent Tonics (Advanced)

Cost: Three Sekhem Traits

As per *Simple Tonics*, but a *Potent Tonic* immediately restores all lost Health Levels to the subject.

Potion of the Armor of Ra (Advanced)

Cost: Four Sekhem Traits

As per the *Potion of Valor*, except that you suffer no wound penalties whatsoever while this potion is in effect.

Potion of Vile Body (Advanced)

Cost: One Sekhem Trait

An advanced permutation of the *Blood of the Snake*, this preparation is a noxious formula that can only be made as a potion. As soon as you drink it, you become immune to all poisons for the duration of its effect.

Furthermore, your bodily fluids all become corrosive venoms. You may spit poison that inflicts two Health Levels of damage on a successful strike (using Physical Traits to hit), and which slowly corrodes nonliving matter (as a rule of thumb, assume that each shot removes one Trait from a piece of gear; when out of Traits, the object is ruined). Your tears have the same effect. Such vitriolic acid inflicts aggravated damage on all creatures. If you manage to breathe directly on someone (which may also require a Physical Test to grapple or a Social Test to entice someone close), you inflict one Health Level of non-aggravated damage on the individual.

Even your blood is corrosive and highly toxic; vampires who drink of your blood suffer one Health Level of aggravated damage for each Blood Trait taken, and anyone striking you with a hand-held weapon or claws damages the weapon as described above (each hit causing the item to lose one Trait until it is destroyed). If you are struck with claws or fangs, your attacker automatically loses the Trait bid, even if he wins the challenge.

AMULETS

Through the creation of an ornamental object, inlaid with precious materials and crafted with time and care, it is possible to imbue magical energies into an otherwise ordinary accessory. Infusing an object with Sekhem allows it to carry a permanent magical effect, one which functions whenever the item is properly worn and used. Due to the difficulty in creating such an object, though, most amulets take several days (at least) to fashion — a mummy may have to rest and recover Sekhem in order to finish the feat of craftsmanship. In such a case, the mummy can do nothing else besides work and rest until the object is either completed or abandoned. Once the mummy has invested all of the required Sekhem, a Static Mental challenge (with a difficulty of twice the amulet's level — two Traits for a Basic amulet, 10 for an Advanced one) is made, with the *Crafts* Ability used for retests. Failure means that the object fails and the Sekhem is lost; success indicates that the amulet functions properly.

Amulets can be used by individuals other than the crafter. However, because their powers are largely permanent, mummies are quite wary of passing them out to others. After all, a vampire with a *Wood Ward* — rendering him immune to wooden stakes — can always become a nuisance 300 years down the line. Thus, most mummies keep their amulets for themselves and make only the very few absolutely necessary. At the Storyteller's discretion, amulets may require periodic upkeep by the mummy; in this case, an amulet gifted to another character may cease functioning after a time unless it is recharged by a Reborn.

A mummy should buy the *Enchantment* path of sorcery to represent the magic necessary to create amulets. However, instead of learning normal *Enchantment* rituals, the mummy most likely learns to create the special types of amulets described here. As always, mummies of unusual cultures may have different forms of craftsmanship.

Amulets must generally be worn to be effective and usually grant benefits only to the body wearing the amulet — a corpse generally gains no benefit from amulets (although this is not true of vampires). Some amulets, however, might be specially designed to function if placed in the wrappings of a dead mummy; these are created, and work, solely at the discretion of the Storyteller.

Simple Ward (First Basic)

Cost: (Ward rating x 5) Sekhem Traits

Wards are designed to protect the wearer from hostile magic. If you wear a *Simple Ward*, you gain one or two additional Traits in defense against specific types of magic (the bonus is determined when the amulet is created).

• A **Heart** ward protects against magic that affects the heart directly and against effects that target the rational mind, such as the *Dominate* Discipline or the Gift: *Ultimate Argument of Logic*.

• A **Name** ward defends against attacks affecting the True Name. Each such ward must be attuned to a particular individual.

• An **Eye of Horus** fights off magics that attack physical health and strength, such as poisons and damaging spells.

Wood Ward (First Basic)

Cost: Seven Sekhem Traits

While you are wearing this ward, your skin becomes completely impervious to wood. Wooden objects instantly rot and fall to dust upon striking you. This can be problematic, as chairs or walls may collapse at your touch, but weapons and debris made of wood offer little harm to you. Against any assault with a wooden implement, you may double your effective Traits.

Lesser Talisman (Second Basic)

Cost: 10 Sekhem Traits

A talisman channels strength and magical knowledge to the Reborn. While you wear the talisman, you gain additional bonus Traits. These Traits may be used or lost as normal, but they are also regained with your other Traits

— in effect, they are just like permanent additional Traits that you possess normally.

A *Lesser Talisman* grants one additional Attribute Trait of the maker's choice. Thus, you could have an amulet granting the Trait *Resilient* or a wrapping gifting you with *Knowledgeable*. However, you may only gain bonus Traits in any given Attribute category from one Hekau source at a time (the strongest one). Thus, if you wear a *Lesser Talisman* that gives you the Physical Trait *Relentless* but later quaff a potion granting *Tough* x 3, you gain only the bonus Traits of the potion until its effects wear off, at which time the amulet reasserts itself. However, you could have a *Lesser Talisman* of *Patient* while also gaining the bonuses from the potion of *Tough* x 3, because they affect different Attribute Trait categories.

Amulet of Cloud Walking (Second Basic)

Cost: Nine Sekhem Traits

Unlike most other amulets, this one must be activated by a magician with at least some knowledge of the *Amulets* path of magic (in a pinch, a character with *Enchantment* will do). The magician must make a Simple Test (win or tie) to activate the amulet, although the magician does not need to be the maker of the amulet or even know this ritual.

While you wear an active amulet of this type, you can walk through the skies at the level of the clouds. Even on a cloudless day, you may walk through the air effortlessly. This allows you to journey from place to place with extreme rapidity — the actual time required tends to vary; accomplished magicians claim that the travel time reflects your belief in how long the journey should take. For game purposes, you can travel great distances in a relatively short time. The Storyteller can allow you to reach just about any location on the same continent in between game sessions. Once you reach your destination, you sink lightly to the ground, and the amulet becomes quiescent once more.

Removing an amulet of this type while in the midst of a journey is an excellent means to a rapid, plummeting death.

Metal Ward (First Intermediate)

Cost: 13 Sekhem Traits

This ward functions just like a *Wood Ward*, except that it works against all forms of metal. Obviously, this is an excellent defense against bullets and similar trivial nuisances.

Certain metals are not affected by a *Metal Ward*; generally, modern and high-tech metals such as titanium, aluminum, carbon steel, depleted uranium and the like are unaffected unless the creator of the ward has the *Science* Ability (in order to key the ward against these modern creations).

Minor Ward (First Intermediate)

Cost: (Ward rating x 10) Sekhem Traits

This form of ward functions just like a *Simple Ward*, but it has a maximum of four Ward Traits.

Scarab (First Intermediate)

Cost: 25 Sekhem Traits

A small colorful beetle, the scarab was perhaps one of the most common amulets in ancient Egypt. The scarab has two primary functions. While you wear a *Scarab*, you gain two bonus Traits to defend against any physically debilitating attack — you get the bonus Traits against diseases and paralytics, for instance, but not against normal blows in combat. Secondly, if the scarab is worn on your body while you are dead, you gain one additional Trait in your Virtue Tests when testing to rise from the dead (see "Rising Anew").

Charm of Invisibility to Animals (Second Intermediate)

Cost: 30 Sekhem Traits

Designed to protect the wearer from the notice of hostile animals (who, according to the Egyptians, could be messengers of the gods), this amulet renders you completely undetectable to all normal animals. Even magical animals, like werewolves, perceive you only dimly; Lupus Garou must defeat you in a Mental Challenge to notice you.

This amulet must be activated by someone with knowledge of *Amulets* or *Enchantment*, although the magician does not need to know this actual ritual or be the creator of the particular amulet. The amulet's effects last until it is deactivated by a similarly proficient individual.

Nature Ward (Second Intermediate)

Cost: 60 Sekhem Traits

This ward functions just like a *Wood Ward* or *Metal Ward*, except that it grants you bonuses to defend against all natural forces. Lightning, hail, heat and fire all bend around you and leave you untouched. You can still suffer the aftereffects of your surroundings — smoke from a fire can choke you even as the fire fails to burn you — but the natural elements themselves cannot touch you.

Magically summoned elements are not affected by this ward, so (for instance) fire conjured with *Thaumaturgy* can affect you normally. However, weather or elemental conditions originally brought into existence by magic and then continuing naturally do shy from the ward; if a thaumaturgist creates a magical fire, but then lets it burn its way toward you, you gain the benefits of the ward, and you are always protected from weather magic.

Buckle of Isis (Advanced)

Cost: 100 Sekhem Traits

The most powerful countermagic available to mummies, this amulet grants six bonus Traits against all forms of hostile magic. Isis, the Egyptian goddess of magic, imbues protection from all magical forces into this ward. Note that this ward is exceedingly expensive and difficult to make; you must

expend significant Traits in *Resources* and/or the *Crafts* Ability, as determined by the Storyteller, to successfully fashion this sort of ward (generally, three levels of each is a good number).

Greater Talisman (Advanced)

Cost: 120 Sekhem Traits

A *Greater Talisman* functions just like a *Lesser Talisman*, except that it grants two additional Attribute Traits.

Major Ward (Advanced)

Cost: (Ward rating x 15) Sekhem Traits

A *Major Ward* functions just like a *Simple Ward* or *Minor Ward*, except that it may claim up to five bonus Traits in warding.

CELESTIAL

The Egyptians predicated much of their dynamic prophecies and magical influences upon the stars and constellations. With the proper use of sky and weather, a magician can create or banish storms, summon down the stars themselves and tell what the future holds.

Mummy characters should buy the *Weathercraft* path (see Chapter Three) to represent *Celestial* knowledge but use the rituals described below.

Grip the Water (First Basic)

Cost: Two Sekhem Traits

Any body of flowing water can be altered with this ritual; you raise or lower the level of water in a given area with your command. You can affect up to a room-sized lake or river with several meters of change or alter a larger area by about a foot in difference (at most). This can allow you entry into submerged areas or make it more difficult for individuals to pass through a particular area. You must make a Static Mental Challenge to successfully affect your target, with the difficulty dependent upon the size of the body of water — three Traits for a puddle or pond, five for a lake or river, seven for a large (building-sized) body of water.

Weather Magic (First Basic)

Cost: Varies; see below

The most basic form of *Weather Magic* allows you to perform minor alterations to the local climate and conditions. The total difficulty of this ritual and the Sekhem Trait cost depend upon the modifications that you wish to make. See the accompanying *Weather Magic* chart for particulars. Total up all modifiers; you may choose the appropriate time for the effects to begin, any time within a week. The Storyteller should make an announcement or note at the beginning of play informing everyone of the special conditions.

SCALE AND CELESTIAL MAGIC

Celestial magic tends to work over large areas for long periods of time. As a result, its effects can be difficult to portray. It's recommended that *Celestial* magic be limited to Narrator characters; if players' characters use *Celestial* magic, the Storyteller should have a means prepared to notify all players in the game of the (possibly abrupt) change in prevailing local conditions.

You can make slight changes in humidity, change a temperature by about 10 degrees Fahrenheit, make or stop a gentle breeze or shift the wind direction subtly with this power.

At this level, any effect with a total difficulty of five or fewer Traits costs only one Sekhem Trait to invoke; more difficult effects cost two Sekhem Traits.

Read the Stars (Second Basic)

Cost: None

With careful astrological correspondences and plotting, you can read the secrets of Heaven itself. Casting this spell allows you to gain fortuitous circumstances when invoking other rituals by choosing auspicious times and events. When you cast this spell, you must make a Static Mental Challenge with a difficulty of the spell that you are attempting to augment. If you succeed, you may then expend *Astronomy* Ability Traits to gain bonus Traits in casting your intended spell, with each *Astronomy* Trait counting as one bonus Trait.

Weather Magic (Second Basic)

Cost: Varies; see below

At this level, you can make small changes in humidity, alter temperature by up to a noticeable 20 degrees Fahrenheit, generate or still a fairly strong breeze and change wind direction significantly (about an eighth of the compass). Effects with a difficulty of five Traits or less cost two Sekhem Traits; higher difficulties cost three Sekhem Traits. Otherwise, this power is identical to the most basic *Weather Magic*.

Call the Stars (First Intermediate)

Cost: Two Sekhem Traits

A spectacular ritual culminating in a fiery display, this spell actually pulls meteorites from the heavens to strike a target area. Small, flaming rocks roar from the skies, battering everything within the game site (an area up to the size of a small town can feasibly be affected). The meteor storm lasts for a full hour and is blatantly unusual. Anyone caught outside during the shower must

Weather Magic difficulties

Add all of the difficulties appropriate to the level of *Weather Magic* and effect in order to determine the final Trait difficulty for the ritual.

Effect	First Basic	Second Basic	First Intermediate	Second Intermediate	Advance
Change humidity	2	2	2	2	2
Change temperature	1	2	2	2	2
Change wind force	1	1	1	2	2
Change wind direction	1	1	1	2	2
Affect small town	1	0	0	0	0
Affect small city	3	2	0	0	0
Affect large city	5	2	1	0	0
Affect small state	-	4	3	1	0
Affect large state	-	-	5	2	1
Affect continent	-	-	-	4	2
Affect hemisphere	-	-	-	5	4
Affect globe	-	-	-	-	5
One hour duration	1	1	1	1	1
One day duration	3	3	3	3	3
One week duration	5	5	5	5	5

A dash (-) indicates that the effect is impossible at that level of mastery.

make a Simple Test each turn (win or tie) or else suffer one Health Level of aggravated damage from the burning stones hurtling at incredible speeds. The meteorites similarly inflict damage upon structures and objects left in the open; flimsy devices and buildings may catch fire or fall apart under the impact of the meteorites.

Weather Magic (First Intermediate)

Cost: Varies; see below

This power is identical to the most basic *Weather Magic*, except that you can alter humidity moderately (about 30%), change temperature by up to 30 degrees Fahrenheit, generate or still a steady wind or change the wind direction by up to 45 degrees. The cost is three Sekhem Traits for total difficulty of five Traits or less and four Sekhem Traits at six or higher Trait difficulty.

Read the Tree of Life (Second Intermediate)

Cost: Two Sekhem Traits

All beings have their fates cast in the stars. Seshat, wife of Thoth, wove the futures of all things into the tapestry of creation. By using this ritual, you can read the warp and woof of that tapestry, gaining knowledge of an individual's fate.

Casting this spell demands a successful Static Mental Challenge with a difficulty equal to the subject's highest Attribute Traits (the more complex the subject, the more difficult the reading). Success allows you to garner one set of information:

• You may learn the subject's true Nature and Demeanor;

• You may discern the true supernatural nature (if any) of the subject (vampire, werewolf, etc.);

• You may determine a brief glimpse of future events for the subject, allowing the individual the opportunity to gain one retest at any time in the next session, though this benefit may not be held more than once at a time by any individual.

Weather Magic (Second Intermediate)

Cost: Varies; see below

At this level of prowess, you can change humidity drastically (up to 50%), alter temperature by up to 40 degrees Fahrenheit, create or remove storm-force winds and change wind direction up to a full compass point (90 degrees). The cost is four Sekhem Traits for a total difficulty of five or less and six Sekhem Traits at higher difficulties. Otherwise, this power is identical to the most basic *Weather Magic*.

Apep Thrashes the Ground (Advanced)

Cost: Nine Sekhem Traits

Like the Midgaard Serpent, Apep is a great serpentine beast that coils deep below the earth's surface. In Egyptian myth, Apep tried to devour the sun, plunging the world into night. Though it never quite succeeded, its anger could shake the world. Even though Apep, or Apophis, is the enemy of the Shemsu-heru, its wrath can be a potent weapon.

You may use this spell to create a great earthquake over a large area immediately upon casting. This spell cannot be halted or delayed once cast; its effects are immediate. People in the area may well be killed, and there is certain to be a great deal of disaster and property damage. The exact effects are completely up to the Storyteller, but at the very least, large amounts of Influence and various *Resources* and *Retainers* should be lost or killed. Characters may find themselves without homes or allies. Use of this spell causes disaster on a massive scale, and as such it always calls for a Virtue Test of *Integrity*.

Casting this spell is quite difficult, requiring successful Static Physical, Social and Mental Challenges against nine Traits each. Failure in any test means that the ritual fails.

Weather Magic (Advanced)

Cost: Varies; see below

The most advanced *Weather Magic* functions like the more basic forms but allows any change in humidity, alteration of hurricane-force winds, any change in wind direction and up to a blistering or freezing 50 degree Fahrenheit alteration in temperature. For difficulties of five Traits or less, this ritual costs five Sekhem Traits; at higher difficulties, it costs seven Sekhem Traits.

NECROMANCY

With their continuous ties to the Underworld through life, death and rebirth, it's no surprise that mummies command a formidable brand of *Necromancy*. The Egyptians had a detailed theory of the afterlife and developed many powers associated with death. As a recipient of the Great Rite, a mummy is practically required to have some knowledge of *Necromantic* magics. Those mummies originally chosen by the Cult of Isis would have been instructed properly so as to fulfill their duties, whereas those people who become mummies through their own arts must perforce have acquired some knowledge of the cycles of death. As a result, all mummy characters have the first Basic level of *Necromancy* automatically, at no cost.

Mummy characters should use the *Ephemera* path (see **Laws of the Hunt**) to represent levels of *Necromancy* but use the rituals listed here. Note that even with *Necromancy* and *Ephemera*, the mummy has no special ability to sense ghosts unless the appropriate Merits are taken.

Body Preservation (First Basic)

Cost: None

This simple spell requires a full day to perform (and thus is usually cast outside the confines of game play). You cast this spell in preparation for death. When used, this spell prevents all decay upon the body for 50 years. This allows you some leeway in collecting Ba energy without having to worry about refreshing the corpse from rot and decay.

Stormwalk (First Basic)

Cost: None

Unlike most forms of Hekau, this one is used by a Ba-spirit, not by a living mummy. While your Ba spirit is in the Underworld, this spell allows you to find your way through the Tempest. You can use this spell to direct you to any destination for one scene. Casting this spell requires the expenditure of one Mental Trait.

Separate Ka (First Basic)

Cost: One Ka Trait, plus one Sekhem Trait for every scene or two hours that the Ka is separated from the body

While the Ka spirit normally appears only to defend the body during cycles of death, this spell allows you to separate your Ka briefly while still living. Your body becomes comatose, and your Ka is free to move about and act as described in the appropriate section. Unlike most magic, this spell requires only a single turn to cast instead of several minutes of ritual.

Summon the Dead (Second Basic)

Cost: One Sekhem Trait

Recognizable by some spiritualists, this ritual allows you to briefly summon wraiths to your presence. You must make a Social Challenge against the wraith in question (for which you will probably have a Narrator as a proxy). If you succeed, the wraith rushes to you as quickly as possible. Note, though, that this spell does not guarantee compliance or friendliness on the part of the wraith. You may only use this spell while you are living; without other magic, you may not even be able to tell that the wraith has responded to your summons. Once the wraith arrives and makes its presence known to you in some fashion, it is free to leave unless you use some other form of constraining magic (or it chooses to stay).

A typical wraith has one or two ghostly powers, generally allowing it to whisper or even manifest as a ghostly image; throw objects about; create haunting effects like bleeding walls, cold spots and infestations of vermin; briefly possess someone; or take control of a technological item. Whether the wraith decides to use these powers on your behalf is another matter.

See **Oblivion** for more information about wraiths.

Revisit Death (Second Basic)

Cost: None

A most useful ritual, this spell allows you to touch a corpse and instantly gain knowledge of the circumstances surrounding its demise. You must be living to perform this ritual, which takes a full 10 minutes to cast. Upon the ritual's completion, you must win or tie a Simple Test; if you succeed, you gain a vision of the moments of the individual's death and surroundings. Although the vision is not always completely clear and can jump disturbingly through events, it serves to grant a view of the individual's death and the surroundings in all directions at that time. Of course, if someone was using special abilities to remain hidden from view at that time, you still cannot sense that individual unless you have the appropriate sensory powers.

Banish the Dead (Second Basic)

Cost: None

With a simple set of gestures and words, you can banish a wraith from your presence. You must make a Social Challenge against the wraith. If you succeed, the wraith cannot be in the same room with you or approach come 50 feet of you for the remainder of the scene or for a full hour, whichever elapses first.

Separate Ba (First Intermediate)

Cost: One Sekhem Trait per hour or scene

With a single turn of concentration, you can separate your Ba spirit, allowing it to roam the Underworld while your body still lives. During this time, your consciousness is tied up in the spirit, so your body is comatose. Because you are not actually dead, your Ka spirit cannot manifest; this spell cannot be used at the same time as *Separate Ka*, either. If your Ba spirit is discorporated due to damage, your body immediately dies and your Ba spirit Withers, re-forming decades or centuries later in the Underworld. This spell is one of the few means by which a mummy could conceivably gain Ba energy while still living.

Animate Corpse (Second Intermediate)

Cost: One Sekhem Trait

By symbolically bringing breath to the dead, you can raise a corpse to a semblance of life once more. Although not the same as the Great Rite, this ritual allows you to breathe into the mouth of a corpse or to massage its chest in an illusion of breathing and cause it to rise as a mindless zombie. The corpse keeps its normal Physical Traits, but its Health Levels are doubled; it must be dismembered or hacked to bits in order to be stopped. It functions under your silent and uninterruptable mental control. The corpse lasts until destroyed or until you send it to rest. You must be in physical, living form to use this spell; you cannot (for instance) cast it on your own body (or another's) while in manifested Ka form.

Call the Khaibit (Advanced)

Cost: Two Sekhem Traits

By casting this ritual over someone who is dying (at the Mortally Wounded Health Level), you draw out the khaibit, the shadow double that holds the recesses of dark emotion. While the spell is cast, the individual sees every moment of selfishness, greed, pettiness, hate and base emotion from his life. At the end, the individual dies, leaving behind all of the remnants of shadow.

This ritual's primary purpose is to free a dying mortal (or Garou or mage, but not a wraith, vampire or Reborn) from his dark passions at the moment of death. As a result, the person goes peacefully to his final reward; the individual does not become a wraith and cannot later have his spirit summoned or controlled.

Furthermore, calling out the khaibit leaves an inky, intangible shadow of hatred behind. The khaibit functions as a materialized Ka spirit, dark and malevolent, seeking to fulfill its own base passions. In this instance, the khaibit is treated as a free-roaming corporeal Ka spirit with the Traits of its original body; it has five Ka Traits of energy. It cannot normally recharge its own Ka Traits, although it can attempt to steal offerings left for another (by making a Social Challenge against the intended recipient of an offering). It seeks to placate its own hungers in this fashion, terrorizing mortals and stealing that for which its now fleshless form still lusts.

This spell can only be cast while you live. If you use this spell simply to summon up a vicious shadow-monster to torment others, you will certainly need to make an *Integrity* Virtue Test.

Reshaping the Lost Soul

Cost: Three Sekhem Traits

Usable by either a living or dead mummy, this spell enables you to change the purposes of a particular wraith. By challenging the wraith's existing ties to the living lands, you can reshape its desires, casting it into a new form. You may engage in a Static Willpower Challenge (difficulty of the subject's Willpower) in order to reshape one of the wraith's Passions or Fetters with this spell. Success lets you declare a new Passion or Fetter in place of the old one. See **Oblivion** for details; in brief, this spell allows you to change the bonds that tie a wraith to the living world, causing it to be tied to different people or objects and drawing strength from emotions of your choice.

Entrap the Ba

Cost: Three Sekhem Traits

A terrifying prison, this spell allows you to trap someone's soul in a specially-prepared prison. By casting this ritual over the subject and holding a container (a gemstone, receptacle or the like), you pull the Ba spirit from the body, forcing it into the trap and keeping it from fleeing to the

Underworld or materializing in the living world. The body is slain in the process (although an already dead subject, like a vampire, may simply be inconvenienced). You must defeat the subject in three successive challenges, one for each Attribute category, in order to enact this spell.

REN-HEKAU

Every creature or thing in creation has its own name, a resonance that shakes the strands of its place within the universe. The most powerful of Egyptian sorcerers recognized the power of these true names, or Ren, and through them were able to control and change the fundamental states of anything that could be named. *Ren-Hekau* is perhaps the most demanding and compelling path of Hekau. The study of *Ren-Hekau* is not simply the study of rituals but of true names as well. Since these names are often lost to antiquity or encoded in puzzles and riddles, *Ren-Hekau* requires diligence and memory beyond that demanded by most sorcery. A mummy character should have a list of known true names; a mummy who does not know the true name for iron, for instance, cannot use an incantation to change or destroy that metal. At the Storyteller's discretion, a player can purchase new true names (for generic objects and animals, not for individuals) at a cost of one Experience Trait each, but usually true names are learned through study.

All inanimate things and animals share common names. Thus, there is a name for snake that commands all snakes; a name for iron, for grass, for heart. Intelligent beings, though — those beings with souls — have their own individual true names. Thus, each individual human or intelligent animal has a specific name. Careful magicians never tell their real full names to anyone, hoping to thwart anyone planning to use this power; in the modern age, though, it is a simple matter to discern the true name of an individual. Modern records make full birth names easily available.

There are five levels of *Ren-Hekau*: the two Basic levels of *Simple Names* and *Natural Names*; the Intermediate levels of *Commanding Names* and *Transforming Names*; and the Advanced level of *Universal Names*. These levels are purchased like any Hekau; the mummy's level of expertise determines the available *Ren-Hekau* incantations, as noted below.

Unlike most forms of sorcery, *Ren-Hekau* relies on the power inherent in fundamental words and as such uses little in the way of ritual. Unless otherwise noted, *Ren-Hekau* spells take only a single turn to cast, regardless of level. *Ren-Hekau* spells are generally limited in range to things within the magician's line-of-sight; the subject of the spell must be able to hear the sorcerer's utterance of the true name.

Asking the Trees (First Basic)
Cost: One Sekhem Trait

Speaking the name of a form of vegetation, you draw that plant's attention and obedience. You can cause plants to perform minor functions; a tree could drop leaves or branches, a flower could bloom, vines could entangle. This can be used to impress or to clear or bar passage through undergrowth. Entangling vines and branches can attempt to grapple (but not injure) with the equivalent of three Physical Traits. You must address a particular plant or grouping of plants using the appropriate true name, so speaking to vines does not necessarily compel grasses.

Forgetting the Stone (First Basic)

Cost: One Sekhem Trait

Speaking the true name of a form of stone or metal, you command the universe to forget its existence, thus removing it completely. The object is not simply destroyed; it ceases to exist. You can affect roughly a man-sized amount of stone with this incantation. Different forms of stone and metal use different true names, so destroying a gun with the incantation to forget iron would leave pieces behind, whereas a vein of quartz inside of a block of granite would be laid bare were the granite eradicated.

Naming the Warning (First Basic)

Cost: One Sekhem Trait

By speaking the Ren of a particular animal, you cause it to realize that you have power over it. This, in turn, causes the animal to fear you; it will not attack, nor will it even approach you for the rest of the scene (though it will defend itself). You must engage in a Social Challenge to force your will through the animal's true name. If the animal is controlled magically by someone else, you must defeat the controller in the Social Challenge; otherwise, the test is against the animal itself. This spell is even functional against supernatural creatures in animal forms.

Command the Beast (Second Basic)

Cost: Two Sekhem Traits

Uttering a charm of command with an animal's true name, you force the animal to obey your will. You can issue verbal commands, which the animal will understand and obey. You must make a Social Challenge against the subject (or the subject's controller) in order to exert this sort of control; the spell wears off at the end of the scene (unless powered with additional Sekhem), at which point the animal most likely flees in terror.

Becoming the Tree (Second Basic)

Cost: Two Sekhem Traits

Combining your own name with the name of a plant allows you to crudely transform yourself to resemble the plant. You can make yourself into a roughly human-shaped mass of grass, flowers or brush or even a vaguely man-shaped tree, as appropriate to the type of true name invoked. During this time, you are aware of what transpires around you as if possessed of your normal senses, but you cannot move (so you cannot change your direction of view, either). Normally, this spell lasts for the entire scene, but you may transform back to human shape prematurely by expending a Willpower Trait. Injury suffered in plant form is applied to your normal body.

Inviting the Stone In (Second Basic)

Cost: Three Sekhem Traits

This spell functions like *Becoming the Tree*, except that you become a form of stone or metal.

Mend Flesh (Second Basic)

Cost: One Sekhem Trait

You can create and repair flesh with the appropriate Ren. Casting this spell instantly heals one Health Level (aggravated or otherwise) upon the subject.

Become Animal (First Intermediate)

Cost: Three Sekhem Traits

This spell functions like *Becoming the Tree*, except that you become a particular animal (determined by the true name that you use). You are fully capable of using the animal's natural abilities in addition to your own capabilities, subject to the limits of physical form.

If you retain animal form for more than one game session at a time, you risk the possibility of losing your intelligence and personality. Make a Simple Test at the beginning of each game session after the first in which you are in animal form; a loss indicates the loss of a Willpower Trait. If you run out of Willpower Traits, you are stuck in animal form for a full month; you may make a Simple Test (win or tie) to recover once per month thereafter. If you become stuck in animal form, you lose your Abilities and special powers until you revert back — they are forgotten and replaced by the bestial instincts of your animal form.

You may use this spell in the Underworld so that your Ba spirit can resemble specific animals.

Command the Thinking (First Intermediate)

Cost: Three Sekhem Traits

This spell functions like the *Command the Beast* incantation but allows you to control mortal or supernatural creatures. You must know the victim's true name, of course, and you must engage in and win a Social Challenge with the victim. The use of an individual's Ren is noticeable, and your assault upon the victim's consciousness is easily tracked; you cannot conceal this attempt at control.

Enslave (Second Intermediate)

Cost: Three Sekhem Traits

Unlike the more basic forms of Ren command, this spell allows you to utterly subjugate a person's will. The victim has no desire except to serve and please you for the duration of the spell. You must engage in a Social Challenge with the target; if you succeed, the target is completely enslaved for the duration of the session (although the use of Willpower can gain a retest as normal and can also be used to throw off the enslavement for a turn). Note specifically that the subject is completely aware of these effects upon the lapse of the spell; this cannot alter memories, for instance. Use of this spell is a good way to suffer Integrity Virtue Tests rapidly; taking over someone else's life isn't exactly pleasant.

Fortify Flesh (Second Intermediate)

Cost: One Sekhem Trait

Drawing in the essences of stone and metal, you make your skin durable and resistant to damage, though it keeps its normal appearance. For the remainder of the evening, you gain the bonus Physical Traits *Resilient* and *Tough* (cumulative with other magic, like amulets and potions), and you gain one additional Health Level — treat it as an extra Healthy.

Naming the Body's Destruction (Second Intermediate)

Cost: Varies; see below

With a challenge pitting your Mental Traits against the victim's Physical Traits, you can speak the true name for a part of the body and destroy it utterly. If you succeed, you can injure or kill a victim with but a word.

A *trivial* effect destroys a single digit, hand, eye, jawbone or other similarly nonessential part of the body. This inflicts one Health Level of damage and costs one Sekhem Trait.

A *serious* effect ruins an appendix, liver, kidney or the like. This causes two Health Levels of damage and causes the victim to lose one Physical Trait every 10 minutes until proper medical treatment is received — once the victim is out of Physical Traits, additional Health Levels are lost instead until the victim dies. This costs three Sekhem Traits. The victim is two Traits up on defense against this effect.

A *critical* effect names the heart, the brain, the spine or some other vital organ whose loss causes immediate death. A successful use of this incantation immediately drops the victim to the Mortally Wounded Health Level (or into torpor, in the case of a vampire). This costs three Sekhem Traits to cast, and the victim is four Traits up in defense against this effect.

All Health Levels lost to this spell are considered aggravated damage. This spell can only be used by a living caster.

Forgetting the Person's Name (Advanced)

Cost: Nine Sekhem Traits

The most powerful and deadly function of true names is the ability to wipe them from existence. Since each individual has a unique name, destruction of that name correspondingly removes the individual from existence (much like erasing tax records at the IRS). Your victim has one chance to force reality to remember him; this spell automatically fails unless the victim is completely out of Willpower. Even then, you must engage in a Static Willpower Challenge, fighting against your victim's normal permanent Willpower Traits instead of his current total. Only if you succeed in such an arduous task can you finish this spell, completely blotting the individual from existence. All memory and record of the individual is gone forever — although his deeds and actions do not vanish, nobody remembers them or the victim.

If you attempt to cast this spell and fail, you must immediately make a Memory test as the forces of forgetting rebound upon you. In any case, use of this dire spell always calls for an Integrity test.

It is believed that this spell is probably the only way to truly and permanently destroy a mummy. If this is true, though, and has been successfully accomplished, no one would ever remember it anyway. It is also believed that there may be a sort of counterspell. Both theories remain speculation.

Whispers to My Body (Advanced)

Cost: One Sekhem Trait per conflict or five minutes

Subtle control and manipulation over your own Ren gives you the ability to alter your body's structure, changing it to suit any form or shape you desire. You can restructure your appearance, liquefy or solidify pieces of your body and stretch, contort or shift with limitless ease.

Your control over your body allows you to seep through small cracks, reach twice as far as normal and twist yourself into unusual shapes. You can also completely alter your appearance or just change yourself subtly as desired; you can switch your normal Social Traits freely with this power, trading an *Alluring* Trait for a *Graceful* Trait, for instance.

In combat, you gain one retest in all attacks, as you allow knives, bullets and the like to slash through you without harm while countering with bony spikes, ridges and slashing appendages.

Because you can be rubbery or liquefied, you risk the possibility of being rent apart; if you allow yourself to be separated (for instance, if a door shuts on your overextended arm), you must immediately make a Simple Test — if you win or tie, you suffer two Health Levels of damage; if you fail, you die instantly from shock.

USHABTI

Relics and funerary pieces are more than just jeweled accouterments to the Reborn. The symbolic magic inherent in specially made pieces of ornamentation turns them into tools and spiritual aides. The effort of crafting a delicate and precise object draws emotion and energy to that object, creating a spiritual counterpart; similarly, the right triggers of magic can release in an item the potential of a thing that it resembles. Upon such sympathetic magics are *Ushabti* founded; the Egyptians buried their dead with tools, devices and artistic ornaments, all of which could provide ghostly aid and actual assistance if properly invoked.

There are five levels of *Ushabti*: *Lesser Ushabti* and *Simple Ushabti* (Basic), *Greater Ushabti* and *Princely Ushabti* (Intermediate) and *Living Ushabti* (Advanced), respectively. As always, knowledge of a particular level of *Ushabti* confers only the ability to learn or activate the appropriate rituals.

Most *Ushabti* appear to be nothing more than finely made trinkets until their powers are activated. A particular piece can only be activated by someone to whom it is attuned during creation; this person need not be the creator but must be someone with at least enough *Ushabti* levels to learn the appropriate ritual. Thus, activating a *Simple Chattel* requires that the owner know at least *Lesser Ushabti* and *Simple Ushabti*, although she need not know the actual *Simple Chattels* ritual — the ritual is only necessary to create the object in the first place.

Building an *Ushabti* figurine requires a series of Static Physical Challenges of precision (difficulty six Traits) as the Reborn carves the model from wood, clay or other materials. These challenges use an appropriate *Crafts* Ability (for purposes of retests, used *Crafts* Ability Traits do not refresh until the creation work is complete). The magician must succeed in a number of successive challenges equal to the level of the spell — a *Greater Relic* spell, which is a Second Intermediate *Ushabti* incantation, thus requires four successes. Each challenge takes a full day to complete, and any failure ruins the work (though the mummy can stop immediately without wasting days on further futile challenges); thus, very detailed or delicate *Ushabti*, figurines of great power, may take several attempts to complete. The full Sekhem Trait cost for creation is paid at the end of the attempt, whether the sculpture succeeds or fails.

Lesser Creatures (First Basic)

Cost: Two Sekhem Traits to create, one Sekhem Trait per session when active

Tiny, well-carved figures of small creatures like ravens and snakes can be animated to serve as pets or spies. Though they have no more intelligence than a typical member of their species, they will follow your simple commands to the best of their ability. Typically, such a tiny creature has only one or two Physical Traits and a single Health Level; it is neither poisonous nor possessed of any special capabilities.

Lesser Servitors (First Basic)

Cost: One Sekhem Trait to create, One Sekhem Trait per session when active

A wooden figure of a servant, this ushabti can be animated as an actual servant. It performs tasks to the best of its nearly-mindless ability, acting like an automaton or zombie. Such a servant has five Physical Traits and a normal number of Health Levels, though it cannot actually fight (it can only attempt to defend itself in combat and is destroyed if it falls to the Incapacitated Health Level). These servitors are suitable for fetching and carrying, cleaning rooms, moving furniture and so on.

Simple Creatures (Second Basic)

Cost: Three Sekhem Traits to create, one Sekhem Trait per session when active

This spell functions like the *Lesser Creatures* spell, except that it can be used to create medium-sized ushabti figures, such as jackals and ibis. Such creatures typically have five Physical Traits and two Health Levels.

Simple Chattels (Second Basic)

Cost: Two Sekhem Traits to create, one Sekhem Trait per session when active

Though a *Simple Chattel* resembles only a tiny model, it is actually a powerful tool. When activated, the object instantly turns into a full-sized replica capable of all of the functions of the normal tool.

Simple Chattels can only make objects no more complex than a wheel or pulley. Swords, axes, furnishings, statues, buckets, bags and the like are appropriate, but no matter how finely crafted, more complex items like computers, radios, guns or spellbooks simply turn into detailed but nonfunctional replicas.

A *Simple Chattel* will not transform if it would be forced into another creature or object upon transformation. For example, you cannot trick someone into swallowing a *Simple Chattel* sword and then cause it to expand in the victim's stomach.

Overseer (First Intermediate)

Cost: Two Sekhem Traits to create, one Sekhem Trait per session when active

Whereas *Lesser Servitors* have only limited volition or intelligence, an *Overseer* can direct and control servitors, coordinating them to perform their tasks. Thus, though a *Lesser Servitor* could be commanded to dig a simple ditch, an *Overseer* could direct up to 10 *Lesser Servitors* in irrigating a field (a more complex form of ditch-digging). *Overseers* otherwise have the same Traits as *Lesser Servitors*. A properly instructed *Overseer* with *Lesser Servitors* can fulfill some of the tasks of *Retainers*, mostly in repair and upkeep — ushabti models obviously cannot fulfill tasks that require social interaction, but they are quite good for building (or destroying) structures, taking care of menial chores and so on.

Greater Chattels (First Intermediate)

Cost: Three Sekhem Traits to create, one Sekhem Trait per session when active

This spell functions like the *Lesser Chattels* spell but allows the enchantment of more complex models: boats, cars, computers and so on. Very large objects (larger than a house) or very complex ones (like advanced particle accelerators and space shuttles) are still outside the range of this spell.

Lesser Relics (First Intermediate)

Cost: Two Sekhem Traits to create, one Sekhem Trait per session when active

This spell functions just like the *Lesser Chattels* spell, except that it imbues sympathetic resonance into the model or object (it can be cast upon a full-size object of appropriate simplicity). Thereafter, the ushabti can be activated to create a relic in the Underworld. The object has a reflection in the deadlands that can be used by wraiths or Ba spirits.

Superior Creatures (First Intermediate)

Cost: Three Sekhem Traits to create, two Sekhem Traits per session when active

This spell functions like the *Simple Creatures* spell, except that the creations may be up to the size of a large dog and have significant intelligence. Such animals are considered to have up to seven Physical Traits and have five Social and Mental Traits as well. Furthermore, they can communicate empathically with you, sending brief flashes of sensation containing information from all senses (in a sort of "psychic snapshot"). These creatures can have a normal number of Health Levels (though, of course, a small spider or other tiny creature created with this spell still has only one Health Level and a few Traits — it simply gains a measure of intelligence beyond that of its mundane counterpart).

Great Creatures (Second Intermediate)

Cost: Five Sekhem Traits to create, one Sekhem Trait per scene when active

This spell functions like the *Superior Creatures* spell, except that it allows for creation of ushabti creatures of any size — elephants and whales included. Such creatures can have up to 12 Physical Traits and double the normal number of Health Levels if they are large enough; smaller creatures still retain the Health Levels and Traits described in the lesser creature spells.

Greater Relics (Second Intermediate)

Cost: Five Sekhem Traits to create, one Sekhem Trait per session when active

Just as special ushabti can duplicate complex items, some skilled magicians can create relic doubles of valuable and unusual tools. You can use this spell to make relics of cars, houses, computers and the like; anything with a complexity suited to the *Greater Chattels* spell is appropriate, and it functions just like a *Lesser Relic*, manifesting in the Underworld when activated.

Guard (Second Intermediate)

Cost: Four Sekhem Traits to create, one Sekhem Trait per scene when active

Whereas the lesser servant figurines can only perform menial tasks, a *Guard* figurine can fight and defend a particular location or attack as you direct. When activated, a *Guard* ushabti has nine Physical Traits and one level each of *Dodge* and *Melee*. *Guard* ushabti typically have some sort of weapon, usually a spear or sword (this can be worth up to three Bonus Traits). These ushabti can follow fairly complex commands, including one or two clauses ("Attack anyone entering the room except me"). They suffer no penalties from wounds and are destroyed at the Incapacitated Health Level.

Lesser Bond of Fate (Second Intermediate)

Cost: Six Sekhem Traits to create, one Sekhem Trait per turn when active

Like a legendary voodoo doll, this figurine calls upon sympathetic magic to tie a model to a particular subject. Any model that could be reproduced with the *Greater Chattels* spell can be made, duplicating a given object. If this spell succeeds, the model and the subject are linked; whatever happens to one affects the other. Thus, you can destroy (or repair) the model, and the same effects will automatically befall the linked object.

Princely Chattels (Second Intermediate)

Cost: Five Sekhem Traits to create, one Sekhem Trait per scene when active

Jet liners, palaces, hyper-advanced computers — these lie in the realm of the most detailed ushabti. With these figurines, you can create models of just about anything, and they will be fully functional when invoked. Some detailed models also require a knowledge of *Science* or *Computer*, as deemed appropriate by the Storyteller. A *Princely Chattel* otherwise functions as described in the *Lesser Chattels* spell.

Greater Bond of Fate (Advanced)

Cost: Seven Sekhem Traits to create, two Sekhem Traits per turn when active

Whereas the *Lesser Bond of Fate* affects only objects of moderate complexity, this ritual can function on just about any inanimate object. As always, you must have access to detailed information about the target object; you cannot craft a working model if the finished product does not represent the real counterpart in every detail. Once finished, a figurine of this type can be linked just like a *Lesser Bond of Fate*, but it can be made for an object of any size or complexity that the Storyteller allows.

Ka Vessel (Advanced)

Cost: Six Sekhem Traits to create, two Sekhem Traits and one Ka Trait per scene or hour when active

Perhaps the most powerful form of servitor statue, this ritual allows you to imbue a special figurine as a physical embodiment for your Ka spirit. The statue is nothing more than a statue, so it cannot actually speak and it moves only slowly, but it is fantastically strong (double all of your normal Physical Traits) and suffers no penalties for wounds, in addition to having two extra Health Levels. Obviously, you can only use this statue when your Ka spirit is separated, so you must either be dead or use a spell to separate your Ka before you may animate this statue. Still, it makes for an effective and terrifying tomb guardian.

Since the *Ka Vessel* is not actually a living physical body, it is not affected by other Hekau that would augment your capabilities, such as potions or amulets, unless they normally function upon you while you are dead.

Living Bond of Fate (Advanced)

Cost: Eight Sekhem Traits to create, three Sekhem Traits per turn when active

With the most powerful mystical resonances, it is possible to imbue a model or doll with a specific individual's sympathetic properties. Thus endowed, the model acts as a bond to one sentient being, just as any other *Bond of Fate* spell links a model to an object.

You must make a Willpower Challenge against your victim when using this spell, pitting your Willpower Traits against the victim's. If you succeed, you may use the model to take control of the victim's actions as long as the spell is active. You can force the victim to move haltingly and suffer any injury that you inflict upon the statue (although you cannot control the victim's speech). Generally, wounds incurred on the statue cause the victim to suffer one Health Level per blow; actually physically destroying the statue may take some effort. The victim suffers damage at a rate of one Health Level per turn as the statue slowly bends or burns; when the statue finally snaps or falls to dust, the victim dies.

Princely Relics (Advanced)

Cost: Seven Sekhem Traits to create, two Sekhem Traits per session when active

Pyramids, luxury liners and high-tech entertainment centers are all possible relics with this ritual. You can make a model corresponding to just about any sort of object; that object then carries a reflection in the Underworld while active. Obviously, such luxuries can be in high demand among the dead, but remember that there are no radio transmitters or electrical sockets in the Tempest. Otherwise, this spell functions just like the *Lesser Chattels* ritual.

Appendix: Frequently Asked Questions

I'm not young enough to know everything.
— James Barrie

Though we do our best to make sure that the rules listed in this and other **Mind's Eye Theatre** books are complete, some things inevitably slip through the cracks. When in doubt, Storytellers should feel free to come up with an interpretation of the rules that make sense in their chronicles. After all, you are the ones telling the story — we're just helping to set the stage.

FREQUENTLY ASKED QUESTIONS

If I am using a power that causes me to win all ties, do I still gain the benefits if I am Wounded, which would normally cause me to lose all ties?

The two effects cancel each other out. Any ties are resolved normally, using each character's Trait totals.

When resolving ties, do I use my total Traits in a category?

No, all ties are handled using your remaining Traits. Thus, if you started out the evening with six Social Traits but have lost two so far, you would only be able to declare a maximum of four Traits when resolving ties or overbid attempts. Some chronicles may decide to use total Traits, rather than current numbers. This is common in games with many new players.

What is a Willpower Challenge?

Just as an Attribute (Physical, Mental, Social) Challenge requires each player to bid an Attribute Trait, a Willpower Challenge requires both parties to bid a Willpower Trait. In the case of a tie, each character's current

Willpower rating is used to determine who wins. As with other Challenges, the loser must forfeit the Trait bid.

I thought a Simple Test either had to be won or tied (or occasionally just won). Why does this book introduce Traits and difficulty numbers?

A Simple Test is any test in which no Traits are risked. In **Laws of the Night** and **Laws of the Wild**, these were usually just yes/no types of determinations. With **Laws of the Hunt Players Guide**, we ran into many situations that employ the same difficulty numbers and resolution as does a standard challenge or Static Test, but no Traits are at risk. So rather than come up with an entirely different type of challenge, we expanded the scope of the Simple Test.

What does it mean if a power, Merit or Background puts me "two Traits up" on a specific type of test? What about a "two-Trait penalty"?

Characters who gain a bonus of this type add two to their Attribute Trait totals when resolving ties or overbid attempts that pertain to that area. In addition, if you are required to bid multiple Traits for some reason, you may count these bonus Traits in that total. However, these bonus Traits may not be used to require an opponent to bid more Traits when challenging you, nor may they be used as your initial bid. If you are suffering from a Trait penalty, you must bid that many extra Traits when taking part in any challenge or Static Test.

Some spells or rituals do not list a specific target number for the Static Test. What target number do I use?

When attempting to affect another character, use her current attribute rating in the appropriate category (Physical, Mental, Social). Effects that target the Umbra or the Shadowlands use the current Gauntlet or Shroud rating. All other Static Tests are assumed to have a difficulty of 6 unless otherwise specified by a Narrator.

Can I attempt to counterspell vampiric Obfuscate or the Garou Gift: Blur of the Milky Eye?

Obfuscate and the equivalent powers are not targeted at an individual. No challenge is required, nor may counterspells negate them.

If a Garou is peeking out of the Umbra, can he see me if I am using Shadow Cloak? What about the Illusion spells of Lesser or Greater Veil?

When Garou look through the Gauntlet, they are peering into the physical world. Anything that would render a character invisible in the physical world would carry over into the Umbra, as would any powers which affect the perceptions of the viewer.

*Can we use the "Optional Rules" that show up in this book in other **Mind's Eye Theatre** games?*

In general, yes. These rules have come up as possible variants and interpretations during playtesting. These options are provided as examples of how a Storyteller can change the rules to suit his particular style. Always remember the Golden Rule: There are no rules.

Index

Laws of the Night 1999

IS YOUR
Mind's Eye Theatre™
LIBRARY COMPLETE?

— The Masquerade —

This classic includes everything you need to enter the world of the Kindred. In this game, you no longer simply play a vampire — you *are* the vampire.

— Laws of the Night —

The quick and easy pocket-reference to **Mind's Eye Theatre**. It allows you to concentrate on the game by putting the rules right in your hands.

— Laws of Elysium —

This resource is the complete guide to creating, maintaining and running a vampire elder. It also contains extended Disciplines for **The Long Night**.

— Liber des Goules: The Book of Ghouls —

Sure, there are plenty of things to do when you're dead, but here you find what you can do when you're not *quite* dead.

— Laws of the Hunt —

Mortals are the playthings and puppets of the World of Darkness — until they decide to fight back. Take back the night with **Laws of the Hunt.**

— The Long Night —

The Long Night takes you into the Dark Medieval world of the 12th century and makes your Kindred character the undisputed master of the night.

— Laws of the Wild —

Completely revised in a handy pocket-sized edition, this book brings the rules of **Werewolf: The Apocalypse** to the live-action stage.

— Oblivion —

"Live"-action roleplaying in the lands of the dead, **Oblivion** takes the passion and horror of **Wraith: The Oblivion** and translates it into the **Mind's Eye Theatre** setting.

— The Shining Host —

A complete **Mind's Eye Theatre** rulebook on the world of glamour, enchantment and age-old mystery — the world of **Changeling: The Dreaming**.

Getting In The Mood

Vampire's **Book of Nod** and **Revelations of the Dark Mother** are "in-character" tomes that tell of the birth of vampires.